P9-DGO-521

ONE
OF US
IS BACK

BOOKS BY KAREN M. McMANUS

One of Us Is Lying

One of Us Is Next

One of Us Is Back

Two Can Keep a Secret

The Cousins

You'll Be the Death of Me

Nothing More to Tell

ONE
OF US
IS BACK

KAREN M. McMANUS

DELACORTE
PRESS

This is a work of fiction. Names, characters, places, and incidents either are the product of the author's imagination or are used fictitiously. Any resemblance to actual persons, living or dead, events, or locales is entirely coincidental.

Text copyright © 2023 by Karen M. McManus, LLC
Front cover photographs (left to right) copyright © 2023 by annebaek/GettyImages, Morsa Images/GettyImages, Peter Bannan/GettyImages; all other photographs used under license from Shutterstock.com.

All rights reserved. Published in the United States by Delacorte Press, an imprint of Random House Children's Books, a division of Penguin Random House LLC, New York.

Delacorte Press is a registered trademark and the colophon is a trademark of Penguin Random House LLC.

Visit us on the Web! GetUnderlined.com

Educators and librarians, for a variety of teaching tools, visit us at RHTeachersLibrarians.com

Library of Congress Cataloging-in-Publication Data is available upon request.
ISBN 978-0-593-48501-9 (trade) — ISBN 978-0-593-48502-6 (lib. bdg.) — ISBN 978-0-593-48503-3 (ebook) — ISBN 978-0-593-70533-9 (int'l. ed.)

The text of this book is set in 12-point Adobe Garamond
Interior design by Ken Crossland

Printed in the United States of America
10 9 8 7 6 5 4 3 2 1
First Edition

Random House Children's Books supports the First Amendment and celebrates the right to read.

Penguin Random House LLC supports copyright. Copyright fuels creativity, encourages diverse voices, promotes free speech, and creates a vibrant culture. Thank you for buying an authorized edition of this book and for complying with copyright laws by not reproducing, scanning, or distributing any part in any form without permission. You are supporting writers and allowing Penguin Random House to publish books for every reader.

For my readers

Contacts

(AP) **Addy Prentiss**
One of the original Bayview Four, Café Contigo ⓘ

(AP) **Ashton Prentiss**
Addy's sister ⓘ

(BR) **Bronwyn Rojas**
One of the original Bayview Four, Maeve's sister ⓘ

(CC) **Cooper Clay**
One of the original Bayview Four ⓘ

(EK) **Eli Kleinfelter**
Lawyer, Until Proven, Addy's brother-in-law ⓘ

(EM) **Emma Lawton**
Phoebe's sister, former Bayview High student ⓘ

(JR) **Jake Riordan**
Addy's ex-boyfriend ⓘ

(KS) **Keely Soria**
Cooper's ex-girlfriend ⓘ

(KM) **Knox Myers**
Member of the Bayview Crew, Until Proven ⓘ

(KB) **Kris Becker**
Cooper's boyfriend ⓘ

(LS) **Luis Santos**
Maeve's boyfriend, Café Contigo ⓘ

(MR) **Maeve Rojas**
Member of the Bayview Crew, Bronwyn's sister ⓘ

(NM) **Nate Macauley**
One of the original Bayview Four ⓘ

(PL) **Phoebe Lawton**
Member of the Bayview Crew, Café Contigo ⓘ

(SK) **Simon Kelleher**
Creator of About That gossip app ⓘ

(VM) **Vanessa Merriman**
Former Bayview High student ⓘ

PART ONE

CHAPTER ONE

Addy
Monday, June 22

"Are we seriously watching this?"

Maeve lifts the remote, then her eyebrows. The coordinated challenge annoys me because she knows perfectly well that we are, in fact, watching this. *This* is the entire reason that we're sitting in front of the television on a beautiful summer day.

"You didn't have to invite me over," I remind her, snatching the remote before she has a chance to toss it across the room. I click the On button, then press Channel until I find the station I'm looking for. "I was perfectly fine at home."

"You're never perfectly fine after one of these," Bronwyn pipes up from the corner of an overstuffed sofa. The Rojas media room is a much more comfortable place to watch TV than my living room, with the added benefit that there's zero chance of my mother poking her head in. I forgot, though, that this enhanced viewing experience would come with a heaping dose of concern. Bronwyn returned from Yale for the summer a couple of weeks ago and immediately started trying to take charge of my life like the bossy older sister I already have.

Not that I'm complaining. I've missed talking to her in the Bayview Four group chat, which we really need to rename now that it's nine people strong: me; Bronwyn; Nate Macauley; Maeve and her boyfriend, Luis Santos; Cooper Clay and his boyfriend, Kris Becker; and Maeve's fellow Bayview High rising seniors Phoebe Lawton and Knox Myers. It's a very coupled-off group chat, with the exception of me and those last two. Possibly only me, since nobody fully buys Phoebe and Knox's insistence that they're just friends.

Bayview Crew, maybe? I pick up my phone and edit the group chat name. It doesn't look half bad.

"Who's this guy?" Maeve asks, squinting at the screen. "Is he going to introduce—"

"No," I say quickly. "This isn't the Eastland High program. That starts at three o'clock. This is . . . I have no idea, actually."

"A town council meeting," Bronwyn says. Of course she'd know; she probably watches this kind of thing for fun. "Looks like they're wrapping up a budget vote."

"Thrilling. But at least it *matters*." Maeve props her bare feet up on the coffee table a little too aggressively, wincing as her heels slam into the marble top. "At least it deserves a platform. Which is more than you can say for—"

"It's local cable, Maeve," I interrupt. "They're not picky about their programming."

My voice is even but my heart thuds uncomfortably, and I'm torn between wishing I were by myself and feeling grateful that I'm not. The town councilman we're watching announces that the meeting is over, and the scene fades as interim music begins to play. Bronwyn, Maeve, and I sit in silence for a few beats, listening to what sounds like a weirdly plucky instrumental version of "The Girl from Ipanema."

Then a half-filled school auditorium appears on screen with the words *Eastland High School: Summer Seminar Series* superimposed along the bottom. Before I can react, Bronwyn abruptly launches herself off her sofa and onto mine, flinging her arms around me.

"Oh my God, what are you doing?" I mutter, dropping my phone onto the cushion.

"You're not alone, Addy," Bronwyn says in a fierce whisper. The smell of green apples surrounds me: Bronwyn's distinctive shampoo, which she's used for as long as I've known her. And probably a lot longer than that, since Bronwyn is nothing if not a creature of habit. One time, when Nate was being extra mopey about their long-distance relationship, I gave him a bottle of it wrapped with a big red bow. He got annoyed, which was the entire point—it's never *not* fun to crack Nate's cooler-than-thou façade—but he also kept it.

"Obviously," I say, spitting a strand of hair from my mouth. Then I sink into the hug, because I actually do kind of need it.

"Good afternoon, Eastland High, and welcome to the start of our summer seminar series." The man behind the podium doesn't introduce himself, probably because he doesn't have to—he's likely a teacher or an administrator. Somebody in charge of shaping the minds of teenagers who look a thousand years younger than I feel, even though I turned nineteen just a few months ago.

"Look at all those eager beavers. School let out two weeks

ago, and they're already back," Maeve says as the man continues with what Principal Gupta liked to call "housekeeping"—all the random announcements that have to be crammed in before any type of school-related event can start. "Good old Eastland High. Remember when you stalked Sam Barron in their parking lot, Bronwyn?"

"I did not stalk him," Bronwyn says, although she technically did. It was a necessary evil, though. Solving the mystery of Simon Kelleher's death hinged on Sam—the boy Simon had paid to create a distraction while we were in detention the day he died. It was the biggest, most horrifying story ever to hit Bayview. Until a few months ago, when a Simon copycat launched a deadly game of Truth or Dare that nearly got all of us blown up at my sister's wedding rehearsal dinner.

Sometimes, I deeply question why any of us continue to live in Bayview.

"I lightly interrogated him," Bronwyn adds. "And it's a good thing I did, or . . ." She trails off as all our phones buzz in unison.

"Bayview Four is lighting up," Maeve reports before I can reach for mine.

"I think we should change it to Bayview Crew," I say.

"Fine by me," Maeve says with a shrug. "Kris says to stay strong, Addy. He also wants to know if you're still up for waffles tomorrow morning. I happen to like waffles, too, in case that's relevant information for the two of you. Luis says *Fuck that guy.* He's not talking about Kris, obviously; he means—"

"I know who he means," I say as the Eastland High speaker raises his hand to quiet the restless chatter that's started up among the audience.

"All of us at the Eastland High Summer Seminar Series realize that there are many other things you could be doing on a beautiful June afternoon," he says. "It's a testament to the importance of today's special topic that you're here instead."

"Special, my ass," Maeve mutters, tucking a strand of hair behind one ear. It's exactly the same shade of dark brown as Bronwyn's, but she recently cut it into a cute, choppy bob. After a battle with childhood leukemia, Maeve spent the first few years of high school trying to get out from behind Bronwyn's shadow, and I think her final form emerged when she stopped echoing her sister's signature ponytail.

"Shhh," Bronwyn hisses, before finally releasing me.

"At Eastland High, we want to inspire you to dream and achieve, but we also want to prepare you for the harsher realities of life," the speaker continues. "The decisions you make as high school students today will shape the trajectory of your future for years to come, and the wrong choice can have devastating consequences."

"Is that what we're calling it now?" Maeve asks. "A *wrong choice*?"

"Maeve, I swear to God—" Bronwyn starts.

"Quiet!" The word bursts out much more loudly and angrily than I intended, startling Bronwyn and Maeve into silence. I'd feel shame at the misdirected rage, which neither of them deserves, if I weren't such a giant ball of stress. Because any minute, I'm going to see . . .

"Nobody knows that better than today's guest. He's here through an educational partnership with the California Department of Corrections, to speak frankly with you about how his actions derailed what was once a bright and promising future. Please welcome our speaker, who's a current inmate at the East Crenshaw Juvenile Detention Facility and a former student from neighboring Bayview High—Jake Riordan."

Bronwyn squeezes my arm and Maeve inhales sharply, but other than that, I've managed to cow them into temporary silence. Not that it matters; if they spoke, I wouldn't hear a word over the blood pounding in my ears.

Jake Riordan.

My ex. The love of my life, once upon a time, when I was too naïve and insecure to see who he really was. I knew he could be jealous, and if you'd pressed me back then—which nobody except my sister, Ashton, ever did—I might have admitted that he was controlling. But I never would have imagined that when I cheated on him, he'd get revenge by teaming up with Simon to frame me for murder, then nearly kill me when I tried to expose him.

Oh, right. Jake wasn't *actually* trying to kill me, according to his very expensive lawyer. *Lack of specific intent,* she said, along with a lot of other legal buzzwords piled onto his defense that, ultimately, kept him from being tried as an adult.

At the time, a lot of people called it a sham of a trial, especially when it was over and Jake was sentenced to a juvenile facility until the age of twenty-five. Everything he did—not just to me and my friends, but to Simon—boiled down to a whopping seven and a half years behind bars. The headlines screamed "Privilege on Display!" and there were a half-dozen online petitions urging the judge to impose a harsher sentence.

But memories are short.

Jake's been a model prisoner ever since he went in, and last December, a true crime show ran a profile on him that was, as the *Bayview Blade* said, "surprisingly sympathetic." Jake was humble. He was remorseful. He was *committed to helping other young people avoid the same mistakes he'd made.* And then, barely two weeks after my sister's wedding at the end of March, Juror X surfaced.

Or rather, his former girlfriend did—a woman who claimed she'd gotten hundreds of texts about Jake's trial from one of the jurors while it was happening. Turns out, Juror X kept her up to date with a constant stream of confidential information and visited news sites that he was supposed to keep away from. When screenshots surfaced on BuzzFeed, Juror X panicked, tried to delete his Internet history, lied under oath, and basically gave Jake's legal team the opening they'd been looking for to ask for a new trial.

Juror X's real name is Marshall Whitfield, which the Internet collectively discovered within a few weeks of the story breaking. He's now gone underground after being doxed, and I might feel sorry for him if he hadn't tossed a grenade into my life.

Now Jake's case is pending, and in the meantime, he's started what Maeve sarcastically calls the Jake Riordan Rehabilitation Tour. The school visits aren't always televised, but when they are . . . I watch. I can't help myself.

"He looks terrible," Maeve says, glaring at the screen.

She's not entirely right. Jake looks older than nineteen, but not in a bad way. He's still handsome, his brown hair cropped short and his eyes a piercing, summer-sky blue against too-pale skin. He's clearly working out more than ever, which you can tell despite the shapeless khakis he's wearing. He approaches the podium to scattered applause, his head bowed and his hands clasped in front of him. No handcuffs, of course. Not for a school visit, although the three officers sitting in folding chairs off to one side are armed and ready for trouble.

But Jake never gives them any.

"I'm here to tell you about the worst time of my life," he says in a low, earnest tone, which is how he always starts. And then, with his hands gripping the edge of the podium and his eyes locked on the students in front of him, he tells them about the worst time of mine.

He's clever. He talks a lot about *pressure, undue influence,* and *duress,* as though he were Simon's reluctant, clueless patsy instead of his eager conspirator. According to Jake, he doesn't even remember attacking me and Janae Vargas in the woods behind her house; all he wanted, he claimed during the trial, was for us to stop threatening him. *Us,* threatening *him.* That didn't go over well in the court of public opinion, though, so he's careful to avoid the topic during school visits. If anyone mentions me, he quickly segues into a monologue about how his poor choices hurt *everyone.* Especially him.

Next November, it will be two years since that awful night in the woods. A lot of good things have happened since then: I moved in with my sister, I made new friends, and I graduated high school. I took some time off so I could figure out what I wanted to do with my life, and I've decided it's going to involve teaching. I got my first-ever passport last month, so that Maeve and I can travel to Peru at the end of July to be counselors for an English immersion program. After that, I'll start applying to college. My dad, although he's still the definition of a hands-off parent, came through with an offer to help with tuition.

The ticking clock of Jake's release has always been far enough away that I could believe I'd be ready once it wound down—older and wiser, settled into the kind of busy, important life where I'd barely think twice about my convict ex being back on the streets.

It never occurred to me, until recently, that the clock could be reset.

"What does Eli say about all this?" Maeve asks as Jake continues his well-rehearsed monologue. My sister's husband heads up a legal-defense nonprofit, so he's our go-to expert for anything crime-related. Even though, as Eli has pointed out to all nine members of the Bayview Crew at one time or another, we rarely listen to him until it's too late. "Does he think Jake's going to get a new trial? Or that he'll be released, or—"

"Eli is busy thinking about who's going to cover for him during paternity leave," I remind her. My sister Ashton's surprise pregnancy—she's due in November—is why I've moved back in with my mother. Mom and I haven't always been on the best of terms, but being excited about the baby has given us something to bond over. Lately, that bonding mostly consists of coming up with grandmother names that won't make her sound old. Current leader: Gigi, because Mom refuses to consider my suggestion of Insta Gram.

"Eli can think about more than two things at once," Bronwyn says. "Especially if you let him know how worried you are."

"I'm not worried," I say, eyes on the screen. My voice is muffled, though, by how hard I'm gnawing on my knuckle.

Jake has wrapped up his speech and started taking questions from the kids. A boy sitting in the front row asks, "What's the food like in prison?"

"In a word? Awful," Jake says, with such perfect timing that everyone laughs.

"Do you get to see your mom and dad?" a girl calls out. The camera jerkily pans her way, and I catch the flash of another girl's coppery curls behind her. It almost looks like—but, no. I must be seeing things. Still, when I glance at Maeve, she's squinting at the television with a puzzled frown.

"Not as often as I'd like, but yes," Jake says. "They haven't given up on me, and their support means the world. I hope I can make them proud again someday."

"Barf," Maeve says, but even she sounds slightly less sarcastic. The Jake Riordan Rehabilitation Tour is *that* good.

Another boy raises his hand, and Jake acknowledges him with a chin lift. It's such a familiar gesture—the way he'd greet our friends in the hallway of Bayview High, one arm wrapped tightly around my shoulders—that I shiver. "If you could go back in time, what would you do differently?" the boy asks.

"Everything," Jake says instantly. He gazes directly into the camera, and I recoil as though he'd just entered the room.

There it is.

That's what I've been waiting for—the reason I keep torturing myself by watching these. I don't want to see it, but I need to acknowledge that it exists. That glint in Jake's eye. The one he can't hide for a full Q&A session, no matter how hard he tries. The one that reflects all the anger he's pretending he no longer feels. The one that says, *I'm not sorry.*

The one that says, *What would I do differently?*

I wouldn't get caught.

CHAPTER TWO

Phoebe
Monday, June 22

I hunch lower in my seat, wishing I'd thought to wear a hoodie even though it's eighty degrees outside and the Eastland High School auditorium doesn't have AC. I knew there might be cameras here, but usually the kids who sit way in the back, like I am, aren't the type to ask questions.

I know Addy watches these things. What am I supposed to say if she sees me? How do I explain . . . this?

Deny, deny, deny, Phoebe. You're good at that.

"Any further questions?" The man who introduced Jake Riordan gets up from the front row to stand beside him. "We have time for one more."

Are you truly sorry?

Would you ever hurt someone again?

What made you like this?

Those are the questions I need answers to. I can't bring

myself to ask them, but I keep hoping that maybe someone else will.

Instead, a girl calls out, "Are you getting a new trial?"

Jake ducks his head. "I try not to think about that," he says. "It's out of my hands. I'm just living the best life I can, one day at a time."

I search what I can see of his face and think, *Please let that be true.*

Like half my classmates, I had a crush on Jake Riordan once. He was a junior when I was a freshman, and he and Addy were already the It Couple of Bayview High. I used to watch them glide through the hallways back then, marveling at how glamorous and grown-up they seemed. When they split up after Simon Kelleher's death, I'm embarrassed to admit that my first thought was *Maybe I have a chance with him now.* I had no idea how unhappy Addy had been, or what Jake was capable of doing. He hid his dark side incredibly well. A lot of people do.

I know how stressed Addy is, and I wish I could talk about it with her—*really* talk about it, not just offer empty reassurances. But I can't. I cut myself off from that possibility back in April, and now the only person I can confide in is my older sister, Emma. Who moved to North Carolina to live with one of our aunts as soon as she graduated two weeks ago, and might as well be on the moon considering how infrequently she returns my texts.

What's done is done, she said before she left. *We had our reasons.*

* * *

14

"Sorry, I'm sorry I'm so late, and thank you so, so much!"

My words are breathless, tumbling over one another as I scurry through Café Contigo to reach Evie, one of the new waitresses, who's ringing up a takeout order at the cash register. I asked her to cover the beginning of my shift, knowing I wouldn't make it back from Eastland in time, but I hadn't anticipated so much traffic. I'm more than an hour late, and Evie, who's been working since the café opened at ten a.m., has every right to be annoyed.

Instead, she gives me a cheerful smile. I wish Evie could bottle her always-positive attitude and sell it, because I would definitely buy. "No worries, Phoebe," she says, handing a bulging paper bag to one of our regulars. "I told you to take your time."

"The doctor's office was so crowded," I murmur, grabbing an apron from under the counter and wrapping it around my waist. Then I pull an elastic from my pocket and yank my hair back into a haphazard ponytail. All my hair doesn't make it through the elastic, but whatever—speed is of the essence here. "Okay, I'm ready. You can go."

"Relax, Phoebe. Grab a drink or something. And maybe check out your hair in the mirror before you try to serve tables like that," Evie says with a grin, tugging at the end of her own bleached-blond braid.

"What?" I ask, just as Luis Santos, Maeve's boyfriend, comes out of the kitchen, stops in his tracks, and starts to laugh.

"Nice horn," he says.

"Oh God," I mutter, catching sight of my reflection in the mirror that lines the far wall. Somehow, I've managed to make myself look like a deranged unicorn. I pull out the elastic, wincing as a few strands of hair come with it, and sink into a chair beside the register. "I'm a disaster. Is your mom mad that I'm late again?"

"She's not here. Pa is," Luis says, and I breathe a sigh of relief. I love both his parents, but Mr. Santos is by far the more lenient boss. "We're not all that busy, anyway. It's too nice out. Speaking of which." His smile widens as the bell on the café door jangles and Maeve steps inside, waving to us with both hands as she crosses the room. "There's my cue to take off. Maeve and I have big plans. Hey, beautiful."

"Hi," Maeve says with not quite her usual level of enthusiasm, even as she melts into Luis for a kiss. I turn away, wishing happy couples didn't send such a stab of jealousy through me. *It's your choice to not be part of one,* I remind myself, but that doesn't help. Mostly because it doesn't actually feel like a choice.

"You rode here, right?" Luis asks expectantly.

"In a manner of speaking," Maeve says, scuffing the toe of one sneaker against the tile floor. Luis raises his eyebrows, and she says, "Mostly, I walked it." He sighs, and she adds, "I'm sorry, but I don't see why I need to get better at riding a bicycle when you're perfectly capable of doing it for both of us."

"You can't ride on my handlebars forever," Luis says.

"Why not?" Maeve counters. "It's not like I'm going to out-grow them."

"Heading for the bike path again?" Evie asks, hiding a smile. Luis bought Maeve a bicycle a couple of weeks ago, determined to make up for the fact that she never learned how to ride one between cancer treatments when she was a kid, but it's slower going than he expected. Maeve doesn't so much *ride* the bike as she straddle-walks it. Or just regular walks, while resentfully wheeling the bike beside her.

"It's going to be *great*," Luis says with what seems like misplaced optimism.

Maeve rolls her eyes and turns to me, one arm still around his waist. "Phoebe, it was the weirdest thing. I was watching Jake's school visit earlier—"

Luis's smile vanishes. "Fuck that guy," he growls. There aren't many things that pierce Luis's laid-back vibe, but his former friend is one of them.

"I know." Maeve gives his arm a comforting squeeze before turning back to me. "I saw a girl in the audience who had your exact hair and . . ." My heart sinks as her eyes rove over my sparkly tank top, which wasn't exactly designed to be overlooked. "Shirt."

"Really? That's so weird," I say, busying myself with creating a less ridiculous ponytail. "I meant to watch, but I got stuck at the doctor's. How's Addy holding up?" I hate lying to Maeve, but I'd hate it even more if she knew what I was lying about.

"Same," Maeve says. She looks like she's about to say more, but she pauses as the door jingles again and a familiar figure enters the café.

"Owen! What's up, bud?" Luis asks as my not-so-little-anymore brother approaches the counter. "Jesus, did you grow another foot?"

"No," Owen mutters, because he's humorless like that lately.

"Your order's on the counter," Evie tells him. She doesn't need to add *It's on the house,* because Mr. Santos never lets my brother pay.

"Thanks," he says in the same monotone, grabbing his takeout without even glancing my way. Maeve catches my eye with a rueful grin, like, *He's thirteen, what can you do?* I force myself to smile back, even though my stomach twists as Owen slouches out the door and lets it slam closed behind him.

"Good talk, Owen," Luis says, and Maeve lightly punches him.

Almost three months ago, when Owen was still twelve, Emma and I learned that he'd posed online as Emma—who'd been posing as me—to chat with a boy who'd roped Emma into a revenge-swapping plan. The boy, Jared Jackson, promised he'd make my ex-boyfriend, Brandon Weber, pay for the fact that Brandon had caused a forklift accident that killed our father three years ago. In return, Emma was supposed to help Jared get revenge on Addy's brother-in-law, Eli, who'd helped send Jared's crooked-cop brother to jail. Emma got cold feet and bailed—but Owen stepped in and kept the pact going.

Then Brandon died in what everyone thought was an accident, as part of a Truth or Dare game that Jared set up. When Owen abruptly stopped communicating, Jared decided to get revenge on his own and plant a bomb at Eli's wedding rehearsal dinner. If Knox and Maeve hadn't stopped him, everyone at that restaurant could have died. Instead, Jared was arrested and promptly gave me up as his accomplice. Emma, who'd landed in the hospital after weeks of guilt-fueled binge drinking, confessed that it was actually her. But we didn't realize Owen was involved until we read chat transcripts between him and Jared and saw a word Owen misspelled while practicing for a spelling bee: *bazaar* instead of *bizarre*.

In that moment—seated at our kitchen table with our

mother and Emma's lawyer—my sister and I made a silent pact to keep that information to ourselves. I couldn't imagine doing anything else, because it was clear from Owen's messages to Jared after Brandon died that he hadn't understood what he was doing. My sweet, innocent, still-grieving little brother never meant for Brandon to get hurt.

But almost immediately, doubts started creeping in. I knew I couldn't tell anyone—especially not Maeve and Knox, after they'd risked their lives to stop Jared—and the secret made me feel horribly isolated once Emma moved away. Owen turned thirteen a few days later, becoming tall and sullen seemingly overnight, and I couldn't stop thinking about how he was the same age Brandon was when he accidentally killed our father. And how, if Brandon had ever taken responsibility for that, he might still be alive.

So now I lie to my friends, semistalk Jake Riordan, and compose late-night texts to my sister that I'm too afraid to send:

What if Owen turns into another Brandon?

Or another Jake?

Do you think we did the wrong thing?

Do you think we should tell someone?

By the time work is over and I've helped Mr. Santos close, I know I should drive straight home. It's almost eleven o'clock, I'm exhausted, and I've got an early shift tomorrow. But when I come to a fork in the road that leads to my house, I take the opposite direction.

I can't help it. Consciously or not, I've been looking forward to this all day.

When I reach a familiar house, I park in the driveway but bypass the front door and head around back instead. Then I hoist myself onto a tree, climb until I'm parallel with a jutting edge of the roof, and carefully step onto it. There's a window in front of me, and when I tug at the sash, it lifts easily. I squeeze through, wishing like always that the space was a little bigger so the maneuver wasn't quite so graceless. Then I land on the hardwood floor, dust off my hands, and close the window before turning to face the room.

"You know you could just ring the doorbell, right?" Knox says.

He's lying in bed, propped up by a half-dozen pillows with his laptop open in front of him, so sleepy-eyed that I'm pretty sure he was dozing before I came in. My heartbeat quickens even as some of the day's tension flows out of me, and I hold on to the edge of his dresser to steady myself while I pull off my sneakers.

"I don't want to wake your parents up," I say. "Besides, climbing through your window makes me feel like I'm in a teen movie, so it's on theme." I cross over to his bed, pull back the navy comforter, and slip in beside him, curling into the white T-shirt he always sleeps in like it's a favorite blanket. "What's up next?"

Knox taps a few keys before angling the laptop toward me. *"She's All That,"* he says. We've been steadily working our way through classic teen movies since school ended, and we've finally reached the nineties. "I think it's the one where the girl takes off her glasses and becomes prom queen."

"She probably lets her hair down too," I say, resting my

head on his shoulder and breathing in the scent of the citrusy soap he uses.

"Life was so simple in the twentieth century," Knox says. I wait for him to press Play, but instead, he drums his fingers against the edge of his laptop, for so long that I raise my head to give him a questioning look. "So," he says, keeping his eyes on the frozen screen. "I'm glad you came, because—I mean, not that I'm ever *not* glad, obviously, it's always good to see you, and it's not like I wasn't expecting you or anything—"

"Knox," I say, fidgeting with the edge of his comforter. "You're babbling." That's never a good sign.

"Right. Sorry." His fingers keep drumming as I study his profile, wondering how there ever could have been a time when I didn't find him attractive. How did I miss those cheekbones? "It's just . . . I wanted to tell you that I kind of think we should stop doing this."

"Doing what?" I lift my head from his shoulder, stung. "Watching movies?"

"No, not that. We should definitely keep doing that. It's more . . ." He gestures to the inch of space between us, now that I'm sitting up straight. "This." I stare at him, and he swallows visibly. "You. In my bed. It's . . . too much."

"Too much *what*?" I ask, pulling his comforter over me like a shield. "I'm not doing anything!"

"Yeah. That's the problem." Knox rubs the back of his neck. "Look, Phoebe, I totally respect that you want to be friends. I'm fine with it, I swear. I never expected anything else."

My heart squeezes at the simple truth of the words. Knox and I kissed once, the night of Ashton and Eli's wedding, and I thought—hoped—it was the start of something great between us. But then Owen happened. I couldn't tell Knox about it, and I couldn't get involved with him while lying about something that important. So when he asked me out, I told him I thought we were better as friends. Even though part of me was relieved at how quickly and easily he swallowed the lie, a bigger part of me absolutely hates it.

"But you being this close . . . look, I'm not, like, *pining* or anything," Knox says, sending another knife through my heart. "It just makes it hard to stay in the friend zone, is all."

Then don't. The words are on my lips, and I want to cover his with mine while I say them, tossing his laptop to one side so I can finally, *finally* pull off that white T-shirt. But of course I can't. And of course he's right, and my one source of comfort was never going to last. This hasn't been fair of me, and it's been superhuman of Knox to put up with it for as long as he has. "I get it," I say numbly, swinging my legs off the side of the bed. "No problem."

"We can still watch the movie, though," Knox says. "Just, you know, downstairs. I can make popcorn, if you want."

Oh God. There's nothing I want less than to traipse into Knox's living room and sit on opposite ends of the couch with a bowl of popcorn between us. Watching a movie I couldn't care less about, since the only reason I came here is to be close to him. But it would be a jerk move to refuse when he's been nothing but honest, so I force a smile and say, "Sounds great."

After all, what's one more lie?

CHAPTER THREE

Nate
Wednesday, June 24

The digital billboard at the edge of Clarendon Street has had the same ad for as long as I can remember—a dancing energy drink—so the fact that it's changed catches my attention while I'm stopped on my motorcycle at a red light.

TIME FOR A NEW GAME, BAYVIEW.

Those are the only words, red against a stark white background. They fade off the screen and I wait, mildly intrigued despite myself, to see what's next. Then the ad copy cycles back to TIME FOR A NEW GAME, BAYVIEW once again. So much for building suspense. Or letting people know what the hell you're promoting. A-plus job, advertisers.

The light changes and I roar through it, following the familiar route to the Bayview Country Club. For a lot of people, summertime in Bayview means beaches, barbecues, and one-upping one another on social media with their no-filter vacation pictures. For me, it means a second job. Construction work by day, serving drinks to Bayview's McMansion crowd at night, then trying to sleep for a few hours in a house filled with five other people who have nothing to do except throw parties they keep trying to drag me to.

Living the dream.

I pull into the parking lot and settle my bike between two freshly painted white lines, then take out my phone to check the time. There's a new text waiting for me—a picture of Bronwyn and Stan, my bearded dragon, sitting side by side on an oversized rock in Bronwyn's garden. Now that she's home from Yale for the summer, she's decided that Stan needs, as she puts it, "more exercise and mental stimulation." So, some days when she's done with her internship, she picks him up, brings him to her house, and hangs out with him in the backyard. As far as I can tell Stan isn't moving any more than he usually does on these field trips, but he does seem to like having a new rock to sit on.

I grin, my mood instantly lifted. My girl's back in town for the next two months, so I guess I am, in fact, living the dream. Bronwyn's prelaw, and she had her pick of internships in New Haven or New York for the summer, but she chose one in San Diego. It's a fantastic job with the kind of woman-owned start-up that she wants to be general counsel for someday, so I don't even have to stress about her giving up opportunities to be closer to me.

Don't let a bird make off with him, I text back.

I WOULD NEVER, Bronwyn responds with a horrified-face emoji.

Of course she wouldn't. There's not a person in the world

24

you can count on more than Bronwyn Rojas. I know exactly how good I have it with her, and that's why I'm doing all this—the jobs, school, the cheap-ass house with too many roommates so I'm not blowing everything I make on rent. One of these days I'm going to be the guy Bronwyn deserves, not the guy she had to save from prison while we were in high school.

In the meantime, though, I have drinks to serve.

I shut off my bike, pocket the keys, and head for the giant pillars that frame the country-club entrance. At the edge of the parking lot, there's a bulletin board filled with flyers hawking landscaping services, tutoring, housecleaning, dog walking—all the stuff rich people can't do on their own, because they're too busy hanging out at country clubs. My eyes land on one I haven't seen before that's a lot more glossy than what's usually there. Bright white, with just a few words in a large red font:

TIME FOR A NEW GAME, BAYVIEW.

My steps slow, and I frown before yanking off the flyer and turning it over. There's nothing on the other side. It's clearly a companion piece to the billboard ad I saw on my way here, and I still don't understand what it's for. Unless . . .

It's probably a company trying to be edgy. But it hits me, now that I'm holding the words in my hand, that some asshole might want to remind Bayview of the Truth or Dare game that killed Brandon Weber. That kind of thing happened a lot after Simon died—copycats of Simon's gossip app, About That, kept springing up around school. Those were created by students, though, not somebody with the kind of money to rent a billboard. Although come to think of it, there are probably plenty of Bayview High kids who could.

"In the market for some tutoring?" calls a voice behind me.

I turn to see Vanessa Merriman in a sheer, nearly see-through white sundress over a striped bikini. Vanessa and I graduated together, and she was Addy's friend until she took Jake's side during their breakup. Somehow, even after Jake wound up in jail, Vanessa never seemed to think she had anything to apologize to Addy for. I guess she's back for the summer from whatever college she went to, which I don't know because I couldn't care less about Vanessa Merriman.

She leans provocatively against the side of the bulletin board and adds, "Maybe I could help you out. I excel in many subjects. Human anatomy, for example." I just stare at her, until she laughs and says, "Come on! Lighten up; that was a joke." She raises a hand like she's about to slap my arm but freezes before she makes contact. "Wait. Weren't you practically blown up a few months ago? How do you still have all your limbs?"

"Reports were exaggerated," I say.

Vanessa cranes her neck, eyes widening as she catches sight of my left arm. I got the worst of Jared Jackson's bomb attempt in March, since I'd been walking with Bronwyn in an arboretum behind the restaurant where Ashton and Eli were having their rehearsal dinner. Knox, who had no idea we were there, tossed the backpack he'd seen Jared leave beneath the restaurant a few feet away from us. We had to run for our lives and didn't make it out of range before the bomb exploded. I'd thrown myself over Bronwyn, shielding her, and ended up with an arm full of shrapnel. The wounds have healed, but the scars will never go away entirely.

"Ouch," Vanessa says. Then she pats my cheek and adds, "Well, it could be worse, right? At least nothing hit that pretty face of yours."

Looks like Vanessa's priorities haven't changed since high school. She reaches for the flyer I'm holding, but I drop it into the trash before she can grab it.

"What was that?" she asks, tossing her hair over one shoulder. Vanessa has expensive-looking hair; the kind that's darker on top and lighter on the bottom, with lots of different-colored highlights. Addy would know what it's called. "Why'd you throw it out?"

"Because it's weird," I say, resuming my trek toward the entrance.

Vanessa falls into step beside me. "Weird how?"

I'm not interested in swapping theories about mysterious billboards with Vanessa Merriman. "Don't you have a pool to get to?" I ask.

"I need a drink first," Vanessa says, slinging her tote bag over her shoulder. Then she starts telling me about the trip to Ibiza she just got back from, and she keeps up a steady stream of one-sided conversation all the way from the parking lot through the front entrance and the main corridor, until we reach the restaurant where I work. She hops onto a stool at the U-shaped bar, takes off her oversized sunglasses, and says, "I'll have a gin and tonic."

"Nice try." I step behind the bar and wave to Gavin, one of the bartenders, who's serving an older couple at the other end of the bar. "But it doesn't matter how good your ID is when you graduated high school with the barback."

"Oh, come on, Nate." Vanessa pouts. "No one cares. It's not like I'm driving."

"Then what were you doing in the parking lot?"

"Okay, it's not like I'm driving *far*."

"Here." I fill a glass with ice, soda water, and a lime. "Use your imagination."

Vanessa sighs and takes a long, resentful sip. "You know what? You're a lot less fun than you used to be."

"I'll take that as a compliment."

She makes a face. "Don't."

"Nate, my friend." Gavin comes over and claps me on the shoulder. His pale skin is still sunburned from the weekend, and his light-brown hair is darkened at his forehead with sweat. There's too much open air around the bar for the AC to make much difference. "Stephanie just called from the road. She's almost here, but I'm already running late to meet someone and need to take off. Can you . . . you know?"

You know is code for *cover for me.* Technically, I'm not supposed to pour drinks since I'm not twenty-one, but country-club management doesn't pay much attention to the bar. Half the time, I'm like a second bartender anyway.

I'd been hoping to grab some food before starting work, since I came here from my day job at Myers Construction. There wasn't enough time between shifts to make going home worth it, and besides, home is worse than ever thanks to my newest roommate. The only guy I semiliked moved out two weeks ago, and guess who moved in? Reggie Crawley, the former Bayview High student best known for being outed by Simon Kelleher for having a camera in his bedroom. In that case, Simon actually did what he always claimed to do: *expose the assholes.* And it's not like Reggie has improved with age; when the *Bayview Blade* interviewed people about a true crime show that made Jake look like a decent guy, Reggie went on record with this gem: "He was always pretty cool to me."

That's not Gavin's problem, though, and he's so generous about splitting tips that I can't insist he hang around until Stephanie shows up. "No problem," I say.

"Thanks, I owe you one," he says, stepping out from behind the bar.

Vanessa perks up, sensing a new target. "Hello, I don't think we've met. I'm Vanessa Merriman," she says, extending one bracelet-clad arm.

Gavin takes her hand. "Nice to meet you, Vanessa Merriman," he says, repeating her name like he's memorizing it. Which he probably is. Gavin is a college student and didn't grow up around here, but he knows more Bayview people than I do. *Bartending trick,* he says. *Improves the tips.*

"Don't serve her," I say, grabbing some clean glasses from beneath the bar and hanging them in the racks above me. "She's nineteen."

"Okay, now, that is just *rude,*" Vanessa whines.

Gavin grins and pulls off the tie he always wears, even though we don't have to. "Sorry, Vanessa. Have fun with the happy hour crowd, Nate."

He takes off, and Vanessa sulkily squeezes her lime in my direction. "Not all of us are happy," she says. Her eyes stray over my shoulder, and then her face takes on a new expression that's almost . . . hopeful? It's a weird look for Vanessa, so I follow her gaze and see a trim, well-dressed, middle-aged woman settling herself into a stool a few feet away.

"Hi, Ms. Riordan," Vanessa calls out. "How *are* you?"

Jake's mom looks our way. It surprised me, when I first started working here, to learn that she and Mr. Riordan still come to the country club. It's not like I spent time thinking about the Riordans, but if I had, I would've assumed they moved out of town like Simon's parents did. Or at least kept a low profile after their only son wound up in the middle of Bayview's biggest scandal. Then I got to know Mr. Riordan and it made sense, because the guy's a grade A dick. He still thinks he's the king of Bayview, and he'll tell anyone who'll listen—and everyone who doesn't, too—that Jake got a raw deal. He acts as though he has no clue who I am, like his son never framed me and my friends for Simon's death. On top of all that, he tips for shit.

Ms. Riordan is different, though. I wasn't planning on saying a word to her unless I had to, but she surprised me, the first night I started working, by taking me aside and apologizing for what Jake did. "He's trying really hard to make up for that," she said earnestly. I don't believe it for a second, but I think she actually does.

"Oh, Vanessa, hello. How lovely to see you," Ms. Riordan says. I know what she came for, and since Stephanie still isn't here, I go ahead and fill a wineglass nearly to the rim with the bar's most expensive chardonnay. Ms. Riordan needs every drop to put up with that asshole she's married to. "Thank you, Nate," she says gratefully, taking a long sip before putting two twenty-dollar bills on the bar. "That's for you. Put the wine on our tab, please."

"Thanks," I say, pocketing them. It's more than a little strange, probably, that my best tips come from Jake's mother, but it is what it is. I don't have a grudge against Ms. Riordan; we even talk sometimes, about safe subjects like the weather and school and work. I know she used to be a hotshot advertising executive, and I think she misses it. I'm not sure how she fills her days now, and it's kind of depressing to wonder.

Vanessa moves seats so she's next to Ms. Riordan, and they start talking while I pull out my phone for a final message check. I have a few more from Bronwyn, and the recently renamed Bayview Crew group chat is going strong. Ever since the NCAA changed its rules about student athletes profiting from their names and likenesses, Cooper's been flooded with endorsement deals. He finally agreed to take one, and his first commercial—for the gym chain where he works out—is airing next month. Naturally, Addy saw that as a reason to have a party.

Viewing party set for Café Contigo, Luis writes. *Can't wait to see our boy make his TV debut. You should've taken that mobile service deal, though. Way more money.*

I couldn't, Cooper messages back. *It kept dropping my calls.*

That's Cooper Clay for you: the kind of guy who insists on actually using something before putting his name on it, and then politely declines a boatload of cash when it sucks.

There's a message from my father too. *Can't find my keys,* he says. *Did you see them the last time you were here?*

Nope, I text back, suppressing a sigh. The thing about Dad is—he's trying. He's been sober for almost four months, and he even has a job now, doing maintenance at Bayview High. I'm not taking bets on how long it'll last, but I'm not trying to tear the guy down either. I relent and add, *Check the side table next to the TV.* Nine times out of ten, that's where he puts them, but even when he's not drinking he can't seem to remember that.

Ms. Riordan's phone rings, and she holds up a finger to halt

Vanessa's Ibiza monologue. "Excuse me one moment, please, this is . . . hello?" She turns away, and Vanessa extends her near-empty glass toward me with a clatter of bracelets.

"More soda water, please, killjoy," she says.

I top her off as Ms. Riordan lets out a loud gasp. "Are you sure?" she says breathlessly. "Please don't . . . I honestly don't think I could take it if . . . really? You're sure. *Really?*" When I look her way, her eyes are brimming with tears. "Oh my goodness. I hoped and I prayed, but I never thought . . . yes. Yes, of course, I know how busy you are. We'll be there tomorrow, nine a.m. sharp. Thank you. Thank you, Carl, from the bottom of my heart." She hangs up and presses her hands to her face.

I've never seen Ms. Riordan so overcome with joy and relief, and it makes my gut twist. There's only one thing that could make her that happy. I exchange glances with Vanessa, who plucks at Ms. Riordan's sleeve. "Everything okay?" she asks.

"It's better than okay," Ms. Riordan chokes out. "Jake . . . he . . ."

She can't continue, so Vanessa prods, "He's getting a new trial?"

Even though I was thinking those exact same words, they still land like a punch. Somehow, I can deal with seeing Mr. and Ms. Riordan, because they've never done anything to me directly. But Jake did. The guy who framed me and helped send me to juvenile detention—the absolute lowest point of my life, when I gave up hope that I'd ever get out—is getting a second chance. The DA's office couldn't wait to put me away, but Jake? Jake Riordan gets a pass, just like always.

Some things never change. They never, ever fucking change.

I yank at the neck of my T-shirt like that'll help me breathe, but it's no good. To hell with the happy hour crowd; I need to get away from this bar. And I need to call Addy, who's going to feel even worse than I do. This is a nightmare come true, and the least I can do is give her a heads-up before she hears about it from someone else.

Ms. Riordan, who's too overcome with emotion to process the fact that her good news sucks for everyone else, roots around in her bag for a tissue before answering Vanessa's question. "It's more than that," she says shakily, pressing it to her eyes. "He's coming home."

CHAPTER FOUR

Addy
Monday, June 29

Cooper's Jeep gives a wheezy rattle as he pulls into a metered parking spot in front of a San Diego office building, and he sighs as he shifts into Park. "Hate to admit it, but I think this thing might be on its last legs," he says.

"Hadn't noticed," I deadpan. On the drive from Bayview, we'd practically had to shout at one another over whatever noise his engine was making.

"Sorry. It wasn't this bad yesterday, I swear. I would've borrowed Kris's car," Cooper says. Then he puts an arm in front of me as I reach for my door handle. "Hang on. Let me check things out first." He gets out of the Jeep and walks around it, scanning the street and nearby buildings before opening my door. "The coast is clear," he says.

"You're ridiculous," I say, smiling despite my horrible mood. Cooper is decked out in full incognito mode—sunglasses, a baseball cap pulled low enough to cover his sandy hair and half his face, and the Oktoberfest T-shirt Kris bought the last time he visited family in Germany—but he still doesn't look anything like the tourist he occasionally pretends to be. Those professional-grade workouts give him away every time.

It's not baseball fans Cooper's worried about, though.

"We're early," he notes, glancing at his phone. "You wanna get some coffee first?"

"No," I say, scanning the windows of the coffee shop on the first floor of Eli's office building. A half-dozen people are scattered across the bench seating, most of them staring at their laptops or their phones. Nothing out of the ordinary, but Eli's office is well-known enough that I wouldn't put it past a reporter to be camped out in their midst. A few of the old standbys hung out around my house for a couple of days after the news about Jake broke, but I've become professional-level skilled at avoiding them. "Let's just go up."

"Yes, ma'am," Cooper says, linking his arm through mine.

I lean into him, relieved at his presence even though initially I'd resisted it. *I'm sticking to my normal routine,* I told everybody when the news dropped last week: that not only was Jake getting a new trial, but he'd been granted bail. *The days of Jake controlling what I do are over.* And I meant it, but it's still nice to have Cooper by my side. Especially since my *normal routine* now consists of picking up restraining order paperwork from Eli.

"I'll bring it to you tonight," Eli said when he called earlier.

"No, I'll come get it. I have errands to run anyway," I'd said. *Normal routine.*

"I'm glad you don't have a game today," I tell Cooper as we

make our way to the elevators. He's playing for an elite summer baseball league, and the schedule is intense even though he doesn't pitch as often as he did during the Cal Fullerton season.

"You and me both," Cooper says, rolling his shoulders. "I overdid it on pull-ups yesterday. Nonny lectured me for half the night." We pass a woman who gives him a long, appraising look—like she's sure she knows him but can't quite figure out how—while ignoring me. The only time I ever feel invisible is when I'm with Cooper, and it's kind of nice.

"Nonny did?" I ask, pressing the Up button. "But she's your number one fan!"

"Yeah, but you know how she's been since she got out of the hospital. Kinda obsessed with joint health," Cooper says. Nonny had knee-replacement surgery a couple of weeks ago, and even though she's recuperating well, I know Cooper worries about her. Other than Kris, there's no one on earth he's closer to.

The elevator door chimes, and when the doors open, we step inside. "Do you think she'll be able to come to your viewing party at Café Contigo?" I ask.

"Doubtful," Cooper says. "Probably a good thing, though, since I'm pretty sure I was terrible in that commercial. Can't believe I let you talk me into a party." His nose wrinkles as the elevator comes to a stop and its doors open to a familiar, pungent smell. "I take it the hair-replacement clinic hasn't moved?"

"Nope," I say, stepping into the hallway.

"Addy!" The door to Until Proven flies open, and Bethany Okonjo, one of Eli's paralegals, comes out to engulf me in a crushing hug. "It's so good to see you!"

"You too," I say, managing to move one hand enough to

pat her back. "Thank you for the, um . . . hug." I was going to say, *extremely normal greeting,* but why be sarcastic toward people who are trying to show you how much they care? That's one of the many, many life lessons I've learned over the past couple of years.

"Eli is wrapping up a meeting, but we've got a conference room all set up for you," Bethany says, releasing me and gesturing through the still-open door. "Winterfell." She catches Cooper's confused look as he finally takes off his sunglasses and adds, "Or for those of you not familiar with our *Game of Thrones* naming system, the small one. Go right in. We picked up a few snacks in case you're hungry."

A few snacks is putting it mildly; it looks like somebody emptied the entire contents of the downstairs coffee shop's bakery case onto the table. That somebody was probably Knox, who waves to us from the larger, glass-walled conference room where a half-dozen people are listening intently to whatever Eli is saying. Now that school is done for the year, Knox is working practically full-time at Until Proven. He was promoted from intern to office assistant last month, so he's finally getting paid with more than free pizza and work experience.

"I have to get back in there, but wave if you need anything," Bethany says before closing the door behind her.

Cooper stalks around the table like a man on a mission. Despite his nonstop training and clean-eating regimen, he's a sucker for carbs. "Yesss, chocolate croissants," he says happily, grabbing two of them. But instead of taking a bite, he folds them into a napkin and places it off to one side. "Kris loves these," he adds.

"Aw, look at you, saving your favorites for him." I sit down and reach for a fruit tart, plucking a glazed strawberry from the top and popping it into my mouth. "The perfect couple remains perfect."

"There's no such thing," Cooper says.

The too-sweet strawberry nearly gets stuck in my throat, and I swallow hard. He's right, of course, because that's what people used to call me and Jake: *the perfect couple.* Seemingly shiny, happy, and ultrapopular, even though both of us were actually second-best at the things we thought we cared most about; Jake was an afterthought behind Cooper when it came to Bayview sports, and I was a perennial beauty pageant runner-up. It turned out, though, that pageants weren't really my thing, and as for Jake, well . . .

"He fooled all of us, you know," Cooper says quietly.

"Not to quite the same extent," I say with a strangled laugh.

"That's not true," Cooper says. "I mean, yeah, I get it was different with you two, but I knew him even longer than you did, Addy. We started hanging out at the end of summer before freshman year, and I never—not one single time—thought he was capable of hurting anyone. Luis had no clue either, and Keely—"

"Could we not mention Keely right now?" I ask.

Cooper blinks. "I thought . . . I thought what happened was a good thing," he says.

"It was," I say, picking at the crumbling edge of my tart. "Or it would be, probably, if I weren't totally *broken.*"

Earlier this month, when my friend Keely Soria came home after finishing her first year at UCLA, we spent most of a Friday night driving around San Diego looking for a party that one of Keely's friends was having. We couldn't find it, so she kept trying slight variations on the address, and it got increasingly hilarious as she drove us from one clearly wrong location to the next. When we finally parked in front of a retirement home, we started laughing so hard that tears leaked out of my eyes. Keely tried to wipe them away and almost stabbed me in the cheek with one of her gel tips, which made me laugh even harder. And then all of a sudden—we were kissing. It was something I hadn't realized I wanted until it was happening, and then it was . . .

Well, not perfect. Like Cooper says, there's no such thing. But it was pretty great.

"You're not broken," Cooper says firmly. "You're cautious, and Keely gets that. She gets that better than almost anyone, I'd say." Cooper and Keely are close now, but they have a past; they'd dated in high school before Cooper was open about his sexuality, and Keely was hurt when she found out. "She's not pushing you, right?"

"Of course not," I mutter. "This is Keely we're talking about. Anyway, she's already gone, remember?" Keely's family always spends the summer on Cape Cod, and she left last week. I hated that I felt a little bit relieved—just like I was relieved when Daniel, the guy I'd been dating a month before that, gracefully accepted my *We'd be better as friends* suggestion. Even though that wasn't what I really wanted.

My love life has followed a familiar, depressing pattern since Jake was arrested: I get excited about somebody new; we have a fantastic, giddy couple of weeks; and then my lizard brain kicks in. Some kind of deep-seated, fight-or-flight fear response that makes me push people away. I don't mind being single—I've come to love it, in a lot of ways—but I want it to be by choice. Not because I'm too afraid for anything else.

Cooper was the first person I told about Keely, since they have a history and I wanted to make sure it wouldn't be weird for him. I think he was touched that I went to him with something of a coming-out moment, even though I'm not entirely sure what it means. I know that I still like guys, and I don't think I've ever been attracted to a girl before Keely, although it's possible I was and didn't know what to call it. When I told Cooper that, he reminded me that labels don't matter. "Just like who you like," he said.

Now Cooper brings me back to the present with a reassuring hand on my shoulder. "Give yourself time, Addy. It hasn't even been two years since everything imploded with Jake."

"And yet, he's gotten out of jail before I've even had a third date," I say, stuffing the rest of the fruit tart into my mouth as Eli finally exits the large conference room and heads our way. He's juggling a big stack of folders, so Cooper lunges for the door and pulls it open.

"Thanks, Cooper. Hi, Addy. Sorry about the wait. Glad you're enjoying the food," Eli says, eyes lingering on my chipmunk cheeks. That was more pastry in one go than I realized.

I chew harder and wave, relaxing at the sight of him. Even though chaos frequently surrounds Eli on account of his job, he's one of the most competent, and therefore calming, people I've ever met. "I can make this quick, because it's all good news. Well, as good as it can be, under the circumstances," he adds, dumping his folders onto the table and rooting through the top one. "We got everything we asked for. Jake can't come within

40

two hundred feet of your home, my and Ashton's home, or Café Contigo. He can't contact you, he can't—"

"How is this even happening, though?" Cooper bursts out in a rare show of anger. He paces toward the window and looks outside, hands on his hips. "There were three eyewitnesses to what Jake did to Addy, *including* Addy. She was in the hospital! Not to mention all the other crap he pulled. Simon would still be here, probably, if Jake hadn't helped him, and maybe things would've changed for him. Why doesn't any of that matter all of a sudden?"

"It does," Eli sighs, running a hand through his hair. It's gotten a little longer—or taller, really—since the wedding, though it still hasn't reached the mad-scientist heights he was sporting when I first met him. "But trial by impartial jury is a fundamental right of our judicial system. Mix that with overcrowding, and Jake's age, and his community service, and, well . . . we are where we are."

Cooper stares out the window, jaw twitching, as Eli takes a seat beside me and grabs both of my hands in his. "Addy, I know this is awful. Nobody believes in the importance of a fair trial more than I do, and I still hate what's happening. But the court understands your concerns, which is why this protective order is extremely thorough. Also, Jake's whereabouts will be carefully monitored, and the new trial will be expedited."

"Am I going to have to testify again?" I ask, my throat drying at the thought. Back then it felt good to confront Jake and be able to calmly state all the ways in which he'd harmed me. But it's not the kind of thing I feel the need to do more than once.

"Possibly not. We can talk about that later, though," Eli

says, releasing my hands. He extracts a stapled packet from his folder and puts it on the table between us. "In the meantime, here's your copy. We can go over everything in full detail, but the most important thing for you to know is that it would be massively, incredibly foolish for Jake to so much as breathe in your direction. Even the slightest violation of this order would send him straight back to jail, and be added to the pile of evidence that convicted him in the first place."

"He didn't worry about leaving evidence the first time around," I say, slumping in my chair. "I wish I was going to Peru now instead of the end of July." Originally I thought I'd be there most of the summer, but then the school I applied to, Colegio San Silvestre, decided to divide its program into two sessions. In order for Maeve and me to be guaranteed spots together, we could sign up for only the second one.

"Don't worry, Addy," Cooper says, folding his arms. "Your friends won't let you be alone for a single minute between now and when you step on that plane. And when we're not shadowing your every move, we'll be keeping an eye on Jake."

"You absolutely will not," Eli says, but I can't help smiling a little at Cooper in bodyguard mode.

"Anything suspicious-looking outside?" I tease.

Cooper's eyes stray back out the window. "There's a beat-up car that's been idling across the street since we got here. Red convertible with a tan top." He leans closer to the glass, squinting. "I'm pretty sure Jake wouldn't be caught dead in a piece of junk like that, but I'd need to get closer to be sure."

"Cooper. Listen. I cannot stress this enough," Eli says, a note of agitation creeping into his voice. "Do nothing. About anything. That goes for both of you. *All* of you. The entire

Bayview Bunch, or whatever you're calling yourselves these days—"

"It's Crew," I break in.

"Whatever," Eli says with a wave of his hand. "I've told Knox the same thing, and I'll fire his ass if he doesn't listen."

"No, you won't," I scoff, feeling a rush of affection as I catch sight of Knox carefully assembling packets at his desk. I barely knew him three months ago, but having someone save an entire wedding party is an intense bonding experience. Now he's like the younger brother I never realized I wanted. He's also very patient about the fact that occasionally, when I think about what could have happened to my sister and nearly every other person that I care about, I feel the need to wrap my arms around his neck and hang on tight for a few minutes.

"I would seriously consider it," Eli says. Unconvincingly. "And as for you—" He frowns as I pick up the restraining order and an envelope drops from between the pages, landing face-down on the table. "Wait a sec. That shouldn't be there."

We both stare at the envelope for a few beats. Eli looks worried, and I flash back to the death threats he got a couple of months ago from Jared Jackson, the boy whose brother Eli helped put in jail. Those letters escalated over time, right until Jared decided to blow up Eli and Ashton's rehearsal dinner. "Is that . . ." I grab for the envelope before Eli can and turn it over with shaking hands. Then I blink a few times as Eli fidgets in his chair. "Baby Kleinfelter Prentiss?" I read. "Are these . . . ultrasound pictures?"

"No," Eli says. "It's the baby's sex, from our last OB visit. We don't want to know, but the nurse gave us the results anyway. Ashton asked me to throw the envelope out without opening it, but doing that felt like bad luck, somehow, so I've been . . . hanging on to it. I don't understand how it got mixed up with my files." Eli gets a little red as I start to smile, Jake temporarily forgotten. "I didn't open it or anything. I wasn't even tempted." He goes redder still. "Much."

"*We* don't want to know?" Cooper asks with a grin. "Or is that just Ashton?"

"Both of us," Eli says. "But I'm slightly more curious than she is."

"How about I keep it?" I say, tucking it into my bag.

"You're gonna look as soon as we get into the car, aren't you?" Cooper asks, finally detaching himself from the window.

"Maybe, maybe not," I say, my spirits lifting a few notches. It's a welcome change, after the week I've had, to be in charge of a mystery where there's no bad answer.

CHAPTER FIVE

Phoebe
Wednesday, July 1

There are only so many things you can worry about at once, and right now, four hours into my shift at Café Contigo, I've hit my limit.

"If you don't like ground beef, or garlic, or onions, or olives, then maybe you don't actually *want* an empanada," I tell the woman sitting at my corner table. "Maybe what you really want is a lump of dough. Unfortunately, we don't serve those."

The customer blinks in shock, as she should, because *wow*, that was rude. I open my mouth to apologize, but my throat is thick and I can't think of anything to say except, *Sorry, but you know the old saying about a last straw? That's you.* Before the woman can call over a manager, though, Evie swoops in beside me, her pad and pen in hand.

"Phoebe, you're overdue for your break," she says in a cheery voice. Her smile is as bright as her voice, but her hands are firm as she guides me away from the table, just as Ms. Santos glances up from the cash register. "Why don't you take a seat and I'll finish up here?"

"Okay," I say stiffly. Then, belatedly, I add, "Thanks," but Evie's already bending over the woman's shoulder, pointing out alternatives on the menu. None of which, probably, are *a lump of dough*. Adding that snotty little suggestion to all the times I've been late this month might be the last straw for Ms. Santos, and nobody would blame her.

I can feel my boss's eyes on me as I debate my next steps. All I want to do is hide away in the kitchen for a few minutes of peace and quiet, but my brother is sitting at a corner table with the remnants of his dinner. Owen's by himself like always, hunched over his phone, his black backpack at his feet and his too-long strawberry-blond hair hanging in his eyes. Family means everything to Ms. Santos, and if I skulk past my lonely little brother without a word, she's going to think even less of me than she already does.

I paste on a smile and slide into the chair across from him. "How was your dinner?"

"Fine," Owen says without looking up. Mom got him fake AirPods for his birthday, and he has one of them tucked into his ear.

"Didn't feel like being at home tonight?" I ask, trying to match Evie's cheerful tone. Owen usually gets takeout the nights that Mom and I are both working. She has a day job as an office manager and sometimes works nights and weekends on her wedding-coordinator business. That slowed down a lot after the disaster of Ashton and Eli's rehearsal dinner, but it's finally started to pick back up.

Owen shrugs, and the silence stretches between us until I try again. "What are you doing?"

"Watching TikTok."

"Anything good?"

My brother finally glances up, and my heart skips at the trace of animation on his face. He's changed so much, so quickly, that it's like an unexpected gift to catch a glimpse of his old self—the sweet, earnest boy who could talk for hours about rewiring a toaster. Then he says, "This guy posted a video about how his girlfriend died in this freak fishing accident. He said she got dragged underwater by a giant carp and drowned, but it turns out she's not actually dead. He made the whole thing up. She didn't even know till she saw the video."

And just like that, Former Owen is gone. "Why would he do that?" I ask.

"To get views," Owen says, like it should be obvious. "And it worked. It's his most popular video by, like, a million." He lets out a little cackle that makes my skin crawl.

"That's not funny," I say testily.

Owen shrugs and swipes at his phone. "I think it is."

I bite my lip to keep from asking, *What's wrong with you?* I know how Maeve would reply—or Knox, or my mom, or pretty much anyone who's observed Owen's recent trans- formation: *He's thirteen.* Which is true, but it's *also* true that Owen kept a deadly game going that ultimately killed my ex- boyfriend. Snickering about somebody faking a death doesn't seem nearly as harmless against that backdrop.

But Owen and I can't talk about that, because he doesn't know that I know. Back in April and May, when it was touch and go whether Emma might get into legal trouble, part of me hoped he might confess—that his conscience wouldn't let her take the fall for him. That he'd at least confide in his family, even if he couldn't bring himself to tell the police. But he never did.

Even though Emma ultimately wasn't charged, it's not like she wasn't punished in other ways: the merit aid she'd been counting on for college disappeared, she lost all her tutoring jobs, and a small but vocal contingent around Bayview made it clear they felt she'd gotten away with murder. It's why she moved across the country to my aunt's, for at least the summer and possibly a lot longer. My smart, studious sister, who's spent half her life planning for college, is suddenly staring at an empty, uncertain future.

Meanwhile, Owen's acting like nothing happened.

"Did you see this?" he asks abruptly, holding out his phone.

I take it apprehensively—I really don't want to watch a toxic video—but it's just somebody's Instagram picture of the billboard on Clarendon: TIME FOR A NEW GAME, BAYVIEW.

"Yeah, I've seen it," I say.

"There's a second part," he says, swiping at what I now realize is a carousel post. The next image is of the same billboard, but this time it reads: THERE'S ONLY ONE RULE. Whoever posted the picture wrote beneath: *Here's my guess: the only rule is THERE ARE NO RULES MUAHAHAHAHA (skull emoji).*

The knots that have taken up permanent residence in my stomach get tighter as Owen says, "Weird ad, huh? Like, what are they even selling?"

I search his face, trying to decipher his blank expression and tone. Do the words bother him because they remind him of the Truth or Dare game that killed Brandon? Do they scare him? Does he think they're funny?

Did he write them?

No. That's ridiculous. My brother might be a technology whiz, but even he can't hot-wire a billboard. Probably. Then again, the words aren't only on a billboard. . . .

"Have you seen the flyers?" I ask, but Owen's eyes are already back on his phone. A few seconds later, he snorts out a short laugh. I clear my throat and add, "Did you hear me?"

"I'm watching skateboarding videos now," he says. "This one guy took a header off a rail and he's covered in blood."

"Stop watching that crap."

"It's dripping into his eyes. Oh, man, he looks dead," Owen chortles, and that does it. My temper spikes, and before I realize what I'm doing, I've grabbed the phone from his hand.

"That's. Not. *Funny*," I growl, yanking out his earbud.

"Ow!" Owen winces and grabs at his ear. "What's your problem?"

"You, Owen. *You* are my fucking problem!"

Oh God. As soon as the words leave my mouth, I realize how loud they are—and how easily they've carried through the small restaurant. Owen's mouth drops open while the entire room stares at us, and my cheeks burn as Ms. Santos glides over from the cash register.

"Phoebe, why don't you take off the rest of the night?" she asks. "You've been here so long already. Evie can handle your tables."

I feel an irrational stab of annoyance at Evie then, for being so goddamn efficient at everything that she makes me look even worse. "I'm fine, I don't need to leave—" I start, but Ms. Santos quickly cuts me off.

"Yes, you do," she says. The rest of that sentence—*or you're not coming back*—is unspoken but heavily implied.

"Okay," I sigh. I can barely look at Owen, who's fiddling with his earbud, but I force myself to ask, "Do you want a ride home, or . . ."

"I'll walk," he says. "I'm gonna stay here for a while."

Ms. Santos pats his shoulder. "I'll bring you some alfajores," she says, before heading into the kitchen. If the customer who wanted an ingredient-free empanada hadn't already been the last straw, this would be it: being tossed out of my home away from home while my brother, the potential budding sociopath, gets a plateful of cookies.

Maybe that's my life now: a series of never-ending last straws.

I get up from the table without another word and skulk into the kitchen to get my stuff. Everyone's too busy to talk to me, or maybe they've already heard that I lost it in the dining room and are giving me *space*. Which is a concept I've hated ever since Emma did it to me after our father died. I don't understand how you can look at someone who's obviously hurting and think, *You know what this person needs? More time in their own head.*

I'm almost at the door when someone calls my name. I turn to see Manny, Luis's older brother, holding a brown paper bag. "Hey, could you take this? It's for Mrs. Clay."

"Of course," I say. Café Contigo doesn't normally deliver, but the Santos family has been making an exception for Cooper's grandmother since her knee surgery. I volunteer whenever she orders while I'm working, because Mrs. Clay—who keeps telling me to call her Nonny—is awesome. Plus, hanging out with her has the added benefit of making me less starstruck around Cooper. It's hard to be intimidated by someone once you've seen their baby pictures.

"Great, thanks. She loves you," Manny says, which lifts my spirits a little.

I step outside and blink at where my car should be—right out front—before remembering how crowded it was when I got here. I had to park a good five minutes away, at the edge of a sloping side alley. I take out my keys as I approach, frowning at the pavement because I don't remember it being quite *that* sloping, and—oh God.

It's not the street that's so uneven; it's my car. The rear driver's-side tire is flat.

"God damn it," I hiss, kicking the tire much too hard. Not *another* last straw. Then I hobble on one foot, pain radiating through my toe, before carefully placing Mrs. Clay's food on the ground so I can dig through my bag for my phone.

I need to call Café Contigo to let them know that someone else will have to deliver Mrs. Clay's dinner, and then AAA. But once I have my phone out I hesitate, overcome with the sudden urge to call Knox. The last time a tire went flat on the ancient Corolla I used to share with Emma, he'd changed it. So slowly and painstakingly that I'd gotten impatient at the time, but now, it's one of my favorite memories of him. One of those hidden sides I kept discovering back then.

Back then. It wasn't even four months ago, but it feels so much longer.

If I called, I know Knox would leave Until Proven without

a second thought. But I shouldn't, right? We've hung out a few times since he kicked me out of his bed, and I'm doing my best to follow his lead and act like everything's normal. The problem is, I'm not sure what that word means anymore when it comes to me and Knox.

"You okay there?"

I glance up, still favoring my sore foot, and nearly fall over.

Jake Riordan is standing on the sidewalk beside my car, dressed in a crisp blue T-shirt and jeans, like he's some kind of regular person and not the monster who's been haunting my friends' nightmares. I can feel my jaw drop—unhinge, really—and my throat works convulsively without managing to push out any words.

"Looks like you've got a flat tire there," Jake says amiably. There's a woman behind him—middle-aged and well-dressed in a stylish floral sheath, with the same blue eyes and chestnut-brown hair as Jake. "You need help changing it?"

I'm frozen in place, still unable to speak. The woman glances nervously at me and touches Jake's arm. "Sweetheart, she probably has someone coming—"

"I don't." I blurt the words without thinking, and before I can take them back, Jake flashes an easy grin.

"You have a spare in there?" he asks.

I glance at Mrs. Clay's food, getting cold on the ground. And somehow, instead of telling Jake no, I find myself opening my trunk.

"I got it," Jake says as I fumble with the latch on the trunk floor. I back away, giving him a lot more space than he needs as he hauls out the tire and jack. He kneels beside my car with practiced ease, as quick and confident as Knox was slow and cautious. After a few minutes of silence I glance at Ms. Riordan, who gives me a tentative smile. I suppose it would be polite to say something to her, or to him, but . . . *what?* How did I even let this happen? And why is he here? Aren't there rules about him prowling the streets, just a few blocks away from where Addy works? I glance at his ankle and catch a flash of black plastic; at least he's being monitored. But downtown Bayview feels like an overly generous geographic area.

"Phoebe, right?" Jake asks, popping the old tire from the rim.

"Huh?" I'm so startled to hear my name that I take another step back.

His head is still down, so maybe he didn't notice. Not that I care, because so what if Jake Riordan thinks I'm rude? Or that I'm afraid of him? I'm not; or at least, I'm not while his mother is standing right there. "You're Phoebe Lawton, right?" he says, grunting a little as he positions the spare tire. "I remember you from Bayview High."

No, you don't, I think. *You remember me from whatever news program you watched in prison.* Jared Jackson's bomb attempt didn't make quite as many headlines as Simon's death, but it was close. All I manage to say, though, is "Yeah."

"Nice to see you again," Jake says, and—*come on.* How am I supposed to respond to that? *Can't say the same, but thanks for the roadside assist?* At least he's practically done already, and . . . nope, not practically, he's done. He heaves my flat tire into the trunk, places the jack and other tools beside it, and closes the trunk.

"Well, that was fast," his mother says, sounding relieved.

Meanwhile, I still haven't thanked him. Somehow, I can't

bring myself to utter those words to Jake Riordan. This entire surreal scenario feels like a betrayal of Addy. The least I can do is not express appreciation for the guy who tried to choke the life out of her, and . . . oh God, they're both staring at me now and I need them to leave.

Say something, Phoebe. Anything.

"I . . . I should really learn how to change a tire," I manage.

Jake stands there with his hands on his hips, eyes glinting as he holds my gaze for a few beats too long. I can't help it; I back up another step. Then he smiles again—more wolfish than charming this time—and says, "It's easy, Phoebe. All you need is practice."

JAKE

Six Years Earlier

"You wanna keep playing or what?" Simon asked.

Jake rolled his eyes, annoyed for reasons he couldn't really explain. No, he didn't want to keep playing. He was bored with the video game they'd already been at for three hours. He was bored, period. Or maybe *restless* was a better word. It was the summer before freshman year of high school, and all Jake could think lately was that there should be more to life by now than sitting in his living room playing video games with Simon Kelleher.

That was fine for middle school, but things were changing. Jake wasn't nearly as tall as his dad yet, but he was finally starting to get there. His football skills had really taken off in eighth grade, to the point where his coach told him he should try out for varsity at Bayview High. Girls were looking at him differently, and when he examined himself in the mirror—which was a lot lately—he knew why. His face was changing in a good way, losing what his mother called, mortifyingly, *baby fat*. Jake Riordan was finally starting to go places.

But Simon? Simon Kelleher was the same angsty, nerdy, scrawny, pissed-off kid he'd always been. Simon hated sports, parties, being outdoors for any length of time, and most people. Last month, all he did was complain when Jake made him watch the Little League World Series, even though the whole town was watching because a Bayview team made it all the way to the semifinals. Cooper Clay, that new kid from Mississippi, pitched an unbelievable no-hitter, and the team missed out on going to the championship game only because of fielding errors. All Jake could think as he watched Cooper—so cool and calm under pressure, clearly destined to be a legend at Bayview High—was *That's the kind of friend I need.*

For now, though, he was stuck with Simon.

The front door opened then, and a deep voice boomed, "Katherine? I'm home."

"Mom's not," Jake yelled back.

He glanced at the clock, surprised to see that it was past six. He knew he shouldn't be, though; ever since his mother had gotten promoted, she'd started coming home later than Dad. Now that he knew how late it was, he decided he was starving and added, "What's for dinner?"

"Hell if I know," Dad said, poking his head into the living room. He unknotted his tie and tossed his briefcase onto the nearest armchair. Jake's father was a lawyer—"Biglaw," he always said, which Jake took to mean he made a lot of money. Enough to pay for this house and buy all his perfectly fitted suits from some legendary London shop. Mr. Riordan stopped by whenever he was there on business, to keep his measurements up to date. "Some kind of takeout, probably. How's it going, Simon? You staying for food?"

"Nah," Simon said, getting to his feet. Another one of the things Simon hated was making polite conversation with adults. "I'm out. See you tomorrow."

"Maybe," Jake said noncommittally as Simon skulked out of the room.

"You talk to your mom lately?" Dad asked, leaning against the door frame. His blond hair had gone prematurely silver years ago, and his eyes were a clear, sharp hazel. He'd been an Ivy League athlete and was still in shape, fast enough to beat Jake in sprints. Jake admired his father; he'd never gone through the kind of *I hate you* phase that Simon was stuck in with his parents. Even though Jake resembled his mother, he mimicked his father's mannerisms so closely that everyone commented on how much they looked alike. It was interesting, Jake thought, how easy it was to make people see what you wanted them to see.

"Not today," Jake said. His mother usually checked in with him at some point, unless she had too many meetings.

"Busy woman," Dad said, pulling his phone from his pocket. "Let me see if we should wait for her or order now. Are you up for Vietnamese?"

"Yeah, sure."

"Not sure why we bothered renovating the kitchen, for all the use it's getting lately," Dad muttered as he swiped at his phone.

Jake knew why: because it looked great. Just like the rest of the house. When Mr. Riordan made partner at his law firm a few years ago, the family had moved onto the street he'd had his eye on for years. "Wellington Avenue," Mr. Riordan would say every time he drove past it. "That's the best of the best, right there."

Most of the time Mom smiled, but every once in a while, she'd wrinkle her nose and say, "Too much house."

"There's no such thing," Dad always replied.

Jake agreed with him. Who wouldn't want five extra bedrooms, a game room, the kind of finished basement you almost never saw in this area, and a giant backyard with a perfectly landscaped pool? Now all Jake needed was the right kind of friends to fill it with.

And the right girlfriend.

Dad frowned suddenly, his phone to his ear. "Who's this?" he asked. "Oh? And you're answering my wife's phone because . . . ? Yes. Please do that." A pause, and then Mr. Riordan asked, "Katherine? You joining us at home anytime soon?"

Jake lunged for his headphones, plugged them into his phone, and turned on some music. He didn't like when Dad sounded like this—as though he was already mad at you before you'd even had a chance to start talking. There was no winning with Mr. Riordan when he took that tone, and he's been taking it a lot lately with Mom.

The best thing to do, Jake decided, was block it out. Because if you can't see or hear something, there's no reason it should bother you.

CHAPTER SIX

Nate

Friday, July 3

"All in favor?" Sana asks. Each of my roommates, except me, raises their hand. Which makes this a done deal, but Sana's a stickler for protocol. "All opposed?"

My hand shoots up. Sana—our self-appointed house leader even though she's been here only a few months—glances my way, and then at the girl perched beside me on one of our lop-sided living room futons. "Bronwyn, you don't live here," she says. "You don't get to vote."

"I'm still opposed," Bronwyn says defiantly, raising her hand higher.

"Noted," Sana says, tapping her knuckles on the coffee table like a gavel. "The motion to let Reggie Crawley stay in the house hereby passes."

Bronwyn sits up straighter—which I didn't think was physically possible—and says, "You're all making a huge mistake."

I rub a hand across my jaw and glare at my roommates. I knew we were going to lose this—that *I* was going to lose this—but the thing about being with Bronwyn Rojas is, you don't get to ignore shitty situations. You have to *do something,* even when it's pointless.

And then you have to keep talking about it. "You're enabling Reggie and putting anybody who comes into this house at risk," Bronwyn continues.

"He says the girl knows about the video, though," Jiahao says, pushing a shock of bleached-blond hair off his forehead.

I roll my eyes. "You seriously believe him?"

"Some people are into that kind of thing." Jiahao shrugs. "Who's to say?"

"How about the people who went to high school with Reggie and know all about his creepy modus operandi?" Bronwyn asks. "He doesn't care about consent. Trust me, that girl has no idea she was being filmed, and she definitely has no idea that he *shared* it."

That's why we're here; because last weekend, I walked in on asshole Reggie Crawley showing a sex tape to Jiahao and another one of our roommates, Deacon. They were stoned and not exactly worried about where and how Reggie had gotten the recording. But I knew.

I went straight into Reggie's room, shut the door and the curtains, and used my phone's flashlight to look for reflections where they shouldn't be. Turned out the camera was on an alarm clock. I smashed it, but it's not like that's going to stop him from getting another one. Kicking him out won't solve the problem either, but at least it would be *something.*

"Didn't any of you see Katrina Lott's TikTok?" Bronwyn asks.

Blank looks all around. None of my roommates except Reggie went to Bayview High, which is where Katrina went too. She graduated the same year as Bronwyn and me, and she unknowingly starred in Reggie's first-ever sex tape. Katrina didn't talk about it back then, and she moved to Portland after graduation. But a few months ago, she posted a video about how violated that tape made her feel. Almost everyone from Bayview High has seen it by now, and it's made me hate Reggie even more.

"You should watch it," Bronwyn says. "I'll send you a link."

"Okay," Sana says. "But for now—majority rules."

Sana won't admit it, but her vote is mostly financial. It's not easy finding new roommates in July, especially in a shack like this one with no air conditioning and stuffy, closet-sized bedrooms. If we toss Reggie, everyone's rent goes up by a hundred and fifty bucks. Sana's even more strapped for cash than I am, and Jiahao, Deacon, and Crystal aren't much better off. Nobody in this house gets any help from their family.

Or maybe it's more that, like me, they won't take it. My mother gives me a check every month, and I deposit it untouched so I can give it back to her in case she backslides and has to go through rehab again. Or my father does.

"We done?" Deacon unfolds his nearly seven-foot frame from an armchair, yawning, and everyone follows suit except me and Bronwyn.

"You guys suck," I grumble.

Deacon shrugs. "Reggie's a dick, but what can you do?"

I exhale a frustrated breath. "I don't know, Deacon. *Kick him out?*"

Sana lingers in the doorway between the living room and the hall as the rest of our roommates file out. Her faded cotton skirt brushes the floor, which is the closest thing to being swept that it's ever going to get. Sana looks like some kind of old-school folk singer, with her flowy clothes and her fondness for wearing a headband across her forehead. She also plays the guitar, badly, and she knows only one song. Years from now, I'm going to be forced to think about this house anytime "Time of Your Life" comes on the radio.

"Reggie will have to be on his best behavior from now on," she says. "Including the Fourth of July party tomorrow. Bedroom door open at all times."

I snort. "Way to lay down the law, Sana. That'll do it."

"It will. Trust me," Sana says before heading upstairs.

When she's out of sight, Bronwyn mutters, "This probably goes without saying, but I *don't* trust her."

"Uh-huh," I say. It's all I can manage right now. I feel the same tightness in my chest that I did at Bayview Country Club; like all the air I should be breathing has been sucked out of the room by a single, poisonous thought: *Some things never change.* First Jake Riordan, and now Reggie. What's the point of doing the right thing when assholes like that never bother, and get whatever they want anyway?

"This isn't over," Bronwyn says. "We just need to take a different angle." Then she looks at me—*really* looks at me—and adds, "It doesn't have to be right this second, though."

That almost makes me smile. "Don't tell me Bronwyn Rojas is going soft."

"I'm not. Just getting better at knowing when to take a break." She shifts toward me and puts her legs across my lap. "We can talk about something else. Like . . . that movie you've been bugging me to watch."

"*Onibaba*?" I ask. I still haven't converted Bronwyn into a Japanese-horror-film fan, but that doesn't mean I've stopped trying.

"That's the one. It's old, right?"

"Yeah, from the sixties."

She lifts one hand to play with the hair on the nape of my neck. "How bloody is it?"

Some of the tension drains out of me as I trace a circle on her knee with my thumb. "Less than average," I say.

"Good to know."

"Plus, women do most of the killing. You'd like that."

Bronwyn leans forward to plant a lingering kiss on my cheek. "Yeah, I would," she murmurs, and I can't help it— I start cracking up.

"This is the most obvious distraction attempt ever," I say.

Bronwyn kisses my other cheek, and then her lips trail down to my neck. "Are you complaining?" she asks with a smile in her voice.

All my negative thoughts disappear as I pull her to me. "Hell no," I say before lowering my mouth to hers. Her body melds to mine, fitting into places I forget exist when she's not around. I push her back against the pillows and kiss her more deeply, my hands sliding beneath the hem of her shirt, until she breaks away with a laugh.

"Not here," she says, adjusting the glasses that have slid halfway off her nose. Her hair is mussed, and her cheeks are flushed bright red. She looks gorgeous. "It's only a matter of time before one of your roommates comes back."

"My room?" I ask hopefully.

"I have to meet Maeve in ten minutes," she says.

"I can work with that."

Before we have a chance to move, though, the doorbell rings. "Not it!" Deacon yells from the kitchen. Bronwyn slides off me, and I reluctantly get to my feet. "I can also work with nine and a half minutes," I tell her as I head for the front door.

I'm expecting the FedEx person, or maybe one of those randos Crystal occasionally does tarot readings for, but that's not who's standing on the doorstep. "Hey, Dad," I say, opening the door wide. "What's up?"

"Hi, Nate." He's holding a cardboard box in one hand and shoves it toward me. "Your lizard powder showed up at the house."

"Sorry," I say, taking it. I started sprinkling a calcium supplement over Stan's food last year—another recommendation from Bronwyn, which actually does seem to perk him up—and the online store I buy from still has my old address on file. Half the time, I forget to check the right box when I order it. "I could've just picked it up, though."

"You're on my way to work," Dad says gruffly, shifting from one foot to the other.

I'm not—he works maintenance at Bayview High and I'm nowhere near the place—but I let it slide as I take him in. He's lost weight since he stopped drinking, and his faded T-shirt and ancient jeans are practically falling off him. I know my mother bought him a bunch of new clothes, but she finally moved out last month, so nobody's making him wear them anymore. My eyes go automatically to his hands, checking for the kind of tremor that would tell me he's slipped up. I'm not sure when I'll stop looking for that.

"You wanna come in?" I ask, even though my mood plummets at the thought of losing what's now barely eight minutes alone with Bronwyn. I don't blame Mom for moving out; it's not like they had a real marriage anymore, and she's spent more than a year helping Dad get on his feet and through rehab. She deserves her own space, and it's not like she can keep him sober. He's the only one who can do that. But he's not used to living alone, so he's always making up excuses to stop by.

"Nah, that's okay. You're busy," Dad says. His eyes stray over my shoulder as he adds, "Hi, Bronwyn. Nice to see you."

"You too, Patrick." Bronwyn comes up beside me, hair smoothed into its usual neat ponytail. I'm not sure when she got on a first-name basis with my father, but he seems to like it. "I'm heading out, but I'm glad I ran into you. I've been thinking—maybe Nate and I could come over and make you dinner sometime next week? My grandmother gave me a new recipe for sancocho soup that I've been dying to try, if you're willing to let me experiment on you."

A smile creases Dad's worn face, and for a second, I see what my mother means when she says *You two look so much alike.* "I'd like that. Very much. Any night that Nate's free," he adds with a hopeful look toward me.

Once again, my girlfriend is a million times better a person than I am, because that invitation should've come from me. "Wednesday, probably," I say.

"Perfect," Bronwyn says.

"Looking forward to it," Dad says. Then he shuffles back

a step, like he's about to leave, but he doesn't. Instead, he asks, "Listen, Nate—are you sure you didn't pick up my keys by mistake? Not the house ones," he adds before I can protest. "I did find those, right where you said they'd be. The work ones. Can't find them anywhere."

"I'm sure," I say, unease creeping over me. Dad's back has finally fully healed after he was injured during a roofing job years ago, which is good news. In related news, though, he's no longer eligible for disability, so he needs to hang on to this job. Otherwise, my mother and I are going to have to pitch in to pay his bills, and that'll mean I have to get a *third* job, and—

Bronwyn's arm links through mine with a reassuring squeeze. I can practically hear her say *One thing at a time,* which is her mantra every time all the balls I'm juggling threaten to come crashing down on my head. "Did you leave them at work, maybe?" she asks.

"I don't think so," Dad says doubtfully. "But it's possible. My brain . . . it gets foggy every once in a while, you know?"

"Yeah. I know," I say. "You need to retrace your steps. Want me to help you look?" I'm not sure what good it'd do, but I have an hour to spare before I need to head to the country club.

"No, that's okay," Dad says, snapping the rubber band on his wrist. Mom told him he should wear one and do that anytime he feels stressed, and now it's a constant with him. "You probably don't want to be around Bayview High today. Or any day, for a while."

I don't like the shifty look on his face. "Why not?" I ask warily. If he's stashing whiskey bottles at work, I will kill him. Not literally. But I'll want to.

"That kid . . . he works out there sometimes," Dad says.

66

"With his parole officer. At least, I think that's who it is. Some kind of cop-looking guy."

I guess my brain can be foggy, too, because Bronwyn catches on a lot faster than I do. "Jake Riordan?" she gasps, tightening her hold on my arm. "Are you serious? Why would he be allowed anywhere near Bayview High?"

"He's using the fields," Dad says. "I guess it's some kind of thing they worked out with the court, that he can run around the track for a few miles." I gape in disgust, and he adds, "He's not allowed in the building or anything."

"Jesus. So much for keeping him on a short leash," I say bitterly. It doesn't matter how hard I try to shove guys like Reggie and Jake out of my brain; they keep coming back. Because people keep *letting* them.

"Yeah." Dad snaps his rubber band again. "I know I wasn't around much when everything happened, but . . . I don't like seeing that kid there. Anywhere, really."

Dad wasn't so much *not around* as he was *passed out,* but the general sentiment still holds. "You and me both," I say.

The more Jake waltzes through town like he's a regular guy, the more people are going to start thinking that he is one. And that *impartial trial* he's supposed to get will suddenly be biased in the wrong direction. Instead of jurors looking at him like a criminal—the way they would've looked at me if I'd ever been in front of them—all they'll see is Bayview's golden boy.

Some things never change.

CHAPTER SEVEN

Addy
Saturday, July 4

There are relaxing Saturdays, there are sociable Saturdays, and then there's this: the Bayview Mall on the Fourth of July with my pregnant sister and my mother, going head-to-head over the fact that Ashton refuses to spend three thousand dollars on a pod-shaped crib from a trendy baby store called Le Petit Ange.

"But Ashton, *look* at it," Mom says, running her hands along the smooth blond wood. "It's so chic. They didn't have anything like this when you and Addy were born."

"It looks like a miniature tanning bed," Ashton says.

I tap my fingers against the clear acrylic front, patterned with laser-cut stars. "Or a really big salad bowl," I say, and my sister snorts out a laugh. The *Bayview Blade* called Le Petit Ange "a one-stop shop for Bayview's trendiest, most style-conscious parents," which is pretty much the opposite of Ashton and Eli. Try telling that to my mother, though.

"You two have no vision," Mom complains. She's dressed to the nines for this shopping trip, in tight white pants, gold sandals, and a patterned wrap top, and I have to admit that she looks great. So does Ashton, in a pale-blue sundress that shows off her tiny bump. I'm dragging down our style quotient in a Café Contigo tank top and shorts, my purple-streaked hair held back with a flower-shaped clip. Which must be crooked, because Mom reaches out to refasten it before adding, "It even converts into the most darling little toddler bed."

"Without rails," Ashton notes, eyeing the glossy photo mounted beside the crib. "The poor kid would fall right out."

Mom waves a manicured hand. "I'm sure you can buy those separately."

"For a thousand dollars," Ashton mutters under her breath.

"At least think about it. I'm going to look at high chairs."

Ashton watches Mom weave her way through clothing displays as she heads for the back of the store. "I don't have the heart to tell her we're getting a hand-me-down crib from Eli's cousin," she sighs.

"She knows you'd never drop three grand on a crib. She just wants the experience of being a doting grandmother in a store like this. All you have to do to keep her happy is buy one small thing like . . ." I gaze at the rack beside us before plucking off a tiny pajama set patterned with white and gray elephants. "These pj's."

Ashton's expression softens as she reaches out a hand. "Those are adorable." Then her eyes widen as she lifts the price tag. "And three hundred dollars." I shove the pajamas back onto the rack as she adds, "This store is not meant for the children of freelance graphic designers and nonprofit lawyers."

"Speaking of . . ."

"Nothing new," Ashton says quickly. She knows exactly where I was going, and I hope she appreciates the fact that I waited more than an hour to ask if Eli had any updates about Jake. I haven't seen him since he was released, mostly because I've memorized where he's allowed to go and made sure I stay far away. The Bayview Mall, for example, is safe territory. "At least, not when it comes to *him*."

My sister never says Jake's name if she can help it. Her tone is a little strained, though, so I ask, "But there's *something*?"

Ashton glances behind us, where Mom is absorbed in browsing high chairs that look like tiny, expensive ladders. "Yes. Maybe. Nothing to do with you," she adds hastily, reading whatever expression must have crossed my face. Panic, probably. "But Eli's worried because . . . Do you remember the billboard that popped up about a week ago on Clarendon Street? The one about a new game?"

"Yeah, of course," I say. My mother is positive that it's some kind of guerilla marketing tactic for Cooper's summer baseball league. She refuses to be swayed by my counterargument that baseball is not a new game, and has more than one rule. "Why is Eli worried?"

"Well, a lot of people were upset about that billboard. It felt like a horribly insensitive campaign, given what happened with Brandon and Jared a few months ago. As if some company was trying to capitalize on the notoriety, although you couldn't even tell who they are or what they were trying to sell. So people complained to the advertising agency that manages the billboard, and it turns out . . ." Ashton pauses as a harried father pushing a double stroller passes us. "It turns out the billboard was hacked."

"Hacked?" I repeat.

"Yeah. It's digital, you know, managed by the company, and somehow, someone got into their system and changed the ad. The agency switched it back, and they're investigating, but they don't have any answers yet. Maybe it was just a prank, but . . ." Ashton reaches out a hand to stroke the soft sleeve of the elephant pajamas. "Eli is worried that it might have been someone from the revenge forum. You know, picking up where Jared left off."

"Oh my God." My stomach plummets. Jared was part of a subreddit called Vengeance Is Mine, inspired by Simon and populated by a lot of angry people with grudges. After Emma discovered that Brandon had caused her father's death, she found her way there and started commiserating with Jared. And the rest, unfortunately, is Bayview history—including the part where my brother-in-law was stalked by a terrorist.

And by extension, so was my sister. I can't help it; my eyes stray to Ashton's stomach, and she instinctively covers it with one hand. "Eli hasn't received any threats," she says quickly. "There's no indication that anyone is targeting him directly, but he's worried enough that there's a task force at Until Proven looking into it."

"Looking into it how?" I ask. "Vengeance Is Mine got taken down."

"Yeah, but you know how these things are. They have nine lives," Ashton says. "As soon as you get one taken down, it pops up somewhere else in a different form."

She's right, of course, but I was hoping we'd go at least a year without having to deal with Simon's legacy again. "We should get Maeve on the case," I say. "She has a knack for—"

Ashton holds up a hand, cutting me off. "Eli doesn't want her involved."

"Oh, come on," I say, tugging at my earring anxiously. "He needs to stop thinking like that. If it weren't for Maeve and Knox, we could all be dead!"

I said that last part a little too loud, and a couple of well-dressed women browsing the onesies rack glance over at us. "Shhh," Ashton murmurs, strolling toward a quieter corner with me at her heels. "I know," she says, stopping in front of a blanket display. "But they're just kids. Still in high school. If there really is something going on with a Simon-Jared copycat, it's not safe for them to get involved."

"It's not safe for *you*," I protest. "Ash, you need to go stay with Dad in Chicago."

I expect her to protest, but she gives me a wry smile. "That's what Eli said."

"So go! Go tomorrow."

"I can't," she says. "Well, I could, but I won't. My life is here, Addy. My husband is here. He's doing important work that sometimes brings him into contact with desperate people, and if I left every time that happened . . ."

"You'd be safe. The baby would be safe." My voice hitches as I think about the envelope in my room that I still haven't opened: *Baby Kleinfelter Prentiss.*

72

"I don't see *you* running off to Dad's," Ashton says.

I thought about it, briefly. My stepmother, Courtney, reached out to invite me when the news about Jake broke, which was nice of her. But we barely know one another, and I couldn't imagine being cooped up in a city apartment with Dad, Courtney, and Courtney's three grade-school-aged kids for a month. "That's different."

"How so?"

"I'm not pregnant, for one thing!"

We have a glare-off that Ashton breaks first with a rueful smile. "I'm sorry, Addy. I went about this all wrong," she says. "I scared you, and I didn't mean to. Eli's acting out of an abundance of caution, okay? Everything will be fine."

"You can't possibly be sure of that." I look over at our mother, who's reached the end of the high chair display. "Does Mom know?"

"Not yet. Not till there's something more to know."

"Probably just as well," I mutter. "It's not like she'd worry."

Ashton purses her lips. "You know she feels horrible about Jake, right?"

"What, that he was released? We all do."

"No. That she encouraged that relationship in the first place."

I blink. Mom was Jake's biggest fan a couple of years ago, to the point where she made me feel like I was lucky to be with him and needed to do whatever it took to keep him. My whole life was like that, even before I started dating: Mom always encouraging me to be the prettiest, most desirable, most pleasing possible version of Adelaide Prentiss. I tried so hard to make myself perfect that by the time I was seventeen years old, I had no idea who I really was. I might still not know, if Simon hadn't forced Jake and me apart. Then, once Jake attacked me and got arrested, Mom flipped a switch and acted as though she'd hated him all along.

"She's never told me that," I say. Not that I've given her much of a chance. I moved in with Ashton as soon as I could after the whole Jake disaster, and now that I've moved back, I'm hardly ever at home.

"You two really need to talk," Ashton sighs. I make a face, and she adds, "Give her a chance, Addy. Have you told her about Keely?"

"God, no." I haven't trusted my mother with my feelings for years, especially when I'm still figuring them out.

"Well, maybe that would be a good place to start. She's—"

"She's coming this way," I mutter as Mom strides toward us brandishing a hanger so tiny, I can't even tell what's on it. When she gets closer, I make out a pair of ivory knit booties with satin bows and fake fur along the top. At least, I hope it's fake.

"I'm getting these for you," Mom declares, before sweeping toward the cash register. I catch sight of the price tag as she passes: seventy-five dollars. Could be a lot worse.

"Thank you!" Ashton calls after her. Then she turns to me with her patented *Time to change the subject* smile. "We should probably give Mom some ideas about where to go to lunch before she drags us to that place where all the entrées are named after cocktails."

"Good idea," I say, pulling my phone out of my pocket. "After that, I have to pick up chips for Nate's party tonight." It's my contribution on his behalf, since he refuses to contribute anything himself. "Let me check what kind he wants."

"Okay, I'll meet you at the register."

I open my contacts but don't pull up Nate's name, because I know perfectly well that he couldn't care less what kind of chips I buy. In fact, his last text to me was *Don't bother, they don't deserve it.* Instead, I start a new message for Maeve:

I need you to look into something for me.

CHAPTER EIGHT

Phoebe
Saturday, July 4

I told myself before I left for Nate's Fourth of July party that I would push aside everything that's been worrying me and just have fun. But now, I can't stop looking at the button on Knox's shirt.

He's wearing a faded blue oxford with the sleeves rolled up, and the second button from the top is only half-buttoned. If I weren't overanalyzing every single reaction I have to him, I'd reach over and fix it. But is wardrobe adjustment allowed within the new Knox-and-Phoebe order? Especially since my hands would probably linger there, brushing off imaginary lint and straightening the collar that doesn't need to be straightened. The button is only an excuse, really. Or maybe it's a metaphor?

"Phoebe?" Knox asks. "Did you hear me?"

"What?" I blink at him and Addy, who's looking adorable in a pale-pink T-shirt dress. Her hair is freshly colored, a beautiful platinum purple that makes her entire face glow. "Sorry, it's just . . ." My eyes drop to the button again, and I extend my hand halfway to Knox's chest with a gesturing motion. "You missed a button. Well, you half missed it."

"Really?" Knox looks down, hands me his cup of ginger ale, and fixes the button himself. There goes my excuse to stare. "Thanks. Can't take me anywhere."

Nate's roommate Crystal drifts by then, waving to Addy before her eyes skip over me and settle on Knox. She breaks into a smile then, reversing whatever course she was on to join us. "You did it," she says delightedly, brushing a lock of wavy brown hair from Knox's forehead. "You grew your hair out! I told him to do that the last time he was here," she adds as an aside to me and Addy. "I said he'd be a total hottie if he did, and I was right, wasn't I?"

I try to hide my jealousy with a cheerful nod, because none of my angst is Crystal's fault. She's still touching his hair, though, and I wish she'd stop. "You were right," I say. Addy smiles affectionately, bumping Knox's shoulder with hers.

"Technically, you said I'd be cute," Knox says, with that crooked grin he gives when he's both embarrassed and proud.

"Did I? Well, I'm upgrading you," Crystal says. Okay, now she's pretending to brush something off his shoulder, and it's completely unfair that she's stealing all my would-be moves. "How old are you, anyway?"

"Seventeen," Knox says.

"Ahh," Crystal sighs, patting his shoulder in a much more

sisterly way. Other than Reggie, all Nate's roommates are in their early twenties. "Way too young." She turns to leave, adding, "Let's talk in a couple of years" over her shoulder.

"I'll be eighteen before you know it!" Knox calls after her.

"Really?" Addy teases as Crystal disappears. "You and Crystal?"

"Probably not. She isn't my type," Knox says. His warm brown eyes settle briefly on mine, and a little thrill goes through me until he adds, "And I doubt I'm hers. She was just being nice. Good to get some positive reinforcement on the hair front, though."

"Knox, if you stopped hanging out in a corner with me and Phoebe, I promise you'd have more positive reinforcement than you can handle," Addy says.

Knox blushes and ducks his head, and I take a long, bracing sip of punch. This entire party, so far, feels like it has been expressly designed to torture me.

Then Addy's eyes widen as she gazes over my shoulder. "Oh, good, Maeve and Luis are finally here." She stands on tiptoes, waving them over. As soon as they're within earshot, Addy calls out, "So what did you find?"

"Seriously?" Maeve asks. "I've barely started."

Addy makes an exaggerated show of glancing at her wrist, even though she's not wearing a watch. "You've had six hours," she says.

"I was on a bike for most of them," Maeve says with a grimace.

I take another sip, trying to get into a party mood. "Were you actually riding?"

"Sometimes," Maeve replies without looking at me, which

is . . . strange. Maeve has trouble meeting people's eyes when she's not being honest, but she's never tried to hide her lack of enthusiasm for bikes. My nerves start to prickle, wondering if Maeve managed to dig something up about the revenge forum that she doesn't want to tell Addy about. But then she squeezes Addy's arm and says, "I've set aside the whole day tomorrow. If Vengeance Is Mine has moved, I'll find it. I promise."

There's something unnaturally stiff about her posture, though, and I don't think it has anything to do with spending hours on a bicycle.

"I'm gonna get drinks for me and Maeve," Luis says, gazing around our circle. Right now it's just me, Addy, and Knox; Cooper and Kris aren't coming, and Nate and Bronwyn are off arguing with some of his roommates. "Anyone need anything?"

"Could you get me more punch?" I ask.

"Sure thing." Luis turns to leave as Knox stares into my empty cup.

"I got you that, like, five minutes ago," he says.

"I'm thirsty," I say. I'm not, though—just on edge, like always lately. Maeve glances between us, for long enough that I find myself saying, "What?"

"Hmm?" she asks, her eyes fastening somewhere over my shoulder.

"You're looking at me funny. Or rather, you're . . . not looking at me," I say.

She finally meets my eyes, and my pulse skitters at her expression. She's worried about something, and that something clearly has to do with me. Did she stumble across Owen during her research? Is he online somewhere, bragging about what he did to Brandon? He's too smart to identify himself, of course, but Maeve is incredibly good at picking up contextual clues about people who think they're anonymous.

"Well . . ." She pulls her phone from her pocket and swipes at the screen. "Like I said, I couldn't find anything related to the revenge forum this afternoon, but . . . did you guys know there's an Instagram page dedicated to Jake sightings?"

Oh God. My stomach drops as Addy sucks in a breath. "I didn't, but it shouldn't surprise me," she says. "What's he doing? Do I even want to know?"

"Nothing to do with you," Maeve says, still swiping. "But Phoebe . . . this is your car, isn't it? And your sneakers."

She holds out her phone and—there he is. Jake Riordan, changing my tire. My bumper and license plate are clearly visible, and so are my pink Nikes. The ones with silver laces that I happen to be wearing right now. My throat goes dry as Knox and Addy peer at Maeve's phone, and then stare, open-mouthed, at my feet.

"I . . . I can explain," I stammer.

"You let him . . ." Addy, her eyes wide and horrified, can't even finish the sentence.

"I didn't mean to!" I say. "It happened really fast—"

"Why didn't you call me?" Knox asks.

There's not enough punch in the world to give me the courage to unpack *that* question. "It's just . . . I was worried about this delivery I had to make for Café Contigo, and I was about to call Triple A, and then all of a sudden Jake was there, and his mom was there, and I went on autopilot or something. . . ."

"When was this?" Addy asks. Her voice is so cold that I'm struck mute, and Maeve has to answer for me.

"Three days ago," she says.

"So we worked all day together yesterday, and it never occurred to you to mention this?" Addy demands.

Only like a million times, I think miserably. But I couldn't bring myself to do it, and I never imagined she'd find out. "I'm sorry," I say, wishing Luis would hurry back with that punch. "It was stupid of me. I didn't talk to him or anything. I . . . I didn't even want to thank him, once he was done, so all I said was that I should learn to change a tire, and he said it takes practice, and—"

I'm babbling now, and Addy's had more than enough. "Oh, well, as long as you didn't *thank* him," she says, and her sarcasm is like a knife to my heart. Addy is the queen of giving people the benefit of the doubt and forgiving their mistakes, but right now, she's too upset for that. "I guess we're all good, then," she adds.

Maeve bites her lip. "Phoebe, that really *was* you, wasn't it?" she asks. "At Jake's Eastland High event. Not some random girl with your exact hair and shirt."

"Oh my God." Addy's breath catches as she turns to stare at Maeve. "I saw her too."

Her. Not *you.* Like I'm outside the circle all of a sudden.

"That was the day we were at your house, right? With Bronwyn?" Addy asks, and Maeve nods. "I almost said something, but I thought for sure I was wrong." Addy's tone gets hard again as her eyes cut toward me. "Why were you there?"

I can't speak. There's no way I can tell her the truth: *Oh, you know, just wondering if a boy who tries to commit murder can actually change, so I don't have to keep obsessing about my brother.*

So that means lying—again—but I can't think of a single good excuse. Not now, with my friends staring at me like I've committed the ultimate betrayal.

"Phoebe, what's going on?" Knox asks. His voice is full of concern, and for some reason, that's yet another final straw. Luis comes back then, balancing three cups, and I grab one so roughly that he almost drops the other two.

"What's *going on* is that I'm a disaster and I'll leave," I say, turning on my heel to stomp away before I burst into tears. I can't wait to get away, and yet—it still hurts when I reach the other side of the room without anyone tugging at my arm. Not even Knox.

The party is full of people I know—Nate and Bronwyn are still in a heated conversation with his roommates Sana and Reggie, oblivious to what just happened. My former best friend, Jules, is across the room with her boyfriend, Sean, and Monica Hill, another girl from my class. Even the Café Contigo staff is here: Manny, Evie, and a server named Ahmed. But I can't bring myself to join any of them, so I just stand awkwardly against the wall next to the hallway until somebody taps me on the shoulder.

"Did you get kicked out of Murder Club?" a voice asks.

I turn to see Vanessa Merriman in a cute red halter dress, a Solo cup in each hand. "Here," she adds, dropping one of them into the cup that I somehow emptied during my walk of shame across the room. "This was for a friend, but you look like you could use it." She leans one shoulder against the wall and adds, "That friend was me, by the way. I don't know why I bother coming to these things."

"Why do you?" I ask, taking a long, grateful sip.

"I just said I don't know," Vanessa says irritably. Her eyes follow mine to the corner where Knox, Maeve, Addy, and Luis are still deep in conversation. "They're all so judgey, aren't they? Like, you pick the wrong side *once,* and all of a sudden you're a pariah."

Vanessa did a lot more than pick the wrong side; from what I remember, she bullied Addy mercilessly after Simon died. And then, for good measure, she bullied Cooper too. But I'm not in any position to remind her of that right now. "They're my friends," I say, even though I'm not sure that's true anymore.

"Then what are you doing all the way over here?" Vanessa asks.

I don't have a good answer for that, so I guzzle my drink as I watch Nate and Bronwyn break away from Sana and Reggie and head for the Bayview Crew corner. Sana pulls my eyes back to her and Reggie when she grabs hold of Reggie's arm, all her hippie-chick floatiness gone, and pulls him closer so she can say something directly into his ear. Reggie shrugs and turns away, leaving Sana wearing a frustrated expression.

"I can't believe that's still going on," Vanessa says.

"What?" I ask. I almost add *Sana and Reggie?,* which would be brand-new information, but Vanessa flicks a hand in Nate and Bronwyn's direction.

"Their little good-girl, bad-boy romance," she says. "I mean, come on. What do they even have in common, besides getting accused of murder together? The sex can't be *that* good."

Aaand, we're done. "Gotta go," I blurt, propelling myself off the wall toward . . . I don't even know where. Bathroom, probably, because I've had a *lot* of punch. There's a surprisingly short line, and I pull out my phone to scroll while I wait and see I have a text from Emma. I've been trying to persuade her to come home for a weekend. I miss her, but really, I need to force her to talk about Owen.

I tap on the text, and all she's said is *I can't afford the plane fare. I still don't have a job.*

It's just an excuse, though, and we both know it. The longer she's away from Bayview, the less she wants to come back.

You can't leave me alone to deal with the mess we made, I write, then erase it before hitting Send. We're not supposed to put any of this in writing.

"Your turn," a voice says behind me, and I look up to see the bathroom door ajar.

As soon as I get inside, it hits me how drunk I am. The black-and-white tile spins, and I can barely manage to undo the braided belt on my shorts. I have even worse luck trying to refasten it once I've used the toilet, fruitlessly searching for the microscopic belt holes until a loud knock on the door reminds me that I've overstayed my turn.

"Almost done," I call, deciding to improvise and tie the belt into a little knot. Which I immediately realize is a bad idea, because I'm never going to be able to get it undone when I go to bed. Oh well, that's a problem for Future Phoebe. Then I wash my hands, staring at my flushed, glassy-eyed face in the mirror.

"Something has to give," I tell my reflection.

These walls must be paper-thin, because another knock sounds on the door as somebody yells, "It's gonna be my *bladder* if you don't get out of there!"

"Sorry," I call, drying my hands on—oh, ew. I thought it was a towel, but it's actually someone's boxer shorts draped over the rack, and now I need to wash my hands again. By the time

I'm done, the next person in line is pounding steadily at the door, and when I open it, I scurry past them as fast as possible. "Sorry," I repeat, eyes on the floor. Vanessa's still standing where I left her, absorbed in her phone, a full cup of punch on the table beside her. Before I even realize what I'm doing, I scoop it up and brush past her.

"Hey, you little lush, that's mine!" she yells, but I pretend I don't hear her and make a beeline for the staircase.

I like it better upstairs; it's darker, quieter, and I don't know anyone. A bedroom door is open—literally tied open, with some kind of sheet contraption fastened around a radiator, which I'd probably be curious about if I were sober—and a bunch of people are hanging around inside, talking. Nobody seems to mind when I drop into a beanbag chair and pull out my phone, spending a good twenty minutes composing a short, typo-free message to Emma:

Please come home.

Then I close my eyes, and by the time I open them, I'm alone in the room. I stand and immediately get dizzy, and I have to brace myself against the wall before making my way to the door. When I reach it, I nearly bump into a boy on his way in.

"Well, hey, Phoebe," Reggie Crawley says. "Long time no see. What are you doing all by yourself in my room?"

I got to know Reggie all too well when Bronwyn stopped tutoring him after Simon died. Emma stepped in to help him retake the SATs, even though she was only a junior, because she'd already aced the PSATs and Reggie's parents were desperate. For two months he was in our apartment three nights a week, leering at me every time Emma's back was turned. He's barely changed since then: same scraggly goatee, same propensity for too-thin V-neck T-shirts, same leather-cord necklace with three silver beads. Already in a style rut at age nineteen.

Reggie leans against the door frame, waggling his eyebrows in what he thinks, wrongly, is a seductive manner. "Waiting for me?" he adds.

I might be woozy, but I have enough presence of mind to give the only possible response to that question. "Ugh, no thank you," I say, pushing past him.

"Your loss," he calls after me.

I stumble downstairs, clutching the banister the whole way, and wonder if I've been gone long enough for Addy to be less angry. But she's not in the Bayview Crew corner anymore; none of them are. It's been taken over by my former friend Jules, and when she waves at me, I'm so relieved at the welcoming gesture that I don't hesitate to approach, even though she's flanked by two of my least favorite people in the world.

"Drink?" Sean Murdock asks when I reach them, holding out a cup. I don't really want it but take it anyway.

"Perfect timing, Phoebe Jeebies," Jules says.

I try to smile at the nickname, but it sounds wrong. That's the old Phoebe—the one who got to judge Jules for dating a creep like Sean and lying to the police about how Brandon died. Jules and I cleared the air after that, but things still aren't the same between us. Partly because I try to spend as little time as possible in Sean's presence, and partly because it's not lost on me that I've turned into a much bigger liar than she ever was.

"Perfect timing?" I echo.

Jules nods and bumps her shoulder into Monica's. "We need some intel," she says.

"About what?" I ask, finishing half the drink I didn't want in a single gulp.

"Slow down, tiger," Sean says, smirking. God, I hate him.

"About Knox," Jules says.

I blink at her, trying to bring her face into better focus, but it's no use. She still looks as though she has two of them. "What about him?"

"Is he single?"

"Whaaa?" That doesn't seem to be enough of an answer, so I add, "Why?"

"Monica's into him," Jules says.

I snort out a laugh, but nobody joins in. "Sorry, were you serious?" I ask.

"Of course," Monica says, twirling a strand of ponytail around one finger. "Why wouldn't I be? He's hot."

It feels like the entire party has chosen tonight to notice, but Monica doesn't get to throw her hat into this particular ring. "You made fun of him all last semester!" I protest.

"I did not," Monica says. "Sean did, but he knows he was wrong. Right, Sean?"

"Me and Knox are bros now," Sean says with perfect meathead confidence.

"No, you aren't," I snap. "He can't stand you. Or you," I add, swinging my gaze back toward Monica. There are three of her now, which is three too many. Or four, even. A negative number of Monicas would be preferable. "Leave him alone."

"Phoebe, you don't own Knox," Jules says bossily. "If you like him, you've had plenty of time to do something about it."

"I don't . . . I can't . . . I have to go," I say, and stumble past them toward the hallway. I try to get my phone out of my pocket as I push my way outside, but my hands are numb and my breathing has gone shallow. My head aches so horribly that I can barely think. I want to call a Lyft, but I don't know if I can even manage to unlock my phone.

I turn around to go back inside, but somehow, that's not where I end up. I'm surrounded by grass and trees, and I collapse into some kind of stone bench. *Something's wrong,* I think as the edges of my brain turn fuzzy. A figure looms nearby, so indistinct that it's barely a shadow, but if I squint hard enough, it looks familiar.

Go away, I try to say, but the words won't come. I'm so impossibly tired.

"Oh, Phoebe," someone says, sounding as though they're talking to me from the end of a long, echoing tunnel. "You've made a big mistake."

Which one? I think.

Then everything goes black.

CHAPTER NINE

Nate
Sunday, July 5

"We should have our half-birthday party here," Addy says, tapping my arm.

"Huh?" I gaze around the back room of Café Contigo, where a large-screen TV has been set up so we can watch Cooper's gym commercial. Right now it's showing a Padres game, but the commercial is supposed to air after the fifth inning. "What half-birthday party?"

"You know how we always have a joint birthday party in March?" Addy asks.

"Twice," I say. "We did that twice."

Technically, Addy did it. We were both born in March, so she decided during the last semester of high school that we should throw a party on the midpoint between our birthdays. She organized the whole thing at her apartment, and I showed up, because it meant a lot to her and there aren't many people

89

I like better than Adelaide Prentiss. Plus, I learned a long time ago that there's no point in resisting Addy when she's in social-director mode. Then she did the same thing this year, although it was a lot more subdued since Brandon Weber had recently died.

"Right. So it's a tradition," Addy says. "But this year wasn't all that celebratory, so I thought—what about a half-birthday party? In mid-September?"

"No, that's too late," Bronwyn protests, extracting the only tortilla chip untouched by any kind of topping from the platter of nachos in front of us. "I'll be back at school by then."

"Oh, right. And we can't do August, because I'll be in Peru, so . . . July fourteenth it is," Addy says decisively. "It'll be, like, a one-third birthday party."

"That's not a thing," I say.

Addy ignores me. "We could invite all the usual suspects," she says, waving a hand around us. We're at a single table ringed with nine chairs, and all of them are filled—with me, Addy, Bronwyn, Cooper, Kris, Maeve, Luis, and Knox—except for one. Phoebe's not here, even though we were all supposed to show up half an hour ago.

"Perfect," Bronwyn says. "But not *just* us, right? I want to invite Kate and Yumiko, and Evan, maybe. . . ." She trails off and shoots me a sideways glance. "Or not."

"Whatever." I shrug. I can be magnanimous about her ex when he has no shot.

She squeezes my arm. "This room might not have enough space for everybody."

"Well, there's always Nate's house," Addy says.

"No way." I can't help the irritated edge that creeps into

my voice. "You might be able to force me to have a one-third birthday party, but you can't force me to spend it babysitting Reggie Crawley."

"Absolutely not," Bronwyn says quickly.

We tried to restart the Reggie discussion with Sana last night, but even Bronwyn had to admit that we weren't getting anywhere. Ultimately, it wasn't the time or the place. But it pissed me off when Sana admitted she hadn't even looked at the link to Katrina's video that Bronwyn sent her, because that would've been bare minimum for taking the problem seriously.

"Okay, yeah, fair enough," Addy says. Then she tugs on her earring—a classic Addy anxiety move—as she gazes at the beaded curtain that separates the back room from the main restaurant. "Last night was a mess, wasn't it? And not only because of Reggie." She tugs harder. "You guys, do you think Phoebe's coming? I was kind of hard on her."

"You were upset," Bronwyn says.

"I was, but . . ." Addy bites her lip. "I keep thinking about what I said to her when she said she didn't thank Jake for changing her tire. I was super mean and sarcastic. And the thing is—that's almost exactly how Jake treated me, way back when I tried to apologize for cheating on him with TJ. He said, *That's all right, then. As long as you're* sorry." From the way she says the words, I can tell they're imprinted on her brain. "You have to give people a chance to explain, right? But I didn't."

I grasp the edge of the table to keep myself from making a cutting remark about Phoebe that I know, deep down, she doesn't deserve. Letting someone change your tire isn't the end of the world, except . . . it's *Jake*. Walking around town playing the good guy, like the past never happened. Anyone in Bayview

91

who's ever been caught up in this town's sick dynamic shouldn't give him anything except a punch to the face.

"The situations are in no way similar," Bronwyn says, which is a more polite way of saying the same thing.

"Yeah, they're different because what I did to Jake was *worse*," Addy says. "Or it would've been, if he was a decent human. I tried texting Phoebe earlier, but she left me unread."

Knox, who's sitting beside Maeve on the other side of the table, twists in his chair. "Wait, are you guys talking about Phoebe?" he asks. "She hasn't texted me back either. I gave her a ride to the party last night, and she just, like, disappeared."

"Didn't she leave with Jules?" Maeve asks.

"No," I say. Everyone stares at me, probably because this isn't the kind of thing I tend to notice. "That loser boyfriend of hers was too wasted to drive, so Crystal took his keys and made them leave with someone else. Phoebe wasn't there."

Addy digs her fingernails into her palm. "I hope she got home okay. I wouldn't worry so much, but Ashton's gotten me all worked up about that billboard. . . ."

"Guys!" Luis calls from the other end of the table. "Pay attention! That was the second out; the inning might be over soon."

Addy ignores him. "I wish we knew what those revenge forum guys are up to now," she says, looking pointedly at Maeve. Who doesn't notice, because she's doing the supportive-girlfriend thing by staring at the television screen almost as hard as Luis is.

"Maeve's working on it," Bronwyn says. "Give her time."

"The billboard's gone back to the dancing energy drink," I say. I'd noticed it on the ride here with a sense of relief. "Guess they fixed the hack."

On the TV screen, the capacity crowd roars with disappointment when the batter hits a foul ball into the stands. "This guy's timing is way off," Luis says, leaning forward intently. "He's gonna pop up any second, just you wait."

"Oh God." Cooper, who's sitting up front with Kris, rubs both hands across his face. "I'd just like to remind everyone that I am *not* an actor. And I wouldn't even have done this except my car's on its last legs, so . . ."

"Cooper, you work harder than anyone I've ever known, and you deserve to be recognized for that," Kris says. "And *paid* for it. Don't you dare apologize."

"You say that now," Cooper mutters, but his shoulders relax a little. I know he's been worried about taking any kind of sponsorship, afraid that companies want him only because of lingering Bayview Four notoriety. And yeah, maybe that's part of it—none of us can ever rule it out fully—but he had a phenomenal freshman year. More than ever, he seems destined for a huge career, and he might as well start getting paid for it.

"I wish Nonny could've come. I love watching her cheer Cooper on," Addy says wistfully. Her phone starts buzzing on the table then, but before she can reach for it, Bronwyn snatches it up and puts it facedown.

"Don't answer," she says. "Luis was right—inning over."

The screen fades to black, and Luis calls, "Here we go!" Maeve shushes him as a sleek gym interior appears, with a huge logo for FiredUp Fitness on one wall. Heavy bass music kicks in as the camera pans to workout machines, lockers, a bunch of weights, and then—Cooper, running on a treadmill like his life depends on getting away as fast as possible.

The room erupts into cheers, so loud that we can't hear

anything else for a few beats. Which is fine, because the commercial is just one shot after another of Cooper working out, barely breaking a sweat while looking like a superhero. "So far, I am *loving* this," Kris says as Cooper squats with a barbell across his shoulders on screen.

Then the music fades as Cooper puts down the weights, reaches for a towel, and turns toward the camera. "Nothing gets me fired up like fitness," he says.

There's a moment of stunned silence in the room, because that was easily the most wooden line that anyone's ever delivered. Cooper sounded like a robot programmed for English by someone who's never actually heard it spoken. But then we erupt into even louder cheers, because Cooper still rules and that was weirdly iconic.

"Oscar! Oscar!" Luis yells. "Or whatever they give for commercials!"

"You looked hot," Kris says, pulling Cooper toward him for a kiss.

"I hate working out, but you *almost* convinced me," Maeve says.

"Y'all are full of it," Cooper says, blushing. But he's smiling too.

After the excitement dies down and the game comes back on, Addy reaches for her phone. "I wonder if that was Phoebe calling earlier," she says, before narrowing her eyes at the screen. "Huh. No. It was her mom."

"Phoebe's mom has your number?" I ask as Knox turns in his seat.

"She was Ashton's wedding planner, remember?" Addy

says, lifting the phone to her ear. A frown crosses her face as she listens to the message. "Okay, this is weird. Ms. Lawton is asking if Phoebe's still with me because she's not answering her phone, which, I mean . . . she was never *with* me, exactly. We didn't go to the Fourth of July party together. Did her mom call you?" she adds, turning toward Knox.

He pulls out his phone, brow furrowed. "No. You should call her back."

"On it," Addy says. She swipes at her phone and lifts it again, plugging one ear. "Hi, Ms. Lawton," she says after a few seconds. "Phoebe's not . . . what?" Her voice gets strained. "No, she didn't. That was never . . . She *what*?"

"What's happening?" Knox asks urgently.

Addy waves him away. "No, we were definitely at the party together, but we didn't make plans for her to stay over. I haven't seen her since last night. Did you try Jules?" Her expression turns grave as she listens to whatever Phoebe's mother is saying on the other end. "Yeah, for sure. Keep me updated, okay?" When she lowers her phone, her face is ghost pale. "Phoebe didn't come home last night," she says, staring around at the ring of concerned faces. "She texted her mom late to say she was spending the night at my house. Why would she do that?"

"Because she was staying someplace else and didn't want her mother to know?" Maeve suggests. Her eyes flick toward Knox, who has the same look on his face that he used to get when his dad—who's my boss at Myers Construction—didn't notice that he'd stopped by the office: like he's crushed and pretending not to be.

"I don't think Phoebe would do that," he says tightly.

95

"If she did, I messed things up for her," Addy says with a grimace. "But why hasn't she checked in with anyone yet? She missed the commercial."

"Try calling her," Bronwyn says.

Addy does, but she's barely lifted her phone to her ear when she frowns and says, "Straight to voice mail."

Maeve has her phone out now, stabbing at the screen. "I wonder if . . . Okay, her Snapchat location is on, and it says she's . . ." She enlarges her screen and blinks at it a few times, before holding it up to me. "She's at your house, apparently."

"Really?" I ask. "She wasn't there when I left. At least . . . I don't think she was."

I slept late, since I had a rare day off today, and didn't leave my room until it was time to come here. Crystal and Sana were gone, and Jiahao and Deacon were watching TV in the living room like usual. Reggie was . . . I don't have a clue where Reggie was, but his door was shut because at some point last night, he'd managed to undo Sana's sheet contraption.

"Oh no," Bronwyn says, like she's reading my mind. "She couldn't be . . . she's not with *Reggie,* is she?"

"No way," Maeve says. "Phoebe would never."

"She was drinking a lot, though," Addy says worriedly.

"Not *that* much," Maeve says, though she looks less sure. "But even if she were . . . um, hanging out with Reggie at any point last night, she would've left by now."

"Unless he's not letting her," Luis says. Maeve punches his shoulder, like she thinks he's making a bad joke, but there's not a trace of a smile on his face.

That got dark, fast. "We better check on her," I say.

CHAPTER TEN

Nate
Sunday, July 5

When we arrive at my house—six of us, minus Cooper and Kris, because they had to take Nonny to a physical therapy appointment—Phoebe's not there.

"Haven't seen her, man," Reggie drawls from his prone position on the couch, a beer in one hand and the remote in the other as he scrolls through Netflix. "Not since last night."

"Since *what* last night?" Bronwyn asks, plucking the remote from his hand. It's a good thing she got to it first, because his *couldn't care less* vibe makes me want to throw it at his head.

"Hey, give that back!" Reggie protests. He lunges at her half-heartedly, slumping back against the cushions when Bronwyn steps out of reach. "I dunno. Since the party."

"Where was she?" Maeve asks. "When you saw her?"

"My room," Reggie says, tugging absently at his cord necklace. All six of us glare at him until he holds up a hand and says,

"Relax, Murder Club. She was by herself, about to leave, when I walked in. Obviously, I invited her to hang out for some one-on-one time—"

"Gross," Maeve interjects.

"But she took off," Reggie says. "And that was that."

Bronwyn and Maeve exchange skeptical glances, but the thing about Reggie is, you can always tell when he's being shady. Right now, he doesn't seem to be. Still . . . "Her phone says she's here," I say.

"Well, she's not," Reggie says, making an obnoxious show of lifting the blanket that's half-covering his legs. "Unless she's hiding. Hellooooo, Phoebe?"

"Fuck you," I say as Bronwyn tosses the remote at him. Into his hands, which is more than he deserves.

"What do you want from me?" he says defensively. "She's not here. End of story."

"I'm going to try calling her again," Addy says. "Maybe we'll hear a ring."

But there's no sound except for Addy's frustrated hiss before she says, "Still voice mail."

"Did we get her location wrong?" Knox asks. "Maybe her phone's off, and it's defaulting to wherever it was when she powered down."

"Since when does Phoebe turn off her phone?" Maeve asks.

"I think we'd better look around," Bronwyn says. "Phoebe might have fallen asleep someplace random, or lost her phone." Her eyes gleam, and I know what's coming—Bronwyn is in take-charge mode. Thank God somebody is. Within minutes, she splits us into pairs and gives everyone an assignment: Addy and Knox will check upstairs, Maeve and Luis have the downstairs, and Bronwyn and I are in charge of the yard.

"I feel awful," Bronwyn says as we make our way outside. "Addy's right; last night was rough on Phoebe. But I was so focused on Reggie, I didn't even notice."

"You and me both," I say, running my thumb over one of the scars on my arm. I don't think much about Jared's bomb anymore; for the most part I came out of it fine, and in some ways, it brought Bronwyn and me closer together. Or maybe it'd be more accurate to say that it brought me and her parents closer together. They stopped worrying that Bronwyn and I were from "different worlds" after I took the brunt of an explosion for her.

But now, the scars remind me how life-or-death this town can be. I hated the idea of Phoebe being with Reggie, but the alternative might be worse. I don't know her all that well—until recently, she was just a coworker of Addy's whose annoying friend planted one on me during the Truth or Dare game—but going through a Bayview crisis together bonds you for life. Plus, Phoebe lost her dad, and her mom's run ragged trying to care for everybody. I know what it's like to feel as though you've got to solve all your problems on your own.

I stop short to scan the small, scrubby yard. There's not much to it—lots of half-dead grass and a few sad bushes, plus a pathway of uneven stones leading to the front door. The sun is hot and bright, and I squint to see better. "Do you know what color Phoebe's phone case is?"

"Pink," Bronwyn says, walking in slow circles across the grass. "It's not here."

"Do you think she might've gone to visit her sister?" I ask. "Maybe she got a last-minute flight or something."

"Maybe," Bronwyn says. "But it doesn't explain why she hasn't gotten in touch with anyone, or why she told her mom she was with Addy." She heaves a frustrated sigh. "None of it makes sense. Ugh, if I'd just spent five minutes *talking* to her last night—"

"Don't," I say, taking hold of her shoulders to steer her behind the house. "No beating yourself up on my watch."

The backyard is bigger and more overgrown. Crystal's attempt at a vegetable garden covers a lot of it, leading to a stone patio flanked by a couple of benches and a moldy fountain that's always at least partially filled with grubby rainwater. "Do you ever sit out here?" Bronwyn asks, stepping carefully through the ankle-high grass.

"God, no," I say. "Why would I—"

And then I catch sight of it: a bright pink rectangle lying beneath one of the benches. Bronwyn gets there a step before I do, lifting the phone to reveal a screen that lights up with a text as she angles it toward us.

Emma: WHERE THE HELL ARE YOU???

"Oh no," Bronwyn says softly.

CHAPTER ELEVEN

Addy
Sunday, July 5

The Bayview Police are nothing if not consistent. No matter what kind of crisis they're faced with, they'll focus on the wrong problem one hundred percent of the time.

"So, there was underage drinking at this party?" Officer Budapest asks, dropping Phoebe's phone into a plastic bag and zipping the top.

We called Melissa Lawton as soon as we found Phoebe's cell. She immediately got into her car and headed for Nate's house, calling the police along the way. Now she's here with Owen in tow, clutching him to her side as we all stand in a semicircle around Officer Hank Budapest. The fact that he was the officer who first questioned us about Simon's death isn't lost on anyone—including him, I'm sure. He didn't exactly cover himself with glory during that investigation.

"Yeah," Nate says, his jaw clenched.

"Who procured the alcohol?" Officer Budapest asks.

"Officer, my daughter is *missing*," Ms. Lawton interrupts, her face tight with worry. "Can we focus on that, please, and worry about the party later?"

"From what you've told me, Phoebe lied to you about where she was spending the night," Officer Budapest says. "Isn't it more likely that she's simply gone somewhere that she didn't want you to know about? It's been, what?" He makes a show of glancing at his watch. "Less than twelve hours since people saw her last?"

"Fourteen," Maeve says, folding her arms tightly across her chest. She looks like she's about to say more—bring up the revenge forum, maybe—but before she can, Ms. Lawton lets out a strangled sound of frustration and clutches Owen tighter.

"Phoebe wouldn't intentionally go anywhere without her phone," she says. "And have you forgotten that she was *stalked* three months ago, by a disturbed young man with a lot of on-line followers? All of whom spend their days fantasizing about revenge? You should be talking with Jared Jackson *right now* about whom he might have incited to go after Phoebe."

Maeve nods emphatically. Owen flushes and stares at the ground, and my heart squeezes in sympathy. From what I've seen at Café Contigo, he and Phoebe haven't been getting along well lately, so he probably feels the same aching sense of regret that I do now that she's missing.

Missing. The word sends a stab of panic through me as Officer Budapest clears his throat. "Naturally, we'll be speaking to Mr. Jackson," he says, although I'd bet my life he hadn't even considered it until Ms. Lawton brought it up. "If you'd like to come with me to the station, we can put those wheels in motion." He runs his eyes over the rest of us, adding, "It might help to have one of you along as well. Maybe . . ."

Bronwyn steps forward before he has time to call her name, which he obviously was going to. No matter the situation, she's always the logical representative. "I'd be happy to."

"Me too," Knox says quickly. "I think I talked to her last."

"All right. That should do for now," Officer Budapest says, tucking the baggie holding Phoebe's phone beneath his arm. "As for the rest of you, we'll be in touch as needed—and keep spreading the word among Phoebe's friends and classmates that you're looking for her, all right? Chances are good that she's with someone you know."

He and the Lawtons head for their cars, and Bronwyn gives Nate a quick peck on the cheek before she and Knox follow them. Maeve glares daggers at Officer Budapest's back as he makes his way across Nate's lawn. "Well, he's as useful as ever, isn't he?" she says. "Acting like Phoebe's some flighty girl who lies to her mom for fun. And oh, by the way, why should we even be worried when she's only been missing for *fourteen hours*?"

"The biggest unsolved mystery in Bayview is why that guy still has a job," Luis mutters, putting an arm around Maeve's shoulders.

"He's not even the worst one. If you look up *incompetent* in the dictionary, I'm pretty sure it's just a picture of the Bayview Police," Maeve says, aiming one last dirty look in Officer Budapest's direction before tilting her head to look up at Luis. "Can you drive me home? I need to get cracking even harder on that revenge forum. If they had anything to do with Phoebe's disappearance, there's bound to be chatter somewhere."

"Your wish is my command," Luis says. "You coming, Addy?"

I hesitate. If I go with him and Maeve, I know I'll distract her from what she needs to do. I can't go home, because Mom's there and she'll only make me more stressed. And if I go to Ashton's apartment, I'll make *her* stressed, which is the last thing she needs, so . . .

"Hang out here for a while," Nate says, sensing my dilemma. "I don't have to be at the country club for another hour, and I can drop you wherever you want to go on my way there. Sana should be back from work soon, and we can ask her if she saw anything last night. She was sober the whole time."

"Yeah, okay," I say gratefully.

"Can you believe we were watching Cooper's commercial less than an hour ago?" Luis asks as we make our way to the front of the house.

"No," Maeve and I say in unison. "That already seems like it happened last week," I add.

"Nothing gets me fired up like fitness," Luis says morosely as he opens the car door for Maeve. It should be funny, but at the moment, it's just—not.

"Me either," Maeve says with equal melancholy. She slips into the car, buckles her seat belt, and closes the door before leaning out the open window. "I'll text if I find anything," she promises.

"Okay, thanks," I say.

They drive off, and Nate and I stand in silence on the sidewalk. For a lot of the past year, ever since Bronwyn and Cooper went to college, it's been Nate and me left behind in Bayview, trying to figure out a way forward without hyperinvolved parents, money, or lots of natural talent. I don't begrudge Bronwyn and Cooper their gifts, not even a little. I feel lucky to know them. But there's something comforting about a friend who doesn't have everything figured out, and who knows how it feels to take one step forward and then get knocked back two or three. Nate and I, with our messy families, uncertain futures, and frequent bouts of self-doubt, understand one another in a fundamental way. When I'm feeling worried and guilty and generally helpless, he's the ideal person to kill an hour with.

"You wanna help me feed Stan?" he asks. "It's cricket day."

"Ew, no." I manage to huff out a near-laugh. "I'm fruit duty only, remember?"

"Suit yourself," Nate says with a shrug. "Come on, let's go in the back way so we don't have to see Reggie." He shades his eyes against the sun as he glances across the street and adds, "Looks like Phil bought another beater."

Nate's elderly neighbor likes to fix up old cars, but they usually have a lot more charm than the faded red convertible that's idling in front of Phil's split-level house. Not that I know much about cars, except . . .

"Wait a sec," I say, stepping closer to the sidewalk. "Okay, this is kind of random, but . . . that looks a lot like a car that was hanging around Eli's office when I picked up my restraining order." I scan the tan, ill-fitting convertible top carefully—it looks as though it was made for a completely different car. "Cooper noticed it and was keeping an eye on it from the window. He joked it couldn't possibly be Jake staking us out, because the car is such a piece of crap."

"Well, I guess it was Phil. Or someone else who doesn't mind cars with more rust than paint," Nate says.

"And ultratinted windows," I say. They're so dark that whoever's sitting in the driver's seat is barely visible. "Doesn't Phil usually work on his cars in the driveway?"

"Yeah. Maybe he's going somewhere."

Just then Phil's front door opens with a loud creak, and Phil himself steps outside in a blue-and-green-striped bathrobe. He bends to pick up his newspaper, then straightens and catches sight of the idling car, Nate, and me. "Nate!" he hollers, pointing the newspaper at the red car. "Do me a favor and remind your friends that you have a driveway."

"They're not—" Nate breaks off, a frown creasing his forehead, then stalks purposefully toward the car. Before he can reach it, though, the engine roars and the car peels away. Within seconds it's gone, leaving a trail of exhaust in its wake. "That wasn't a friend of mine," Nate calls to his neighbor. "Not one of yours either?"

"Nope. Damn kids," Phil says, before shuffling back inside.

Nate returns to the sidewalk, still frowning. "The license plate is caked with mud," he says. "I couldn't read any of it."

My stomach flutters with unease. "There's no way that was Jake, right?" I ask. "Because he can't . . ." *He can't be here,* I was going to say, but actually, he can. Nate's house isn't part of the safe zone.

"Beats me, but I don't like how whoever's driving took off as soon as I headed their way," Nate says. "Especially after a day like this one."

"Do you think the car has something to do with what happened to Phoebe?"

Nate exhales a noisy sigh. "Hell if I know, Addy."

His phone starts ringing then, playing a cheery musical

tone that couldn't be less Nate-like if it tried. Nate blinks, looking as confused as I feel, and then a deeply annoyed expression crosses his face as he pulls the blaring phone from his pocket.

"Is that . . . is that 'MMMBop'?" I ask. Despite the tension of the day, the last word comes out as an incredulous laugh.

"Maeve thinks she's funny," Nate says sourly.

"MMMBop, boppaly roomba," I sing, earning a glare from Nate as the music ends and he holds the phone to his ear. "What? Sorry I don't know the words. You should teach me."

"What's up, Dad?" Nate asks, a little too loudly. After a beat of silence, his frown deepens. "What kind of problem?" Another beat. "I'm gonna need more than that. Seriously? You can't . . . okay, fine. Relax. I'll be there in five minutes."

"What's going on?" I ask once he's hung up.

"I don't know, but my dad's freaking out about something," Nate says, stuffing his phone back into his pocket. "How would you feel about a quick trip to Bayview High?"

CHAPTER TWELVE

Addy
Sunday, July 5

It's been more than a year since I graduated, but when I hop off the back of Nate's motorcycle in the Bayview High parking lot, time slips away and for a few seconds, I feel like *her* again: Adelaide Prentiss, the always-anxious princess of Bayview High. I used to linger in this parking lot until the bell rang every morning, locked in Jake's embrace and worrying about a half-dozen petty things at once: his mood, my hair, and whatever was front and center in my latest friend drama—like whether the snotty remark I'd made about Vanessa's new boyfriend would get back to her (it did) or whether I'd get more votes than Keely for prom queen (I didn't). Running beneath all that, even before everything imploded with Jake, TJ, and Simon, was my deepest, darkest, most constant fear: *I'm not good enough, and I never will be.*

I don't miss high school for a lot of reasons, but I especially don't miss that.

Nate must be experiencing similar déjà vu, because we haven't even gotten our helmets off before he mutters, "I could happily live the rest of my life and never come back here."

"Same," I say, fastening Nate's extra helmet over his handlebars. We cross the parking lot and head for the break in the fence that surrounds Bayview High's athletic fields. "Have you heard anything else from your dad?"

Nate checks his phone. "Nope."

"He wants you to meet him in the equipment shed?"

"Yeah. I guess he finally found his keys, at least."

"Where *is* the equipment shed, exactly?"

"Behind the baseball diamond," Nate says, and I can't help being relieved that he didn't say *the football field.* I'd much rather this trip down memory lane include a detour through Cooper's old stomping grounds than one that belonged to . . .

"Jake," I say, right before my throat closes up.

It's like I performed the worst magic trick ever, and the corner of my brain that's currently reliving Bayview High conjured him out of thin air. Because all of a sudden there he is: less than fifty feet away, dressed in a T-shirt and gym shorts. He's standing beside home plate, next to a burly man who turns our way as I stop dead in my tracks.

"Oh, *fuck,*" Nate says under his breath. "God damn it, I'm such an idiot. My dad told me he works out here sometimes, but I didn't think . . . I never should've brought you here. I'm sorry, Addy. Let's go."

"No," I say as Jake's head swings in our direction. This was bound to happen eventually, wasn't it? I can't spend my life skulking around the edges of a safe zone to avoid Jake's wrath; I did enough of that when we were dating.

We stare at one another for a few endless beats. My heart pounds in my ears so loudly that I can't hear whatever Nate is muttering under his breath, and black spots dance across my vision. For one horrifying second, I'm afraid I'm going to pass out, but then the dizziness passes and a strange feeling of calm settles over me. This is the worst thing I could have imagined a month ago, but I'm still standing.

I will *always* keep standing.

Jake raises one hand slowly in—not a wave, exactly. More like a placating gesture.

"We didn't think anyone was here," he says. "I'll go."

Those are the first words Jake has spoken to me since the night in the woods behind Janae's house, when he put his hands around my neck and said, *You should be in jail instead of Nate, Addy. But this works too.*

I push the memory away and say, "Do what you want," in a loud, clear voice. "It has nothing to do with me." Then I force myself to continue walking toward the bleachers, with Nate silently keeping pace by my side.

That's another good thing about Nate: he knows when to shut up.

"Addy," Jake calls after me. Of course he can't leave well enough alone. He made a solid attempt at acting conciliatory for the benefit of whoever the guy next to him is, but Jake has never been able to let me have the last word.

"You okay?" Nate asks once we've disappeared from sight beneath the bleachers, raking one hand through unruly dark hair. "I'm really sorry about that. You handled him like a pro, but you shouldn't have had to. My dad's call got me kind of rattled, and—"

"I'm fine," I break in, a little surprised to realize it's true. Maybe because an unexpected Jake sighting is only the second-worst thing to happen today. Also, I hardly ever get to see Nate flustered, so I should enjoy it while I can. I pat his arm and add, "I understand. But your friends are here for you, Nate. Nobody will judge you for being a secret Hanson fan."

"You know what? I'm keeping that ringtone. Fuck all of you."

"That's the spirit. Now where is the—"

Before I can say *equipment shed,* Patrick Macauley materializes in front of us, and I register the small, squat building behind him. He's wearing a faded T-shirt and jeans that look too big for him, a ring of keys clipped to one sagging belt loop. I've seen Nate's dad in passing only a few times since Nate and I started hanging out, and I'm struck by how careworn he looks. Every line of his face is etched with tension as he calls out, "Is the ambulance here?"

Nate and I exchange startled glances. "Ambulance?" Nate asks, a hard edge creeping into his voice. "What's going on? Are you drinking?" Nate had to call an ambulance for his father more than once when Mr. Macauley's alcoholism was at its worst, so I'm not surprised that his mind instantly goes there. But Mr. Macauley doesn't seem drunk; he seems worried.

"No, no," Mr. Macauley says, snapping a rubber band on his wrist. "It's not for me; it's just . . . I thought they'd be here by now. I called them right after I called you. I should've called them first, but I—I got a little panicked. It felt like this was my fault, somehow." He unclips the keys from his belt and stares at them like he has no clue how they came to be in his possession. "Because of these, I guess."

"Your fault? Because of . . ." Nate trails off, too confused to do anything except focus on the keys. "Where'd you find them?"

Mr. Macauley snaps the rubber band again. "Well, I did what you said. I retraced my steps at work, went to all the places I'd been last week, and when I got to the shed—there they were, dangling from the lock. But then I opened the door, and . . ." He looks over his shoulder. "We better get back. I shouldn't have left her, but I heard voices and I thought . . ."

Cold sweat pricks the back of my neck. "Left who?" I ask.

Nate strides past both me and his dad quickly, pushing the door fully open. He sucks in a sharp breath and disappears inside the shed. I follow him, blinking as my eyes adjust from sunshine to the dimness of the musty shed. Nate is crouched on the ground beside one of the walls, leaning over—

"Phoebe!" I cry out.

I nearly trip in my haste to reach her, heart racing as I drop to my knees beside Nate. Phoebe is slumped against the wall like a discarded rag doll, her clothes streaked with dirt and her bronze curls hanging limply over her pale, still face. All I can think is: *We're too late. Something terrible has happened, and we're too late to stop it.*

Then Phoebe's head jerks up, and her lashes flutter. "Oh, thank God," I say breathlessly at the same time Nate growls, "What the hell is that?"

"Huh?" I ask, cupping Phoebe's chin with one hand and staring into her eyes. "Phoebe, can you hear me? It's Addy and

Nate. You're okay. Help is coming." Her eyes close again, but her breathing is steady, and she looks unhurt, except for . . .

"Her *arm*," Nate says as my eyes drop and I let out a shocked gasp.

The word is written on Phoebe's left arm in what looks like black Sharpie, each capital letter so big and bold that it should've been impossible to miss:

PRACTICE

CHAPTER THIRTEEN

Phoebe
Tuesday, July 7

"Thanks for the ride," I say stiffly as I get into the passenger seat of Cooper's car.

"Of course," he says over a loud, rattling hum. "Sorry about the noise."

"It's fine," I say, clipping my seat belt. It doesn't sound good, but in the greater scheme of things . . . who cares? This is the first time I've left the house in almost two days, and I'd probably still be in my room if Cooper hadn't offered me a ride to Café Contigo to meet up with the rest of the Bayview Crew. Even my mother, as horrified as she is about what happened on Fourth of July weekend, feels like I'm safe with Cooper around.

"Nonny wanted me to give you these," Cooper says, reaching into the back seat to hand me a Tupperware container. "They're cookies. She says she hopes you'll come by sometime when you're feeling up to it. Doesn't have to be to deliver lunch."

"Tell her thanks," I say, swallowing hard. "And I will." Then my throat closes up before I can tell him that I'm sorry I missed his commercial. I watched the clip last night, and it almost made me smile.

"How are you doing?" he asks as he backs out of my driveway.

"Okay," I say. A small, simple word that does nothing to convey the weekend I had. I don't remember much of it, because according to toxicology reports, there were traces of Rohypnol in my system when Bayview Memorial Hospital got back the results of all the tests they gave me. "Roofies?" I'd asked the doctor, clutching the edges of my hospital gown tightly around me. "So somebody . . ."

"Somebody drugged you," she confirmed.

A wave of nauseated horror washed over me. I've never been so drunk that I've blacked out, so maybe I should've realized sooner that something was deeply wrong. But I didn't understand, until right that second, how *calculated* my lost night had been. When I'd woken up with Addy and Nate beside me, my mouth dry and my head aching, I thought maybe I'd wandered into the shed on my own. Even after I saw the word on my arm, I thought some jerk did it at the party. But as soon as Detective Mendoza said *Somebody drugged you,* all I could think was: *Who? And why?*

When I came to, my clothes were dusty from the shed, but not torn or out of place. The knot I'd tied in my belt in Nate's bathroom was still there. That was a comfort, but it didn't change the fact that somebody doctored my drink, took me from Nate's backyard, and then *wrote on me.* My arm is scrubbed clean, but every time I look at it, I'm positive that I can still see a faint outline of the letters. That I can feel them, like they were burned into my skin.

"A sick, nasty prank," one of the nurses said at the hospital when he thought I couldn't hear. "The kids in this town are flat-out horrible, aren't they?"

They can be. But somehow, I don't think *prank* even begins to cover what happened to me. The police asked where I'd gotten my drinks that night, and the last one I remembered was the one Sean handed to me. While I wouldn't put it past Sean Murdock to roofie someone, the doctor at Bayview Memorial said the drug shouldn't have kicked in that fast, and the double vision I'd experienced while talking to Sean, Jules, and Monica probably meant it was already in my system. Plus there's no way Sean brought me to the Bayview High equipment shed; Crystal took his keys and sent him home with one of her friends.

Before that, I'd gotten drinks from Knox and Luis—both of whom I'd trust with my life. Vanessa gave me a drink after I stalked away from the Bayview Crew corner, and then I stole another one from her, which the Bayview Police found interesting. I suppose I could've grabbed a drugged drink by mistake, but if somebody was targeting Vanessa, why am *I* the one who was taken from Nate's house and dumped in a shed?

And then there's the time I spent in Reggie's room, which I barely remember. Could someone have handed me a drink there? Was it Reggie? I don't think so, but parts of the night have such a surreal quality that I'm not sure what really happened from the time I left the bathroom until I staggered out of Nate's house.

I'm positive I didn't send that text to my mother about staying over at Addy's—for one thing, no matter how out of it I was, I wouldn't have forgotten that Addy was mad at me; and for another, there's no way I could've sent such a long message with no typos at that point in the night. But if I didn't, who did? It had to be someone who knows who my friends are. Somebody who probably held my phone up to my face to unlock it, searched for "Mom" in my contacts, and made sure that nobody would check up on me for a good long while.

Oh, Phoebe. You've made a big mistake.

Did someone actually say that, or was I dreaming? I can't be sure, especially because it's exactly the kind of thing I'd say to myself.

I shake off my thoughts and try to focus on the road. "You missed the turn for Café Contigo," I say as Cooper sails past it.

"Yeah, I know," he says. "I thought I'd take you someplace else first, if that's okay? It's right down the street."

My curiosity is piqued despite myself. "Where?"

"The auto shop where Manny used to work," he says, making another turn.

"I . . . um, okay," I say, confused. "Are you getting your car fixed?"

"No, nothin' like that," Cooper says. He pulls into a deserted lot surrounded by a chain-link fence and parks beside the most decrepit car I've ever seen. It's missing all four tires and both the front and back bumpers, and it's covered with rust and dents. "This just got stripped for parts, and it's getting hauled to the junkyard soon. Before it does, well . . . let me show you."

We get out of Cooper's Jeep, and he picks up an oversized hammer leaning against one side of the car. "After Simon died, when things got really bad, Luis brought me here," he says. "There was another car just like this one. He handed me a sledgehammer and told me to whack the hell out of it until I felt better. Seemed like a dumb idea until I actually did it. It helped, so I thought maybe it'd help you too."

I blink at him, frozen in place, and he swings the sledge-hammer lightly, making a small dent in the driver's-side door. "Phoebe, I can't relate to everything that happened to you Saturday night," he says. "But I know what it's like to feel like your life doesn't belong to you anymore. And to feel like you can't talk about it."

Cooper swings the hammer again, his gaze locked on the car. "When I told Nonny what happened, you know what she said? She said, 'That's terrible, especially because that girl is already in a world of pain.'" My eyes sting as he continues, "I asked her what she meant, and she said, 'Well, she hasn't said anything specific. But I can tell.' Nonny's never wrong about stuff like that." Cooper turns and holds the sledgehammer out to me. "You don't have to say anything. But if it'd help to take a swing at something—go ahead."

I gingerly grab the handle. It feels good in my hands, but my feet stay rooted in place, long enough that Cooper adds, "And if this was a bad idea, we can leave."

"No," I say, taking a deep breath as I lift the sledgehammer over one shoulder. "It wasn't." I step toward the car, take aim, and hit the driver's-side door with every ounce of strength that

I have. It makes an incredibly satisfying dent, so I pull back and hit the car again. Then I move toward the hood before taking another swing. And another, and another, and another, for every single awful thing that's happened over the past few months. Learning how my dad died, the Truth or Dare game, Brandon's death, the blowup with Emma, Jared's plot, Nate's injury, Owen's lies. Feeling like I had to separate myself from Knox and Maeve and Addy and everyone I care about, and then getting *drugged and dragged into a goddamn shed . . .*

I hit the car so many times that, if my arms were as strong as the hurt and anger coursing through me, it'd be pulverized into dust. It's not, but it's an even bigger mess of deep dents when I finally stop, breathing heavily, and look into Cooper's kind, judgment-free eyes.

"Thanks," I say. "You were right. I needed that."

CHAPTER FOURTEEN

Phoebe
Tuesday, July 7

When Cooper and I finally make it to Café Contigo's brand-new roof deck, the rest of the Bayview Crew—Nate excepted, since he's working—is already there. Evie is circling the table with a tray of drinks, and she briefly squeezes my shoulder when I pass. I haven't seen anyone since the party Saturday night, other than Nate and Addy in the shed the next day, and I don't remember much about that. Everyone called and texted and offered to stop by, but I couldn't face them until today.

So I wasn't sure what to expect, but . . . it's nice. Lots of hugs, concern, and righteous anger on my behalf. For a few minutes, I feel like I'm back in the pre-Jared days, when I was part of the team and didn't have anything to hide. It helps, probably, that I'm too physically wrung out from beating up the car to feel tense. And that the roof deck isn't yet open to the public, so it's perfectly private.

Finally, after Evie's dropped off a tray of apps, Maeve opens her laptop with a flourish. "Okay, well, if we're ready to start sharing information—I have some," she says.

My stomach flutters with fear that she found something related to Owen. But if she had, she wouldn't be looking straight at me, eyes warm with concern.

"We're ready," I say, with a glance toward Knox beside me. He's a little green from the height, and clutching his glass of Sprite with both hands. "As long as everybody's comfortable staying on the roof deck? We could always move—"

"I'm fine," Knox says, releasing his death grip on the glass. "Go ahead, Maeve."

"So, I've spent the past forty-eight hours hunting down the revenge forum, pretty much nonstop," Maeve says, suppressing a yawn, and it's only then that I notice the dark circles under her eyes. Of course she did; Maeve on a mission can't be stopped.

"Except for those two hours you slept on me this afternoon," Luis says fondly.

"You should have woken me up," Maeve says, casting a severe look his way. "I lost valuable time. But anyway, what I found is—nothing."

"Nothing?" Addy echoes.

"I mean, not *nothing* nothing," Maeve clarifies, shifting in her seat. "I was able to track down a bunch of the guys who used to post on Vengeance Is Mine, and—"

"How did you manage to do that?" Kris breaks in.

"Simple," Maeve says calmly. "I had screenshots saved with their user names, so I started with those, but also, they gave away a lot of personal details about themselves when they thought their posts were being erased."

"Don't even question her methods," Bronwyn says, taking a sip of her drink. "Mere mortals can't possibly understand."

"Ultimately, a bunch of them congregated on Toq," Maeve says.

"Talk?" Kris asks.

"Yeah. It's pronounced like *T-A-L-K,* but spelled *T-O-Q,*" Maeve says. "It's one of those free-speech apps that sprang up when certain people started getting too horrible to be allowed on regular social media. It's full of racists and conspiracy theorists, which makes it a highly effective place for these losers to hide. Nobody in their right mind wants to spend time there." She makes a face and holds up her phone. "I should know. I have an account now. My name is Tami Lee Spencer, and you don't even want to hear what my hobbies are."

"Yikes." Knox grimaces. "Way to take one for the team, Maeve."

"The Vengeance Is Mine guys all joined a couple of months ago, and they post pretty often. They've referred to Jared more than once—by his initials, JJ, but you can tell it's him," Maeve says. "The thing is, none of them seem to care about what happened to him. They're not mad or plotting on his behalf. Mostly, they think he's a loser for getting caught."

"Have they mentioned Eli?" Addy asks. "Or Until Proven, or—"

"No," Maeve says. "I've read all their posts on Toq, plus similar stuff on other apps, but I figured that wouldn't be enough for you, so . . ." Her mouth puckers like she bit down on a lemon. "Since last night, Tami Lee has been messaging privately with the anonymous poster known as Jellyfish."

Knox's mouth drops open. "Wait . . . you mean that guy

who was always whining on Vengeance Is Mine about getting back at his teacher?"

"That's the one," Maeve says. "And he's *still* whining about that. In between trying to convince Tami Lee to attend a monster-truck rally with him."

Luis clutches his chest. "I can't believe you're two-timing me with a guy named Jellyfish," he says. "A monster-truck rally sounds kind of fun, though, doesn't it?"

"No," Maeve says.

"Give it a chance. Ask yourself, *What would Tami Lee do?*" Luis says. Then his expression turns grave as he adds, "He can't trace who you really are, can he?"

Maeve shakes her head decisively. "There's no way. I've been careful." She turns to Addy and adds, "I've been working on worming my way into his confidence. He brags about a lot of dumb stuff, but nothing related to Phoebe, the Truth or Dare game, or the hacked billboard. No reference to Simon or Eli or Emma, or even Jake. Not from Jellyfish—his name is allegedly Axel, by the way, which is probably as real as Tami Lee—or any of these guys. I'll keep monitoring, obviously, but I honestly don't think they're planning anything."

Cooper puts down his fork, and I realize that he's steadily polished off half the appetizers while Maeve was talking. I, meanwhile, haven't taken a single bite. I lift an empanada and nibble its edge as Cooper says, "Well, that's good news, right?"

"I think so. For Eli and Ashton, anyway," Maeve says as Addy visibly exhales. "But it doesn't give us much to go on in terms of the hacked billboard, or what happened to Phoebe. All the chatter about that is happening on social media. It's not underground."

Addy pokes her fork into an untouched scoop of guaca-mole on her plate. It doesn't look as though her appetite is any better than mine. "What if . . . does anyone think *Jake* could've taken Phoebe?" she asks.

A shudder runs through me as Kris asks, "But he's being monitored, isn't he?"

"Supposedly," Addy says. "The thing is, though . . ." She turns compassionate eyes toward me. "Sorry to bring this up, Phoebe, but is it okay to talk about your arm for a minute?"

"It's fine," I say, the phantom letters prickling as I take another bite of empanada.

"I've been thinking about what the writing could possibly mean," Addy says. "And then I remembered what you told me when Jake fixed your flat tire. You said you didn't want to thank him, so you said something like, *I should learn how to change a tire.* Right?" I nod, and she adds, "And then he said, *All it takes is practice.*"

The entire table falls silent. Kris freezes with his fork halfway to his mouth, Knox's jaw drops, and Bronwyn's and Maeve's eyes both get so round that they've never looked more alike. The empanada in my mouth tastes like dust, and I need a big gulp of Diet Coke to get it down my throat. Cooper is the first to speak, with a lightly exhaled "Nooooo. It can't . . . that's gotta be a coincidence, right? Practice for *what*?"

"For me," Addy says.

"Addy, no!" Bronwyn exclaims, and then it's chaos at the table, everyone trying to reassure her at once. "That's impossible," Maeve says, her voice carrying above the noise. "People would know. He's wearing an ankle monitor!"

"But he's allowed to be at Bayview High," Addy points out.

"He could've been the one who stole Nate's father's keys. He was even there the day we found Phoebe."

"With his parole officer," Cooper says. "And there has to be some kind of time limit, right? I'm sure if Jake was there late at night when a girl goes missing, someone would notice."

"You have a surprising amount of faith in law enforcement for someone who lives in Bayview," Addy says drily. "Plus, all Jake needs is one friend with Maeve-level skills to spend half an hour on the dark web or whatever, learning how to get around an ankle monitor." Maeve opens her mouth to protest, then closes it, because—yeah. She could probably figure that out. "And Cooper, you remember that red car you saw at Eli's office? The one with the tan convertible top? Well, Nate and I saw it again near his neighbor's house, right before we left for Bayview High the day we found Phoebe. And Jake knows exactly where the equipment shed is, and—"

"Addy, stop," Bronwyn says, sounding a little desperate. "It's not logical—why would Jake do something like that? All he needs to do is keep his head down, and . . ." She trails off, clearly not wanting to finish that sentence with *He'll be a free man.*

"Since when is Jake logical?" Addy asks.

"Okay, that's a fair point," Bronwyn concedes. "I don't blame you for being worried, Addy. But he couldn't have had anything to do with the billboard or those flyers around town. That started before he was released."

Addy snorts. "Do you remember that article in the *Bayview Blade* about Jake? It said he had dozens of pen pals. *Dozens.* God only knows what kind of stuff somebody might agree to if they were completely snowed by him." She turns toward me, her expression urgent. "Phoebe, did you see anyone who looked like Jake at the party? Or a red car? Or is there anything else you haven't told us yet that might be helpful?"

Everyone looks at me and I flush, eyes dropping to my plate. I think about what Cooper said earlier at the auto shop: *I know what it's like to feel like your life doesn't belong to you anymore. And to feel like you can't talk about it.*

It would be such a relief to blurt out the truth about Owen. But Emma finally called on Sunday afternoon and promised to come home as soon as she could find an affordable flight. "I'm sorry I haven't been there for you," she said. "It's been rough around here, but that's no excuse. Just don't do anything until I get home, okay? There are complications."

I was too worn out to ask *What complications?,* so all I said was "Okay."

But I need to give Addy *something.* "I remember wallpaper," I say.

Addy blinks. "Huh?"

"I told the police," I explain. "I don't know if it's even a real memory, but . . . I feel like I woke up at one point, and I was someplace I didn't recognize, and all I could see was wallpaper. Green, with twisty vines. But maybe it was just a dream, because I don't remember anything else, and—"

"Vines," Addy interrupts, her face so pale that you can see the light dusting of freckles across her cheeks. She turns to Cooper and adds, "Are you thinking what I'm thinking?"

"I . . . probably not?" Cooper says cautiously.

"The sunroom. In the Ramona house."

I gaze around the table to see if I'm the only one who doesn't catch the reference, but everyone else looks equally confused.

126

Whatever Addy and Cooper are talking about, it's shorthand only they know. "The Ramona . . . what? No," Cooper says. "Those weren't vines in that room. They were more like . . . wheat."

"They were vines," Addy says insistently. "And they were green."

"What are you guys talking about?" Bronwyn asks, looking between them.

Addy tugs on her earring. "I've seen green-vine wallpaper before. *Not* wheat," she adds, with a pointed glance at Cooper. "At a vacation house in Ramona, you know, near the Cuyamaca Mountains? Just about an hour from here." She takes a deep breath before adding, "It belongs to Jake's family."

SIMON

Six Years Earlier

Jake's vacation house reminded Simon of Jake's family: bland, impractical, and more than a little pretentious.

Take the living room furniture, for example. What kind of family with a teenage boy would fill an entire room with stark-white furniture? The Riordans, that's who. They had only themselves to blame for Simon propping his dirty sneakers up on one end of the couch while he opened a notebook and uncapped his pen. He was finally alone, since Mr. and Ms. Riordan were out *antiquing*, whatever that was, and Jake was taking a nap in his room.

Or pretending to be asleep. Either way was fine with Simon.

He flipped pages until he got to what he was looking for: *People I Hate.*

Concise and to the point; Simon didn't like wasting words while cataloging grievances. He'd added *Bronwyn Rojas* last week, after they'd attended the same preparatory Model UN summer program. Bronwyn lived in Bayview, too, but she'd gone to St. Pius for elementary and middle school, instead of Buckingham Academy like Simon and Jake, so Simon had never met her before. He could tell instantly that they'd be in all the same honor classes in high school, and that she'd possibly challenge him for top grades. *She's not smarter than me*, Simon decided as the dark-haired girl made her points of inquiry. *But she'll probably work harder.*

Brownnoser, he'd written in his notebook then. *Irritating voice. Insecure.* He'd also written *Ugly*, but then, after some consideration, crossed it out. Simon prided himself on being harsh but fair, and other people's physical attributes always tested his objectivity. Just because he didn't find Bronwyn Rojas the slightest bit aesthetically pleasing didn't mean that someone else might not think differently. Someone with terrible taste, clearly, but still.

Today, though, Simon wasn't interested in adding to Bronwyn's entry. Instead, he flipped to a blank page and started writing.

> Jake Riordan
>   Sucks at video games
>   Watches reality television unironically
>   Stares at himself in the mirror
>   Fake

Simon kept writing, pen digging into the thin paper of his notebook. He'd thought about making an entry for Jake before, of course, because Jake could be fucking annoying. But he hadn't done it, out of some kind of misguided loyalty that, he now realized, wasn't returned.

Jake and his father liked to get up at seven a.m. to go running, and they knew better than to invite Simon along. Simon usually liked to sleep until noon, but he was restless in his uncomfortable bed—the mattress was like a gigantic pillow, much too soft for his liking—so today he got up earlier than usual and went outside. Then he wandered around the Riordans' two acres of land, so bored that he was literally kicking rocks until he heard voices.

"Then why did you invite him?"

It was Mr. Riordan, huffing from whatever exercise they were doing now. The grounds were littered with fitness equipment that was meant to look like part of the landscape. A pull-up bar built into a tree, for example. That's probably what they were using, because Jake was obsessed, suddenly, with having biceps. And *abs*.

"Who else am I supposed to invite?" Jake asked sulkily.

"Whoever you want," Mr. Riordan said. "For crying out loud, Jake, you're a Riordan. Since when do Riordans need to settle for the Simon Kellehers of the world? You should be hanging out with what's-his-name from Mississippi. The baseball phenom."

Simon paused at the edge of a clearing, trying to analyze the effect that Mr. Riordan's words had on him. He'd never liked Jake's father, but he hadn't considered that the feeling might be mutual. He was surprised, he supposed, but ultimately indifferent, because he didn't care what Scott Riordan thought.

But Jake, on the other hand . . . Jake was actually complaining about Simon? Now, *that* was offensive, especially since Simon had always taken a certain amount of pride in being Jake's friend. Jake was irritating, sure, but he had the potential to be a lot more. A person of consequence at Bayview High—a place that Simon was determined to rule once he got there. Simon had always assumed that Jake saw the same potential in him.

"Cooper," Jake said. "I'm trying."

That was news to Simon. He didn't have a hate page for Cooper Clay yet, but it was probably only a matter of time. Nobody on the receiving end of that much mindless worship could escape being an asshole.

"Well, try harder," Mr. Riordan said. "Or come here on your own and use the time to work out. Mark my words: there's something creepy about that Kelleher kid."

"I know," Jake said. "You're right, Dad. You're always right."

Now Simon carefully wrote *Daddy's boy* on his list. Then he paused when the sound of tires crunching on gravel reached his ears. It looked as though the Riordans were back from antiquing, and that was enough to propel Simon off the couch and into hiding. He headed for the second floor, to a small balcony off the guest bedroom where he could hear anyone coming up the driveway without being seen. He was seized with a sudden certainty that the Riordans would be talking about him—they'd probably spent their entire antique trip plotting how to send him home early—and he wanted to know exactly what they had to say.

As it turned out, though, Simon wasn't the center of their universe. "I can't believe you, Katherine," Mr. Riordan said tightly. He didn't slam the car door, because it was a brand-new BMW, but Simon could tell from his voice that he wanted to. "This is a family trip."

"I know, and I'm sorry," Ms. Riordan said. "But we're in such a crucial point in the campaign. I wish I could trust someone else to oversee the creative, but I can't."

"You need to learn the art of delegating," Mr. Riordan said.

Boring, Simon thought. He'd heard enough and was about to withdraw from the balcony when Mr. Riordan added, "Otherwise, you're going to continue setting a poor example for Jake."

"Poor example?" Ms. Riordan echoed. "For taking my job seriously?"

"For caring about it more than you care about this family."

"But I . . . but that's . . ." Even on the second floor, Simon could hear Ms. Riordan take a deep, steadying breath. "How can you say that, Scott, with all the traveling you do? At least my work is local! I've never missed a Pop Warner game, or a parent-teacher conference, or—"

"So it's my fault you're obsessed with work?" Mr. Riordan asked.

"I'm not *obsessed*—"

"Just go, Katherine," Mr. Riordan broke in. His tone was curt, dismissive. "I'll take care of our meal for the evening. Like I always do." The front door slammed, and then there was nothing but silence for so long that Simon assumed Ms. Riordan had slipped away too.

"Like it's so hard to order takeout," she finally muttered, and Simon nearly laughed out loud. Ms. Riordan had a spine, after all. Too bad she used it only when she was alone. She was quiet for a while longer, and when she spoke again, her voice was transformed. It was bright and energetic—the kind of tone where you could tell the person was smiling, even if you couldn't see them. "I'll be there in an hour," she said. "I just need to pack a few things." After a few moments of silence, she added, "I can't wait either."

Simon peered over the edge of the balcony as Ms. Riordan hung up the phone, turning in his direction. All she'd have to do to see him was glance up, but she didn't, and Simon got a good look at her face before she went inside.

Her expression made one thing clear: Ms. Riordan liked her job a lot better than she liked her husband.

CHAPTER FIFTEEN

Nate
Wednesday, July 8

There's something interesting about watching people who think they're alone. Like Ms. Riordan, who finally dropped the smile she'd been wearing after her tennis partner left their corner table at the Bayview Country Club bar. Now her head's down, and she's rubbing both temples like she needs to scrub whatever they just talked about from her brain.

Or Vanessa, who's pretending to be absorbed in her phone in the hallway leading from the pool to the bar but keeps glancing at Ms. Riordan like she's waiting for her to look a little less miserable. Vanessa's the type who's always putting on a performance, so it's weird to see her looking unsure of herself, especially when it comes to Ms. Riordan. Addy's words at Café Contigo pop into my head then: *Do you remember that article in the* Bayview Blade *about Jake? It said he had dozens of pen pals.* Is it possible that one of those pen pals was . . . Vanessa?

Curiosity keeps me eyeing a still-oblivious Vanessa for long enough that Gavin, the bartender on duty today, bumps my arm with his as I wipe down the counter.

"Thought you were all about that girlfriend of yours," he says.

"Huh?" I ask, a half second before his meaning hits me. "Oh, hell no," I say, turning away before Vanessa catches me staring too. The last thing I need is her jumping to the same conclusion. "Just zoned out for a sec."

"You sure?" Gavin asks with a smirk. I glare hard enough that he holds up a conciliatory hand. "All right, all right. Didn't mean to question your OTP. I'm only asking because I think she's cute. Vanessa, not Bronwyn. Well, Bronwyn is *also* cute, but she's very taken and you're kind of mean and I'm scared of you, so. . . ." He raises both hands in surrender, and I snort out a reluctant laugh. "What do you think? Is she single?"

"You're back to talking about Vanessa, right?"

"Obviously. I don't have a death wish."

"I have no idea."

He runs a hand through his hair. "Can you find out for me?"

"No," I say shortly, and he sighs.

"Worth a shot," he says as a group of men who look like they just finished a round of golf settle themselves at the end of the bar. "How much longer are you here for?"

"Half an hour," I say.

"Got plans tonight?"

"Yeah. Bronwyn and I are making dinner for my dad." Or more accurately, I'll end up making most of it, because Bronwyn is such a careful recipe follower that we won't eat until midnight otherwise. The amount of time she can spend measuring a single cup of rice is mind-boggling. Maeve is even worse. The Rojas sisters have a lot of skills, but none of them are kitchen-related.

"How domestic," Gavin says with a grin. Then he waves at the golf guys and calls out, "Be right with you, gentlemen."

While we were talking, Vanessa sidled her way up to Ms. Riordan's table, and she's now perched at the end of a stool, talking animatedly. I gaze around the U-shaped bar to see if anybody's trying to catch my attention. The blond moms in the corner are still working on their peach margaritas, the two old men across from me are too busy arguing about somebody running for Congress to touch their whiskey, and the lone guy who just walked up is—

"What the hell do you want?"

The words burst out of me in a growl before I remember where I am, and that I'm not supposed to snap at people leaning over the bar with money in hand. Even when they're Jake fucking Riordan.

"Great to see you too, Macauley," he says.

I brace my forearms on the bar so I don't take a swing at him. That *asshole*. Walking around in his polo shirt and salmon-colored pants like he's the same pampered jock he always was. Like he shouldn't be behind bars for the rest of his life after what he did to Addy. To me. And Bronwyn, and Cooper, and Janae, and Simon . . .

Jake tosses a twenty onto the bar. His hair's starting to grow out, making him look more like his old Bayview High self. "Chardonnay, please," he says.

"Fuck off," I say.

He raises his eyebrows. "It's for my mother."

"I don't care."

"You're gonna make her walk over here and order herself?"

He's not getting it, so I enunciate my words slowly and clearly. "Fuck. *Off.*"

Instead, Jake slides onto a stool with a smirk. "It must drive you crazy, huh?" he asks in the kind of buddy-buddy tone the golf guys use when they try to make me talk sports. "That even though I spent a lot more time than you did behind bars—wrongly, I might add—you still have to serve me. And you always will." His eyes glint as he folds his arms on the counter. "Ten years from now, I'll be able to buy this club ten times over, and you'll still be here trying to scrape enough credits together for a shitty associate's degree. Maybe even selling drugs again. That was the most money you'll ever see at one time, wasn't it?"

My vision goes red as my right hand curls into a fist. I can hear Bronwyn clearly in my head, saying, *Don't react; he's not worth it,* but the thing is—she's not here, so she doesn't have to look at Jake's smug, incredibly punchable face.

"You know what I can't wait for?" Jake continues. Still smiling and relaxed, like he's about to say *Our five-year reunion* or reminisce about all the great times we never had at Bayview High. His tone hardens, but it's too low for anyone except me to hear. "For you to lose it all, Macauley. Your job, your pathetic friends, your addict parents, and most of all, your tight-ass girlfriend. Because once she's gone, you're gonna spiral so fast that—"

I'm not even thinking when I lunge for him, only to find myself being roughly yanked back, arms pinned to my sides. "Let's not get fired today," Gavin mutters in my ear. He's surprisingly strong as he shoves me behind him, startling the peach-margarita moms. "Get out of here, Nate. Go ride your bike or something. Your shift's almost done; there's no point hanging around here and letting this asshole bait you. You touch him, he's gonna have you arrested for assault. Don't give him what he wants."

Jesus, I hate that he's right. I hate that the only choice I have is to walk away with Jake's words echoing in my ears and to let Gavin smooth things over. I hate that Jake is back in my world and there's nothing I can do about it. And maybe most of all, I hate the fact that in less than five minutes, he managed to yank all my worst fears out of my brain and shove them in my face.

Some things never change.

Ms. Riordan's already at Jake's side, fussing over him, her voice pinched with worry, and Jake raises both hands. "I'm going, I'm going," he says. "I've got shit to do anyway." He levels his gaze at me with a sardonic wave. "See you around, Macauley."

"Is that . . . ," one of the margarita moms asks.

"You know perfectly well who it is," another one says. "It's appalling that he's allowed to come here. We should complain to management."

The third woman takes a long swig of her drink before saying, "Go ahead and hit him, Nate. I'll tell everyone it was self-defense."

"You're not helping, ladies," Gavin says.

He finally releases me when Jake is out of sight. "Don't worry about that guy," he says, jaw tight as he watches Vanessa lead Ms. Riordan back to the corner table. "I'm a big believer in karma, and Jake Riordan has a massive reckoning coming his way."

"Yeah, that's what I thought, too," I say. "Too bad the legal system thought different."

"Have faith in the long game," Gavin says. "Patience is a virtue."

"Whatever." I should thank him, I know, but I don't have it in me, so I grab my keys from beneath the counter and take off without another word. I unlock my phone on the way to the parking lot, pulling up a new message from Bronwyn. She left her internship early to go shopping for dinner tonight. *Look at this haul,* she wrote, alongside a picture of a bunch of vegetables she picked up at a farmers' market. *I tagged you in my IG story, which you would know if YOU EVER WENT THERE.*

I stare at my phone for a few seconds. There's a knot of resentful, self-hating fury inside me that makes me want to text back: *forget dinner.* Forget everything, Bronwyn, because you're too good for me and one of these days you're going to realize it. I'd rather you do it now than later, because it's only going to feel worse the more time we're together.

Then I take a deep breath and hold it as long as possible before sending back a normal response. *Maybe someday,* with a heart so she knows that if I ever start using any of the social media accounts she created for me, it'll only be to make her happy. Bronwyn has proved a hundred times over that she's in it for the long haul with me, and I'm not going to let Jake Riordan make me question it. Or ruin it.

It's unreal, though, how fast the inner voice you thought was gone can jump back into your head to tell you how much you suck. Addy must be feeling the same way, and I have a sudden urge to find her and tell her that she's awesome and destined for a brilliant life. But then I remember she's having dinner with her sister and Eli, so I settle for a text: *You're great.*

Addy responds instantly. *Are you drunk?*

I pocket my phone, mood slightly lifted. She knows I'm not.

CHAPTER SIXTEEN

Nate
Wednesday, July 8

"Padres are looking good this year," my father says.

"Yeah," I say. "Real good."

I wouldn't know, since I don't watch baseball unless Cooper's playing. But it's one of my father's favorite conversational topics, and it doesn't require much effort on my part. I'm always on edge when I come to this house, flashing back to when I used to live here. It's a lot neater than it used to be, and Dad has fixed a few things—the cabinet under the sink that I kicked in after Simon died, for example, isn't splintered anymore. But it's still the kind of place that makes you feel like giving up before you even start trying.

Bronwyn knows that, so I was hoping she'd show up early. But when Dad runs out of baseball steam and I glance at my phone, I realize that she's actually five minutes late. Which is like an hour for anyone else. "It's weird that Bronwyn's not here yet," I say, opening my messages to see if I missed one from her.

"What time did she say she was coming?"

"Six-thirty," I say, texting *You almost here?* to her. I wait for gray dots to appear—Bronwyn returns texts like she's being graded on speed—but there's nothing.

Dad frowns at his watch. "Really? She's late? That's not like her."

A chill settles over me. No, it's not. My father has barely started getting to know Bronwyn, but he knows that. I pull up her Instagram; her latest story is the picture she took at the farmers' market, with the caption: *Next stop, Andre's Groceria!*

If she's not checking texts, she's definitely not checking Instagram, but I still send a comment: *CALL ME.* Then a second one: *please.*

Relief floods my veins a few seconds later when my phone rings with a FaceTime request, but . . . it's not Bronwyn. It's Maeve, who's frowning when I pick up. "Sorry to interrupt your cozy family dinner," she says. "But can you tell my sister that if she's going to change the Netflix password, she needs to save it on *all* devices because—"

"Maeve." I stop her. "She's not here."

"What?" Maeve blinks. "I thought you guys had plans."

"We did. We do," I say as apprehension fills my chest like a lead balloon. "But she's late, and she didn't answer my last text."

Maeve bites her lip. "Mine either."

"Fuck." I'm on my feet then, barely registering my father's worried look as I launch myself out of the kitchen. I yank open the front door and head down the stairs, bypassing the second step out of habit, even though my father finally got around to filling in the giant crack that used to be there. Then I stare at the driveway, like I can make Bronwyn's Volvo appear by sheer force of will. "When did you last talk to her?"

"Um, maybe an hour and a half ago? She was buying vegetables, and she wanted to know what kind of lettuce makes the best salad and I said, *How should I know?* Like that's obviously not information I would have, so I tried to get Luis on the line but he's at work and didn't pick up, and . . ." Maeve's voice gets a little shaky. "And then we hung up, and I haven't heard from her since. What about you?"

"About the same." The lead balloon in my chest gets bigger, squeezing all the air out of my lungs as I stalk to the end of my driveway and look both ways. A car is approaching from the right, but even from a distance I can tell it's not Bronwyn. As it speeds past, I say, "I don't like this. What do your parents say?"

"They're at a charity thing," Maeve says. "They—wait, hang on. Addy's calling me. I'm going to add her." A second later, Addy's face pops up beside Maeve's on my screen. "Addy, have you heard from Bronwyn?" Maeve asks urgently.

"I called to ask *you* that," Addy says. "She's left me unread for almost an hour, which is so unprecedented that I started thinking about what happened to Phoebe. . . ."

"Fuck. *Fuck!*" My heart hammers as I pace the driveway, raking a hand so hard through my hair that I'm surprised I don't tear it out. An image pops into my mind then, of Jake Riordan leaning over the country-club bar with that smarmy grin of his. *You know what I can't wait for? For you to lose it all, Macauley.* And then he had the goddamn nerve to talk about Bronwyn: *Once she's gone, you're gonna spiral so fast. . . .*

Gone. I thought that asshole was talking about her dumping me. But what if he meant something else? I flash back to finding Phoebe in that shed, drugged and unresponsive. I don't know why Jake would mess with Phoebe when she had nothing to do with putting him in jail, but then again, she was just *practice*. Bronwyn, on the other hand . . .

A wave of white-hot rage crashes over me. If Jake Riordan touches a single hair on Bronwyn's head, it'll be the last thing he ever does. I'll kill him. I will *kill him*.

"Can you track her on her phone?" Addy asks.

"She never turns that stuff on," Maeve says. "She thinks it's creepy."

"Okay, well, I don't really understand why she thinks *that's* creepy, but she's fine with broadcasting her whereabouts to all of Instagram— Nate, *calm down*," Addy says at whatever furious, frustrated noise I just made. I don't even know. I can't think; I can barely breathe right now. "It's going to be fine. We need—"

"I'll kill him," I snarl.

Dad's hovering in the doorway as I turn back toward the house. "Everything okay?" he calls, but I can't answer him. I need to get on my motorcycle and go—somewhere. Where would Jake go if he decided to rope Bronwyn into some twisted little game?

"Kill who?" Addy asks. "Nate, you're making me dizzy." My phone is dangling loosely from one hand, facing the ground as I stride for my bike.

"Jake," I grit out, swinging one leg over the seat.

"What? *Explain*," demands Addy's disembodied voice.

I bring my phone back in front of my face and somehow

manage to get words out about what happened at the country club, although I don't know if they make much sense. "So I'm going to find him, and find *her,* and make sure he knows that messing with Bronwyn Rojas is the worst mistake a person could make," I finish. Saying her name calms me down a little, grounding me in a way that only Bronwyn can. If something were really wrong, I'd know, right? I'd feel it, way worse than the aching dread I'm feeling now. There has to be a whole other level of pain when your soul gets ripped in half.

"Find them where?" Maeve asks.

"I have an idea," Addy says, just as I'm about to drop the call to start my motorcycle. "Jake's vacation house in Ramona. The wallpaper, remember? I think Phoebe might have been there the night she was drugged, and if I'm right, then—"

"Give me the address," I say.

"No," Addy says firmly. "There's no way I'm letting you tear off on an hour-long drive by yourself. You'll crash from all that adrenaline. Give me five minutes to grab my keys and pick up Maeve, and we'll all go."

CHAPTER SEVENTEEN

Addy
Wednesday, July 8

I've made the trip to Jake's house in Ramona dozens of times, but never like this: with Nate losing his mind beside me and Maeve leaning over the center console from the back seat, staring intently at my speedometer.

"Sixty-five miles per hour is a baseline, Addy," she says. "They *expect* you to go faster."

"I'm almost at eighty."

"Are you sure? Because it feels like we're going backward."

"I don't want to get pulled over," I say, glancing into my rearview mirror as I change lanes. "I mean, under different circumstances a police escort might be helpful, but . . ."

"But all they'd say is *Oh, she's only been missing for two hours,*" Maeve snorts. "And then something super useful like, *What are you planning to do? Break and enter?*"

"Yes," Nate growls. It's the first thing he's said in almost half an hour that's not just a guttural sound of rage, so: progress.

"We're almost there," I say, tapping my brakes as I exit the highway. It's strange to be on this road again; the last time I went with Jake to Ramona was a couple of weeks after I'd hooked up with TJ Forrester. I was so tense during the ride, afraid that I'd let something slip and ruin everything. I had no concept, back then, what "ruin" could look like.

I hate everything, now, about my time with Jake, but at least it gave me this address. At least we're doing something, instead of sitting around waiting and worrying. It's much better for my mental health to be on the move, although my heart doesn't fully agree with my head; my pulse spiked as soon as I spotted the sign for the exit, and it's been pounding ever since. This trip feels like half wild-goose chase and half suicide mission. What, exactly, are we going to do if Jake really is here with Bronwyn? Maybe we should've rounded up the entire Murder Club, but I could barely get Nate to wait until Maeve and I showed up. He would've spontaneously combusted if I'd so much as mentioned making a few extra stops.

"Do you have any weapons in this car?" Maeve asks suddenly, as though her mind is running along the exact same track.

"Weapons?" I repeat. "What exactly do you think I do in my spare time?"

"No, I mean . . . like a baseball bat or something. Maybe Cooper left one behind?"

"Cooper doesn't walk around with bats, Maeve."

"Sure he does. It's practically his job," Maeve says, sitting back in her seat. "Or do you have, like, a snow scraper? Under your seat, maybe?" she adds, her voice muffled.

"Okay, first of all, why would I have a snow scraper when we live in Southern California, and second of all, since when is that considered a weapon?"

"Isn't it pointy?" Maeve asks. "To stab the snow?"

"You think snow needs to be *stabbed*?"

"I mean . . . you know what I mean. Break the ice or whatever."

"Never move to New England, Maeve," I mutter as I stop at a red light. "You wouldn't last a single winter."

She reemerges over the center console with a sigh. "It was just an idea."

Before I can respond, Nate's phone erupts into "MMMBop" from where it's clutched in his hands like a drowning man's life preserver. Even Maeve can't bring herself to snicker as she asks, "Is it Bronwyn?"

"It's . . . I don't recognize the number," Nate says, holding up his phone to show us the screen.

Maeve's scream is so loud that I jump, taking my foot off the brake, and we lurch forward. Thank God there's no one in front of me, or I'd have smashed right into their bumper. "It's my home phone! Pick up, pick up—"

Nate's already on it. "Hello?" he asks, setting his phone to speaker.

"Nate, I am *so* sorry!" Bronwyn's voice fills the car, and then it's chaos—Maeve starts screaming again, I'm half crying and half hysterically laughing, and Nate repeats Bronwyn's name over and over, like it's the only word he can remember. By the time we settle down, the light's been green for a while and the cars behind me are honking furiously.

"Let me pull over," I say.

"Bronwyn," Nate says again, his voice cracking with emotion. "Jesus. We thought . . ."

"Where have you *been*?" Maeve yells. "We were worried sick!"

"Maeve? Are you . . . who's there?" Bronwyn asks as I pull into a near-deserted gas station and shift into Park.

"Me, Nate, and Addy," Maeve says. "Bronwyn, what happened? Are you okay?"

"I'm fine, mostly. It's just . . . everything went wrong," Bronwyn says. "I wanted to have raspberries and cream for dessert, but I couldn't find any good ones, so I thought I'd pick some near Marshall's Peak. You know that giant bush near the rocks? But when I got there, nothing was ripe. So I thought I'd look around for any other bushes that might be farther along, and I wandered too far and ended up by a river that I'd never seen before. I took out my phone to look at Google Maps, and then—I dropped it. Right into the river. I tried to go after it, but I slipped on a rock and twisted my ankle, and when I tried to stand up I fell even harder. By the time I managed to get back on my feet and out of the water, my phone was gone."

"Oh my God," Maeve says, her eyes bright with unshed tears. "I want to make fun of you, you absolute klutz, but I can't because we were *terrified*!"

"I was afraid of that," Bronwyn says. "I know the timing couldn't be worse to go dark, after what happened to Phoebe.

But it took me forever to find the way back to my car, especially because I was limping the whole time. I was getting a little afraid, honestly, that I'd be one of those people who gets lost for days when they're barely a half mile from where they started."

"Legitimate concern," Maeve says, wiping her eyes.

"I figured it out eventually, but then I got stuck in rush-hour traffic," Bronwyn continues. "I kept thinking about pulling over and asking to borrow somebody's phone, but the thing is, I don't know any of your numbers off the top of my head. That's a lesson learned, by the way. All of us should memorize at least one phone number, it doesn't even matter which one—"

"We'll all memorize yours," Maeve says. "Obviously."

"Whatever works. Anyway, I kept driving until I got home and could look them up, and now . . ." Bronwyn exhales a long breath. "Here I am, calling as soon as I could. I'm so unbelievably sorry I missed dinner, Nate."

"Do you have any idea how much I love you?" he asks roughly.

"I do," she says, her voice softening. "I love you too."

"Maeve and I also love you," I chime in, slumping against the window. My entire body's gone limp with relief, because for once, the worst-case scenario didn't happen.

"Back at you," Bronwyn says. "Where are you guys?"

"Oh, well, that's a fun story," Maeve says. "We're in Ramona."

"What?" Bronwyn asks. Even though we're not on FaceTime, I can picture the exact confused expression she's making. "Why?"

"Because we thought Jake drugged you, kidnapped you,

and stashed you in the same vine-wallpapered room that Phoebe thinks she remembers," Maeve says. "In retrospect that was clearly an overreaction, but it made sense at the time."

"Oh my God," Bronwyn gasps. "You must have been in a panic!"

"No, we were totally calm," Maeve says. "Nate definitely wasn't planning to murder Jake or anything like that."

"I still might," Nate says tersely. "As a preventive measure." He stares longingly at the phone, like he wishes it was a genie's lamp he could rub to make Bronwyn appear. "We're coming home. I need to see you."

"I need to see you too—"

"Hold on," I break in. "Sorry to interrupt this adorable virtual reunion and delay the in-person one, but . . . we're less than two miles from Jake's place. Now that we don't have to rescue a hostage, we can switch gears and do something else."

Maeve arches her eyebrows. "Like what?"

I hold up my phone. "Take a picture of the sunroom wallpaper so Phoebe can tell us if that's what she saw Saturday night."

CHAPTER EIGHTEEN

Addy
Wednesday, July 8

"There it is," I say when we near the end of a long, winding road. "You can see Jake's house behind those trees on the right."

I can hear Maeve shift in her seat behind me, getting closer to the window, and then she sucks in a breath. "There are lights on," she says. "Somebody's here. Abort! Abort!"

"There are always lights on," I say. "Jake's parents have them on a timer. These vacation homes get broken into if they seem empty for too long." I slow to a crawl, inching along until I spot a familiar paved indent along the side of the road and ease my car into it. "The driveway is about fifteen feet ahead," I tell them. "We can keep driving or park here and walk."

"Park," Maeve says instantly. "In case you're wrong about the lights."

I turn off the car, and when the headlights go out, the road turns pitch black. When we climb out of the car, goose bumps erupt all over my body. I wrap my arms around myself, wishing I'd thought to bring a sweatshirt like the one Maeve grabs from the back seat. "Here," Nate says, shrugging off his leather jacket and thrusting it toward me.

"You're not cold?" I ask, even as I slip it on gratefully.

"Nah," he says.

"He's warmed by the flame of love, which even the river beside Marshall's Peak couldn't extinguish," Maeve says dramatically.

"Shut it," Nate says, but he's still too relieved to sound truly annoyed.

"Shhh," I say as we approach the Riordans' driveway. A couple of flickering sconces light the stone pillars on either side of the entrance, but once we pass them it's dark again. The driveway is long, and I can't see anything except the wood-and-glass monstrosity looming a couple dozen yards ahead of us. I've never liked this house—there's something cold about it—but there's no denying that it makes a statement.

"Jesus," Nate mutters. "That's their *second* home?"

"Third," I whisper. "They have a place in Barbados too. That's the sunroom right in front of us—the one with all the windows above the patio area."

"Why is there wallpaper in a sunroom?" Maeve whispers.

"It's just one wall. It's supposed to complement the plants outside."

"Oh, good," Nate says. I can't see him well, but I can practically hear his eyes rolling out of his head. "Wouldn't want them to clash. Where's the spare key?"

"Beneath one of the planters at the side door. At least, that's where it used to—"

Maeve grabs my arm and I stop in my tracks. "Addy," she hisses. "There's a car."

She's right. It's parked on the most deeply shadowed part of the driveway, so I hadn't noticed until we were practically on top of it. My heart pounds as I take in the familiar lines and say, "Not just *a* car. Jake's car."

"Why is he here?" Nate mutters, jaw tensing as he stares at the house. "Is this whole probation deal a joke?"

"I told you—dark web," I say. "He's moving around way too much for someone who's following court orders."

"Okay, well, time to go," Maeve says. "We tried. Good effort, team."

"Wait," I say. "We know Bronwyn isn't there, but what if someone else is?" I can't stand the thought, suddenly, of coming all this way and then turning around empty-handed. I know exactly what Jake is capable of. What if I could prove it now, when he's probably feeling invincible? "I think we should still check it out."

"I strongly disagree," Maeve whispers, backing up.

"Well, I'm going," I say, turning to Nate. "You in?"

He sighs. "If you're in, I'm in."

Maeve fades into the shadows. "I'll keep an eye out."

Nate and I creep closer to the house, skirting past the front and around the side. I know from spending nights here that the lack of outdoor lighting makes it impossible to see anything outside except your own reflection in the windows. We pass the cavernous living room, with its wall-mounted television turned to a sports channel, but I don't see people anywhere.

"Seems quiet," Nate murmurs.

"There's a whole downstairs area that we can't see from here," I whisper, crouching beside one of the planters next to the side door. It's meant to look heavy, but it's not, and it lifts easily to let me slide my hand beneath. I feel around for the extra key, my fingers scraping against rough concrete but nothing else.

"Looking for this?" a voice asks, and I drop the planter with a loud clatter.

Nate steps in front of me, partially obscuring my view of the figure on the steps below us: Jake, dressed in sweatpants and a hoodie, his ankle monitor visible beneath his sock, holding up the spare key. I gape at him, too shocked by his presence to respond, and his mouth curls into a sardonic grin. "I saw your car while I was out running. Way to violate your own restraining order, Addy. Guess you can't stay away, huh?"

He takes a step forward, and so does Nate. "Back off," Nate says.

"You're trespassing, Macauley. I could go inside and call the cops on you right now," Jake says. But he stays put, looking Nate up and down. "Or we could settle things another way. Pretty sure I could take you, seeing as I spent a lot more time behind bars than you did. You learn things." Jake's eyes drift back toward me, and I force myself not to shrink into Nate's jacket. "Then Addy and I can have a conversation that's long overdue."

"Over your dead body," Nate says in an ice-cold, *Don't-fuck-with-me* tone that would intimidate most people.

Not Jake, though. "Yeah?" he asks, crackling his knuckles. "You wanna try me?"

"Jake!" A familiar voice drifts from inside the house, snapping me out of my frozen state. I scramble to my feet as Jake's father adds, "You talking to someone?"

"Just a neighbor," Jake calls back. "Be right in."

His lips twist again, eyes glittering as they capture mine. I can't look away, no matter how much I want to. "Oh well. The timing's not right for a reunion, but here's the thing, *Ads*." His old nickname for me sounds like a threat. "I'm getting this monitor off, and soon. We both know it. And if you think I've forgotten about what you did to me, if you think I forgive you for that? You thought wrong. We have a score to settle. Get used to living life looking over your shoulder, because one of these days, I'm going to be there." Jake levels another stare at Nate as he circles around him and inserts the key into the lock. "And he won't."

He opens the door and then, thank God, he's out of sight. But I still can't breathe properly; it's like I've forgotten how. "Don't listen to that prick," Nate says in a harsh whisper. "He's messing with your head."

"No. He's just telling the truth," I say, the weight of the words dropping my voice so low that I'm barely audible. "I knew he felt that way. All he did was confirm it. He's right about the restraining order too." Tears gather behind my eyes, and I blink them away. *Not here.* "Let's go. This was such a stupid idea. I never should've talked you guys into coming here."

"We all agreed," Nate says as we start back down the driveway. "And it was pure bad luck that he saw us. Who the hell goes running this time of night?"

"We didn't even get a picture of the damn wallpaper," I say. Which is the least of my problems right now, but if we had, maybe I could convince myself that there's a silver lining to hearing Jake speak words straight out of my nightmares.

"Don't be so sure about that."

Maeve's voice floats toward us from the darkness, and within seconds she appears, holding up her phone. "I'm not a very good lookout, because I never saw Jake coming," she says in a breathless whisper. "But he didn't see me either. So while he was being his usual asshole self, I climbed up to the patio. The door to the sunroom was unlocked, so—" She hands me her phone. "There you go. A crystal clear picture of the wall-paper, in all its hideous glory."

CHAPTER NINETEEN

Phoebe
Thursday, July 9

"That's not it," I say.

"You're sure?" Maeve asks, holding her phone up higher.

"I told you when you texted me last night. The patterns are nothing alike."

"Yeah, but I thought you might think differently if you saw the original," Maeve says, enlarging her screen. "Plus you were drugged, so . . ."

"I know what I saw, though. Or what I dreamed, and it wasn't that."

"Damn it," Maeve sighs as she closes the picture of the Ramona-house wallpaper. "We're back to square one, then, and Addy got terrorized for nothing."

"Sorry," I mutter, and she squeezes my arm.

"No, no, that's not what I meant. It's just—ugh, it was a *night*."

"You should've called me," Cooper says from the front seat. Kris is driving, and Maeve, Luis, and I are stuffed into the back seat of Kris's Honda Civic.

"And me," Luis says, frowning as he smacks his fist into his palm. "We could've taken care of Jake right then and there."

"Next time, tough guy," Maeve says, kissing his cheek. "You didn't see Nate. There was no holding him back. He was either going with me and Addy, or by himself."

"*Nobody* should have gone," Kris says, his tone equal parts exasperated and forbidding. Sometimes, that extra year he has on Cooper and the rest of the OG Bayview Four seems more like ten. "That was an absolutely terrible idea."

"Yeah, we get that now," Maeve says. "Don't rub it in when you see Addy, though."

"Well, of course I would never—" Kris starts.

"There," Cooper interrupts. "Turn left at the light after this one. The Subaru dealership is one block after that."

We're on a new-car reconnaissance mission, because Cooper's Jeep finally stopped running, and the cost to fix it was ridiculous. Nonny offered to give him a down payment for a new car—apparently, she bought a lot of Apple stock in the nineties—and he'll pay for the rest with his FiredUp Fitness endorsement.

I didn't expect to be part of this car-buying field trip, but I was at Café Contigo when everyone stopped by to pick Luis up, and Cooper persuaded Mr. Santos to let me come too. He's been looking out for me like that ever since our car-smashing trip, and it's helped me feel less alone. So once I'd gotten permission from my mom—after what happened at Nate's Fourth of July party, I have to check in with her before making even the slightest variation in my schedule—I was all in.

"Subaru?" Luis asks, sounding pensive. "What kind of Subaru are we talking about? Something sporty, or—"

"An Outback," Cooper says.

Kris pauses at a red light and puts his hand on Cooper's arm. "Cooper. Darling. Love of my life. You know I support you in all things, but are you sure that you want your first new car to be a station wagon?"

"It's Nonny's favorite," Cooper says. "She's always wanted one."

"How am I supposed to drive when you say things like that?" Kris demands. He shifts the car into Park, grabs Cooper's face between both of his hands, and plants a lingering kiss on his lips. After a few seconds a horn beeps discreetly behind us, and Kris releases Cooper with a wave in the rearview mirror before driving through the now-green light. "Trust me, what Nonny wants is for you to get something that you'll enjoy driving."

"I don't even know where to start," Cooper protests.

Luis's eyes gleam. "That's why I'm here. Turn right, Kris. We're going to Mandalay Motorcars." Kris obeys, and a huge glass-and-chrome building looms on one side of the road, surrounded by a multicolored sea of impossibly shiny cars.

"Oooh. *Where luxury meets destiny,*" I say, quoting the ubiquitous TV ads.

"I don't really understand that tagline," Maeve says.

"Bayview companies aren't known for their cutting-edge slogans," Luis says. "Do you remember Guppies? That fake Swedish Fish candy they used to manufacture here when we were kids? *The sweetest treat you'll ever meet,*" he sings in a rich tenor.

I blink at him. "Damn, Luis. You can *sing.*"

Maeve squeezes his arm. "He's full of surprises."

Luis smiles modestly. "It's no *Nothing gets me fired up like fitness,* though."

"I'm never gonna live that down, am I?" Cooper sighs.

Luis claps him on the shoulder. "At least you're getting a new car out of it."

Kris pulls into the overflowing parking lot and carefully navigates into one of the last remaining spots. He is, without question, the only Honda in sight. "All right," he says, pulling his keys out of the ignition with a flourish. "Here we are. Mandalay Motorcars, where cars cost more than houses."

"Wait. What?" Cooper pauses with one hand on his seat belt buckle, his handsome face a mask of apprehension. "Maybe we should talk about this."

Luis, on the other hand, can't wait to get out of the car. "This is a dream come true!" he crows, then takes off for the entrance before anyone else has even closed their door.

Maeve stares after him. "Well, would you look at that? It took a few months, but I've finally discovered what makes Luis Santos nerd out," she says.

"Come on," Kris says, slinging an arm around Cooper's shoulders and propelling him across the parking lot. "We're just looking. It'll be fun."

Maeve and I follow at a slower pace, and I tug on her sleeve as she stops to gaze at a sleek gray Porsche. "Are you still keeping an eye on the revenge forum guys?" I ask, trying to sound casual. I've been doing my own surveillance on Owen this week, trying to creep on his browser history—which is useless, because he clears it every time, and I'm not nearly tech-savvy enough to figure out a work-around.

"Yeah," Maeve says, making a face. "Still messaging with Jellyfish too. It's getting harder for Tami Lee to put him off, though, so I might need to ghost. I'm ninety-nine percent sure he and his buddies have nothing to do with what's happening in Bayview."

"Why not one hundred percent sure?" I ask.

"Human unpredictability," she says with a shrug. "People are full of surprises, even when you think you know them." My stomach gives an uncomfortable little twist, but Maeve is still looking at the car as she adds, "I mean, that was the whole point of Simon's app, wasn't it? He went about it the wrong way, but it's like he told Bronwyn once: *if people didn't lie and cheat, I'd be out of business.*"

"Yeah," I say, as my stomach dips again. "He wasn't wrong."

"The problem with Simon was, he never had any compassion about *why* people lie," Maeve says. "Most people aren't malicious; they're afraid. There's nothing scarier than letting people see the parts of yourself that you wish weren't there."

It is really, *really* hot in this parking lot. I pull at the hem of my T-shirt and ask, "Should we go in, or—"

"I owe you an apology, Phoebe," Maeve says abruptly.

I blink. "You owe *me* . . . for what?"

"For busting out that picture of Jake changing your tire at Nate's party, instead of talking with you first," she says, cheeks flushing. "I was so startled that I didn't stop to think. I blind-sided both you and Addy, and if I hadn't done that, the rest of that night would have gone differently. You wouldn't have gotten so drunk, and—"

"Maeve." I stop her. "I'm the jerk who let Jake change my tire. I should've been up-front about that, and also about . . ."

I trail off, and Maeve finishes, "Going to his event at East-land High?"

"Yes," I say, eyes on the ground. "That too."

"Why did you?" she asks softly. "And why didn't you tell anyone?" When I don't answer, she adds, "Come on, Phoebe. That's the point of having friends, isn't it? So you can have the scary conversations?"

I swallow hard against the lump in my throat. What if having the scary conversations means that you *lose* your friends? On top of everything else you've already lost? "I—I guess I wanted to see for myself if Jake was . . . any different," I stammer. "If there was any chance he'd really changed, because . . . because . . ."

Oh God. Am I actually going to say it?

Emma asked, *Don't do anything until I get home, okay?* But she's still not here. It's been five days since I was drugged, dragged away from Nate's party, and treated like somebody's living notepad, and my sister is still waiting for a price drop on Expedia. What kind of superhuman ability to constantly shove down trauma does she think I have?

"You guys!" We glance up as Luis leans out of the dealership's front door, waving wildly. "Come on, you need to get in here. We're test-driving a Lamborghini!"

"This version of him is *so* not attractive," Maeve groans, but her eyes say otherwise as she waves back, a smile tugging at her lips. Then she turns to me, her expression full of understanding, and says, "You were worried about Addy, right?"

"Yes," I say, because it's true.

And because it's so, so much easier than saying anything else.

CHAPTER TWENTY

Phoebe
Thursday, July 9

Cooper didn't come close to buying anything at Mandalay Motorcars, because the prices terrified him. "Nonny's not giving me a blank check," he said after finally wrangling Luis back into Kris's car. "Plus, I need the monthly payments to be low. The FiredUp Fitness contract is only for a year, and who knows what'll happen after that. I have to save for a rainy day."

"Cooper, you are *such* a Taurus," Kris said affectionately. "You're right, though. This was fun, but next time we'll look a few levels down from Mandalay Motorcars."

"Leave it to me, Coop," Luis said. "I know exactly what you need."

"Somehow I doubt that," Cooper sighed.

The boys argued good-naturedly for the rest of the ride, and then Kris dropped me back at Café Contigo. I worked on autopilot until ten o'clock, doing my best to copy Evie and be a model employee. At the end of the night I even started marrying ketchup bottles, which I usually leave to her. "It's okay, Phoebe; I can finish up," she said when she saw me.

Do you ever get tired of being so perfect? I almost snapped, but I managed to stop myself and thank her instead. Then I called my mother and told her, "I think I might stop by Knox's for a little while."

It's a mark of how much my mother likes Knox that she didn't tell me to come straight home. "All right, but don't stay too late. I want you home by eleven," she said.

"I will be," I said. Then I trudged to my car, drove to Knox's house, and stared into his softly glowing window like a creeper for fifteen minutes while I debated whether or not to drive away. I couldn't, though. Maeve's words kept running in an endless loop through my brain while I was at work, so much so that I almost called her a dozen times before my shift was over. But in the end, there was someone else I thought I should talk to first.

So now I'm climbing through his bedroom window, once again.

"Thought your window days were over?" Knox says from his usual spot in bed as I heave myself over the sill. He's smiling, but he also looks confused. Ever since he asked me to give him space, I ring the doorbell when I visit.

"I need to talk to you," I say, perching at the edge of his desk chair. "But I don't want your parents to know I'm here. And you have to swear that you won't tell anyone."

Knox doesn't even hesitate before saying, "Okay." He yanks

his covers to one side and moves to the end of the bed, facing me. "What's up?"

How do I start? I don't know where to look, so I pick up a loose paper clip from Knox's desk and start twisting it out of shape. "It's about . . ." My mind is churning, and I grasp for something—anything—that will help anchor a conversation that I'm terrified to have. "Do you remember when you asked me out, after Ashton and Eli's wedding?"

Oh God. Where did *that* come from?

"Yup," Knox says, succinct.

"I said no," I say, twisting the paper clip harder.

"I remember," Knox says. His tone is even; the only hint that it bothered him is the way he unconsciously rubs the back of his neck.

"But I wanted to say yes," I say. Then I look up and—*oh no.* Knox's entire face has softened into a shy, disbelieving, completely adorable smile, and I have somehow screwed this up even worse than I thought possible. Before we've even gotten to the bad part. "Phoebe, do you have any idea—" he starts.

Whatever happens, I *cannot* let him finish that sentence. "But I couldn't, because there was something you didn't know," I break in. "About how the Truth or Dare game ended."

"What about it?" Knox asks. His expression is more puzzled now, but he's still fighting off a grin. I am the *worst* for starting like this, and yet—maybe it was the only way. Because now I can't chicken out, like I did with Maeve at Mandalay Motorcars. I have to tell him.

So I do. Every awful, sordid detail about what Owen did, and what Emma and I did to cover for him. I keep my eyes on the paper clip while I talk, twisting it into a dozen different shapes, my voice low and strangely calm. You'd never know, to hear me, how desperately my heart is trying to break free from my rib cage.

I keep going until there's nothing left to say. I thought I'd feel relieved once it was all out, but I don't; the words hang in the air long after I've stopped speaking, taking up all the space left by Knox's silence.

"Wow," he finally says. I can't read his tone at all.

"Yeah," I say.

And then neither of us speaks for an excruciatingly long time.

When I can't stand it any longer, I look up just as Knox swings his legs over the edge of the bed so his knees are touching mine. "You know I'd bury a body for any one of my sisters, right?" he asks. "I wouldn't even ask why."

"Oh God." My eyes fill with tears and I clap my hands over my mouth, hardly able to believe the olive branch he offered. "I thought you would hate me. You and Maeve were so brave, you saved everyone, and you wouldn't have had to if Owen had let Emma walk away—"

"Yeah, that part's not great," Knox says with a grimace. "But I understand why you did it. And why Owen's been so miserable. This must be eating him alive. It's okay, though, now that you're telling people. He can get the help he needs."

The relief flowing to my veins comes to an abrupt stop. "Telling people?" I echo. "I'm not telling people. I'm telling *you.*"

"Well, yeah. First me, and then other people, right?"

"No!" The word bursts out of me before I fully intended to say it; after all, I'd been thinking along the exact same lines. But now that the possibility is out there, I feel nauseated at the thought. *There are complications,* Emma had said.

"No?" Knox asks, eyes widening. "But then . . . then it just keeps going, doesn't it? It's an endless cycle. Simon wanted revenge, Jake wanted revenge, Jared wanted revenge, Emma wanted revenge, Owen wanted—"

"Stop it!" I put my hands over my ears like a little kid. "Owen didn't want this. He never meant for it to happen. He didn't understand what he was doing."

"What's going to happen when someone wants revenge on Owen?" Knox asks quietly. "What if that's why you got kidnapped on Saturday?"

My vision gets hazy. For a few seconds I'm back in the equipment shed, scared and disoriented, with no clue how I got there. *What if* . . . no. It's impossible. "No one knows," I say. "Except me and Emma, and now you, and you *promised*—"

"I'm not going to break my promise," Knox says, knotting his fingers together. "But I wish you'd consider breaking yours. Last Saturday could have been a lot worse. If there's one thing we know about Bayview, it's that things tend to get worse before they get better."

I can't let myself think about that. "Owen's just a kid; everyone will judge him like they judge Emma—"

"Brandon was just a kid, too, when he goofed around with the forklift that killed your dad," Knox says. "He never took any responsibility for that, and Emma set him up to die because of it—"

"She didn't mean to! You know she didn't mean to. She

thought he might get . . ." I swallow hard around the lump in my throat. "Injured."

"Is that really so much better?"

Yes. No. I don't know. There's no good answer, so I don't give one.

"Phoebe, everything else aside, you're not doing Owen any favors by keeping quiet. If you think it's been hard on you, can you imagine what it's like for him? The guilt he must feel?" I silently stab the tip of my finger with the paper clip until I draw blood, as Knox adds, "Have you forgotten what it was like to watch that video?" He doesn't have to say which video; Brandon jumping to his death while Sean, Jules, and Monica screamed in the background will be burned into my brain for the rest of my life. "Or the bomb that nearly killed a few dozen people and tore up Nate's arm, or—"

"I haven't forgotten any of it!"

I don't realize that I'm yelling until a light knock sounds on the door, and Knox's mother pokes her head in. "Everything okay, sweetie?" she asks, before catching sight of me. "Oh, hi, Phoebe. I didn't hear you ring the . . ." She trails off as her eyes take in the still-open window and the breeze rustling Knox's curtains. "Are you all right?"

"I'm fine," I say. "I'm sorry for disturbing you. I was . . . blowing off steam." God, I wish I had a sledgehammer and a junkyard car right about now.

"Why don't you kids talk downstairs?" Ms. Myers says. "There's leftover pizza if you're hungry."

"No, that's okay, I . . . I was just leaving." I stand, still clutching the paper clip; I'm not sure I'm capable of releasing it at this point. "I need to go."

"Are you sure about that?" Knox asks, unable to hide his frustration. This was a mistake, and I wish I'd never come. Telling Knox didn't fix anything; it only made it worse, because now he's looking at me like *that*. Like he never really knew me at all. And maybe he's right.

"I'm sure," I say, and brush past Ms. Myers.

CHAPTER TWENTY-ONE

Nate
Friday, July 10

Thursday was my night off from the country club, and I spent it with my not-missing girlfriend. It was the best night I've had in a while, and it more than makes up for the fact that today . . . today, I'm probably going to be fired.

Gavin was fast on Wednesday, but not fast enough. A lot of people saw me lunge for Jake, and after the showdown we had at his Ramona house, I wouldn't be surprised if Jake uses that to get rid of me. Just because he can.

So when I show up at the bar, the first thing I do is scan the half-full barstools warily, expecting to see Jake's smug, expectant grin. Instead, I spot Vanessa, a tall glass in front of her, topped with a maraschino cherry speared by a toothpick. "Don't worry," she calls, biting into the cherry. "He's not allowed to come here anymore."

Some of the tension flows out of me as I step behind the

bar and wave at Stephanie, the bartender who's working to-night instead of Gavin. I'm not about to let Vanessa know I was worried about Jake, though, so I say, "Who?"

She rolls her eyes. "You know who. A bunch of women complained that they don't feel safe with Jake at the club. Also, a few of them said he threatened you."

I blink at her as I start pulling glasses out of the dishwasher behind me. "Really?" I ask. He did, sort of, but there's no way anyone except me could have heard. "Who said that?"

"I don't know their names, but . . ." Vanessa points her toothpick at the corner where the margarita moms always sit. "They have your back."

Suddenly, this shift is going a lot better than expected. And Vanessa Merriman, of all people, is the bearer of good tidings. In fact, it's almost like she was waiting here to tell me. I fold my arms across my chest, lean against one of the pillars that an-chors each end of the bar, and say, "What's your deal, Vanessa?"

"Oh, is it question time?" she asks, sipping her drink. "Fun. Here's one for you. Why are you so rude?"

"Come on. You're always here, and you're always on your own. That's not the Vanessa Merriman I remember from Bay-view High."

She arches her brows. "I hope you're not implying that I'm here for *you*."

"I'm not," I say. And it's true. Vanessa's default setting is *flirt*, but in all the time she's hung around here, I've never got-ten the sense that she means it. "Are you here for Gavin?"

She furrows her brow and asks, "Who?" Which: ouch. Poor Gavin. I regard her steadily, weighing how to word my next question, until she snaps, "What? Just come out with whatever judgey little thing you're about to say, Nate."

Well, she asked for it. "It crossed my mind that you might be here for Jake."

Vanessa scowls. "Seriously? Yeah, I love assholes who abuse their girlfriends and help disturbed boys ruin lives. Totally my type. God, Nate, I can't believe you said that."

She looks genuinely upset. "Sorry," I say. "I didn't know you felt that way." And then I feel compelled to add, "I don't think Addy does either."

Vanessa pokes her straw into the bottom of her drink. "She knows I'm sorry about everything that happened senior year."

"You told her?"

"No, but of course I am. I'm not a *monster*."

"That's not how apologies work."

"Ugggggghhh," Vanessa mutters, poking harder. "I know, okay? I'm working up to it. I was going to say something at your party, but I drank too much too fast and couldn't do it. But trust me, I was as horrified to see Jake the other day as you were. I never thought he'd be allowed to hang out here. I've only been coming for . . . his mom."

That shouldn't surprise me as much as it does, considering that Vanessa was practically stalking Ms. Riordan the last time she was here. But if there's no Jake connection, I don't understand what Vanessa is after. "Why?" I ask.

"Because she used to be a huge deal at Conrad and Olsen." Seeing my blank look, she adds, "The biggest ad agency in San Diego. They have offices everywhere—London, Paris, Sydney, you name it. I wanted to intern there so badly this summer, but they never even called me for an interview. I think they're still mad at my dad."

"Your dad?" I ask, squinting at the glasses in front of me. The dishwasher sucks, so most of them are still kind of wet. I grab a towel and start drying them, adding, "For what?"

"His company hired them for an ad campaign a few years ago, but he ended up hating the creative and wouldn't pay them. It was a whole thing." She stabs her straw again. "He was right, incidentally. The creative was *terrible*. They need my help, desperately. Anyway, Ms. Riordan used to be the co-managing director, and I thought maybe she could put in a good word for me. She said she would, but . . . I don't know. It doesn't sound like she keeps up with them much anymore. They had a big restructuring after the other managing director died. She wouldn't come out and say it, but I have the feeling that she basically got pushed out."

"That's too bad," I say, and I mean it. Ms. Riordan has always seemed like she has way too much time on her hands, and wishes she didn't.

"Yeah, no nepotism for me," Vanessa says moodily. "Although maybe it's for the best, now that Conrad and Olsen is getting so much bad press."

"They are? How come?"

"Because they manage the Clarendon Street billboard. You know, the one that got hacked?"

"Really?" I ask, pausing my drying. Maeve keeps looking for a connection between that billboard and what happened to Phoebe, but she hasn't found one yet. Jake seems like a dead end, since his sunroom wallpaper doesn't match what Phoebe remembers. It's interesting, though, that his mother used to work at that agency.

What does Maeve always say about coincidences? *Don't trust them.*

"Yeah. They lost a bunch of accounts over that," Vanessa says. "I mean, the lack of security alone is a massive red flag. Maybe I dodged a bullet."

"Okay, so if Ms. Riordan can't help you out, and you're not into Gavin—"

"Seriously, who is that?" Vanessa interrupts.

The next time I see Gavin, I'm going to have to tell him to set his sights somewhere else. "Why do you keep coming here?" I finish.

I mean it as a joke, kind of, but Vanessa flushes and stares at the counter. "I don't know if you've noticed, Nate, but everyone I graduated with hates me."

"Not everyone," I say, and she gives me a wry smile.

"Am I growing on you? Like mold?"

"You're not the worst person who's ever come here."

She snorts. "Thanks for your support."

"Look, I just think . . . if you wanna have a conversation about what happened in high school, I'm not the person you should be having it with," I say. "You might've given me a hard time occasionally, but I gave it right back. I said stuff to you that I wouldn't say today, no matter how mad I was, and you know what? I'm sorry about that. I'm sorry I talked shit about your sex life in the cafeteria after Cooper was outed."

Vanessa blinks, startled. "Are you apologizing for standing up for Cooper?" she asks. "Because I was out of line that day."

"I'm apologizing for how I did it. I shouldn't have gone there."

"I . . . okay." Vanessa bites her thumb, and now her whole neck is a splotchy red, like she's got anxiety-related hives. "I see what you're doing. But like you said, you and I were equal-opportunity assholes. You're not the one who basically kicked a couple of golden retriever puppies while they were down. Plus, do you have any idea how hard it is to apologize to people who don't want you anywhere near them? Who assume you're going to say the worst thing possible as soon as you open your mouth?"

I do, actually. I also know what it's like when people start giving you a chance. And I can't believe I'm about to say this, but . . .

"You want to come to a one-third birthday party next week, Vanessa?"

I'm at your house, Bronwyn texts just as I get off from work at nine o'clock. *With your dad.* I send back a question mark, and she adds, *I stopped by his place to apologize for missing dinner the other day, and we decided we'd make you something to eat tonight.*

I'm pretty sure there was no *we* about it. My father wouldn't think of that on his own, but he'd cheerfully walk through a burning house if Bronwyn asked him to do it. We have that in common. *Sounds great,* I text back, although I'm a little apprehensive about how long it might take the two of them to come up with something that resembles dinner.

I shouldn't have worried, though, because when I get there, my roommate Crystal has gotten in on the act. Crystal is almost as good a cook as Luis, and her specialty is making meals out of ingredients that don't seem like they should go together. "Fruit salad with mint and maple syrup," she calls out as I enter the kitchen, handing me a bowl.

"Really?" I ask, dropping a kiss on the top of Bronwyn's head before sitting down beside her at the white table that Jiahao got at a discount when he worked at IKEA.

Bronwyn beams at me. "It's so good." Then she reaches over and taps my father's arm. "Would you rather have regular salad, Patrick?"

My father has barely touched his bowl, but now he scoops up a mouthful. "Oh, no, this is great," he says after he swallows. "I'm just not very hungry."

"You'll want to save room for the coconut-milk omelet," Crystal says. She cracks a couple of eggs into a bowl, then looks over her shoulder as she starts whisking them and asks, "Nate, have you talked to Reggie lately?"

"No." I try a forkful of fruit salad and—yeah, it's weirdly good. "Why?"

"Well, he didn't come home last night," Crystal says. "Which isn't unusual, I know, but he and Deacon had big plans to play in some video game tournament, and Reggie never gave a heads-up that he was going to miss it. And then, you know how Reggie works at the Apple Store with Deacon's friend Ariana? She said he didn't show up for work today. So I've been texting him to check in, but I haven't heard anything back."

I pause with my fork halfway to my mouth and exchange glances with Bronwyn. Reggie almost never bothers telling any of us his plans, but even so, this sounds too much like what happened to Phoebe for comfort.

"I saw him Wednesday night, but not since then," I say. "What about you?"

"Same," Crystal says. "Oh, no, wait—I saw him yesterday morning before I left for work. So it hasn't been all that long, but—"

"But it's been more than twenty-four hours," Bronwyn breaks in. "And he's blown off two things without notice. Reggie's not the most considerate person around, but he worships video games and Apple products. Have you talked to his parents?"

"I don't know them," Crystal says. "Do you?"

"A little," Bronwyn says. "I used to tutor Reggie in high school, so I've met them, but I don't know their phone numbers. I wonder if . . ."

"What?" I ask when she trails off.

Her worried gray eyes bore into mine. "I know this probably sounds paranoid, but . . . should we check the equipment shed?" she asks. "Just in case?"

"It doesn't sound paranoid at all," I say.

"Wouldn't it be taped off because of what happened to Phoebe?" Dad asks.

"I doubt it," I snort. "The Bayview Police aren't that efficient."

"Even if it is, we can probably get around it," Bronwyn says, putting her fork down with a clatter. "I hate to eat and run, Crystal, but I'd feel a lot better if we checked it out."

My dad speaks before I can answer, pushing his nearly untouched salad bowl away. "Then we should go," he says.

CHAPTER TWENTY-TWO

Nate
Friday, July 10

Fifteen minutes later, Bronwyn, Dad, and I are trekking across the Bayview High baseball field, flashlight apps shining. "Behind the bleachers," I say, leading the way.

"It's so quiet," Bronwyn murmurs. "Peaceful, almost."

"Don't be fooled," I mutter, aiming my light at the equipment-shed door. "Well, it's closed," I say, reaching out to try the knob. "And locked."

"Somebody had my keys for a while, though. They might've made a copy," Dad says, pulling them out of his pocket. "Hang on."

He fits a key into the lock and tugs, opening the door with a long, prolonged squeal. A vision of Phoebe sprawled on the floor flashes through my mind, and my pulse spikes as I stare into the darkness within. Then Dad's flashlight app illuminates the space, and . . .

"There's no one here," he says, as Bronwyn steps inside and trains the beam of light from her phone against each wall in turn.

"Thank God," she murmurs.

I'm not as relieved, though; not after what my father said about his keys. He's right—whoever took them could have free and clear access to every part of Bayview High. "Dad, what else is locked up around here?" I ask.

"Huh? Everything," he says.

"Yeah, but . . . if somebody wanted to, I don't know, *keep playing a game,* what kind of location do you think they'd choose?"

Dad looks baffled, but Bronwyn catches on fast. "You think whoever put Phoebe here might've taken Reggie somewhere else?" she asks.

"I don't know," I say. "But it's possible."

"Hmmm," she says, tapping her chin with a finger. "This shed is separate from the rest of the grounds at Bayview High. Are there any other freestanding buildings?"

"Not that I'm aware of," Dad says.

"Okay, well . . ." She gazes at the mess of equipment and mats that are piled high against the walls. "Let's suppose that TIME FOR A NEW GAME and THERE'S ONLY ONE RULE actually mean something. Along with the writing on Phoebe's arm. *Practice.* It's all sports related, and so is this shed, so—"

"The gym," I say. "Or the locker rooms, maybe."

"Exactly," Bronwyn says. "Can you get us in there, Patrick?"

"I can, but . . ." Dad snaps the rubber band on his wrist. "The school has security cameras everywhere. They'll know we were there. Maybe we should call the police, tell them what we're worried about."

"But you're not breaking in," Bronwyn says. "You have keys. You're being a responsible and concerned employee."

Dad looks conflicted, and I don't blame him. He needs this job. "Or," I say, "your asshole son could've taken the keys without your knowledge."

"No," Bronwyn protests. "He can't have his keys stolen *again*."

"Look, I'll just—I'll go alone, okay?" Dad asks. "You two stay here."

"How about we come with you to the fence, at least?" Bronwyn suggests.

Dad locks up the shed, and we reverse course until Bayview High looms in front of us, dark except for a few lights burning in the entrance. "Be right back," Dad says, setting out for the parking lot. Bronwyn shivers as she watches him go, and I wrap my arms around her.

"Cold?" I ask.

"No." She rests her head against my chest. "Worried. This feels all wrong."

I tighten my hold and breathe in the scent of her green-apple hair so I don't accidentally blurt out what I'm thinking: *Whatever's happening, at least it's not happening to you.* It's the wrong sentiment for the moment, and anyway, Bronwyn already got a front-row seat Wednesday night to how badly I'd handle that. We stay like that for a while, until the sound of footsteps causes us to break apart. My father is jogging our way, which is something I haven't seen him do in at least ten years.

He looks tense and winded when he reaches us and bends over, palms against his knees, to catch his breath.

"Security cameras are out," he manages to say.

"Out?" Bronwyn echoes. "What do you mean?"

"Their lights aren't on," he says, straightening. "The little red lights that mean they're recording. I noticed it for the one on the back door and thought it was a fluke, but the hallway cameras aren't working either. I took a quick look in the gym—nobody there, by the way—and it's the same thing."

"Maybe there's a power outage?" Bronwyn says, gazing at the building. "Although the outdoor lights are still on, so . . ."

"Come on, Dad," I say. "Let's check the locker rooms."

I expect my father to protest, but he doesn't. He lets me take his keys and lead the way to the rear entrance, where—just like he said—the corner-mounted security camera is dark. I unlock the door and push, entering the halls of Bayview High for the first time in more than a year. The first thing I see is the back stairwell, and my mind flashes to being there with Bronwyn after we'd been questioned by the Bayview Police about Simon's death. I'd apologized for stealing baby Jesus during our fifth-grade Nativity play and given her a burner phone in case she wanted to talk more.

I tried to act like I didn't care whether she used it or not, but all I could think as I handed it over was *Don't throw it out, okay? Pick up when I call.* And she did. She let it ring six times first, but she did.

Not everything that happened at Bayview High was bad.

Bronwyn links her fingers with mine as we push through the double doors and enter the main hall, lined on either side with lockers. "Do we need to go through the gym to get to the locker rooms?" she asks. "I can barely remember."

"No," Dad says. "There's a side hallway running behind the gym that we can use." He leads the way past the trophy case, adding, "It's been strange working here. Spending so much time walking these halls, when I barely set a foot inside while you were a student, Nate." He clears his throat. "Wish I could've gotten my act together when you needed the help."

"Don't worry about it," I say. I always get uncomfortable when my father does this, because I never know what to say back. "Everything worked itself out."

"*You* worked it out," he says. "With Bronwyn."

"Yeah, well . . ." I've never been so glad to see the door to the boys' locker room. "Here we are." I push against it, expecting the resistance of a lock, but the door swings open. "Smells the same as ever," I grimace, stepping inside.

"I haven't been inside the boys' locker room before," Bronwyn says. "Should we . . . would it be okay to turn on the lights, do you think?" She feels along the wall until she finds a switch, and a burst of fluorescence floods my eyes.

"Ow," I mutter, blinking. "Okay. Let's see. The showers are over here, and—"

I stop in my tracks, holding out my arm to keep Bronwyn from going any farther. "What?" she asks, craning her neck over my shoulder. I hear her sharp intake of breath, and I know I haven't prevented her from seeing what I see. A spatter of thick, dark-red liquid on the floor. Right before the corner you turn to get to the main locker area.

"Blood," Bronwyn breathes.

"Stay here," I tell her. Like she'll listen. Instead, she's right by my side as I tread carefully past the blood spatter, turn the corner, and . . .

"Oh my God!" Bronwyn's hands fly to her mouth, and the new phone she bought yesterday drops to the ground with a clatter. I manage to keep hold of mine, stomach churning as I take in the scene in front of us.

"Jesus," my father says, sagging against the wall.

It's Reggie. He's gagged and blindfolded, tied to a plastic classroom chair that's overturned on the floor. There's a gaping cut on his forehead, a puddle of blood around his head, and more spatters on the corner of the wall between the shower and locker areas. His skin is grayish, his body stiff. There's a word scrawled across his right arm, in the exact same block letters someone used to write on Phoebe.

MAKES

PART TWO

CHAPTER TWENTY-THREE

Addy
Tuesday, July 14

I take the envelope and hold it up to the light of my vanity mirror. No—not see-through. I'll have to open it to know whether to expect a niece or a nephew in the fall. Maybe if I do, the excitement will help balance the nightmare this summer is turning out to be.

But then again, it might just be one less thing to look forward to.

My phone rings, and I drop the envelope when I see that it's a FaceTime from Keely. "Hiiii!" she says when I pick up, waving from what looks like an oceanfront deck. Stars twinkle behind her as she adds, "Happy one-third birthday, Addy!"

"Thanks," I say, propping the phone up against my mirror. There's a brief second where I'm not sure what to feel, and then I take in Keely's bright doe eyes and the glowing tan of her skin and—yes, there they are. Butterflies. "You look pretty. I miss you," I blurt out, before my lizard brain kicks in and makes me say something like *How's the weather there?*

Keely gives me a huge, dimpled grin. "I miss you too. And your hair looks *amazing*. Very celebration-ready. You know, I actually thought about flying out there for your party, but then I heard about Reggie and I wasn't sure you'd even have it."

Keely was going to *fly out*? All the way from Cape Cod? That's—I don't know. That seems like a lot. I scrunch down in my chair and say, "It's been way toned down. Nate and I have terrible timing when it comes to these parties. The last one was barely a week after Brandon Weber's death, and now . . . same thing, pretty much, with Reggie." Gloom settles over me again as I tuck the envelope from Ashton's obstetrician back into the top drawer of my vanity. Now is definitely not the time for happy news. "It's so awful."

"I can't believe Nate and Bronwyn were the ones to find him," Keely says. "That must have been so scary. Do the police have any idea who could've done it?"

"If they do, they're not telling," I say. "But you know Bayview. There are always a half-dozen people being sketchy at any given moment."

"I do know Bayview," Keely sighs. She tilts her head and adds, "And I know you. Be careful, okay? Just focus on getting to Peru. You have two weeks, and then you can exhale. Things could look completely different when you come back."

"They could," I say, picking at a hangnail. "And you'll be back at UCLA by then, so—I guess I'll see you at Thanksgiving, maybe?" I huff out a sort-of laugh and try to tamp down the butterflies because really, who am I kidding here?

We're on totally different schedules, and even if we weren't, I'd just ruin things and then ruin our friendship too.

"That might be a good thing," Keely says.

I blink, stung. I'm supposed to be the one doing the pre-emptive rejecting here. "Why?" I say.

"You remember when Cooper and I broke up?" she asks.

It's such an unexpected question that all I can do is nod. "Well, he and I are fine now, but back then I was really hurt," Keely says. "I thought I knew him, and that he felt the same way about me as I did about him. It made me think—if I could be so wrong about that, what *else* am I wrong about? And it felt like the answer was: everything." I pick harder at the hangnail as she adds, "It made me doubt myself, especially when it came to relationships. I didn't want to start anything when I felt like I couldn't trust myself, let alone anybody else."

"You dated Luis, like, two weeks after you and Cooper broke up," I remind her.

"Only because I knew it would never get serious. Plus, that was a classic rebound move. I guess I wanted to feel good about myself again. It didn't work, though." She tucks a strand of hair behind one ear, displaying the multiple delicate hoops that outline the shell of her ear. "I think what I'm trying to say is, I know what it's like to be completely fooled by the person who's supposed to be in love with you—and my person was *good*. Cooper never meant to hurt me, which is why we were able to stay friends. But it still took a long time for the voices in my head to quiet down anytime someone tried getting close to me."

"Lizard brain," I mutter.

Keely blinks her mile-long lashes. "Huh?"

"That's what I call it. The lizard brain takes over when it senses danger, which is . . ."

"Which is probably all the time, when you're recovering from a Jake and not a Cooper," Keely finishes. "Especially a Jake who's suddenly in your backyard again." The breeze sends Keely's hair across her face, and she pushes it back with one hand. "I guess what I'm saying, Addy, is there's no rush with you and me. I liked kissing you, but I also like *you*. So let's keep talking like we always do, and not worry about anything else." A mischievous smile tugs at her lips. "In other words, you don't have to look terrified when I mention flying out."

"I was not terrified!" I protest, and she laughs.

"You fully were. Lizard brain, ignite."

"Okay, maybe a little," I admit.

"I get it. I really do." Her gaze moves off-screen as she adds, "Okay, be there in a sec." She turns back to me and says, "I have to go; we're playing late-night mini golf. Post pictures from the party, okay?"

"It's not so much a party as a Murder Club debrief now."

"Still," she says, blowing me a kiss. "Put on one of your tiaras and be the queen that you are. You've earned it."

"I really do miss you," I say, feeling a thousand times lighter as I blow a kiss back.

"I know you do," she says, winking before she disconnects.

I feel so much better, suddenly, that I call out a cheerful "Come in!" when my mother knocks on the door. She looks confused when she opens it, because that's hardly my typical greeting. Usually, I just grunt.

"Your ride is here," Mom says, leaning into my room. "What's got you so happy?"

"I was talking to Keely," I say.

"Oh?" Mom says. Then she looks more closely at me, just as I catch my own face in the mirror. I look giddy, glowing, lit from within—as if the blown kisses I'd exchanged with Keely were real. "Oh," Mom repeats, in a completely different tone. "Oh, really?"

Ugh, I don't want to have this conversation with her. I don't want to hear *Since when do you like girls?* or *She's out of your league.* "It's nothing," I say, grabbing a tube of lip balm from the top of my desk and stuffing it into my pocket. "I better not keep Luis waiting."

"Well, if it's something—"

"Don't, Mom, okay?" I feel a little light-headed as I face her, thinking of all the times she stood in that exact spot and lectured me about what to wear and how to act around Jake. It's been almost two years since he showed his true colors, but it feels as though nothing has changed between my mother and me. No matter what I'm doing, it's always the wrong move. "I just want to get to the party on time."

"I'm not trying to stop you," Mom says, stepping out of my way. I thud down the stairs, shoulders tensing when she calls after me, "All I was going to say is—"

Why do you always need to have the last word? I think as I tug open the front door, waving toward Luis's headlights. *You and Jake both.*

"—if it's something, then she's a lucky girl," Mom finishes, and I'm so caught off guard that I nearly catch my fingers in the door when I close it.

CHAPTER TWENTY-FOUR

Addy
Tuesday, July 14

"Practice makes perfect," Maeve says, staring at her laptop in the Rojas media room, which is filled with the entire Bayview Crew. "That has to be the phrase that someone's building toward. *Practice* on Phoebe's arm, and *makes* on Reggie's. Don't you think?"

"Maybe," I say as a familiar sense of unease settles into my stomach. I knew the good mood that Keely put me in wasn't going to last. "But the bigger question is, who's the someone? Jake? He told Phoebe to *practice,* remember?"

I look toward Phoebe, anxiously—she's sitting on a sofa beside Cooper and Kris instead of Knox for a change—but it's Bronwyn who answers. I'm pretty sure I know why; she never likes me to fall down a Jake rabbit hole for too long. "True, but even if Jake has managed to get around his monitoring system, why would he target Phoebe?" she says. "There's no bad blood between them. Or Reggie? Reggie supported Jake in that *Bayview Blade* article, remember? Said he used to be nice to him, or something like that."

"He said, *He was always pretty cool to me,*" I quote. I have that stupid article practically memorized. "Okay. Fair point."

Phoebe leans forward. "It's interesting that you said *building toward,* Maeve," she says. "Things *are* escalating. I . . . I wasn't tied up like Reggie was. I don't think whoever did this wanted me dead, or even hurt." She swallows hard as Cooper slings a comforting arm around her shoulder. "I think they just wanted me found."

"It's possible they didn't want Reggie dead either," Bronwyn says. She exchanges a loaded glance with Nate. "We're not supposed to talk about what we saw, but . . ."

"Murder Club cone of silence," Nate says. Everyone murmurs in agreement, except for Maeve, who probably already knows whatever Bronwyn is about to say.

"It looked almost like Reggie died accidentally," Bronwyn says. "The floor was all scraped up from the chair, and the part of the wall that was spattered with blood looked like the height Reggie would have been while sitting in the chair. Nate and I think Reggie was trying to get free, but tipped over and slammed himself into a sharp corner of the wall."

My stomach rolls. I never cared for Reggie Crawley in high school; most of the time, I could barely stand him. But no one deserves to die like he did.

"So, whoever did this wanted to—what? Terrorize him?" Cooper asks. "Send a message? I can think of a few people who'd want to do that. Katrina Lott, for one. But it's a stretch to think she'd come all the way back from Portland to kidnap

Reggie. Plus, what does she, or anybody else, have against Phoebe? There's no connection."

"Well, both Phoebe and Reggie were at Nate's Fourth of July party," I say. "And you guys talked for a while, right, Phoebe? Did anyone see you together?"

"I don't think so," Phoebe says. "As far as I can remember, everyone who'd been hanging out in his room had left by the time he came in."

Bronwyn puts her legs over Nate's lap, her brow furrowing as she plays with his hair. "Whoever it is, they're both frighteningly competent and staggeringly incompetent," she says. "They were able to make kids vanish and take out an entire security-camera system—"

"That wouldn't be hard if it's a local system," Maeve interrupts. "All you'd have to do is erase the footage of you entering the building, then shut the whole thing down."

Luis shoots her a look that's half admiration, half alarm. "Sometimes I don't know whether to be turned on or terrified by you," he says.

Maeve smiles serenely. "Both is fine."

Bronwyn clears her throat. "As I was *saying*—they could do all that, but they couldn't keep Reggie alive?"

"Maybe they didn't want to," I say, my skin prickling. "Maybe Reggie's death was only supposed to look like an accident. Just like Brandon's."

"Right. Just like Brandon's," Knox echoes. He tries to catch Phoebe's eye, but she just stares at the floor. The energy between those two is seriously off, which I'd ask about if we didn't have bigger problems. "Any chatter from the revenge forum guys, Maeve?" he asks.

"They're talking about it," she says. "Like everyone else is. Wondering if it's a Jared copycat, now that Reggie turned up dead. But they're not taking credit. And nobody's saying anything about *practice makes perfect.*" A faraway look comes into her eyes. "I can't stop thinking about that phrase, though. What if it's connected to the TIME FOR A NEW GAME billboard? I mean, Bronwyn and Nate found Reggie because they were thinking in terms of a sports theme; first the equipment shed, then the locker room. Could *practice makes perfect* be the 'one rule' the ad mentioned?"

"But what's the game?" I ask, exasperated. "It's not like Truth or Dare, where people got texts and instructions. One hacked billboard, and that's it?"

"Maybe only the person behind it gets to play," Maeve says, plugging her laptop into a cord running across the end table beside her. Within seconds, search results fill the wall-mounted television screen. "I've been Googling the phrase, obviously, but I haven't found much. Just a bunch of songs, Wikipedia entries, some kind of summer enrichment program . . ."

The sound of a doorbell interrupts her. "Who could that be?" Bronwyn says as she detaches from Nate. "Everyone is already here." She gets to her feet and crosses the room to peer at the small screen beside the doorway. Then she frowns. "Hold on . . . am I seeing things, or is Vanessa Merriman at our front door?"

"Oh, shit," Nate says in a tone so unfamiliar that I need a few seconds to place it. He sounds . . . *guilty.* He leans forward, his elbows on his knees, and says, "Okay, yeah, that's my bad. There's been so much going on, I forgot to tell her it's not a party anymore."

"Nate!" My jaw drops as I glare accusingly at him. "You invited Vanessa to our one-third birthday party? Why would you do that?"

He stands and raises one hand in a conciliatory gesture. "Sorry. I meant to give you a heads-up before everything happened with Reggie. Vanessa hangs out at the country club a lot, and she said she wanted to apologize for how she treated you and Cooper in high school, so I thought . . ." He trails off as the entire room gapes at him. "I thought wrong, obviously. This was a terrible idea. I'll tell her it's not a good time."

"*Vanessa* wants to apologize?" I ask. "Seriously?"

"She said she does," Nate says.

"Well, it's not like this so-called party could get any worse," I say. "We might as well hear what she has to say."

"You sure?" he asks. I nod, and he turns to Cooper. "Coop?"

Cooper shrugs. "Why the hell not?"

Nate disappears into the hallway, and Bronwyn watches him go with a mixture of trepidation and pride. "He means *so* well," she says.

A muscle in Kris's cheek twitches. "Is this the girl . . . ," he starts.

"From the cafeteria," Cooper confirms, and Kris's expression gets deadly.

"Oh, I'd say that whatever apology she wants to give is too little and far too late," he says darkly, folding his arms across his chest.

I hear murmured voices and footsteps, and then Nate returns with Vanessa in tow. She's dressed for a much more exciting night than this one, in a short, sparkly dress and strappy heels. Her ombré hair is pulled back into a loose ponytail, with a few caramel-colored strands framing her face. "Huh," she says as she walks in. Her eyes scan the room, taking in all of us sipping soft drinks while angled toward the television screen displaying Maeve's laptop screen. "This is almost exactly what I thought a Rojas party would be like."

Nate exhales in frustration. "Really? That's how you're gonna start?"

"No, I . . . here." Vanessa thrusts a silver foil–wrapped bottle at me. "Happy, um, quarter birthday or whatever." I take the bottle without correcting her, and she adds, "It's pink champagne. The kind I brought that time you, me, Keely, and Olivia had a beach day without the boys the summer before senior year. Remember that?"

"Yeah," I say. It's one of my favorite memories from that summer, and probably the single-best memory I have of Vanessa. "Thanks."

She fiddles with the bracelets on her arm, like she's waiting for me to say more. When I don't, a long silence fills the room until Nate prompts, "And?"

"And I'm really sorry," Vanessa blurts out. "I'm sorry that I took Jake's side, and that I slut-shamed you, and that I tried to turn all our friends against you—"

"You didn't try," I break in, feeling a twinge of the hurt that was my constant companion back then. "You succeeded." Even Keely stopped talking to me for a while.

"Except Cooper," Vanessa says, her eyes flicking his way. "I'm sorry I was a total homophobe to you, Cooper. That was gross and wrong. There's no excuse for any of the things I did back then, so I won't try to make one. I was an insecure asshole, but lots of people are insecure assholes and don't do what I did.

I really am sorry, though. And I'm glad you guys are doing amazing and have like a million friends, so . . ." She twists her bracelets again. "I guess you could say that karma works."

Maybe it's the way she's playing with her bracelets—it reminds me of how I tug on my earrings when I'm nervous or worried—but I find myself softening toward her. Her apology doesn't make everything okay, but at least she finally made one. And with Reggie in the back of my mind, I don't want to hold grudges against former classmates, even the awful ones. You never know when you're going to see a person for the last time.

"I forgive you," I say.

"Really?" Kris blurts out. "That's generous of you, Addy, but as for me . . ." Everyone turns his way, and his cheeks stain a deep, angry red. "I realize this isn't my apology, but I'm the one who had to pick up the pieces with Cooper that day." His green eyes bore into Vanessa's, who flushes but doesn't look away. "He was devastated, because you were *awful*."

"I know," Vanessa says.

"Do you?" Kris bites out. "Do you have any idea what it's like to be falsely accused of murder, outed to your entire school, and then mocked by people you thought were your friends in the course of a single day?" His voice rises with every word as I catch Bronwyn's eye and she mouths *Whoa*. I've never seen Kris like this; I'm not sure I even realized, until right this second, that he was capable of being so angry. Nate's wide-eyed and frozen, like he can't believe he inadvertently released Kris's inner Hulk. "And it's not just about what you did to Cooper. Poor Addy had to deal with your abuse for weeks—"

"Hey," Cooper breaks in, his eyes on Kris and his voice low

and soothing—like he has, in fact, seen Kris this angry before and knows exactly how to calm him down. "We got through all that, right? I did things I'm not proud of back then—"

"You were never cruel!" Kris says.

"You're right," Vanessa says. Her chin is still up, but her neck is nearly as red as Kris's face. "I was horrible, and I'm sorry."

"Well, maybe you should consider making your regret tangible," Kris snaps. "With a donation to the Trevor Project, for example."

"Okay," Vanessa says, nodding eagerly. "I will."

"Good." Kris looks a tiny fraction less pissed off. "It's a start."

Silence falls. Nate throws such a desperate look toward Bronwyn that, despite the tension in the room, I have to choke back a giggle. It'll be an ice-cold day in hell before Nate Macauley attempts to play the role of peacemaker again. "That's probably enough on this topic for one night," Bronwyn says smoothly.

Cooper squeezes Kris's hand before saying, "I appreciate your apology, Vanessa."

Vanessa gives him a rueful smile, maybe noticing that he said *appreciate*, not *accept*. "You always were a lot nicer to people than they deserve, Cooper. Well, listen, I didn't mean to bring down the party. I'll let you guys get back to . . ." Her eyes drift across the Rojases' television screen. "Looking up old ad campaigns?"

"Ad campaigns?" I ask, putting the bottle of pink champagne down on the nearest side table. It was a decent gesture from Vanessa, even though a champagne toast is the last thing I feel like having right now. "What do you mean?"

Vanessa waves a hand toward Maeve's Google search results. "Isn't that what that is? *Practice makes perfect.* Remember those ads from middle school? From that SAT tutoring company, when there was all that controversy because parents were like, *There's no such thing as perfect.* But the company still doubled its business." She catches Nate's eye and adds, "That was a Conrad and Olsen campaign, by the way. It's the one that put them on the map."

There's something familiar about the name, but I can't place it. Nate obviously can, though. "Really?" he asks, his tone suddenly sharp. Maeve started Googling again while we were talking, and a YouTube ad springs to life on the television screen. Three "teens"—all of whom are unquestionably actors in their twenties—are sitting in the world's most stylish library, surrounded by a mountain of books. "Practice," says one girl, tapping her pencil to the beat of a pulsing music track. "Makes," says another girl, flipping long braids over one shoulder. "Perfect," finishes the boy with a roguish grin, blue eyes flashing.

Now I remember the ads; they were everywhere the summer before I started high school. They totally worked on me; I'd asked my mother about SAT tutoring even though the test was years away. She'd rolled her eyes and bought me a padded bra instead.

"You sure about that?" Nate asks Vanessa.

"Positive," she says. "I studied it last semester."

"What's Conrad and Olsen?" I ask.

The commercial finishes, and Maeve hits Replay. It's more than a little chilling, suddenly, to watch the smiling actors speak the words that somebody wrote across Phoebe and Reggie's arms. *Practice. Makes.*

"They're the ad agency that manages the hacked billboard," Nate says. "And where Jake's mother used to work."

Ohhhh, of course. Ms. Riordan had given her notice at the agency by the time I met her, but she'd mentioned it more than once. I always wondered why she'd left; from the way she talked about it, it seemed as though her job had been . . .

"Perfect," says the blue-eyed boy.

CHAPTER TWENTY-FIVE

Phoebe
Thursday, July 16

"I'm so sorry," Emma says again.

I take in my sister's familiar form sitting across from me at our kitchen counter: auburn hair held back with a headband, skin that's pale even in summer, and straight, even features. A face as familiar as my own, and one I haven't seen for over a month. But that's not the timeline that kills me. "Twelve days, Emma," I say in a voice that I have to fight to keep steady. "It took *twelve days* since I was drugged and kidnapped for you to come home."

"I know," Emma says. "It took a while to find the right flight, but—" She holds up a hand as I huff out a disbelieving snort. "Seriously, Phoebe, I have *no* money, and I can't ask Mom. She already spent a fortune on a lawyer for me. Plus . . . it's been really hard to do things lately. Not because I'm drinking," she adds quickly before I can ask. "Never again, I promise. But the idea of traveling seemed impossible. Most days, I can barely get out of bed." She gazes around our quiet apartment; Mom is still at work, and Owen is playing video games at a friend's house. "I almost can't believe I made it here."

"Really?" My heart squeezes at the sadness in her voice. "Are you . . . Emma, it sounds like you should be talking to someone. . . ."

She lets out a strangled laugh. "Who am I supposed to talk to?"

"Well, me for starters," I say. "But maybe also a therapist."

Emma snorts. "With what money?"

"I have money—" I start, but she shakes her head.

"Look, I made my bed when I started that pact with Jared, and I have to lie in it. I deserve to feel this way. You don't, though, and I hear you about Owen. Maybe we aren't helping him as much as we thought we were. But Phoebe . . ." She swallows hard. "I gave false information to the police when I told them I had no idea who could've written those messages to Jared after I told him to end the game. I could be charged for that if they decide to get tough."

"So I'll tell them," I say. I hadn't been grilled the way Emma was, once she admitted that she'd been posing as me all along.

"People will hate you," she says.

"They already do," I say, stomach twisting as I think about Knox.

"And they'll hate Owen." Emma bites her lip. "We can't rush into this, Phoebe. We really need to think about it. I haven't even seen him yet—"

Heavy footsteps sound in the hallway then, and a key turns in the front-door lock. "Speak of the devil," I murmur as Emma twists in her seat and the door opens.

"Owen!" she cries, getting to her feet. "Oh my God, you're huge!"

"Hey." Owen takes his time dumping his backpack in the corner, like always, as though Emma's been gone an hour instead of a month. She flings her arms around him anyway, making fussing noises as I pull out my phone and check the time. I need to leave in five minutes for an appointment, which will give Emma the chance to observe Owen one-on-one.

"So, how've you been?" Emma asks when she finally disentangles from him. "Tell me everything."

Owen shrugs and heads for the refrigerator. "Nothing to tell," he says.

"There must be something," Emma insists. "How are you spending your summer?"

"Sleeping. Video games," Owen says, popping the top on a can of Fanta.

"Well, that sounds fun," Emma says brightly. "Have you seen many of your friends?"

Owen shrugs, and Emma's smile gets more fixed. *Welcome to my world,* I think as a text from Bronwyn pops up on my phone. "Reggie's funeral is tomorrow," I report. "Everybody's meeting up at Café Contigo tomorrow at ten if you want to come with me."

"Oh yeah, of course," Emma says. "We can all go."

Owen snorts. "Not me."

"Why not?" Emma asks, frowning.

Owen chugs half his soda before answering. "It's so fake," he says. "Everybody hated Reggie, so why are they pretending to be sad all of a sudden?"

"Owen!" Emma's mouth drops. "That's a horrible thing to say!"

"It's true, though," Owen says.

"Reggie is *dead*," Emma says. "Just like . . ." Her throat works, and I know she's trying to bring herself to say *Just like Brandon*. She can't do it, though. "Someone dying is a tragedy regardless of whether you got along with that person," she finishes.

"Maybe with someone like him, it'd be a bigger tragedy if he got to keep being an asshole," Owen says, leaving his soda can on the counter as he lopes toward his room.

Emma stares after him, open-mouthed. I'm horrified, too, but there's also a sense of relief that she's seeing what I've been seeing. I'm not paranoid or overly sensitive; Owen is being legitimately awful. It would be bitchy to tell Emma *I told you so*, though, so all I say is "See you in a couple of hours," before grabbing my bag off the counter and heading for the door.

"Phoebe Lawton?" The young man behind a sleek chrome desk adjusts his headset and raises perfectly groomed eyebrows at me. "Lucinda will you see now. Straight down that hall, third door on your left."

"Thanks so much," I say, springing off the rock-hard, ultramodern chair in Conrad & Olsen's reception area.

Last night, after Vanessa left the Rojases' house, the Bayview Crew spent hours searching for any information we could find about the Practice Makes Perfect campaign. When we were scrolling through the "Leadership Team" section on Conrad &

Olsen's website, one name stood out to me: Lucinda Quinn. My mother coordinated Lucinda's wedding five months ago, and she was a frequent, chatty guest in our house during the weeks before the big day. She's also, according to her biography, an eight-year veteran of Conrad & Olsen.

It felt like a gift; a small connection I have that might lead to something useful. I don't know how to bridge the gulf that still exists between me and all my friends, but I know how to pick Lucinda's brain under the guise of career planning.

"Phoebe, hi! It's so great to see you!" Lucinda is still a whirlwind of energy, hopping up from behind her desk to engulf me in a tight hug. She's even shorter than I am, with pixie-cut dark hair and trendy purple glasses, wearing a charcoal-colored dress that's so oddly constructed, and yet so flattering, that it must have cost a fortune. "Goodness, you've had a rough go, haven't you?" she adds, patting my shoulder. "I heard about all that mess with your sister and Jared Jackson. I am *so* sorry you had to go through that."

I'm sure she is, because she's a nice person, but she can't hide the spark of curiosity in her eyes. I don't mind, though; I was counting on it. "It's been *awful*," I say in a hushed tone, dropping my gaze to the floor. "He was obsessed with me. Well, he thought it was me."

"I heard," Lucinda says, stepping past me to close her office door. She gestures to the chair opposite her desk and says, "Please, sit. Tell me what happened." So I do, in as much detail as I can stomach. It's just a rehash of the headlines, really, but with enough of a personal spin to make Lucinda feel like she's getting inside information.

That way, maybe she'll do the same for me later.

"What a nightmare," she says sympathetically when I've finished.

"It really was," I say. Emphasis on the past tense, because as far as Lucinda knows, that's all the trauma I have to share. The Bayview Police are holding back information about what was written on Reggie's arm, so there's no public link between my kidnapping and Reggie's death.

"But here you are, spending your summer planning for the future. I admire that, Phoebe. Your mom must be so proud of you."

"I hope so," I murmur, feeling like a complete heel. My mother is still compulsively checking in on me whenever I'm not at home, and *proud* is the last thing she'd be if she knew the real reason behind this visit.

Lucinda folds her hands on her glossy black desk. It's very stark and very chic, kind of like Lucinda herself. "So, what do you want to know about the advertising industry?"

I give her my best wide-eyed ingenue look. "Everything?"

Lucinda smiles kindly. "Maybe I could tell you how I got my first job?"

"That would be amazing."

The conversation flows easily after that, because Lucinda's friendly and I'm genuinely interested. But I keep looking for an opening to pivot, and once Lucinda starts reminiscing about her favorite campaigns, I find it.

"It's interesting how some ads stick in your mind," I say. "Like Mandalay Motorcars. They've been using the same tagline forever. Or the, um, Guppies candy theme." I have to move on from that one quickly, though, because I honestly can't remember that little jingle that Luis sang. "And I'll never

207

forget this Practice Makes Perfect campaign for SAT tutoring that was everywhere when I was in middle school. I was kind of obsessed with it back then."

"Oh God, that campaign," Lucinda says, cringing. "Did you know Conrad and Olsen did that?" I make what I hope is a surprised face, and she adds, "It was one of the first accounts I worked on when I started here, and to be honest—I always thought it was kind of basic. I mean, *practice makes perfect*? That's not exactly breaking new ground from a messaging standpoint. It was effective, though."

"Maybe it was the actors," I say. "They made studying look cool."

Even to my own ears, that sounds like blatant sucking up, but Lucinda beams. "*Exactly.* I was in charge of casting the girls, and that was my goal—to make them aspirational. They were phenomenal talents. One of them landed a national ad for Toyota a few months later."

"I had a crush on the boy," I lie. "Do you happen to know his name? I'd love to know what he might be working on now." That was something even Maeve's Google skills couldn't uncover, although she'd managed to track down the two girls.

"Oh, *that* I had no say in," Lucinda says, rolling her eyes. "It's a good thing that kid had a cute smile, because he couldn't read lines to save his life. We had to do something like a hundred takes before he managed to say 'perfect' right. I doubt he ever got another role."

"Why'd he get hired if he was so bad?" I ask.

"He was our comanaging director's son," she sighs.

"Really?" I sit straighter in my chair. "And the comanaging director was . . . ?"

"Alexander Alton," Lucinda says, frowning a little.

"Do you not like him?" I ask.

"Of course I did," Lucinda says. *Did?* "Why?" she asks. "Was I making a face?" She gives herself a little shake. "Sorry, I went down memory lane for a second. I loved Alex; he was a wonderful mentor. I just get sad thinking about what happened to him."

My pulse starts to pick up. "What do you mean?"

"He drowned six years ago," Lucinda says. I let out a startled gasp as she adds, "It was such a tragedy. He had three kids—Chase, the actor, had just turned twenty-one, and the twins were still in high school. They'd started driving lessons a couple of months earlier, and Alex used to joke that being in the car with his youngest son was like taking his life into his hands. We never imagined . . ." She exhales a long sigh. "Anyway, their mom moved away afterward, somewhere in the Midwest. Close to family, I think."

"Wow, that *is* sad," I say, mind racing. I knew someone high up in the firm had died—Vanessa mentioned that to Nate when she talked about the restructuring that led to Jake's mother leaving—but that small detail seems more significant when it's someone with a direct tie to the Practice Makes Perfect campaign. "Drowning is such a . . ." *Such a what? Suspicious kind of death?* "You don't hear of it happening to many people," I finish limply.

"I know," Lucinda says. "We were shocked. The whole firm went into mourning."

"That must've been so hard, with Mr. Alton being in charge and everything. Although, you did say he was the *co*managing director, right?" I ask, trying to recall what Nate had said about

Ms. Riordan. "So I guess there was another leader who could, um . . ."

I trail off, not sure how to finish that sentence, but Lucinda breaks in before I have to. "In theory, yeah, but that didn't really work out. The other managing director left soon after." She tilts her head, eyes gleaming like they did when I first showed up, and I'm pretty sure I know what she's thinking. *Fresh gossip.* "You might know her, actually, since you live in Bayview. Or know of her. Katherine Riordan, her son is—"

"Jake Riordan," I say. "We went to school together before he got arrested."

Lucinda purses her lips. "I cannot *believe* he's getting a new trial," she says. "Such a travesty. I always liked Katherine, but that boy should've been put away for life."

"Agreed," I say fervently. I could talk trash about Jake forever, but that's not why I'm here, so I put on a thoughtful expression and ask, "Why did his mom leave Conrad and Olsen?"

"Well, the official story was that she left to spend more time with Jake," Lucinda says. "And maybe she did. God knows, that kid must've needed more supervision. But mostly, Katherine just couldn't do the job anymore. Alex's death really rattled her. She'd been in Mexico on a shoot when he died, and when she came back she took almost a month off. Even though we were insanely busy and desperate for some kind of direction. And once she returned, well . . ." Lucinda shrugs. "She wasn't the same."

"Wow." I don't know Jake's mother at all, except for a few sightings at school events, but that seems like unusual empathy for a Riordan. "Was she close with Mr. Alton?"

Lucinda smirks. "Rumor has it."

My jaw drops at what she's implying. *"Really?"*

It's too much reaction. Lucinda clears her throat in a business-like way, like she just remembered she's at least fifteen years older than I am and shouldn't be gossiping as if we're both in high school. "The important thing is, Katherine needed to switch gears, and we needed a leadership change. Somebody who could take the firm into the twenty-first century, because honestly, with that Practice Makes Perfect crap we were kind of stuck in the nineties. We didn't even have an Instagram account six years ago. Like, you'd say *digital* to the creative team, and all they could think was *billboard.*"

She glances at her watch, like she's about to tell me she's out of time, so I blurt out my next question before she can speak. "Speaking of which, did you ever find out who hacked the one on Clarendon? The billboard, I mean." An irritated expression crosses Lucinda's face, like she doesn't appreciate the reminder of all the bad press, and I rush to add, "I was so scared when I first saw it, like the Truth or Dare game might be starting up again."

"Oh, goodness, sure," Lucinda says. She rearranges her features to be more sympathetic, but I can tell she's still kind of annoyed. "Well, don't worry about that. There were some very old security protocols in place, but they've been updated. You won't see anything more like that." She looks at her watch again. "I need to get ready for my next meeting, but it was lovely talking with you, Phoebe. I hope that some of what I told you was helpful?"

"Absolutely," I say, closing out the app on my phone that I've been using to surreptitiously take notes while Lucinda talked. *Chase Alton nepotism/Alex Alton drowned/Affair with Jake's mom?* "I learned a lot."

JAKE

Six Years Earlier

"All of this will be yours someday, Jake," Dad said, waving a hand toward the crystal-blue pool in the Riordans' backyard. "If you want it. Maybe you'd rather have an apartment in the city, though. Some of the new high-rises going up downtown are incredible."

"I don't know, Dad," Jake said, adjusting his sunglasses. "That's so far away."

"Not as far as you think," his father said. "Time flies. You'll be in high school next month, and then it's only four short years till graduation. You'll need to start thinking about the right college, the right job, the right girlfriend. . . ." He chuckled at Jake's expression. "Trust me, kid, you'll be fighting them off soon."

"Hope so," Jake muttered.

"You will," Dad said, stretching his arms above him on the lounge chair.

"What does the right girlfriend even look like?" Jake asked.

Then he felt compelled to half answer his own question. "Besides hot, I mean."

"Someone who supports you," Dad says promptly. "Someone who understands that you're the kind of person who's going places, and will help you get there."

"Like Mom." Jake said it as a simple statement of fact, but when his father didn't answer, Jake twisted in his seat to look at his father. "Right?"

"Your mother is an incredible woman," Dad said. With his sunglasses on, it was impossible for Jake to read his expression. "She's also very driven, which is something I didn't realize about her when we first met."

"Is that a bad thing?" Jake asked cautiously.

"Of course not," Dad said. Jake couldn't read his tone either. "If it's what you want. Some couples enjoy having competitive careers. Others might prefer a more complementary relationship. I know you better than you know yourself, Jake, and I have a feeling that you'd be happier with the second scenario. The kind of sweet, supportive girl who knows that your successes are her successes too."

"Yeah," Jake said. That did sound good. His father's words made him uneasy, though. It's not as though Jake hadn't noticed the tension between his parents this summer; he couldn't miss it no matter how hard he worked at being oblivious. But nothing was actually going to come of it, right? The Riordans of Wellington Avenue were a force in Bayview, and they were supposed to stay that way. Jake didn't want to start high school like some kind of pathetic latchkey kid shuttling between houses, no matter how nice the houses were. "You and Mom are okay, though, right?"

"Of course we're okay," Dad said, swinging his legs over the edge of his lounge chair. "So okay, in fact, that I'll bet she'll make some of that chicken salad we like if we ask very, very nicely. Come on, let's head inside. The sun's getting too bright, anyway."

"Okay," Jake said, pushing down his concerns. If his father said there was nothing to worry about, then he wasn't going to worry.

"By the way, I've been talking with some of the coaches at Bayview High about hosting a mixer for the incoming freshmen players before school starts," Dad said as they made their way around the pool. "We have plenty of space, and it would be a great opportunity for you to start hanging out with the right kids."

"Sounds good," Jake said.

"Simon isn't doing any sports, is he?"

"Are you kidding?" Jake snorted. "What would he play?"

"I don't know. Croquet, maybe?" Dad asked, and they both laughed.

"You say that like Simon could aim any kind of ball," Jake said as they reached the patio. "He can't even handle ping-pong. You should see him with a paddle." Jake swung one hand around his head like he was brandishing a flyswatter, and his father chuckled again.

"I'm sure he'll understand not being invited, then," Dad said.

The sliding glass door was normally closed, but Jake realized as they approached that he'd left it partially open the last time he went inside for a drink. The double-glazed glass usually prevented any sound from the house reaching outside, or vice versa, but now, Jake could hear his mother's anguished voice loud and clear.

"It's not that simple, Alex," she said. "I wish to God it were, but it's not."

Jake paused, ready to stop, but his father's hand on his shoulder kept him going. Scott Riordan continued to stride toward the door like he hadn't heard anything.

"Don't you think I want that too?" Mom said. "I want it more than anything, but there's Jake to consider, and—"

And then Dad pulled the door the rest of the way open, and Mom stopped talking. By the time they reached her, her phone was facedown on the dining room table, and she was wearing a near-perfect replica of her usual smile. "How was the pool?" she asked.

"Beautiful, but a little too hot," Dad said. "And then we got hungry. I don't suppose we could impose on you for some chicken-salad sandwiches?"

"Of course," Mom said, picking up her phone and hurrying for the kitchen. "Coming right up. I just need to thaw the chicken."

Beyond the conversation Jake and his father had overheard, that was the second sign that something was wrong. *Coming right up?* That wasn't how Mom talked to Dad lately; she was more likely to say *I'm right in the middle of something* or *Could I get a little help?*

The third sign was the reflection of Dad's face in the gilt-edged dining room mirror. Scott Riordan was smiling faintly, like he always did when he got his way. But his eyes were glittering as they followed his wife's progress into the kitchen, and Jake could read their expression even though he'd never seen anything quite like it before.

His father was utterly furious.

CHAPTER TWENTY-SIX

Nate
Saturday, July 18

My mother's apartment is so neat, it looks like some kind of showroom. Bronwyn is perfectly at home here, eating breakfast and chatting with Mom about Yale, but I'm constantly distracted by how different everything looks from our old house.

"Why do you have so many limes?" I ask, staring at the ceramic, citrus-filled bowl in the middle of the kitchen table.

"Well, they're pretty, aren't they?" Mom asks. "And they taste good in drinks." I must look up too sharply at that, because she adds, "Like seltzer."

"I love them," Bronwyn says, giving me a look that says, *Relax.*

I'm trying. But I can't shake the feeling that my mother invited us here for some particular reason, and historically speaking, my parents' reasons for anything are never good. "So, what have you been up to lately, Mom?" I ask, a little too abruptly.

We've both been working so much that it's been a few weeks since I've seen her in person.

"Trying to keep up at the office, mostly. We're so busy," Mom says, taking a sip of orange juice. She's still working for a medical transcription company, but she's a manager now. "I was sorry to miss Reggie's funeral. I heard it was a lovely ceremony."

"I guess, yeah. As good as it can be," I say.

While I sat in a pew at St. Anthony's Church between Bronwyn and Addy yesterday, I couldn't help remembering Simon's funeral. I went to that with my parole officer and got pulled aside by the police for questioning as soon as it ended. I had no idea, back then, that my entire life was about to change. A lot of it has been for the better, and yet—yesterday was the third funeral I've attended for a Bayview High student in less than two years.

Last night, Crystal told all the roommates that Reggie hadn't been wearing his signature leather-cord necklace when he died, and his parents had asked about it. I guess it was a gift from his mom, so we tore the damn house apart looking for that thing. No luck, though. I felt like shit afterward, because it was the first time I'd considered Reggie as anything other than a giant pain in the ass. A guy who wore a necklace from his mom every day might be someone who could've grown out of being a dick if he'd managed to make it out of Bayview alive.

Mom seems to be thinking along the same lines as she shoots me a rueful smile. "Sometimes, I wonder what life would have been like if I'd actually taken you to Oregon all those years ago," she says.

"It would have been *terrible*," Bronwyn says instantly. Both my mother and I turn her way, and her cheeks get red. "For me, I mean."

I shake off my gloom about Reggie and tease, "What are you talking about? You'd be living your best life, dating some Yale legacy, while I—"

"Pined away over your fifth-grade crush," Bronwyn says, her lips curving up.

It doesn't matter how many times she smiles at me like that; I still forget how to breathe for at least a few seconds. "Accurate," I manage to say.

"It all worked out for the best, then." Mom sounds like she means it, even though she got the short end of that stick.

"You must get tired of living here, though," I say. "What with all the . . ." I was going to say *murders,* but stop when Bronwyn shakes her head. "Yuppies," I finish.

"It's where *you* live," Mom says, like that settles the matter. Plus, she probably doesn't mind the yuppies. She's started doing yoga with a few of them from her office, and it's been great for her. She looks healthier than she has for a long time.

"Yeah, but . . ." *But I'm an adult now. I have my own place. My life is on track.* I can't say any of that, though, because what it'll really sound like is *I don't need you.* And that's not true, even though I suck at showing it. "But you must miss your old friends."

"We talk all the time," Mom says. "They're not going anywhere."

Are you? I think.

Old habits die hard, even with both my parents being weirdly functional. My mother doesn't deserve my doubt, though—she's been here for a year and a half, working and taking her meds, going to yoga, and she just made us *waffles,* for crying out loud. Whole wheat, because she knows Bronwyn likes them. She's not the same person she was ten years ago, or even one year ago, so maybe I can finally stop waiting for that other shoe to drop. I shift my focus and ask, "You think Dad's going to get fired over the keys?"

Him, I can still worry about.

"No," Mom says. "He was careless, yes, but if it weren't for him—plus you two—poor Reggie might not have been found for a long time. But even if that job doesn't work out, it might not be the worst thing in the world. . . ." She searches my face then, like she's looking for some kind of signal. "Have you and your father talked recently?"

"Yesterday," I say, finishing the last of my waffle.

"About anything in particular?" she asks.

That pings my emergency parent radar. "What's he up to?" I ask, pushing my plate away.

Mom sighs. "Oh, Nate. He's not *up* to anything."

"Then why—"

Bronwyn's phone chimes and she announces, "Cooper's here," then turns to my mother and asks, "Can we help you clean up before we leave?"

"No, no, go ahead. Enjoy the beach," Mom says with a shooing motion. She looks wistful as she adds, "You kids could use the break."

We're out the door before I realize I never finished my question.

* * *

It should've taken less than fifteen minutes to get to the beach, but with Cooper at the wheel, it was almost twice that.

"This car is wasted on you," I tell him as he finally inches into an empty spot in the parking lot. Luis talked Cooper into buying a black Subaru WRX—a slick, sporty little sedan that didn't cost a fortune. It probably goes a lot faster than thirty miles per hour, too, but we wouldn't know that thanks to Cooper's obsession with the speed limit.

"I've never had a new car before," Cooper says, adjusting his sunglasses and pulling a baseball cap from the glove compartment.

"Should we be taking it to the beach, then?" Bronwyn asks nervously. "We're going to be covered in sand when we get back in."

"It's okay; I have a vacuum cleaner," Cooper says earnestly. Kris, who's halfway out the passenger door, swallows a grin as he passes me on the way to the trunk. He opens it and carefully pulls a blanket, chairs, and an umbrella from the small space, looking so much like a dad that even Bronwyn, who's usually the organized one, can't help but laugh.

"Don't forget the cooler full of juice boxes," she teases.

"It's full of water bottles, but yes," Kris says, handing everything except the umbrella off to Cooper. "Could you grab it, Nate?"

I do without being a smart-ass, because this might be our last beach day for a while. Addy and Maeve are leaving for Peru on the last day of July. Cooper's summer league wraps up in early August, so he and Kris are visiting Kris's family in Germany after that. And way too soon, it's going to be time for Bronwyn to go back to Yale. So even though it's a weird time in

Bayview, we decided to act like a normal group of friends and spend Saturday together.

Besides, if we waited for it to *not* be a weird time in Bayview, none of us would ever leave the house.

"Maeve says they're to the left of the lifeguard tower," Bronwyn reports, scanning her phone as we cross the parking lot. It's a perfect summer day, hot and sunny, the sky a bright, cloudless blue. The air smells like a mix of salt, sunscreen, and sugar wafting from the cotton candy machine in the snack shack to our right. "She says to look for her hat."

"Okay," I say, although I'm not looking at anything except Bronwyn while she pulls off her T-shirt and stuffs it into her beach bag. My girlfriend in a bikini top and cutoffs is quite possibly the greatest sight on earth.

"Her hat?" Cooper asks as we reach the sand. "There are hundreds of people here. How are we supposed to . . . oh." He trails off, and I follow his gaze until I spot a striped straw hat the size of a small planet. "She always finds new levels to covering up, doesn't she?"

"You know how Maeve feels about sun exposure," Bronwyn says.

Or the beach in general. When we reach her, Maeve is sitting cross-legged on a chair in the center of a large blanket, wearing a long-sleeved shirt, floaty white pants, and sunglasses that cover almost half her face. There's a laptop balanced on her knees and a giant bottle of sunscreen beside her chair. "Oh, good," she calls out as we approach. "Finally, an umbrella."

"Yeah, thank God," I say, dropping the cooler at the edge of the blanket. "Looks like one of your wrists is getting sunburned."

"Really? Which one?" Maeve asks, reaching for the sun-screen.

"Where's everyone else?" Bronwyn asks, stretching out on the blanket beside Maeve's chair. I sprawl beside her and pull her close, nuzzling the space between her neck and her shoulder, and she laughs when I hit a ticklish spot.

"Knox and Addy are getting ice cream, and Luis and Phoebe are swimming," Maeve says, gazing resentfully out to sea. "I tried to tell them how bad the undertow is today, but apparently neither of them cares about water safety."

"And how have *you* been enjoying yourself on this glorious day, Maeve?" Kris asks as he finishes setting up the umbrella and opens a folding chair with a flourish.

"Research," Maeve says, adjusting the hood on her laptop against the glare of the sun. "Alexander Alton's death is *highly* sus. His car was found parked near a beach about ten miles from here, like he'd randomly driven there and decided to go swimming without telling anyone. It was pure luck his body washed up at all, but it took over a month. Not a lot left to examine at that point." She grimaces. "And he left his phone in his office, which—who does that? Maybe it was a mistake, but maybe someone was covering their tracks."

"What did the family say?" I ask.

"Back then? Nothing," Maeve says. "Or at least, nothing I could find. They didn't give any interviews." She taps her keyboard. "So of course, I looked them up next. Chase Alton was easy to track down. He's the ultimate cliché—a wannabe actor waiting tables in Los Angeles, hoping for his big break. That's what he told Tami Lee, anyway."

Bronwyn props herself up on one elbow, frowning. "I thought you retired Tami Lee?"

"She's retired on Toq," Maeve says as Kris starts handing out bottled water. "Now she's in Chase's Instagram DMs, telling him how much she loved his commercial way back when."

"You sure that's a good idea?" Cooper asks, unscrewing the cap from a water and taking a long pull. "If he has anything to do with what's been happening, that might tip him off that someone's onto him."

Maeve shrugs. "I had no choice. He has zero acting credits beyond that, and I needed an in. He was chatty at first, but he got a little quiet once I started asking about weekend plans. Either Tami Lee is coming on too strong, or that isn't information he wants to share." She drums her fingers on the arm of her chair. "I found an obituary for their mom too. Drunk-driving accident last year."

"Oh no," Bronwyn says. "Was she—"

"The driver? Yeah," Maeve says. "You're seeing the pattern, right?"

Bronwyn and I exchange glances. "Not entirely," I say.

"It's Jared Jackson all over again. When Jared's brother went to jail, their whole family fell apart—the dad's health got worse and the mom overdosed—so Jared became obsessed with Eli, even though it was hardly *Eli's* fault that Jared's brother was a criminal. But that's why Jared met Emma, who was fixated on Brandon for accidentally killing her dad. It's another Bayview family destroyed, and what is Bayview best known for? Revenge." Maeve adjusts her hat as she gazes out to sea, where Phoebe and Luis are dots in the water. "I don't think it's

223

a coincidence that all the hints flying around town lead back to another ruined family. Two dead parents in the space of a few years is pretty traumatizing. Especially if the first death wasn't an accident after all."

"So, what are you saying?" Cooper asks. "This guy Chase is pulling a Jared?"

"Maybe," Maeve says. "It would help to know what really happened to Alexander Alton back then. I wonder if the woman who was allegedly having an affair with him might know." She tilts her head my way and taps her chin with one finger. "If only one of us had regular access to the place where Ms. Riordan goes to drink her sorrows away."

"What? No," I say, alarmed. "I barely know the woman. I can't suddenly ask about some maybe-affair from years ago."

Maeve scowls at me. "Come on, Nate, you work at a bar. If you haven't figured out how to pull people's sob stories out of them by now, you're doing it wrong."

Cooper tugs his T-shirt over his head and tosses it to one side. "Plus, you're a new man, Nate," he says. "Look how you got Vanessa to come around."

"I didn't do anything," I say automatically. Although . . . maybe I did? Inviting Vanessa to the party didn't go as planned, but it ended better than it started.

Kris leans forward. "Vanessa," he says thoughtfully. "Now, that's an idea."

Cooper blinks. "What's an idea?"

"She knows Jake's mother, right? And Vanessa has a certain . . . listen, I'm not going to say *charm,* but there's an aggressive kind of sociability happening with that girl that might be useful." Kris grabs Maeve's sunscreen, pops the top, and squirts a bunch into his hand. "She wants to make up for being awful during high school, right?" he adds, spreading sunscreen across Cooper's shoulders. "Maybe she could start there."

"Why would Ms. Riordan tell Vanessa something so personal?" I ask.

Kris shrugs. "That's Vanessa's problem to solve."

"What about the younger brother and sister?" Cooper asks. "They're twins, right? What's their deal?"

"Christopher and Chelsea Alton," Maeve says promptly. "I guess they're one of those families that picks a naming theme and runs with it. Chelsea is studying art history at Oxford, and she has a pretty consistent social media presence." She hands her laptop over to Bronwyn, who perked up at the word *Oxford*. It's one of Bronwyn's dreams to study there her junior year, which might finally spur me to get a passport.

"Oh my God, she's at the Bodleian Old Library," Bronwyn murmurs. I lean over Bronwyn's shoulder, squinting at the Instagram page of a brown-haired girl posing in the courtyard of an imposing Gothic building. "I've always wanted to go there."

"Christopher, on the other hand, is a total void," Maeve says. "Zero social media accounts. No word about him since his high school graduation notice."

"Well, that's suspicious," Kris mutters.

Luis comes running up to the blanket then, soaking wet and shaking hair out of his eyes, with Phoebe close behind him. "The volleyball net is free," Luis reports breathlessly. "Addy and Knox are there, saving it. Come on, let's play."

"Yessss," Cooper says, springing to his feet even though Kris is still massaging his shoulders. "Just like old times."

"Only for some of us," Bronwyn says, but she's already twisting her ponytail into a bun.

"I call Bronwyn's team," Kris says, giving her a high five. "I love when you get into attack mode."

I'm not much of a volleyball guy, but . . . "Same," I say.

"This all sounds very sandy," Maeve says doubtfully.

"Come on, Maeve," Cooper says. "Stop obsessing about true crime and play some damn volleyball." He slings an arm around Luis, who clasps his hands together in a praying motion. Phoebe grins, shooting Maeve a look that says, *You're outnumbered.*

Maeve heaves a sigh. "Okay, fine, but give me a few minutes. I need to put on another layer of sunscreen first."

Luis beams. "I'd expect nothing less."

"Just let me shut down my laptop and—wait," Maeve says. She pulls off her sunglasses to peer at her screen. "Tami Lee has a new DM from Chase Alton."

Luis frowns. "From *who*?"

Cooper punches his arm. "Kid from the commercial. Keep up."

"The last thing I said to him was *If you're bored this weekend, you should come to San Diego*," Maeve says. Her eyes widen as she adds, "And he said, *Maybe I'm already there.*"

CHAPTER TWENTY-SEVEN

Addy
Saturday, July 18

We switched up rides on the way home from the beach—
Maeve and Bronwyn taking their boyfriends to their house for
a Rojas family dinner, and Phoebe tagging along with them for
a ride home along the way. She said it was so she and Maeve
could continue their discussion about what Phoebe learned at
Conrad & Olsen the other day, but I think it's actually because
she and Knox suddenly can't be within five feet of one another.

"What's going on with you and Phoebe?" I ask as we climb
into the back seat of Cooper's car. I breathe in the new car
smell, and send a silent apology Cooper's way as the sand from
my flip-flops nestles into the pristine rug at my feet. "You guys
barely said two words to one another all day."

"Nothing," Knox mutters in a very *something* voice. He's
gotten lightly tan this summer, his brown hair glinting with
highlights from the sun. If he were a different kind of guy, I'd

wonder if he's starting to get conceited about his recent glow-up. But since it's Knox, I'm pretty sure he hasn't noticed. "It's a big group, is all. You can't talk to everyone." He shifts restlessly in his seat as Cooper carefully backs out of the parking spot. "Look, I've been wondering about something. Do you think we should bring Eli in on this *practice makes perfect* stuff?"

It's an obvious change of subject, but I let it slide—especially because I need to shut down that line of thought, pronto. If my sister had any clue what I've been up to lately, she'd have a heart attack. I can't let that happen while she's pumping blood for two. "No," I say. "Why would we do that? There's nothing solid to tell him."

"There's a connection, maybe, between Jake's family and what happened to Phoebe and Reggie," Knox says.

"The most tenuous connection ever," I say. "Can you imagine trying to have that conversation with the Bayview Police? *Oh, hi, we think the words written on Phoebe's and Reggie's arms might be related to a six-year-old advertising campaign created by Jake's mother and a dead guy she may or may not have been having an affair with. Also, bonus, we're catfishing the guy's son.*"

Knox rubs his jaw. "Well, we wouldn't say it *exactly* like that," he says. "And anyway, I said tell Eli, not the police. He's a much better sounding board."

"You don't wanna do that," Cooper calls from the front seat as he merges onto the road with excruciating slowness. "He said he'd fire you if any of us got caught up in stuff like this."

"He was kidding," Knox says, but he doesn't sound entirely convinced.

"I think we need Vanessa's intel first," Kris says. "Otherwise, we'd just be repeating an old rumor, and a potentially damaging one at that."

"You're assuming Vanessa can *get* intel," Cooper says. "Nate didn't seem so sure."

Kris shrugs. "Nate has never appreciated the power of gossip," he says.

My thoughts swirl as they continue to talk. I started dating Jake during the first month of our freshman year, but I didn't meet his family until Thanksgiving. I was thrilled to get an invite to dinner with the Riordans, especially since Mom was still married to her second husband, Troy, and planning to drag me to his parents' house. The Riordans seemed like an oasis back then; the house was so perfectly decorated, the food so gorgeously presented, and Jake's parents so charming and glamorous, that I felt like I'd stumbled onto a holiday-movie set. The night felt magical to me, and I spent as much time as possible at Jake's after that. I can't remember when or how I learned that Ms. Riordan had recently left her job, but I remember thinking how jealous my mother would be that Ms. Riordan had *everything*—not only the perfect house, the perfect husband, and the perfect son, but a perfectly clear schedule.

I wish I could time travel back a few years, now that I know how much toxicity can hide beneath *perfect,* and view the Riordan family through older, wiser eyes.

It's been more than a week since my run-in with Jake at his house in Ramona. At first I'd been relieved to hear nothing from him or his lawyer, because he was right—I'd violated my own restraining order by going there. He could have reported me and twisted what happened to get the restrictions on him lifted. But he didn't, and after a few days, a new dread started creeping in. All I could think about was what Jake had said right before he went inside: *Get used to living life looking over your shoulder, because one of these days, I'm going to be there.*

He's not going to say anything. Why would he? I gave him exactly what he wanted that night: confirmation that I'm still afraid of him. Now all he has to do is bide his time until a joke of a legal system hands him full freedom.

"Turn left for Addy's street," Kris says, jolting me back to the present.

"I know," Cooper says. He slows as he approaches my house, but then comes to a complete stop when we're still a block away.

"Do you *also* know this isn't Addy's house?" Kris asks teasingly.

"I do," Cooper says. "But I know that car too."

I follow his gaze and draw in a sharp breath. Parked down the street, across from my house, is the same ancient red convertible with the tan top that we'd seen idling outside Eli's office, and later at Nate's house. The one that Nate's neighbor Phil most definitely doesn't own. That's three times now—and this time, it's at my house.

One of these days, I'm going to be there.

Unease twists my stomach as Cooper inches the car forward. "Let's get a little closer," he says. "Try to get a look at the driver."

"Whoever they are, they have tinted windows," I say, trying to keep my voice matter-of-fact. "Nate was only a few feet away, and he couldn't tell who it was."

Knox leans forward. "Maybe it's Chase Alton," he says.

"Maybe he wasn't kidding when he told Maeve he was already here. Maybe he's been here all along."

Or maybe it's Jake, I think, but I can't bring myself to say it.

When Cooper is almost to the car, it pulls out and starts down the street, away from my house. "Follow them," Knox says instantly.

"What?" Cooper taps his brake. "You think? We don't know—"

"Follow them," Knox repeats.

So Cooper does—hesitantly at first, until the red car picks up speed as it leaves my street for a busier road. Then Cooper accelerates, too, weaving through traffic until he's only a couple of cars behind it. "How does a person drive around with their license plate so covered with mud that it's impossible to read and not get pulled over?" he mutters as the red car shifts lanes.

"Oh, you know," Knox says. "The Bayview Police can't be bothered with stuff like that. They have their hands full with not solving murders."

"Whoever it is, they're going kind of fast for this neighborhood," Kris says. "Do you think they spotted you?"

"I think they might've noticed me creeping up at Addy's house, and that's why they took off," Cooper said. "But we're far enough away from them now." We're approaching a stoplight that suddenly changes from green to yellow, and the pickup truck in front of us slows. The red car, on the other hand, sails right through the intersection.

"Run it!" Knox says, smacking the back of Cooper's seat.

"There's a car in front of me!" Cooper protests, slowing to a stop.

The light turns red, and Knox lets out a frustrated grunt.

"Well, that's that," he mutters, slumping against his seat. "We lost them." The red car's taillights flash in front of us for a few more seconds, then disappear around a curve in the road.

"Don't be so sure," Cooper says. "This is a short light. And as Luis likes to remind me, this car can go from zero to sixty miles per hour in five-point-three seconds."

"It can do *what*?" Kris asks just as the light changes. Cooper lets the car in front of us make it about halfway through the light, and then—he *floors* it, zipping around the pickup truck and onto the now-open road. "Oh, okay," Kris says, sounding both surprised and impressed. "Here we go."

The Cooper who drove from the beach to my house with carefully modulated speed is gone, replaced by someone who suddenly figured out what the gas pedal is for. Within seconds, I spot the red car's taillights, and Cooper slows down. He keeps a few cars between us until we approach another intersection, and then narrows the gap so that we both make it through another yellow light. "Fall back," Knox says once we're though. "Don't let them see you."

"So what's the plan here?" I ask, my heart beating uncomfortably fast. Cooper was right the first time we saw that car outside Eli's office; Jake wouldn't be caught dead in it. Unless the entire point of driving it is to be unrecognizable. Could we *actually* be following Jake? I can't do that twice in one month; or at least, I can't get caught doing it. "We're not going to confront this person, are we? That seems like a bad idea."

"Let's at least see where they're headed," Cooper says.

We're approaching a major intersection, and the red car suddenly veers across two lanes to make a right turn onto a side street. Horns blare as Cooper mutters, "Damn it," and turns the wheel sharply to follow.

"So much for being stealthy," Kris says, bracing himself against the center console as Cooper executes a hairpin turn. "Listen, Cooper, I have to admit—you in NASCAR mode is pretty hot. But whoever's in there clearly doesn't want to be seen."

"Which is why we need to see them," Cooper says doggedly.

We're on the side street now, houses flashing past us as Cooper keeps within a car's length of the red car. The driver makes another signal-free turn that Cooper easily follows, his new car handling like a dream. "That was a stop sign, you asshole," Cooper says as the red convertible flies through an empty four-way intersection. Then he follows.

"Cooper, slow down," Kris says. "We're in a residential area. Plus we have no idea how desperate this person is. They could have a weapon, or—" He breaks off suddenly as a building comes into view, and the red car careens wildly into its parking lot.

"Or they could be going to the Bayview Police station," Knox finishes.

"What the hell?" Cooper says. He slows and pulls into an empty spot behind two squad cars. "Please tell me I didn't just run a stop sign while chasing a cop. How am I supposed to explain that to my coach?"

The red car hasn't bothered to park; it's stopped haphazardly off to one side, engine running. The driver's door opens, and I take a deep, steadying breath for whoever I'm about to see. It can't be Jake, right? Maybe it's Chase Alton, or a cop who's going to arrest Cooper for reckless endangerment, or—

"Who is *that* guy?" Knox asks wonderingly.

A short, thin, thirtyish man with wispy dark hair gets out, not bothering to close the door, and stalks toward Cooper's car. Cooper opens his door and makes a move to get out, but the man makes a wild pushing motion, like he's trying to shove Cooper back into the car without actually touching him.

"Don't come any closer, or I'll report you!" he yells.

Cooper climbs out of the car and steps onto the pavement anyway. "Report me for what?"

"Harassment!" the man calls back. "You think you're the first person who's ever tried to run me off the road? Trust me, you're not, and you . . ." Then he trails off and seems to shrink a little, shoving his hands into the pockets of his ill-fitting pants. "Wait a minute. You . . . you're the baseball player, aren't you?"

"I'm *a* baseball player," Cooper says. "And how am I harassing you, exactly, when you're the one who's been following my friends?"

I don't know who this rabbity guy is, but he doesn't seem dangerous. I unbuckle my seat belt, step out of the car, and stand beside Cooper. The man goes rigid at the sight of me, his eyes widening. "Ohhhh," he breathes. He looks wildly over his shoulder toward the police station, and then at his still-running car, as though he's debating which one to make a break for. "Okay, this . . . this was a mistake." His gaze shifts back toward Cooper as he adds, almost accusingly, "You have a new car."

"How would you know that?" Cooper asks, a hard edge creeping into his voice. The man doesn't reply, staring at me so intently that my skin starts to crawl. "And why are you looking at her like that? Who are you?"

"I'm . . ." The man glances over his shoulder again. A couple of people in civilian clothes exit the station, talking animatedly as they head for the side parking lot. Kris and Knox get out of the car then and stand beside Cooper and me, arms folded like twin sentries. It's the first time I've ever seen Knox look even a little bit intimidating.

"You're who?" I ask.

The man swallows so hard that I can see his Adam's apple move from six feet away. "I'm Marshall Whitfield," he says.

It takes a few seconds for the name to register—*Oh my God, it's Juror X*—and Cooper is already striding forward. "You son of a bitch," he spits out. Both Kris and Knox grab hold of his arms, and it takes every bit of their combined effort to hold him back. I've never seen Cooper this angry; despite his strength, he's always been the gentlest person I know. But right now, he looks more than ready to start swinging. "You're the reason Jake Riordan is walking free, and you have the goddamn nerve to come to Addy's house and scare the life out of her? What the hell is wrong with you?"

"It's not like that!" Marshall protests. He starts backing away, as if he doesn't trust Kris and Knox to keep Cooper in check. I do, though; I can already tell that Cooper is calming down from the deep breaths he's taking. "Believe it or not, I was trying to help. The thing is . . . look, I lost my job and my girlfriend and my apartment after what happened—"

"Good," Kris snaps.

"—and basically nobody will talk to me except my cousin,

235

so I ended up crashing on his couch with nothing to do. And I thought, well, since I'm the reason Riordan is out, maybe I could keep an eye on some of the people he's got a grudge against, make sure he doesn't try anything. . . ."

"Are you serious?" I interrupt, resentment flooding my veins. I can't believe this man is standing in front of me—the man who single-handedly gave Jake a new trial—telling me that he's trying to *help* me. "And what if he does? What would you do?"

"I . . . well . . . I'd stop it," Marshall says.

"Bullshit," Knox says bluntly, releasing Cooper's arm. "You couldn't even deal with getting tailed for a few miles. Why are you really here?"

"I told you. To help," Marshall says. His pale skin reddens as he adds, "If I did that, then, you know . . . maybe there could be some quid pro quo. . . ."

Kris narrows his eyes. "Quid pro what now?"

Marshall holds up his palms toward me in a supplicating gesture. "Look, I realize I messed up your life, but I messed mine up too. My family is barely speaking to me. No one will hire me. The reason I thought you guys were running me off the road is because it's happened before when people recognize me. I get death threats all the time. So I thought, you know, if I helped you out, then maybe you could see your way to helping me out."

"Helping you out," I echo flatly. "How so?"

His voice takes on a pleading tone. "Just some kind of statement on one of your social media platforms asking people to back off. They'd listen to you."

Cooper inhales so sharply that I can tell he's desperate to

answer for me, but he manages to hold himself back. Knox snorts out a disbelieving laugh, and Kris is utterly silent.

There are a lot of things I could say to Marshall Whitfield right now, on top of all the things I've been wishing I could say for months. But none of it will make a difference, so I say the only word that matters. "No."

"Won't you at least consider it?" he asks. "I know I haven't done anything to help you with your ex, but I could help out in other ways, maybe." His expression gets shifty. "There's plenty going on with your friend group, right? I've seen some stuff."

Seen some stuff. What a creepy little manipulator. "Marshall, listen to me," I say, carefully enunciating each word. "If you set foot near me or any of my friends again, I absolutely will make a statement on social media. I'll tell everyone that you've been stalking me."

Marshall's eyes grow wide and alarmed. "What? You can't do that!"

"Why not? It's true," I say. "Or maybe I should tell the police right now."

The door to the police station opens then, and a uniformed officer strides outside. Marshall Whitfield doesn't hesitate; he sprints for his car and gets back behind the wheel, quickly shutting the door behind him. The officer ignores him, heading straight for us, and as he gets closer, I recognize Detective Mendoza. He's interviewed all of us at least once, so he definitely recognizes the boys, but he doesn't give them more than a passing glance. Just like Marshall Whitfield, he seems entirely focused on me.

"Addy," he calls. "I take it you've heard."

"Heard what?" I ask as Marshall zips out of the parking lot.

He stops short, brow creased. "Oh, I . . . so . . . your lawyer hasn't been in touch?"

My *lawyer*? My pulse skitters as I ask, "About what?"

Detective Mendoza studies me with such an unfamiliar expression on his usually impassive face that it takes a few beats for me to realize that he looks *concerned*. "Okay, well, this isn't how I envisioned having this conversation, but . . . listen, why don't you come inside?" His eyes flick away from me, scanning Cooper, Kris, and Knox in turn. "We're going to want to talk to all of you, because Jake Riordan has disappeared."

CHAPTER TWENTY-EIGHT

Phoebe
Saturday, July 18

Jake Riordan has disappeared.

"Disappeared like escaped, or disappeared like . . . Reggie?" Luis asks.

We're on the Café Contigo roof deck once again, which Luis's parents have closed for an emergency Murder Club meeting. This time I'm not sitting next to Knox, but even from across the table I can tell that his fear of heights has been over-shadowed by the latest news. He looks tense but not scared. Unlike Addy, who looks flat-out *terrified*.

"Seems like the former," she says, tugging hard on her ear-ring. "His ankle monitor was found in his yard. Cut off, some-how."

"Dark web," Maeve mutters. "You were right."

"But it doesn't make sense," Bronwyn says. "Jake had a good shot at getting his conviction reversed. Removing an ankle monitor—that's a felony, isn't it?" She raises her eyebrows at Nate, who shrugs.

"You tell me," he says. "You're the legal expert."

"I think it is," Bronwyn says. "And even if it's not, it would look horrible to a jury." She turns back to Addy and adds, "What did Detective Mendoza say?"

"It's not like he was sharing theories," Addy says. "Just asked if Jake had made contact and told us to *stay vigilant*." She rolls her eyes. "Thanks for the tip."

"Did you tell him what happened at the Ramona house?" Nate asks.

"God, no," Addy shudders. "I'm not looking to become a *suspect*." Her eyes are glazed, and her voice drops to a near whisper as she adds, "You guys, Jake is out there. He's *out there*."

She looks so scared that I can't help blurting, "Maybe not. Maybe he's 'Perfect,' and someone took him." I flash finger quotes before rubbing my arm, trying to imagine someone as physically intimidating as Jake Riordan getting the same treatment that I did.

Bronwyn loops a comforting arm around Addy's shoulder as Maeve says, "Or maybe we're wrong about all of this, and we've been following a dead end. Because we were definitely wrong about one thing." As usual, she's been tapping on her laptop throughout the conversation. "Chase Alton had nothing to do with anything."

I rub my arm harder, wishing I could make the phantom letters disappear for good. Sometimes, it feels like they'll be with me for the rest of my life. "How do you know?"

"He's not in LA anymore; he's in New York. Apparently, he's been all hush-hush about starring in a new play, but he just started posting about it," Maeve says. "Super off-off-off Broadway, but it did get a couple of reviews. Neither of which have been posted by Chase, because the critics weren't exactly kind to him." She deepens her voice. *"Newcomer Chase Alton was so wooden, audience members could be forgiven for mistaking him for a prop."*

Bronwyn cringes. "Ouch."

"I thought he told you he was in San Diego?" Nate says.

"I know, right?" Maeve widens her eyes in fake surprise. "Can you believe the guy I was catfishing actually lied to *me*? The nerve. Although technically, I guess, he didn't lie. He said *maybe*. He was leading Tami Lee on, letting her think he was geographically available." She stabs at her keyboard. "That girl has the worst taste in men."

"So that leaves us where?" Addy asks before answering her own question. "Nowhere. We have zero clues. Everything's been a wild-goose chase and a waste of energy." She slumps in her seat, looking more defeated than I've ever seen her.

"There's still Christopher Alton," Maeve says. "The younger brother. Chelsea's twin. She and Chase are both living very well-documented lives, but him? I can't find a trace." She glances around the roof deck. "Can anyone think of a mysterious guy in his early twenties who's popped up in Bayview recently?"

"That would be convenient, wouldn't it?" Cooper says, shifting in his seat. "What about Ms. Riordan? Anything new there?"

"Well, I did what you said before all hell broke loose," Nate says. "I sicced Vanessa on her, so . . . who knows." He shrugs. "Maybe she'll come up with something."

"Call her off," Addy says wearily. "All of this is pointless."

"Nothing's pointless. We learned that the hard way with Jared," Knox says before getting to his feet. "I need the restroom. Anyone want anything from downstairs?" There's a chorus of despondent noes around the table, because every single one of us has lost our appetite.

Knox pushes through the door to the stairwell, and once he's disappeared, I'm hit by a wave of loneliness so deep that it makes my chest ache. Even though I'm surrounded by friends and we're worried about a lot of the same things, it still feels like there's an invisible wall separating me from everyone else.

"I should probably go," I blurt out. "I left Emma by herself."

"Does she want to come here?" Cooper asks.

I can't look him in the eye. He's been so nice to me, and all I've done in return is stop visiting his grandmother because I'm afraid of saying something I shouldn't. "No, she's still tired from her flight," I say.

That's a lie; I'd invited Emma, but she insisted on staying home, even though Mom was coordinating a wedding and Owen was at a sleepover. "I'd feel totally out of place," she said. I came without her because I wanted to support Addy, but Addy won't miss me; she's surrounded by people who love her. Emma's all alone.

"Tell her we said hi," Maeve says.

"I will," I say. "Keep me posted on anything new."

When I get downstairs, Evie beckons to me from the cash register. "Hey, Mr. Santos wanted to send an order of nachos to the roof deck," she calls out as I approach. Her face is flushed, strands of hair escaping from her usually neat braid. "They just came up in the kitchen. Would you mind bringing them with

242

you when you go back upstairs? Ahmed and I are swamped, and people are getting impatient."

"I'm leaving," I say absently. My eyes drift over her shoulder to the clock on the wall, my mind already miles away from Café Contigo.

"Oh. Okay." Evie's forehead creases as she jabs at the register, then raps it hard on one side. Sometimes, you have to practically beat that thing to get it to open. "Don't worry about doing me a favor, I guess. It's not like I've ever done any for you."

I blink, startled at the crack in her usual calm. "I . . . what?"

Evie stops pounding the register and puts her hands on her hips, surveying the packed dining room behind us. Now that she's mentioned it . . . yeah. A lot of people are craning their necks, trying to get her attention. "Half the time around here I do both our jobs," she says. "Would it really kill you to bring a plate of nachos to the roof deck?"

My cheeks get warm with shame. She's right; of course she's right. I've leaned on her all summer, too caught up in my own problems to even thank her properly. "I'm sorry," I say. "I was distracted. Of course I can help."

Ahmed comes sailing out of the kitchen then, an overloaded plate of nachos on one shoulder. "Rooftop-bound," he calls to Evie.

She snorts lightly without looking at me. "Ahmed to the rescue, yet again."

My face is a full-on fire now. The problem with being in perpetual crisis mode is that you forget that other people might be having a hard time too. Or maybe that's just me. Addy's had an even worse summer than I have, but she's managed to keep things together at work. I should've been splitting my tips between Evie and Ahmed for months, because I definitely didn't earn them. "I really am sorry, Evie," I say as she bangs on the register again. "I owe you one. Multiple ones. I promise I'll be better about—everything."

The cash register finally pops open, and Evie grabs some change before slamming it shut again. "It's fine, Phoebe. Just think about other people occasionally, okay?" she says, her bright, practiced smile falling back into place as she waves to a table behind us. I wish I could defend myself—lately, it feels like all I *do* is think about other people—but the truth is, none of those people are her. And mostly, I think about how to keep lying to them.

Knox emerges from the restroom corridor then, and I tamp down the immediate urge to flee. We haven't had a one-on-one conversation since the night in his room, and it's been making me miserable. Chances are, I'm not the only one who feels that way.

Think about other people occasionally.

"Hi," I call out.

"Hey," Knox says cautiously.

Now what? There's so much I want to tell him that my brain feels hopelessly tangled, and the only thing that comes out is "I, um, wanted to say goodbye."

Ugh. It's better than ducking out the door like a coward, but not by much.

"You're leaving?" Knox asks.

"Yeah, to hang out with Emma."

"Right," Knox says. "Of course." And then silence falls,

like we're a couple of distant acquaintances with no common ground.

"I hate this," I burst out, twisting my hands together.

"Me too," Knox says, and I wonder if we're even close to being in the same ballpark about what we hate. There's so much to choose from.

Before I can ask, though, my phone trills like a bird in my pocket. It's Emma's unique text tone; before she got back to Bayview, she'd been so impossible to pin down that I didn't want to miss a message.

Even without the birdcall, this one would be hard to miss. *COME HOME RIGHT NOW!!*

I've barely put my key into the lock when Emma yanks the door open and pulls me inside. "What's your problem?" I yelp, stumbling on the threshold.

"You took forever," Emma says tightly, shutting the door behind us.

"I took ten minutes, which is exactly how long it's supposed to take. Trust me, I know. Any delay means I get a frantic call from Mom." I drop my keys and bag on the kitchen island and put my hands on my hips as I stare at my sister, searching for some kind of clue in her expression. "Why the urgency? Are you mad at me about something?"

"At you? No," Emma says.

My pulse spikes. "Then who?"

Emma bites her lip. "Well, I . . . since I was by myself tonight, I thought I'd take the opportunity to look through

Owen's stuff. You know, kind of check up on him and make sure he hasn't been talking to anyone he shouldn't. I tried looking through his computer, but there's no browser history—"

I hold up a hand. "I could've told you that," I say. It's minimum concerned-sister snooping to check browser history, but Owen wipes his constantly. "If you'd bothered to ask."

I expect her to get defensive, but instead she says, "I know. I'm sorry."

Oh no. A penitent Emma *cannot* be good. "And?" I ask.

"And then I checked Owen's room. He didn't take his backpack with him tonight—"

"Really?" I interrupt, surprised. That thing is practically sutured to his shoulder.

"Yeah. Ben's mom showed up earlier than expected, so everything was kind of disorganized. Anyway . . ." Emma goes behind the kitchen island, bends down, and hauls Owen's battered black backpack onto the countertop. "I went through it bit by bit. I was almost done, feeling like a jerk because there was nothing out of the ordinary and then . . . I found *this*, stuffed way down in one of the inside pockets."

I don't want to know. I'm positive, with every fiber of my being, that I don't want to know what my sister found in Owen's backpack. But she pulls it out anyway and holds it up. "Phoebe, does this . . . I mean, *did* this belong to Reggie Crawley?"

My heart rockets into my throat as I take the familiar necklace from her. Same leather cord, same three silver beads that glinted in the dim light of his bedroom the last time I ever spoke to Reggie. "Yeah," I say, turning it over in my hand. "It did."

CHAPTER TWENTY-NINE

Nate
Sunday, July 19

"All in favor?" Sana asks.

My roommates and I barely lift our hands. We look like the most reluctant, depressed group of volunteers ever. Even Stan, who's hanging out on an end table like the house mascot, doesn't blink. "Okay, no one's opposed, so the motion to hold off on renting Reggie's room until September passes," Sana says, rapping her knuckles on the coffee table. "Remember, everyone has to pay an extra hundred and fifty dollars in August."

"We know," Jiahao grunts. Nobody's thrilled about that, but the alternative—having a bunch of murderino rubber-neckers traipse through our house with no intention of actually renting the room—is ten times worse.

Jake Riordan is still missing, and all Bayview can talk about is where he's gone and whether he had anything to do with what happened to Reggie. Opinions are split about whether

Jake took off or something happened to him, but either way, there's an all-out manhunt going on. So far, though, there's no sign of him. Mr. Riordan was all over the local news yesterday, telling reporters that Jake was optimistic about his new trial and never would have tried to escape.

"Also, Reggie's parents are coming to box up his stuff to-morrow, so be prepared for that," Sana says grimly, getting to her feet. "They might be here for a while."

"Any sign of his necklace?" I ask, holding my hand out to Stan so he can crawl up my arm. He starts toward me, but gives up after two steps. The older Stan gets, the less inclined he is to move unless you bribe him with food.

Sana shakes her head, gathering her flowy skirt in one hand as she steps into the hallway. "Not yet," she says. "But it's bound to turn up eventually."

Sana, Crystal, Jiahao, and Deacon all take off, so I'm the only one around to respond when the doorbell rings. I brace myself for the possibility that Reggie's parents decided to show up early, but when I open the door, all I see is my dad.

"Hey," I say, stepping back to let him in. "I didn't know you were coming."

"Yeah, sorry, I would've called, but . . ." Dad trails off, glancing around the empty hallway. "You the only one home?"

"No, everyone's here, just . . . around," I say, waving a vague hand.

"Is there somewhere private we can talk?" Dad asks. "Your room, maybe?"

Oh Christ. Here it is. I don't know what's wrong, but I could tell that he and I were having some kind of calm before the storm. "Sure. Let me get Stan," I say tersely. *It's fine*, I tell myself as I pluck Stan off the end table and make my way upstairs with Dad trailing behind me. *Whatever it is, I won't be any worse off than I was two years ago.*

Except what if I am? Dad's wearing badly fitting clothes again, which is all he has because he's lost so much weight. What if he's sick? Maeve showed me pictures, once, of herself as a kid with leukemia, and I barely recognized her. It wasn't only the lack of hair; it was that she was so thin and frail, she looked like a gust of wind would snap her in half. It'd be the shittiest thing ever if Dad finally kicked the booze only to get hit with something worse.

"So this is your room," Dad says, gazing around us. I guess I could've given him a tour at some point, but it never occurred to me that he'd want to see it. The space is small and dark, filled with secondhand furniture and horror-movie posters. The only bright spots are things that Bronwyn's given me, like the antique desk lamp with a green glass shade that she picked up when she first came home for the summer. "Looks good."

"It's all right," I say, depositing Stan into his terrarium before I sit at the edge of my bed so Dad can take the desk chair. "What's up?"

He lowers himself into it carefully, like he's afraid it might break. "Well, I haven't known how to tell you this—"

"Just say it."

I don't mean to sound like an asshole, but it comes out that way. Ten years of frustration and disappointment find their way into three little words, and I might as well have said, *What have you done this time?*

Dad flushes and ducks his head. "You always expect the worst," he murmurs.

Do you blame me? I almost say but bite it back just in time. I can't snap at a guy who might be about to deliver bad news. "Sorry," I say instead.

"No. I'm sorry. This isn't how I wanted to start." He swallows hard, and I wish I could fast-forward through whatever he's about to say. Anticipation is always the worst part. "The thing is . . . do you remember my uncle Pete? The one from Tacoma?"

"Huh?" I blink. Of all the possible openers, I didn't expect this one. "Not really." My dad's parents are both dead, and the rest of his family stopped speaking to him years ago.

"Well, he got in touch when I got out of rehab," Dad says, snapping the band on his wrist. "You know, Pete had his struggles with addiction, too, so he's been a help to me over the past few months."

Unlike me, probably. "That's good," I say. "Glad you have somebody."

"Well, not anymore. Pete passed a few weeks ago."

"Jesus, Dad!" I stare at him. I know we don't talk much, and I never met my great-uncle, but . . . "Why didn't you tell me?"

"I meant to. But it's complicated, because it turns out, Pete left me some land. Your mom's been helping me sort through all the red tape, but the long and the short of it is that some developers want it and we're gonna be able to sell it." Dad takes hold of his rubber band again, but for once, he doesn't snap it. "When everything's said and done, it should clear a couple hundred thousand dollars."

"Holy shit." I stare at him, unable to process the last part of the sentence. The Macauley family has never come close to that kind of money; it wasn't that long ago that I couldn't pay a nine-hundred-dollar ambulance bill. "Are you serious?"

Dad huffs out a short laugh. "Believe me, I'm as shocked as you are. I had no idea Pete had any kind of property. He never talked about it. That's why I waited a while to tell you—I wanted to make sure it was real. But it is, and Nate . . ." He rubs a hand over the graying scruff on his jaw. "Once everything is settled, I'm gonna give you half."

"You . . . you want to give me a hundred thousand dollars?" The words sound ridiculous coming out of my mouth. A thousand dollars would have felt like impossible luck, but one hundred times that is unreal. Crap, of course it's not real. This is a dream, and it's going to suck when I wake up and still have to come up with an extra hundred and fifty dollars to cover Reggie's rent next month. I twist the skin on my arm, hard, but Dad's still sitting in my desk chair, his worn face lit up with a smile.

"Well, not all at once," he says. "There are tax implications. Your mother's a lot smarter about that stuff than I am, but we're figuring it out. The thing is, Nate—you didn't get to have a childhood because of me and your mom. We never gave you any shot at a future. You did all of this"—he waves an arm around my shitty room, like it's some kind of accomplishment—"on your own. So if this family finally gets a piece of luck dropped in its lap, it should be yours." He rubs his jaw again. "I wanted to give you the whole thing, but your mom convinced me you'd try to give it back, and she's probably right. You worry about us too much. So I'll set myself up, maybe get some job training or pay off the house, and you can enjoy your half, free and clear. And I want you to enjoy it, okay? I know you'll be smart, but have some fun too."

"Some fun," I repeat numbly. Those aren't the right words to say in a moment like this, but I can't think of any others. I can't even begin to grasp what my father is telling me.

"It'll be a few months till everything's settled, so don't spend anything yet," Dad says with a crooked smile. "But I promise, it's coming. You can count on me for this, okay? I even made a will, in case anything happens between now and then." I stare at him, wordless, and his smile dims a little. "You don't believe me, do you?"

"I . . ." *Jesus Christ, Macauley,* say something. *Anything.*

"You need to let everything sink in," Dad says, getting to his feet. "That's to be expected. It's a shocker, I know, so take some time—"

Then he can't talk, because I've launched myself at him, hugging him so hard that I've squeezed the breath out of him. I've barely touched my dad in ten years, unless I was trying to haul him off the couch for some reason. I'm not hugging him because of the money, even though it probably seems that way. It's more because, if he's doing this—planning not only for my future, but his—then maybe he's making real progress.

Some things do change, after all. I have, and so has my mother. Why can't he?

Dad pats my back and then clutches my shirt until I finally let go. "Thanks," I say, my voice thick. It's not enough, but it's all I can manage right now.

"You're welcome," he says. "I'm gonna head out, but . . . maybe we could catch a ball game, one of these nights? I know you're not a big Padres fan, but—"

"No, yeah, sounds good." Maybe I'll even watch some of it.

Somehow I manage to follow him downstairs and keep some kind of conversation going, even with my brain buzzing a mile a minute. And then he's saying, "Talk soon," and shutting the door behind him, and I'm alone.

So that's . . . that. He's not relapsing and he's not dying. He's got a pile of money, which means he doesn't have to live on a razor-thin edge of getting by anymore. And neither do I.

Holy shit, neither do I.

I could . . . finish up school at a four-year college. Move into a better apartment. Visit Bronwyn while she's at Yale. Buy some kind of fixer-upper and flip it, maybe, thanks to everything I've learned from Mr. Myers. Or do none of that—well, except for visiting Bronwyn—but know that I *could.*

The sound of "MMMBop" comes out of my pocket then, and I almost don't mind how fucking cheery that song is. For once, it fits my mood. I hope it's Bronwyn calling, because she's not going to believe this.

It's not, though. The screen says *Vanessa,* and before I even have a chance to say hello, she says, "You better be home, because I'm almost at your house."

"I—yeah, what's up?" I say, rubbing my temple like that'll clear my head.

"I'm coming from the Riordans'," she says.

"You owe me, Macauley," Vanessa says, flinging herself onto one of our couches. She looks completely out of place on the faded brown fabric in her pristine white sundress and silver sandals. "You owe me so hard." Then her nose wrinkles as she gazes at whatever stain she sat next to. "Ew. What is *that*?"

"Impossible to say." I sit beside her, my nerves still jangling from the conversation with my dad. *A hundred thousand dollars.* I could buy a new couch to replace this piece of crap we got for free off Craigslist. How much do couches even cost? No, forget it; I'm not wasting money on this house. I have a weird urge to tell Vanessa what happened, just to tell somebody, but there's no way I can tell her before Bronwyn. *Focus, Nate.* "Why do I owe you?"

"Well," Vanessa says, "I stopped by the Riordans' house a couple of hours ago with a homemade galette—"

"What's that?" I break in. Sounds like a weapon.

"It's a type of French pastry. Sort of like a free-form tart. I make them with fruit from our yard," Vanessa says, narrowing her eyes when I blink in surprise. "What? Like I can't cook? Anyway, nobody answered the bell at first. So I kind of shouted my name from the doorstep, saying that I'd brought food and hoped everyone was doing okay, and then . . . Ms. Riordan opened the door. I gave her the galette and asked her how she and Mr. Riordan were doing. She said they're hanging in there, and Mr. Riordan was at work, and I was like, *He went to work on a Sunday?* And she said that he always works weekends."

"He does," I say. I've heard that enough from Ms. Riordan at the country club.

"Whatever. What I really meant was *Why the hell is your husband at work when your son's missing?*" Vanessa says. "But she answered that for me. She said they're doing their best to stick to a normal routine, and I said, *Wow, it must be hard on you to be here by yourself waiting for news.* Then she invited me in."

Well, damn. Vanessa Merriman for the win. "I'm impressed," I admit.

"She was a *wreck,*" Vanessa says. "And already kind of drunk, so . . . I just sort of encouraged that, you know? Poured some more wine for both of us, although I didn't drink any of mine. We talked about Jake, and I'm one hundred percent positive that Ms. Riordan has no idea where he is or what happened to him. She's devastated. She went on and on about how she's failed Jake, about how she and Mr. Riordan weren't good role models for him, and then, after about three glasses of wine, she finally told me."

Vanessa pauses, and I can tell there's a part of her that's enjoying the drama. A pretty big part. She's earned it, though, so I take the cue. "Told you what?"

"That she did, in fact, have an affair with Alexander Alton," Vanessa says, pushing her stack of bracelets up her arm. "It was a huge deal. She met him right after she graduated from college, when he was separated from his wife. He was, like, ten years older, and she totally worshipped him. They were a couple for almost a year, but he broke her heart when he decided to give his marriage another try. His kids were little, so he felt like he owed it to them." Vanessa rolls her eyes. "I don't know, maybe he could've thought about what he owed his *wife,* who'd given birth to those children, but whatever. Men are pigs."

"Present company excepted, right?" I ask.

She snorts. "Let's hope so, for Bronwyn's sake. Anyway, it sounded like Mr. Riordan was a rebound from that, honestly. She married him super quick, and she didn't see or speak to Alexander Alton for years, until they started working together at Conrad and Olsen when Jake was in middle school. You can guess what happened, right?" There's another dramatic pause, as Vanessa bats her eyes for an imaginary camera. "They fell right back in love, and this time, Ms. Riordan says that Alexander was serious about ending his marriage. She was serious about ending hers too. But then, while she was in Mexico for work, he drowned."

"Mysteriously," I say.

"Yeah. She had a total breakdown after that." Vanessa carefully shifts a few inches to the left, like she's trying to avoid the stain on the cushion, but there's not much point. She's just going to end up on a different one. "I felt bad for her. I mean, cheating's not great, but it sounds like she's been carrying a torch for this guy for years. Even after he died. She kept saying, over and over, *I loved him. I loved him so much. We were going to build a life together. He was supposed to be my ticket out.*"

"Out of where?" I ask. "Bayview?"

"I asked the same thing," Vanessa says. "And she said, *My marriage.*"

CHAPTER THIRTY

Addy

Monday, July 20

I can't stop watching the news.

"Now one teen is dead, and another—the notorious Jake Riordan, who helped Simon Kelleher frame the Bayview Four—is missing." Liz Rosen from Channel 7 is at it again, breathlessly acting as if the total lack of updates over the past twenty-four hours is actual news. "An entire town remains on edge, wondering what's next, and—"

Then Liz disappears as the television screen goes blank. "Hey," I say, twisting in my seat as my mother lowers the remote. "I was watching that."

"I'm staging an intervention," Mom says. "This isn't healthy, Addy. If anything important happens, we'll hear it from Eli."

"Eli's out of the loop," I grumble, even though it's not my brother-in-law's fault that I heard the news about Jake from

Detective Mendoza. I got multiple panicked voice mails from Eli while I was at the station, so he wasn't far behind.

"I want you to promise me something," Mom says, carefully lowering herself into a chair across from me. Her lime-green sheath dress looks great but isn't made for sitting. "Don't go running around town like you did after Simon died, putting yourself in Jake's path. Let the police do their job."

"Seriously, Mom? When have the Bayview Police *ever* done their jobs?"

Mom ignores that extremely valid point. "You're leaving for Peru next Friday, Addy. If you stay at home that entire time—"

"I'm not sitting at home for eleven days," I break in, even though I've considered it. Somehow, no matter what my mother suggests, I find myself wanting to do the opposite.

"We need to take precautions with that monster at large," Mom says. I must be rolling my eyes, because she purses her lips and adds, "What's that look for?"

"Nothing," I mutter, but then all of a sudden, I'm tired of holding my tongue. "I mean . . . sure, he's a monster now, but he wasn't always, was he?" Mom flushes as I continue, "We're terrible judges of character, aren't we? You and I used to think Jake was the greatest guy ever. So great that I was lucky to have him and had to watch my step in case he ever figured out that I wasn't good enough for him. Ashton's the only one who ever saw through him, but we wouldn't listen." I can't bring myself to say the rest: *And when I say we, I mean you, Mom, because how was I supposed to know? I was just a kid.*

I expect her to murmur some excuse and make a beeline for the nearest bottle of wine, because that's Mom's go-to coping mechanism for any conversation she doesn't want to have. Instead, she smooths a wrinkle from her dress and says, "I know. I let you down, Addy." That's so unexpected that I just blink as she adds, "The thing is . . . I've never been very good at being on my own. I was unhappy for most of your childhood, and I thought it was because things didn't work out with your father, and then with Troy. I thought if you and Ashton could avoid my mistakes—if you could find the right person and build a life together—then everything would be different for you. But it didn't work out that way, did it?"

"Bit of an understatement," I say.

"Ashton figured it out first," Mom says. "I couldn't believe it when she left Charlie. I thought she was giving up, and that she wanted you to do the same. But she was so smart, wasn't she? So strong. And you are too."

"Oh," I say. Eloquent as ever, but she's kind of throwing me for a loop here.

"I hate what Jake did to you, Addy, but even before that, I hate the way that he made you feel. And I'm sorry I let that happen." Mom's run out of wrinkles on her dress, so now she's smoothing out the cashmere blanket beside her. "I wasn't much of a mother to you, was I?"

"At least you were here," I say, and add, "No, I'm serious," as Mom huffs out a mirthless laugh. "Dad wasn't. He pretty much forgot about us once he met Courtney. Nobody could ever say that you were, um, uninvolved." One of my earliest memories is of my mother brushing my hair for a pageant, carefully separating the strands into sections and coaxing them into soft waves. I remember watching her face scrunched with concentration in the mirror and loving that all her focus was on me.

Maybe I didn't always get the healthiest form of her attention, but it was there. And it's still here, even though I've been treating her like a distant, somewhat annoying roommate ever since I moved back.

"Indeed," Mom says drily. "Well, I could have done worse, I suppose, because you've turned into an extraordinary young woman. I hope you know that, Addy."

This is the part where we should probably hug, but the women in my family aren't great at that. Even Ashton and I tend to collide awkwardly when we try. Before I can make an attempt, though, Mom reaches over and tucks a stray strand of hair behind my ear. "I do wish you'd go back to your natural color, though. Your hair was always your best feature."

Normally that would annoy me, but there's something almost comforting about Mom not changing too much, too fast. So instead of snapping that I like my hair just fine, I say, "You're going to be a great grandmother."

Somehow, she manages to both brighten up and cringe at the same time. "How on earth did I get to the grandmother phase of life already?" she asks.

"Insta Gram," I say.

"Absolutely not."

"Grandrea?" It's a play on her first name, Andrea, but I can tell from her face that she doesn't like it, so I try again. "Big Momma?"

"Stop it."

"G-Ma?"

"Geema?" From the way she says it, I can tell she's picturing an entirely different spelling. "You know, that's really quite cute."

"G-Ma it is, then," I say with a smile. We'll work on the spelling later.

"A hundred thousand *what*?" I ask Maeve.

She mimes zipping her lips. "I wasn't supposed to tell you, so you have to act surprised when Nate does, okay?" She flips open her laptop as she sprawls beside me on my bed, grabbing an extra pillow to put between her and the headrest. "It just slipped out. I'm so freaking excited for him. What a game changer, huh?"

"No kidding. Meanwhile my estranged parent and I finally had a heart-to-heart, and all I got was a pat on the back," I say, rolling my eyes so that Maeve knows I'm kidding. Because yeah, of course I'd love that kind of windfall, but I also love that it's going to Nate. I worry about him sometimes, feeling trapped in Bayview while the rest of us—even me, although it's taken me a while—make plans to move on. Now he has options.

"It's cool that your mom is being supportive, though," Maeve says. "Even if it took another Jake disaster to get you there."

"Yeah. It was nice," I say, resting my head on her shoulder as she toggles between websites on her screen. "So, what's the latest? Is what Vanessa learned from Ms. Riordan helpful?"

"I think so," Maeve says. "I mean, we already had a pretty good idea that she and Alexander Alton were having an affair, but it's nice to have it confirmed. The question now is— did Alexander really drown or not? And if he didn't, who's responsible?" She waits a few beats before adding, "You know what I always say, right?"

"Don't trust coincidences?" I ask.

"Not that."

"Everyone gives themselves away online eventually?"

"Wow, you've really been paying attention," Maeve says, sounding gratified. "But no." Her voice drops to a low whisper. *"It's always the husband."*

I lift my head so I can stare at her. "You've literally never said that."

Maeve huffs in annoyance. "Okay, well, I don't have to, because every true crime podcast ever has said it for me," she says.

"So you think Mr. Riordan . . ." I trail off, trying to remember the last time I'd seen Scott Riordan. It was at Jake's trial, of course. He was seated as close to Jake as he could get and never looked my way once. Not even while I was testifying.

". . . killed Alexander Alton?" Maeve finishes. "It's a possibility, right? He had motive, and if he's anything like Jake—"

"He is." I gulp. "In lots of ways, but . . . would Ms. Riordan still live with him after something like that?"

"Maybe," Maeve says. "If she didn't know. Or if she was afraid of what he might do to Jake, or to her, if she left."

"Okay, supposing that's true," I say. "How does it connect to what's happening now?"

"Well, let's assume that Jake hasn't disappeared on his own. Like Phoebe said, maybe he's the *perfect* in *practice makes perfect*. Alexander Alton's last campaign."

"But why would his family do anything to Phoebe, or to Reggie?"

"I don't know," Maeve admits. "Alexander's death is the

only real clue we have, though, so I've been focused on his family. But his wife is dead, Chase and Chelsea are accounted for, and guess what? I found Christopher." She opens a tab showing a row of smiling people standing in a semicircle around a guy holding some kind of plaque. "Let me introduce you to Penner Insurance's Employee of the Month."

"Are you sure that's him?" I ask, squinting at the screen. As soon as Maeve enlarges her screen, though, I see the resemblance to Chase. "Where is Penner Insurance?"

"Ohio," Maeve says.

"Maybe he's on a leave of absence or something," I say.

"According to this article, though, the Employee of the Month ceremony happened the day Reggie disappeared," Maeve says.

"Oh," I say, momentarily stumped.

"Yeah. Oh."

"So, what next?"

Maeve sighs. "Beats me. I have zero alternate theories. I was going to ask Phoebe to set up another fake interview at Conrad and Olsen and see if she can learn anything more about Alexander Alton. Who knows—maybe there was bad blood with some colleague who hated him. Advertising's a cutthroat business, right?" She shrugs at my dubious look. "I know, I know, I'm grasping at straws. Doesn't matter anyway, because Phoebe's been totally MIA."

"She has?" I ask, alarmed. "Since when?"

"Not literally," Maeve says quickly. "She's working with Luis at Café Contigo right now. But she keeps putting me off every time I try to talk strategy. She says that she and Emma have a lot of catching up to do."

"I'll bet," I say. There's more I could add, because Phoebe's been acting strangely all summer, but I don't want to get too far off track. "I guess it could be a disgruntled-colleague situation, but . . . that kind of thing doesn't feel personal enough for Bayview-style revenge. You said it yourself, right? *It's Jared Jackson all over again. Another Bayview family destroyed.* Alexander Alton drowned, and his wife was so devastated that she died in a drunk-driving accident." I hadn't been on the beach blanket that day for the original conversation, but Maeve has repeated it more than once since then.

Maeve beams at me. "I *did* say that. You're such a good listener, Addy."

"I listen, and I learn," I say. "You've managed to track down actual calendar events—a play's opening night, and an Employee of the Month ceremony—that make it impossible for Chase or Christopher to be in town. But what about Chelsea? I know she's all the way in England, but it's summertime. What if she's using old pictures?"

"I thought of that," Maeve says, toggling to another tab. "But she's been posting selfies at this seminar series that's happening right now."

Chelsea Alton's Instagram page is up on Maeve's screen, and she clicks on the first picture. "See, here she is at a lecture that was given by a World Bank economist a couple of days ago, and—"

Maeve breaks off, inhaling sharply, but I don't understand why. There's nothing alarming about the smiling girl posing next to a bespectacled man behind a podium. "What?" I ask.

"Ohhhh, you sneak," Maeve breathes, fingers flying over her keyboard.

"What?" I repeat, more insistently.

"Hang on. I have to screenshot this before it disappears, because it probably will soon. Check out the first comment on this picture," Maeve says, handing me her laptop.

It's a comment posted by a girl with the user name @sophiehh13, whose avatar photo . . . looks a lot like Chelsea Alton. The comment reads, *Stop stealing my pics you psycho!!!*

"Wait, what? Who is that?" I ask.

Maeve clicks on the user name beside the comment and loads a new Instagram page belonging to someone named Sophie Hicks-Hartwell. Her bio reads: *Tea enthusiast. Oxford student. Probably sleeping.* Every picture that Maeve has shown us in the past from Chelsea Alton's feed is on Sophie's as well—plus a lot more of her hanging out with friends at parties, restaurants, and what looks like a dorm room.

"Damn," Maeve says with what almost sounds like admiration. "I fell for the oldest trick in the book. Here I was, catfishing Chelsea's older brother, and it never occurred to me that she might be doing the same thing to anyone checking up on her. Sophie Hicks-Hartwell even looks like Chase Alton, doesn't she? The problem is, Chelsea allowed too many followers. That makes the account look legit, but also lets in people who might know the girl whose pictures she's been using. Which is probably exactly what happened."

Maeve returns to Chelsea's page, where Sophie's comment has already been deleted. "Chelsea jumped all over that notification, but it's too late," she says. "We already know she's lying, so all we need to know now is—"

"Where is she?" I finish, staring at the screen.

SIMON

Six Years Earlier

Jake Riordan was so predictable. He'd been pulling away from Simon all summer, but now, when he wanted to do something sneaky, whom did he call?

It was the right call, obviously. But still predictable.

"Alexander Alton," Simon said, shoving his phone in Jake's face. "Her comanaging director at work. They couldn't be more of a cliché if they tried."

Jake stared at the phone, his jaw working. "No way. She can't be hooking up with this guy. He's not even good-looking."

"If you say so," Simon said, shrugging.

Jake threw the phone down onto the couch and folded his arms across his chest. "What did you hear, again, at the Ramona house?" he asked.

"That she was packing up a bag and couldn't wait to go," Simon said. He couldn't remember Ms. Riordan's exact words, but that seemed close enough.

"It doesn't make sense," Jake said, frowning. "My dad is perfect!"

Simon managed to hold back his snort, but just barely. "People have affairs for all kinds of reasons," he said, gazing around Jake's cavernous living room. It was a bright and sunny Saturday afternoon in August, and Mr. Riordan had made a big show of "hitting the links," as he called it, when Simon showed up. Ms. Riordan, on the other hand, was nowhere in sight. "Where is Mommie Dearest, anyway?"

"Lunch with a friend," Jake said.

"Uh-huh," Simon said, hoping his sarcasm wasn't lost on Jake.

It wasn't; one of Jake's hands curled into a fist that he slammed repeatedly into his palm. "This is nuts. She's going to ruin *everything*."

"I have an idea," Simon said. Jake had only wanted a name, but Simon, of course, went the extra mile. Information was power, after all. "Let's ride our bikes past the guy's house and see if your mom's car is there."

Jake's eyes popped. "It's the middle of the day!" he protested. "She'd never do that."

"No offense, but I don't think you know much about what your mom would or wouldn't do in any given situation," Simon said. "Especially this one."

Five minutes later, they were pedaling toward Alexander Alton's house.

Secretly, Simon didn't actually think that Ms. Riordan would be there. According to his research, the guy had a wife and three kids, so home base wasn't a good choice for an afternoon tryst. But Simon was enjoying Jake's angst, and even more, he enjoyed the thought of whatever chaos might erupt if they caught sight of a stray Alton.

And what if, by chance, Jake's mother's car really *was* in the driveway? Simon permitted himself a small smile as he coasted down a hill. Her secret would be out, thanks to him, and he couldn't wait to see what might happen next.

He had to remind himself, when there was no shiny red BMW in the Altons' driveway, that he hadn't really expected one. No reason to be disappointed.

"She's not there," Jake said, clearly relieved, as he stopped in front of the house. "Told you so."

"Not now, anyway," Simon said, gazing at the empty driveway of the neat, compact bungalow in front of them. It was set off by itself at the end of a long, winding road and was barely the size of Jake's living room. "I thought this guy had a big-deal job? Why is his house such a piece of crap?"

"Ad agencies don't pay like law firms," Jake said. He sounded almost forlorn as he added, "My mom doesn't get it. If it weren't for my dad, we'd be living like this too."

"Who knows? Maybe you will," Simon said, dropping his bicycle to the ground. "Let's check out the rest of it."

"What? No!" Jake protested. "Somebody might be home."

"So what?" Simon asked, loping across the street. "We're just a couple of kids cutting through a yard. Happens all the time."

Jake was too much of a coward to follow, though. He stayed behind on the sidewalk as Simon made his way up the Altons' driveway. The house, with its french-blue paint and bright white trim, wasn't as bad as he and Jake had made it out to be.

It had a bay window on one side and an attached garage on the other, with a small porch full of flowering plants surrounding the front door. You couldn't see any other houses from the Altons' yard, which Simon considered a real-estate plus. His own neighbors weren't nearly distant enough.

Simon headed around the back, curious if there might be a deck or a low-enough window that he could peer inside. Before he got far, though, a voice called out, "Um, excuse me. Who the hell are you?"

He turned to see a girl a little older than him, lying on a hammock strung between two trees. Simon should have noticed her, probably, but no matter. This was what he'd come for, after all: an up-close-and-personal look at the Altons.

"Simon Kelleher. I live down the street," he said, the lie slipping out easily. "Sorry about the trespassing. I thought I could get to my house from here, but apparently not."

"*Nobody* can get to their house from here." The girl swung her legs over the edge of the hammock, then stood and strode through the overlong grass until she was a few feet away from Simon. This must be Alexander's sixteen-year-old daughter Chelsea, unless the Alton family was in the habit of letting random kids use their hammock. She struck Simon as too territorial for that to be the case, though. "I've never seen you before," she said, eyes narrowing.

Same, Simon thought. But that wasn't surprising, even though they were only a few years apart in age. From his research, he knew that Alexander Alton's wife was a teacher at Dartmoor Prep, a private school in Eastland, and that all the Alton kids went there. Free of charge, probably, although

Dartmoor was already the cheapest private school around. Could it even call itself a prep school, Simon wondered, with such abysmal Ivy League acceptance rates?

"I'm relatively new to the area," Simon said. Another lie; he'd lived in this cursed town his entire life.

Chelsea shrugged. She clearly wasn't the sociable type, which Simon could respect. He wouldn't make polite conversation with somebody trespassing in his yard either. "Well, you can go now," she said, making a shooing motion with one hand. "Back the way you came."

Simon wasn't quite ready for that. "You probably know my friend," he said.

"Who's that?" Chelsea asked. There was a cool, appraising wariness in her eyes that interested him; it was the same look he sometimes saw reflected in his own mirror. She'd be a worthy adversary, he thought. Or ally. Who knew where fate might take them if the Riordan-Alton affair exploded as spectacularly as Simon hoped it would.

"Jake Riordan," he said, watching her carefully.

There was no flicker of recognition on the girl's face. "Never heard of him."

"Don't worry," Simon said. "You will."

CHAPTER THIRTY-ONE

Phoebe
Tuesday, July 21

When a key turns in the lock, Emma and I both jump as though a gun went off.

We've been on edge ever since finding Reggie's necklace in Owen's backpack Saturday night. "Whatever happened, we can't cover for him this time," I said, even while desperately praying that Owen would have a reasonable explanation for the necklace. He found it, maybe? He bought an exact replica? Because nothing else made sense: not Owen targeting Reggie Crawley, no matter how much he might have disliked him, and certainly not targeting *me*.

He wouldn't, right? Even putting aside the impossible logistics of a thirteen-year-old boy masterminding all of this, Owen would never, ever do that.

"No covering," Emma agreed. "But we can't jump to conclusions either. We need to talk to Owen before we do anything."

Neither of us slept Saturday night. Or the next night, after Mom told us that Owen was extending his sleepover until his friend Ben had to leave for a family vacation. And then, last night, Maeve sent a text to the Murder Club group chat: *All-points bulletin for Chelsea Alton, who as it turns out is NOT in Oxford. I'm working on getting a yearbook photo or similar.*

That set my thoughts spinning in a terrible direction. It had been comforting to remind myself that Owen couldn't possibly pull off something like this without a Jared Jackson lurking in the background, calling the shots. But now . . .

"Do you think Chelsea Alton could be some kind of Jared?" I asked Emma, showing her Maeve's text. "Pulling strings, manipulating vulnerable people, and—"

"Don't jump to conclusions," she said tightly.

That was the last she'd let me say on the subject before we flopped down onto our beds for yet another sleepless night. When Mom got up for work this morning, Emma and I were already at the kitchen island, yawning over massive cups of coffee.

"Why are you two up?" Mom asked.

"Early shift at the café," I lied. I'm off today, but I don't usually get out of bed before ten o'clock unless I'm working.

"Couldn't sleep," Emma said. At Mom's worried look, she added, "Phoebe snored *so* loudly last night. I'm not used to sharing a room."

"Oh well," Mom said, relaxing. "It's probably good that you're up. Owen's due back soon, so make sure he eats something, okay? Ben's family is vegetarian, and you know how picky Owen can be."

"I know," Emma said.

Now Emma and I are sitting ramrod straight on stools behind the kitchen island, watching the lock on our dead bolt turn with agonizing slowness.

"Oh God," Emma murmurs. "It's like we're in a horror movie, isn't it?"

"For the past three months," I say.

The door creaks open and Owen steps inside, a blue duffel bag slung over one shoulder. His strawberry-blond hair hangs in his eyes, and the T-shirt he's probably been wearing since Saturday is a wrinkled mess. "Hey," he grunts at Emma and me, shoving his keys into his pocket as he heads for his bedroom.

"Not so fast," Emma says in her most commanding voice.

It used to make me snap to attention when we were younger, but Owen doesn't even hesitate. "I'm tired; I need sleep," he yawns, pulling his door open. When it clicks shut behind him, the tiny noise feels like a slap in the face after everything we've done for him. Even if he didn't know we were doing it.

"The nerve of him," I say, jumping to my feet and pulling Owen's backpack off the floor. I stride for my brother's room with Emma at my heels, then loudly rap on the door and shove it open before Owen has a chance to answer.

"What are you doing?" he yelps. He's sitting on his bed with one sneaker off, and he glares at me as he unties the other. "Get out. I said I'm going to sleep."

"Not till you explain this." I drop his backpack onto the rug and settle myself down beside it, keeping a watchful eye on my brother's face. Emma sits next to me, her expression grave.

Owen scowls. "What are doing with my stuff?" He lunges for the strap, but I lift the backpack out of his reach. Emma plucks it from my grasp and fishes in the front pocket. "You guys suck," Owen complains, shoving at my arm. "Give it back." He's on the floor now, tugging at the backpack with both hands, and he falls backward when Emma lets it go.

"Why do you have this?" she asks, holding up Reggie's necklace. The silver beads rattle against one another, and I turn my gaze to Owen to see his reaction.

"What's that?" he asks, sitting up. And he looks . . . genuinely baffled.

"You tell us," Emma says.

"Tell you what?" Owen asks. "Why'd you put that in my backpack?"

"We didn't," I say. "We found it there."

The scowl returns to Owen's face. "You can't go through my stuff!"

"Too late," I say, taking the necklace from Emma. "You need to tell us how you got this, Owen."

"I *didn't* get it," he says irritably. "It's not mine."

Emma and I exchange glances. I've been bracing myself for all kinds of reactions from Owen, but I wasn't expecting his typical sullenness. He doesn't look guilty or afraid; he looks annoyed. "Are you telling us that you don't recognize this?" Emma asks.

"Yeah, that's what I'm telling you."

"Then why was it in your backpack?" she asks.

Owen shrugs. "How should I know? Maybe it was there when we got it from Goodwill and I never noticed."

"Owen," I say, carefully folding the necklace into my palm. "This necklace belonged to Reggie Crawley. It went missing when he did, and his parents have been looking for it."

Owen blinks. "Reggie? But that's . . . I don't get it." It's as if he's so confused that he's forgotten to be irritated with us; he looks at Emma and me in turn with wide, guileless eyes. "Reggie's never been near my backpack. How could he put it there?"

"We thought *you* did," Emma says. Owen's mouth opens to protest, but before he can, Emma takes a deep breath and adds, "We thought that you might be involved, somehow, in what's been happening in Bayview lately. The flyers about playing a game, and maybe even—"

"Me? Are you serious?" Owen swings his head between Emma and me, his voice pitching up so high that he sounds like a preteen again. "Why would you think that?"

I pin him with my gaze, my heart cracking as I stare into his light-brown eyes, so similar to mine. And to our father's. "Because we know you were involved in the Truth or Dare game, Owen. We know you stepped in when Emma bowed out and kept the game going with Jared. When we read the chat transcripts with Emma's lawyer, there was a message that spelled the word *bizarre* as B-A-Z-A-A-R. Just like you did when we practiced for your spelling bee." Owen doesn't say a word, but his eyes get shiny and his cheeks flame. "Emma and I protected you. We pretended not to understand what it meant, and we let Emma take the fall. And—"

But before I can get out another word, my brother bursts into noisy sobs that make his entire body shake. He draws his knees to his chest and wraps his arms around them, crying like he used to when he was an overtired toddler. Harder, even, than he did at Dad's funeral. For a few beats, Emma and I are both too shocked to move. Then we're on either side of him, propping him up as he sags against us.

"I'm s-sorry," he chokes out. "I d-didn't mean . . . I never wanted B-B-Br . . ."

He's sobbing too hard to continue, but I understand his meaning. *I never wanted Brandon to die.* It's what Emma and I believed all along, and it's why we were willing to lie to protect him. I think Emma always understood the burden we were taking on, and she did it willingly, as penance for her own part in Brandon's death. I was a lot more naïve; I thought that once Owen was safe I'd be able to go back to normal, not realizing that the secret would start to feel like a ball and chain wrapped around my neck. And I never fully processed—even when Knox tried to tell me—what keeping silent would do to Owen.

"It's okay," Emma murmurs.

"It's *not*," Owen rasps. "It's all my fault. Everything. Brandon dying, that bomb going off, Nate getting hurt, you having to move away—"

"That was Jared's fault," I say. "He used you, just like he used Emma."

"B-but I let him," Owen chokes out. "I *w-w-wanted* him to."

"You didn't know what you wanted," Emma says. "Neither did I."

It takes a long time for Owen's sobs to die down, and when they finally do, he can't look at either of us. "I guess you're gonna tell, huh?" he asks.

"I think we have to," Emma says. "Starting with Mom. She'll know what to do next." Emma meets my eyes over Owen's bent head. "We should have done that as soon as we realized you were involved. We didn't do you any favors, Owen."

"I don't want to go to jail," he whimpers.

"You won't," Emma says with so much confidence that I almost believe her.

Maybe I would, if it weren't for the brand-new problem that we have. "Owen, we need to figure out what happened with Reggie's necklace," I say. "How could it have gotten into your backpack?" I believe, one hundred percent, that he didn't put it there—there's no way he could have faked that kind of surprise or the breakdown he had when we finally confronted him about Jared. "Who else had access to your backpack?"

"I don't know," Owen gulps, wiping his eyes. "It was here all weekend."

"What about before that?" I ask. "Did you leave it anywhere?"

He takes a deep, shuddering breath. "I mean, sometimes I leave it on my chair in the library when I go to the bathroom. Same for Café Contigo." His brow furrows. "Those chairs don't have anything to hook onto, so it falls onto the floor a lot. Ahmed picked it up for me once, and then then last week . . ." He trails off.

"Last week what?" I prompt.

"A girl was holding it when I got back from the bathroom. You know her. That kind of hippie-looking girl who lives with Nate?"

"Sana?" I ask, blinking in surprise.

"Yeah. She was like, 'Oh, some stuff fell out of your bag; I put it back in,'" Owen says. "Then she zipped up the front and handed it to me."

I catch Emma's eye. Her face is a confused blank because she doesn't know Sana, and mine is the same because I do. I never imagined for one second that Nate's roommate could be involved in any of this—but then again, she was Reggie's roommate too. "When exactly was this?" I ask. "Was it after Reggie died?"

"Yeah. It was . . ." Owen scrunches his face. "Last weekend, I think?"

"Nate knows this girl?" Emma asks.

"Nate *lives* with this girl. And Reggie did, too," I say. What had Maeve's latest text said again? *All-points bulletin for Chelsea Alton, who as it turns out is NOT in Oxford.*

"What's her deal?" Emma asks.

"I don't know, she's just . . ." I'm not sure how to finish that sentence. *She's just there?* I don't know much about Sana, and I wonder if Nate does either. Is there any possibility that she's not who she says she is? I know she's lived in Nate's house for only a few months, and she's never mentioned family during our infrequent conversations. She doesn't look much like the pictures I've seen of Chase or Christopher, but she's around the right age. And she was arguing with Reggie the night he disappeared. At the time I assumed she was lecturing him about being gross, but maybe there was something else going on.

"I think I need to talk to Nate," I say.

CHAPTER THIRTY-TWO

Phoebe
Tuesday, July 21

Unfortunately, talking to Nate is easier said than done.

He hasn't answered any of my texts. *He's working,* Addy responded when I asked where he was. So I drove to Myers Construction headquarters, and now I'm picking my way through a parking lot littered with pickup trucks, cement mixers, and other yellow, industrial-looking vehicles with names I don't know on my way to the main office.

"Help you, miss?" a gray-haired man in a yellow vest calls before I get there.

"I'm looking for Nate Macauley?" I say, shading my eyes against the sun.

"He's at a site," the man says.

"Do you happen to know where?" I ask. "I need to talk to him. It's kind of an emergency."

"Sorry to hear that," the man says. "Let me check."

Another text from Addy comes through while I wait: *Every-thing OK? I've been meaning to catch up with you. Want to get coffee?*

Ugh, I do, but not now. *Maybe later,* I write.

"No luck, miss," a voice calls. The yellow-vested man is in front of me again, his expression apologetic. "Nate's not on the schedule, so it was probably a last-minute add. If you want to come back in an hour or so, Keith Myers should be here then. He owns the place, and he always knows exactly where every-one is."

I don't bother telling this helpful man that I already know who Keith Myers is, seeing as I've climbed through a window in his house multiple times. "Thanks so much," I say.

I head back to my car but don't unlock it, hovering next to the passenger-side door while I debate what to do next. Wait for Mr. Myers? Meet Addy for that coffee after all? Go to Nate's house and confront Sana, demanding to know whether she slipped a dead boy's necklace into my brother's backpack?

No, that's a terrible idea. Obviously. But maybe I could do some indirect poking around. I could drive to Café Contigo and ask Ahmed and Evie whether they ever noticed anything. That would kill some time before Mr. Myers returns.

Are you at work? I text to both of them. Ahmed doesn't reply, but Evie answers instantly. *No, home today,* she writes. I have more questions, but I can't ask them over text. Leaving a digital footprint on this subject is probably a bad move.

I glance around me. The last time Evie and I had a conver-sation about Bayview, she mentioned she lived in an apartment complex called something like Glasstown. *It's kind of in an in-dustrial area,* she'd said. *That's why it's so cheap.* I plug *Glasstown* into Google Maps and get nothing closer than Sacramento. But when I try *glass,* the first result is *Apartments at Glassworks,* just 0.2 miles away.

Worth a shot.

I follow the directions on my phone until I reach a four-story, gray-brick building. The entire front lobby is made of glass, but other than that, the name seems like false advertising. It's the right address, though. There are sixteen buttons on a pad beside the front door, and all of them except apartment twelve have names beneath them. None of them are Evie's, so I'm about to press the button for twelve when the door opens.

"Hey," the guy leaving the building says, holding the door open for me.

"Thanks," I say, ducking beneath his arm.

Inside, there are hallways to both my left and right, and an elevator in between. A quick walk around shows four apartments on the first floor, so I figure that Evie's is probably on the third. I take the elevator upstairs, my phone chiming as the doors close.

It's Nate, finally. *What's up?*

I need to talk to you. Are you around? I write back.

I'm at work, but I'll be done at 3.

Can I stop by?

Sure, Nate texts, dropping a pin with his location.

Thanks!

I pocket my phone as the doors open and step onto the dimly lit third floor. I make my way down the right-side hallway first, then backtrack after passing apartments nine and ten. Number twelve is in the left-hand corner, and I say a quick prayer that I guessed right before knocking on the door. There's nothing but silence for a few beats, and then a familiar voice calls, "Hello?"

"It's Phoebe," I say.

The door opens and Evie stands within the frame, a puzzled look on her face. "Hey. What are you doing here?"

"I need to ask you something," I say, brushing past her to enter the apartment. I definitely don't want to have this conversation in the hallway.

"I'm kind of in the middle of something," Evie says.

"This won't take long. Wow, cute place," I say, gazing around me. I could've guessed that Evie's apartment would be as bright and organized as she is: the living room walls are painted a cheerful blue, the love seat is decorated with a half-dozen patterned throw pillows, and there's lots of botanical-themed art everywhere. A small kitchen is to my right, and there's another room to my left that . . .

"Oh my God."

The words slip out of me before I realize I've said them, as I stare at the green vine-patterned wallpaper that's been haunting my dreams ever since the night I was kidnapped. Delicate stems and heart-shaped leaves, twisting and turning every which way. I'd convinced myself that the wallpaper didn't really exist. That my drug-addled brain conjured it out of nothing, creating a false memory that sent Addy, Maeve, and Nate on a dangerous wild-goose chase to Ramona.

But it does exist, after all. Here, in Evie's apartment, which means . . .

"What," Evie says, but there's nothing question-like about the word. When I look at her impassive face, I get the eerie sense that she can see inside my brain—that she knows exactly where my thoughts are headed, and she's simply waiting for me to get there.

All Sana did at Café Contigo was pick up a backpack that somebody else had already slipped Reggie's necklace into. Somebody who was at Nate's party the night I disappeared, who's been at the edges of every Murder Club conversation over the past few weeks, and who had plenty of opportunity to wait for my brother to leave his backpack dangling from a chair at Café Contigo while he used the restroom.

"Evie?" I ask. "Is that really your name?"

Her eyes are like chips of blue ice as she closes her front door with one swift motion and says, "You shouldn't have come here, Phoebe."

CHAPTER THIRTY-THREE

Nate
Tuesday, July 21

"Cheers," Addy says, clinking her glass with mine, and then Bronwyn's and Cooper's.

It's just seltzer water, since I'm not rich enough—or old enough—to uncork a bottle of champagne at the bar where I'm supposed to be working. But I still grin when I take a sip. "Who would've thought, huh?" I ask. Then I feel compelled to add, "Nothing's a done deal, though."

"Nate, please allow yourself to be happy," Addy says, reaching over the counter to grab a lime wedge that she squeezes over her drink. "Your dad will come through."

Cooper gazes around the half-full bar that Gavin started managing without me once my friends showed up. "Are you gonna quit this job?" he asks.

"No. Why would I? The pay's great, and Gavin does all the work," I say as he sails past the bar carrying a tray of dirty glasses.

"One of these days, we're going to have a discussion about workload balance," Gavin calls over his shoulder.

I wave him off and reach into my pocket. "Hey, guess what I found while I was cleaning out the old junk in my closet—"

Addy cuts me off with such a loud gasp that I whip around, half expecting to see Jake behind me. Then she says, "I'm sorry, did you say you were *cleaning your closet?*" She clasps a hand over her heart as Bronwyn tries—not very hard—to hold back a snicker.

"Look at him, so fancy already," Cooper says with a grin.

I huff out a reluctant laugh. I should've expected that reaction, considering my track record of doing the bare minimum in that house. But last night, I looked around my room and realized that even if I don't move out, I can make it less depressing—paint the walls, put up some shelves, and throw out or donate stuff I never use. "Can I finish?" I ask.

"Who even *are* you?" Addy says. "But okay."

"I found my last burner phone," I say, laying it on top of the bar between Addy and Bronwyn. "I charged it to see if I'd left anything stupid on there, but it's empty. Guess I never got around to using this one. Still, maybe I should take a hammer to it or something."

"Ooh, no, let me have it," Addy says, picking it up and turning it over in one hand. "We can use it as a prop at our next joint birthday party."

I raise my eyebrows. "I thought we were giving up on those?"

Cooper shakes his head and says, "The track record's not good."

"Okay, maybe just a regular party, then," Addy says, stuffing

285

the phone into the pocket of her shorts. "Or a farewell party for me and Maeve."

"You're going to have the best time in Peru," Bronwyn says, gray eyes shining behind the new pair of glasses she picked up this morning. They look almost exactly like her old ones, but I know better than to tell her that. "This has been a rough summer, but at least some things are starting to look up."

Addy grimaces. "Don't jinx us. It's still Unsolved Mystery Central around here."

"I know," Bronwyn says. "And I've been thinking about that." She glances around us, then leans in closer and lowers her voice. "Maybe we should hand everything we have over to the Bayview Police. Let them know about the advertising campaign, the affair, the fact that one of Alexander Alton's kids is posing as someone else. They can look into it, and we can . . ." She straightens in her seat as the margarita moms pass behind her. "We can be normal and enjoy the time we have left to hang out together."

"Normal?" Cooper snorts. "Never heard of it."

"I get what you mean, Bronwyn," Addy says, "but the Bayview Police are so useless. I feel like they'll totally dismiss us. And with Jake still out there . . ." She gives a little shiver. "I'd rather see what Maeve manages to learn first."

"Not *just* Maeve," Bronwyn says. "I've been busy too." She holds up her phone to display a text message string. "Maeve had no luck finding any photos of Chelsea from that private school in Eastland the twins went to—they don't do yearbooks, apparently—but you know how the family moved to Ohio after Alexander died?" We all nod. "A girl in my dorm is from the town next to where they lived. She's going to see if she can dig up anything."

"Oh, but we should turn things over to the police, huh?" I tease.

"The more we can hand them, the better," Bronwyn says loftily.

Gavin bustles past again with a bottle of wine in each hand, and I realize the bar's suddenly gotten a lot more crowded. "Not to interrupt your party, but I wouldn't say no to a little help," he huffs.

"Sorry, man. On it," I say.

For the next half hour everything's a blur; I ring up orders, serve drinks, talk with regulars, and collect empty glasses. Stephanie shows up early—for once—but it's busy enough that Gavin keeps working too. After a while, Cooper leaves to meet up with Kris, and then Bronwyn gets to her feet. "I better go. Family-dinner night," she says, before wrapping her arms around Addy and squeezing hard. "Call me later, okay?"

"I will if I don't suffocate," Addy says, her voice muffled in Bronwyn's shirt.

"Sorry, I'm feeling nostalgic," Bronwyn says, releasing her. "Just imagining the four of us two years ago versus now. Can you believe we barely knew one another the summer before our senior year? Well, you and Cooper did, but not like you do now." Then she leans over the bar, takes my face in her hands, and gives me a long, lingering kiss. "You know what the best thing about your dad's gift is?" she whispers as a few people around the bar whistle and clap. "It makes your future easier, but it doesn't make it possible. You did that by yourself."

"You helped," I murmur, pressing my forehead to hers.

"I love you so, so much," Bronwyn says.

It's one of those perfect moments that I try to grab hold of even while it's happening, because I know I'm going to want to remember it. "Love you more."

"Impossible," she says, giving me another quick peck before turning away. I watch her leave for as long as I can before all the credit cards being waved in my face distract me.

It's past seven when the bar finally slows down. Gavin sighs deeply as he refills a drink for Addy, who ordered a salad for dinner. "That was a zoo. And it's way past quitting time for me," he says, glancing over his shoulder at Stephanie chatting with the margarita moms. "I'm going to the restroom and then I'm heading out. Can you let Stephanie know?"

"Yeah, sure," I say.

Addy watches him go and asks, "Anything ever happen with him and Vanessa?"

"No. Vanessa was decidedly not interested." I raise my eyebrows. "What about you?"

"I'm not interested in him either," Addy says.

"You know what I mean. Are you and Vanessa talking again, or what?"

"Oh my God, Nate, you're such a mediator all of a sudden." Addy rolls her eyes, but a reluctant smile tugs at her lips. "We're talking a little. She wants to fly us both out to visit Keely for a long weekend before I leave for Peru. It's short notice, and as my mother keeps reminding me, I still have a *lot* to do before I'm ready to leave the country for a month, but"—she shrugs her shoulders—"who am I to turn down such a generous offer?"

"Who indeed," I say, pulling out my phone to check messages. I have a few from my parents, and one from Bronwyn—but still nothing from Phoebe, who'd asked to meet up a few hours ago and then blew me off. *Sorry, something came up,* she'd texted when I asked if she was still coming. After that: silence. "Have you heard from Phoebe lately?" I ask.

"No, why?" Addy asks. When I tell her, her eyes go round. "And you're only mentioning that now?" she asks accusingly. "We need to be constantly vigilant, Nate!"

"I know that. I checked in with her."

"Did you actually talk to her, or text?"

"Text," I say.

Addy frowns. "Do I need to remind you that somebody used Phoebe's phone to text her mom about sleeping over at my house the night she went missing?"

I stare at her. "Well, fuck. I guess you do."

Addy whips out her phone. "I'm sure I'm being paranoid, but let me check with the rest of the gang and see if anyone else has heard from her." She's quiet for a couple of minutes, fingers dancing across her phone, until her frown deepens. "Nothing so far. I asked Ashton if she could stop by their apartment, but she's not home. Maybe I should go myself, except—ugh." She drops her phone onto the counter with a sigh. "I walked here. It's going to take me forever to get to her place. When do you get off again?"

"Not till ten," I say.

"Let me see if Bronwyn can drive me."

"Hang on," I say as Gavin emerges from the restroom and waves a goodbye. I beckon him over, calling, "Hey, Gavin, could you give Addy a ride? She's going to a friend's place in Bayview. It's not far from here."

"Of course," Gavin says with a dramatic sweep of his arm toward Addy. "Your chariot awaits, milady."

"Thanks," she says, hopping off her stool. "I'll let you know what I hear."

"All right," I say, unease twisting my gut. I'd thought it was weird that Phoebe didn't show up, but not weird enough that it worried me, especially once she answered my text. Addy's right, though; I should have double-checked. Especially with Jake still missing.

As soon as his name enters my head, the bar gets strangely quiet. When I look up, I see Ms. Riordan walking toward me with slow, careful steps. She's dressed to the nines, like usual, but her makeup looks as though she missed a few spots. "Hello, Nate," she says, taking a seat on an empty stool and placing her purse on the bar. "Chardonnay, please."

I can tell she's already had a few of those. "How are you doing, Ms. Riordan?" I ask.

She folds her hands on the bar in front of her. "How do you think I'm doing?"

"Not good," I say.

Ms. Riordan lets out a low, brittle laugh that sounds more like a sob. Then she leans forward, eyes locked on mine. "Are you looking for him?" she asks in a low voice.

"For who?" I ask, filling a glass with water and placing it beside her.

Her mouth tightens. "No. Don't do that. Don't pretend you don't know what I'm talking about. I know what he's done to you, and your friends, but I also know . . . you're not vindictive." She swallows hard. "If you find him first, he'll be okay."

I give up any pretense that we're having a normal conversation and place my palms on the bar, leaning forward so that only she can hear me. "Find him before who?"

Her eyes fill with tears. "I don't know."

"You sure about that?" She doesn't respond, and I lower my voice even further. "What happened to Alexander Alton?"

Ms. Riordan goes rigid. "How did you . . ." She gazes around wildly, like she's expecting Alexander himself to pop out from behind the bar. Then she grabs her purse and clutches it to her chest. "You don't know what you're talking about," she hisses. "This was a mistake."

"Don't leave," I say as she gets to her feet. "You're right, you know. I'm not vindictive, but someone else is. Reggie Crawley's dead because of them. So how about you cut the bullshit and tell me how that guy really died?"

"I—I don't know," Ms. Riordan says brokenly. "I was in Mexico, and he . . ."

"And he what?" I ask.

Tears spill from Ms. Riordan's eyes and her face creases in pure misery. "I asked him to—" she starts, but she's interrupted by a loud, commanding voice.

"Katherine! There you are. Time to head out."

Scott Riordan is striding toward the bar wearing one of his usual power suits, his forehead covered with a thin sheen of sweat. The fixed grin on his face does nothing to conceal how angry he is at seeing me leaning over his wife. "Come on, Ms. R.," I say in a harsh whisper as he approaches. "Last chance. Who killed Alexander?"

Ms. Riordan's eyes fasten on her husband as she pastes on

her own phony smile and murmurs, "I expect your guess is as good as mine." Then she squares her shoulders and makes her way toward Mr. Riordan.

Who, unless I'm reading her wrong, she just accused of murder.

Mr. Riordan puts a possessive arm around his wife's shoulders and steers her toward the exit. Once they're out of sight I pull out my phone to call Bronwyn, but before I can, a new message from her flashes across my screen. *OMG CALL ME!!!* it says, immediately followed by a photo. I enlarge it and see a yearbook page full of smiling high school kids. *Chelsea E. Alton,* the first caption reads, and it's . . . holy shit, it's a years-younger version of that girl Evie from Café Contigo. Alexander Alton's daughter has been here all along, serving us food and eavesdropping on our Murder Club meetings.

But that's not the worst part.

The worst part is the picture a few rows down from her. A kid wearing a suit and tie, beaming a familiar smile. He's heavier now than he used to be, but I still would've recognized him even without the caption beneath his name: *Gavin P. Barrett.* My fellow bar worker and all-around good guy apparently knew Chelsea Alton way back when and has been with her in Bayview the entire time people were disappearing.

And I just handed Addy over to him.

CHAPTER THIRTY-FOUR

Addy
Tuesday, July 21

"Sorry about that pit stop," Gavin says, pocketing his wallet as he opens the car door. "Didn't realize I was running on fumes."

"No problem," I say absently, my arm stretching beside me as I feel around on the floor for my phone. I dropped it right when I was trying to check in with Bronwyn, and now it's taunting me with constant buzzing. "I didn't realize this place even existed. Where are we?"

Gavin starts the engine. "Cheapest gas in Bayview. Well, the Bayview-Eastland line. We're just a few blocks away from the old Guppies candy factory. Remember those?"

"The gummy fish?" I ask, still feeling around on the floor for my phone.

"The sweetest treat you'll ever meet," Gavin sings in an off-key voice. "Those were terrible commercials. No wonder they

went out of business." He makes a sharp turn out of the gas station and adds, "Is that your phone buzzing?"

"Yeah, I dropped it in no-man's-land," I say, turning in my seat to check out the floor behind us. "It's been ringing up a storm ever since."

"Want me to pull over?"

I right myself and dust off my palms. "No, it's fine. I'll get it once we're there."

"You sure?"

"Well . . ." I hesitate. If someone's messaging me about Phoebe, time might be of the essence. "Yeah, okay. Thanks."

Gavin gazes around us. "This is kind of a quiet road, but it's narrow too. Let me find someplace where we won't be in anyone's way in case they . . . ahh." He grins as we pass a chain-link fence. "The Guppies parking lot, at our service."

"I'm surprised they haven't done anything with this building," I say as it looms into sight.

"It'll probably get turned into condos eventually," Gavin says, pulling into the deserted parking lot.

Minutes later, I'm hovering beside the open passenger door as Gavin, grunting, pushes the seat back as far as it can go and sweeps his hand beneath it. "You weren't kidding about no-man's-land," he says. "I can hear it, but I can't tell where it is. Let me get a flashlight out of the trunk and try from the back seat."

"Sorry about this," I say as he pops the trunk.

"I'm the one who's sorry. Didn't realize my car was the Bermuda Triangle," Gavin says. Flashlight in hand, he opens one of the rear doors and slides into the back seat.

An engine roars behind us. I turn, mildly curious about

who else decided to hang out in the deserted Guppies parking lot, and blink in surprise at the sight of a familiar motorcycle charging our way. Nate stops a few feet from me, whips off his helmet, and holds it out. "Here," he calls over the still-roaring engine. "I don't have an extra, so you need to put this on."

I blink, confused. "What are you . . . how did you know we were here?"

"Snapchat location," Nate says. His eyes rove over Gavin's car before he pushes down his bike's kickstand and dismounts with the engine still running, crossing the space between us to shove the helmet into my hands. "We need to leave, Addy. Now. No questions, okay?"

I gape at him. I've never seen Nate so deadly serious. "Okay," I say, twisting to look over my shoulder. "But I need my phone. Gavin's looking for it, it's stuck somewhere under—"

"Get it later," Nate says, just as Gavin emerges from the car, triumphantly holding up my phone.

"Found it!" he calls. Then his eyebrows lift in surprise. "Nate? What are you doing here? Thought you were working late."

Nate's eyes flick between Gavin and me. "Family emergency," he says.

"Oh God, really?" My heart plummets. And just when things were going so well for him too. "Okay, let me grab my phone and I'll go."

"Wow, sorry to hear that," Gavin says as I head his way. "You've got messages coming in like crazy, Addy. Here you—"

He breaks off as I reach him, eyes fixed on my screen. "What?" I ask. I hold out my hand, but Gavin doesn't give me the phone. Instead, he stares at Nate.

"So that's why you're here," he says heavily. "You know."

"Know what?" I ask. I try to pluck my phone out of Gavin's hand, but he twists away and holds it out of my reach. "What are you . . . Gavin! Give me my phone."

"Leave it, Addy!" Nate calls, heading our way.

"You don't understand," Gavin says, a note of desperation creeping into his voice. All of a sudden, he's between Nate and me. "I'm trying to help you guys. Chelsea . . . listen, Chelsea's in kind of a crisis, okay?"

"Chelsea?" I repeat, stomach twisting.

"Evie from Café Contigo," Nate says. "Her real name is Chelsea Alton, though. And our friend Gavin here graduated high school with her in Ohio."

My jaw drops as Gavin says, "I swear to God, I'm trying to help."

He holds up both hands, my phone still in one of them. "If Chelsea's name means something to you, then I guess you know her dad died when she lived in Bayview. I got to know her once her family moved and I—I fell for her right away. Even though she's always had kind of a wall up." He swallows hard. "She's been through a lot, you know, losing both of her parents, but especially her dad. They were close, and she's never really gotten over it. She tends to dwell on stuff, but lately, it's been more than that. She got this idea in her head that her dad didn't drown after all. That somebody might've killed him."

"She *got this idea*?" Nate repeats. "How does someone get an idea like that?"

"I don't know," Gavin says miserably. "She wouldn't tell me, but she insisted on moving back to Bayview. So of course, I tagged along too. Had to take a break from school, but that's what you do when you're head over heels for someone, right? You'll do anything for them." Nate's expression thaws a fraction, because—yeah. He knows what that's like.

Gavin rubs a hand across the back of his neck and adds, "Chelsea didn't like that, though. She broke up with me almost as soon as we got here. And then . . . things started happening."

"Things?" I echo.

"That billboard from her father's old company. Phoebe disappearing. And Reggie . . . and Jake . . ." Gavin's jaw tenses. "I don't know what's going on. But it doesn't feel like a coincidence, you know?"

"Yeah." Nate studies him, eyes narrowed. "We know."

"And then . . . then I found this." Gavin crosses over to the still-open trunk and leans inside. "In Chelsea's apartment."

"Thought you said you guys were broken up?" Nate says.

"We are, but I have a key, and I got worried, so . . . come look." Gavin pulls out a blue-and-gold jacket. "I'm no expert, but I watched the news coverage of what happened in Bayview like everybody else, and this damn football jacket got imprinted on my brain. I think . . . I think it might belong to Jake."

"Let me see," Nate says, crossing over to the trunk.

Gavin tosses him the jacket and Nate holds it up, frowning. "This isn't—" he starts, but before he can get out another word, Gavin's a blur of motion, lunging for Nate so quickly that I don't understand what's happening until there's a sickening, crunching sound and Nate collapses on the ground with Gavin standing over him, a crowbar dangling from one hand.

A scream erupts from my throat and then gets immediately cut off because Gavin's on me now, pinning my arms with one hand as the other covers my mouth. "I didn't want to do that," he says, breathing heavily. "I really didn't. But I meant what I said. I'd do anything for Chelsea, and she has to finish what she's started."

Tears fill my eyes as I watch a dark-red stain appear beneath Nate's head. "She's doing you a favor, Addy," Gavin continues. "You know better than anyone that Jake Riordan is a fucking menace to society. All you and your friends had to do was stay out of the way, and me and Chelsea would've taken care of him. You weren't supposed to figure things out this fast. And now . . . now I don't know what the hell to do with you." He starts dragging me toward the trunk, and I fight him every step of the way, my eyes on Nate's still form.

Then I see one of Nate's fingers twitch. Relief floods me— *he's alive*—followed by sickening dread at how small the movement was. And then, I go limp.

Nate needs help, fast, and I can't help him unless . . .

I stare up at Gavin, making my eyes as beseeching as I can. "I want to help you," I say, my voice muffled against his hand.

He pauses, lifting his palm a fraction from my mouth. "What did you say?"

"I want to help you," I say. "With whatever you're going to do to Jake."

Gavin snorts. "You want to help me after what I did to Nate? I don't think so."

"Nate isn't my friend. He let Jake walk all over me." The lies drip off my tongue like poison. Nobody in their right mind would believe them, but Gavin clearly isn't in his right mind, and I can't think of a better plan. "All of them do. We're supposed to be Murder Club, but nobody has the guts to commit an actual murder, even when somebody deserves it as much as Jake. So if that's what you're doing, I'm in."

Gavin stares at me. "You really think I buy that?" he asks. My heart sinks, but then his eyes start to gleam. "Might not be a bad idea to have you around, though. We need a way out of this, or at least a distraction until we can disappear, and you might be it. You've got a pretty big grudge against him too." He gives me another shove until I'm facing the still-open trunk and says, "Go ahead. Get in." When I don't move, he barks out a short laugh. "You didn't think I was going to let you ride shotgun, did you?"

Oh God. He's still holding my phone, and—

And I have another one.

Nate's last burner phone is still nestled in my pocket. "Okay," I say, climbing into the trunk before Gavin can ask me to empty my pockets. "I meant what I said. You'll see."

He looms over me. "Hold out your hands." My heart sinks even further when he grabs a piece of rope and loops it around my wrists. He pushes me down, and rough carpet scrapes my cheek as he does the same thing to my ankles. Then he grabs a piece of cloth and ties it over my mouth, knotting it so hard at the back of my head that I let out a strangled grunt of pain as strands of my hair break. Still, I don't struggle. "You're making this very easy," Gavin says, almost conversationally. "Chelsea always says not to trust easy."

I meet his eyes, willing mine to stay dry and unblinking. He stares at me for a few seconds, and then darkness descends as he slams the trunk door.

I take a few deep, steadying breaths. This isn't ideal, but my wrists aren't so tightly bound that I'm unable to move my hands. My knees are already at my chest, my hands by my hips, as I slide my fingers into my pocket and feel the cool metal of the phone.

Nate's phone. Nate, bleeding out on the ground.

No. Don't think about that.

I focus on slowly pulling out the phone as the roar of Nate's motorcycle stops and a car door slams. Then the car's engine starts, making everything around me vibrate, and the phone nearly slips out of my now-sweating hands. *No, Addy, focus. Take it slow.* I pause, shifting my weight a little as the car begins moving. Then I hold the phone carefully between my bound hands and flip the lid, letting out a choked sob of gratitude when it lights up. Fully charged, just like Nate said.

Now what? I could try getting my gag off so I can call 911, but I'm afraid of wasting precious time on something I might not be able to do. Instead, I hit the button for Messages, then start slowly and carefully pressing buttons. Bronwyn hadn't been kidding, after that day she lost her phone in the river near Marshall's Peak, about making all of us memorize her number. She drilled me until it was stuck in my brain.

Once her number is entered, I start the message. It takes forever to type with my hands bound, the car roaring beneath me and sending me flying whenever Gavin takes a corner too fast, but I keep at it, writing just enough to make sure that Bronwyn will understand and know what to do. *NATE HURT GUPPIES FACTORY PKG LOT SEND HELP. ADDY.* Then I hit Send and pray for reception.

My message disappears, and I hold my breath as I stare at the screen. One beat, two beats, three beats, four, five, six . . . The screen darkens, and the tears I've been holding back ever

300

since Gavin hit Nate threaten to leak out of my eyes. I take more deep breaths, reminding myself that this was only plan A. Even if the phone won't send messages, an emergency call might still work. I just need to focus my attention on getting the gag off. I put the phone down and lift my hands, twisting them behind my head and feeling for the edge of the knot. It's there, but my angle is all wrong, and my breathing is starting to get a little panicked, making me light-headed. I stop moving and force myself to exhale slowly.

Then a couple of things happen at once. The phone buzzes, startling me so much that I recoil and crack my head against the side of the car. Almost immediately after that, the car lurches to a stop. I strain my ears, barely breathing, listening for any sounds that might give me a hint as to where we are. Stopped at a red light, maybe? Stuck in traffic?

Then the roar beneath my head subsides, leaving behind nothing except silence. The engine is off, and wherever we are now is very, very quiet.

I'm afraid to take even a split second to look at the return message before pressing the Off button to silence the phone. I try to maneuver it back into my pocket, but footsteps are approaching way too fast. All I can do is shove the phone into the corner and pray it's not visible before the trunk opens with a loud creak and light floods my eyes.

"All right," Gavin says. "Let's do this."

CHAPTER THIRTY-FIVE

Phoebe
Tuesday, July 21

I wake up with a horrifying sense of déjà vu—my head hurts, my throat is dry, my vision is hazy, and I have no idea where I am. Except this time it's a hundred times worse, because as soon as I try to move, I can't. It takes a few moments of confused, futile struggling to realize that I'm tied to a chair. *Just like Reggie.*

The thought is enough to still my movements. I start taking deep, measured breaths, trying to calm my racing heart and get my bearings. I'm in a small room with a single window covered with what looks like plywood. There's a desk in one corner, piled high with boxes, and empty bookshelves lining the wall in front of me. The air around me is dusty and smells faintly of mildew. I don't think this is Evie's apartment; not only does the room look like it hasn't been used for years, but the flooring and the crown molding around the windows and door frame are completely different.

And she's not Evie; she's Chelsea Alton. I keep forgetting that.

I carefully twist my hands back and forth, testing the bonds that are holding me. The time in Chelsea's apartment is slowly coming back to me: how I tried to leave and she stopped me, the way the two of us struggled for what felt like hours until she managed to get her arm across my throat, choking me to the point that I thought I was going to die. I saw my mom's face in my mind's eye then, and the last thing I remember thinking was *She's already lost so much.*

But not me, as it turns out. Not yet.

Chelsea could have killed me. She could easily have killed me, instead of bringing me here. And while that part's not great—*Never let them take you to a second location* is the first rule of any self-defense class—it gives me enough hope that when I hear footsteps approach, I don't fully panic. I keep taking deep breaths, slowing my pulse enough that when the door opens and Chelsea appears, I manage to rasp out "Hi."

She shakes her head, almost like she's amused. "Hi yourself, Phoebe."

"What's . . . what's going on?" I ask. "What are you doing?"

"Don't you already know?" Chelsea asks. "You're the one who came looking for me, after all."

"But I didn't . . . I didn't know who you were until I saw your wallpaper. I remembered that, from the night you . . . from the night of Nate's party." It's ludicrous when I'm sitting here tied to a chair, but for some reason, I don't want to say *From the night you* kidnapped *me.* It feels vital to be as non-confrontational as possible. "I was coming to ask you about Sana, because Owen thought she might have put Reggie's necklace into his backpack."

"You found that?" Chelsea frowns. "Too bad. That was for later."

"For later?" I echo. "You were . . . framing Owen?"

"I mean, it wasn't the primary plan," she says. "More of a side benefit."

"But why?" I ask. "Owen's just a kid!"

She crosses her arms. "You really don't remember?" I stare at her, confused, until she heaves an exasperated sigh. "You weren't the target at Nate's party, you know. That was Vanessa. I drugged her drink, but then you grabbed it and took off. By the time I saw you again, you'd already downed the whole thing."

Vanessa? I want to ask why—I can't see where Vanessa fits into any of this—but there are bigger questions pressing on my brain. "So . . . that was you in Nate's backyard? I wasn't imagining things? You were there, and you told me I'd made a big mistake."

"Well, you did," Chelsea says, sounding irritated. "You screwed up both our nights. But I was going to *help* you. Take you home and deal with Vanessa another night. You passed out almost as soon as I got there, so I started tapping your cheeks, trying to wake you enough that you could walk. When you came to, you started babbling about how you *couldn't take it anymore.* And you told me what Owen had done."

Oh God, I don't remember any of that. "What . . . what did I tell you?" I gulp.

"Everything," Chelsea says, and my stomach plummets. "And listen, I get wanting Brandon Weber to pay for what he did. As a general rule—I'm good with revenge." My blood chills as she adds, "But I'm sick to death of toxic boys doing whatever they want with no consequences. All you did with Owen was create another Brandon, and you couldn't even see it. So, you became the target instead." Her eyes gleam. "My practice."

Makes perfect.

I can't bring myself to say the words or ask about her father; I'm afraid that sharing too much of what we know could make her angry or put my friends in danger. My dry throat burns when I say, "But you . . . you didn't want to hurt me, right?" It comes out like a plea, and my heart sinks when she remains stone-faced. "Or Reggie?" I add. "Bronwyn said . . . she said that was an accident."

A muscle in Chelsea's cheek jumps. "Bronwyn's a smart girl," she says.

"And now . . ." I trail off, knowing what I have to ask but afraid to go there. There's a third person missing, and while it seems likely that he's Chelsea's ultimate target . . . what if she's *working* with him? What if we have all of this wrong? Is Jake going to suddenly pop around the corner, laughing at how we've been running around in circles, grasping at bits and pieces of information without ever seeing the big picture?

I shudder at the thought. Despite the position I'm in, I'm not as afraid of Chelsea as I probably should be. But I would be absolutely terrified to see Jake.

I swallow hard and ask, "What happens now?"

"Chels!" Another voice booms from somewhere else in the house, startling me. It's a guy's voice, but not one I recognize.

Chelsea leans out through the doorway and calls, "Hang on, Gavin." *Gavin?* I know that name from somewhere, but my brain is spinning too fast to place it.

"I can't *hang on*," the voice calls back. "I need you in the kitchen, now. We've got a situation."

"Where are we?" I ask, suddenly petrified of being left alone. I don't like the sound of *a situation* at all. "Whose house is this?"

"Mine," Chelsea says. "I grew up here. My family still owns it. It's been empty for years, though." She gazes at the cobwebs lining the bookshelves and adds, "Gavin helped me bring you here before he went to work. Maybe I should've left you in the apartment, but . . . it seemed safer to have everyone in one place."

"Everyone?" I gulp. "Who else is here?"

"Chels!" Gavin calls urgently. "Did you hear me?"

"Coming!" Chelsea calls, her eyes still fixed on me. "Phoebe, do you have any idea how difficult it's been to act like Little Miss Perfect at Café Contigo all summer? Smiling at those Bayview assholes while you barely lifted a finger? I'm *exhausted*. So do us both a favor, and don't make things any harder than they have to be. I'm out of patience." She turns for the door and adds, "Also, my brother used to practice his drums here. The room is soundproof, so you're only going to give yourself a sore throat if you start screaming."

"Wait, please!" I say. Panic is starting to squeeze my lungs, making it hard to breathe. "What are you going to do next?" Chelsea doesn't reply, and desperation turns my voice raw. "Who else is here?"

"You'll see," she says before stepping through the door and closing it behind her.

CHAPTER THIRTY-SIX

Addy
Tuesday, July 21

"What. The. Hell," Chelsea snaps, staring at me.

I don't have the words to say anything back. My heart was beating wildly when Gavin hauled me out of the trunk, afraid that he'd spot the burner phone and then . . . what? Read the message, realize that I hadn't said anything to incriminate him, and go back to the parking lot to finish what he'd started? To finish Nate?

Assuming that Nate isn't already done.

The fear of that made me so nauseated and light-headed that I could barely register my surroundings once I was out of the car. We were in a garage, the small, neat type that's usually attached to a house; the large door was closed behind us, and there was a smaller one to our left. Possibly close enough to other houses that somebody could hear me scream, because Gavin kept my gag on until he carried me inside the house.

Then he shoved me onto a kitchen chair and unbound my legs, wrists, and finally my mouth while he yelled for Chelsea and I struggled to catch my breath and figure out my next move.

"What is she doing here?" Chelsea demands.

"They know, Chels. Bronwyn found our senior yearbook. Nate came after me while I was giving Addy a ride to Phoebe's place—"

"Phoebe's place?" Chelsea interrupts, her eyes boring into mine. "Why?"

"I . . . I was worried about her," I say. "She's not answering her phone, and—"

"She's here," Chelsea says. My heart sinks as she adds, "But . . . God." She rubs her palms over her cheeks. "This is all happening way too fast. Where is Nate?"

"I bashed his head in with a crowbar and left him in a parking lot," Gavin says.

I let out choked sob as Chelsea's mouth drops open. "You did *what*? Nate isn't . . . he wasn't supposed to get hurt!"

"Well, what the hell do you think I should've done, Chels? They knew, and they were coming for you. It was a spur-of-the-moment decision. You think I wanted that? I told you from the start not to pull that crap with the ad campaign and the billboard! You could've flown under the radar with all this, but you just had to *make a statement*." Gavin throws up aggrieved finger quotes. "Now Nate's fucked, and I had to bring Addy along, and Bronwyn knows who we are. So it won't take much time to figure out *where* we are. This house is in your name."

"Is Phoebe okay?" I ask.

Chelsea ignores me, her eyes pinned on Gavin. "True, but why would anyone think to come here? If anything, they'd show

308

up at my apartment. But they shouldn't, because changing your name isn't a crime. Bronwyn can't prove I did anything else, so who's going to care? Not the Bayview Police, that's for sure."

Oh, how I wish she weren't right.

"Nate's out of the picture," Chelsea continues. "Phoebe and Addy are here, so . . . it's contained. For now. We still have time." It gives me hope that she lumps Phoebe and me together like that; as though Phoebe, too, is here against her will but unhurt. Then my heart gives a relieved leap when Chelsea levels a dispassionate gaze at me and adds, "I guess you can join Phoebe in the downstairs office for the time being."

"Addy said she wanted in on whatever we're planning with Jake," Gavin says.

Chelsea snorts. "And you believed her?"

"No, but . . ." Gavin runs a hand through his hair. "We're kind of screwed here, Chels. People are gonna come after us way sooner than you thought. But if we release a video of Addy killing Jake, and if we can make it look like she and Phoebe worked together . . ."

A shiver goes through me as Chelsea passes a hand over her forehead. "Jesus, Gavin," she says. "Please stop trying to think."

"How is that a worse idea than anything you've come up with?" he demands.

My eyes dart between the two of them as my mind spins. There are cracks here, and I need to try to exploit them. Chelsea's right that Bronwyn doesn't have much to go on, but Chelsea doesn't know about the burner phone. If my message really did go through, then Bronwyn knows that Nate's been hurt, and she knows where to find him. If she can help him in time, maybe we have a chance. "Can I ask something?" I say.

Chelsea fixes her gaze on me. "Fire away."

"What really happened to your father? This is about him, right?"

She nods, eyes flicking toward her boyfriend. "Gavin kept saying we shouldn't tie anything to my dad's job. And okay, yeah, maybe taking over that billboard was a little self-indulgent, but . . . there's nothing wrong with *making a statement*," she says, her tone turning resentful. "Everyone in this town has forgotten my father. It's like he never existed—like his life, and his death, didn't matter to anyone except me and my brothers."

"I'm sorry," I say. And despite everything she's done, I mean it.

Chelsea takes a deep breath, and I wait for a rant that never comes. Instead, she exhales and regards me with something that could almost pass for affection. "Part of me *wanted* you guys to figure it out. You and your friends have been stuck in the middle of everything that's wrong with Bayview for years, and I'm trying to bring this mess of a town full circle. But I thought it would take you a lot longer, so . . . job well done, I guess."

I don't have a response for that—*Thank you* feels wildly inappropriate—and after a few beats Chelsea adds, "I take it you know the official story of how my father died?"

"The news reports said that he drowned," I say.

"I never believed it was an accident," she says, her face hardening. "Dad was an excellent swimmer. But there was never any proof, you know? He'd been in the water too long to determine anything definitively. The case was closed, we moved away, and

I tried to get on with life. Even though my father was the only person who ever really got me."

"I'm sorry," I say again.

Her lips thin. "We all have shit to deal with, right? My mom totally lost it, so I couldn't. Somebody had to hold things together. Chase is useless, and Chris has always lived in his own little world. Then Mom died, and Chase took off for Los Angeles, and Chris and I were by ourselves in the middle of nowhere. I thought, *Well, I guess this is my life now.* Until a few months ago, when . . ."

Chelsea trails off, and I prompt, "When what?"

Her mouth curves into a half smile that I instantly distrust. "You know what?" she says. "Let's have Jake tell you that."

"What?" My heart jumps into my throat, then tumbles into the pit of my stomach. "N-no, I can't. . . ." I start to back away, and Gavin seizes both of my arms. He pushes me out of the kitchen, toward a staircase that's suddenly looming like a guillotine. Coming closer and closer, even though I'm resisting with every cell in my body. "I don't want to see him, I—"

"Don't worry," Chelsea says calmly. "He can't hurt you."

That's no comfort, but it doesn't matter. The more I struggle, the clearer it becomes that Gavin's going to get me up those stairs whether I want to go or not. I can keep fighting until he's angry and possibly get myself tied up again, or I can conserve my energy. I give in and let Gavin frog-march me up the stairs, down a hallway with open doors on either side—all leading to dark, quiet, empty rooms—until we reach a closed door at the very end.

Gavin opens the door and shoves me inside in front of him,

and then he's pulling it closed behind a fast-moving Chelsea and I'm . . . I'm looking at Jake.

He's tied to a chair, his mouth covered in duct tape, wearing the same clothes his parents described at the news conference announcing that he'd gone missing: a Bayview Wildcats T-shirt and jeans, both looking stained and worse for the wear. His arms are bound behind him, but I can make out the beginnings of the word PERFECT written across one of them in large block letters.

"You know the drill," Gavin says as he steps behind Jake and rips the duct tape off so quickly that I wince. "Raise your voice and this goes right back on."

For a second, Jake and I just stare at one another. My emotions are churning, fear being taken over by shock and . . . God, is that pity? Buried somewhere deep inside me, coming out because no matter what he's done, he's another human being and this is terrifying and—

"You bitch," Jake snarls.

My blossoming pity dissolves like ash in my stomach as Chelsea positions herself beside me. Gavin stands in front of the door, arms crossed like a sentry, and Jake strains against the ropes holding him. "Addy has a question, Jake," Chelsea says.

"I *knew* you were with them," Jake says, practically spitting the words. If eyes could incinerate, I'd be in flames.

"Addy wants to know what happened to my father," Chelsea says, as if Jake hasn't spoken. "How he really died."

Something besides rage flickers across Jake's face then, but I can't make it out. "Addy can go to hell," he says.

"Should have known you wouldn't cooperate," Chelsea says. She crosses to the only piece of furniture in the room besides the chair Jake is tied to, a beat-up dresser that looks like someone put it together without the instructions, and opens the top drawer. When she pulls out a gun, Jake inhales as sharply as I do.

He hasn't seen that before, I think as his face pales. *She's escalating.* "That thing's not loaded," he says, like he's trying to convince himself.

"Yes, it is," Chelsea says calmly. "I could use it to make you talk, I suppose, but I'm not sure I could stomach your version of the truth. So let me help you along."

JAKE

Six Years Earlier

Simon was like a leech, Jake thought. When Jake had told him he didn't feel like staying overnight at Simon's after all, that he wanted to be home with his own gaming system, he'd expected Simon to take the hint. Not stuff extra clothes and a tooth-brush into a backpack and come along.

"My mom's not home," Jake said as they coasted on their bikes down his street. "She's in Mexico for work."

"Oh, for *work*," Simon said in that smarmy, know-it-all voice he'd taken to using every time Jake's mother came up. Jake wished, now, that he'd never confided in Simon. Things at home seemed to be going better, and he almost could've for-gotten that anything was wrong between his parents if Simon didn't keep bringing it up.

"For work," Jake repeated firmly. "And my dad's not home either. It's his poker night."

"You didn't tell him we were coming?" Simon asked.

"No, why would I?" Jake asked. He wasn't expecting a *we*, after all.

Jake's house came into sight, and Simon slowed his bicycle. "Looks like your dad *is* home," he says. "And he has company."

Jake blinked at the unfamiliar blue car parked next to his father's BMW. "None of my dad's friends drive a *Honda*," he said, injecting as much disdain as possible into the last word. "Maybe somebody's delivering food."

"Good. I'm starving," Simon said. They dropped their bikes in the yard, and then, instead of heading for the front door, Simon crossed over to the Honda and peered into its back seat.

"What are you doing?" Jake asked irritably. "Come inside."

"There's a Conrad and Olsen folder in the back seat," Simon said, cupping his hands over his eyes and leaning in to get a better look. "Isn't that where your mom works?"

"Yeah," Jake said, nerves prickling.

"And a briefcase," Simon said. He tugged on one of the rear door handles and, to Jake's surprise, easily pulled it open. "Unlocked. How trusting."

"Knock it off!" Jake pulled Simon away from the car and shut its door. "It's probably still a delivery person, you know. Conrad and Olsen pays crap. You'd need a second job if you don't have someone else supporting you."

"Suuuure," Simon said, but he followed Jake into the house.

They could hear raised voices as soon as they stepped into the entryway, and Jake put an arm out to keep Simon from going any farther. The voices were coming from the kitchen, which wasn't visible from where Jake and Simon were standing. "Look, Scott, I'm sorry," said a man Jake didn't recognize. "I didn't think you'd come home—"

"You didn't think *I'd come home*?" Jake's father practically shouted the words. "To my own fucking house?"

"I'm sorry," the other man repeated. "I'll go."

"I don't think so," Dad said. "Not until you explain what the hell you were doing in my bedroom, packing up my wife's clothes?"

"Oh, snap," Simon breathed, eyes wide. "It's going down."

"Shut up," Jake hissed, pulling him farther into the living room. They crouched behind the sectional sofa, beside an accent table filled with Mom's favorite vases.

"Scott, come on," said the man—who must be Alexander Alton, Jake thought with a stab of hatred. "I'm really sorry this happened, but . . . you know what I was doing. Katherine and I care deeply for one another, and she thought it would be better to make a clean break when she got back from Mexico. I was just getting a few things—"

"Stop right there," Dad snarled. Jake knew that tone; his father's hands must be balled into fists by this point. "Don't you dare talk about my wife like that. Whatever delusion you, or she, might've been under ends now. You never should've come here."

"You're right. I'll go." Simon and Jake both crouched down when they heard footsteps, but they stopped as soon as they started. There was a moment of silence, and then Alexander said. "Get out of my way, please."

"I have a *son*," Dad said. "Did you even think about him

while you were running around behind my back, trying to break up his family?"

Jake expected Alexander to argue, but his voice got so quiet that they almost couldn't hear him. "Of course. I think about Jake every day."

"What? Why?" Dad demanded. His tone grew harsh when Alexander didn't reply. "Why the hell are you looking at me like that?"

"Katherine said that she . . . I thought you knew," Alexander said.

"Knew what?"

"Nothing. Never mind." There was more movement, and scuffling sounds, then Alexander's voice again. "For God's sake, Scott, let go. Have you lost your mind?"

"Possibly," said Jake's father. "What did you think I knew?" Alexander didn't respond, and Dad's next words came out as a growl. "I'm done asking nicely."

There was a long beat of silence, until Alexander Alton let out a strangled sound of pain at whatever Jake's father was doing. When he spoke next it was in an entirely different voice; the placating tone was gone, replaced with a cold fury that almost masked the fear beneath. "Jesus Christ, Scott, you're such a goddamn bully. Do you really have to wonder why Katherine wants to get away from you? Why she wants to get our son away from you?"

Jake thought his heart had been pounding before, but now he realized that was just a warm-up. It was slamming against his chest now, and his entire body vibrated along with it.

"Our son?" Dad repeated harshly. "What son?"

Jake closed his eyes, wishing he could close his ears, too, as Alexander said, "Jake."

"What in God's name is wrong with you? Jake is *my* son," Dad said.

"No, he's not," Simon whispered.

Right when Alexander Alton said the exact same thing. Except Alexander also added, "He's mine."

He's mine.

Jake squeezed his eyes shut more tightly as heat flooded his face. No. This was impossible. He was Scott Riordan's son. He'd always been Scott Riordan's son, and he would always *be* Scott Riordan's son. He wasn't an . . . *Alton.* Was that what this man was trying to say? It was impossible, and it was ridiculous, and Jake needed him to stop talking.

And then, after a loud crashing noise, he did.

"Get up," Jake's father said roughly. "Get up, you lying son of a bitch." He breathed heavily for a few endless moments, and when he spoke again, it was with less certainty in his voice. "Get up and take that bullshit back."

Simon exhaled slowly. He was staring intently at the wall that separated the living room from the kitchen, as though he had X-ray vision and could see straight through it. "You know what?" Simon murmured. "I don't think he's getting up."

CHAPTER THIRTY-SEVEN

Addy
Tuesday, July 21

I stare at the gun in Chelsea's hand and ask, "How do you know this?"

"Simon Kelleher told me," she says.

The name frays the last of my nerves. "*Simon?* You knew him? He told you what happened and then—what? You didn't say anything for six years?"

Chelsea shakes her head. "I didn't know him. I met him once, the summer my father died, when he was cutting through my backyard. And he didn't tell me anything back then. I got a letter with all the details a few months ago." From my startled look, she adds, "He'd used some kind of service that sends mail on a future date. It was dated three days before he died. He wrote that he was *tying up loose ends*." She glances behind her, where Gavin is still standing guard at the door. "Gavin said the letter was someone's idea of a sick joke, but I didn't think so. There were too many details that made sense."

My pulse hitches as questions spin through my brain. Jake's head is bowed now, his eyes on the floor. "But why didn't Simon tell anyone when it happened?" I ask.

Chelsea barks out a laugh. "Why do you *think*? Jake made him promise not to. But we all know how Simon felt about secrets, right? They have to come out eventually."

Jake's head snaps up. "Simon was a liar," he growls.

"Simon never lied." The words slip out of me before I can stop them, and I look away from Jake before I have to see what I'm sure is a rage-filled reaction. "But Chelsea—why didn't you tell someone? As soon as you got the letter?"

"Because it was right around the time that the whole Juror X thing exploded," she says. "I knew there wasn't any point. Even if I could prove the letter was from Simon, who would care? They didn't care that Jake tried to kill you." My hand goes instinctively to my throat as she adds, "You thought Jake helped Simon with his revenge plan because of *you,* didn't you? Because you cheated, and Jake wanted to get back at you."

A strangled sound comes out of me. "Well, yeah," I say. "He made that pretty clear." I'd come to understand after the whole TJ nightmare that cheating was unforgivable to Jake, but I never could've imagined the twisted reason why.

"That was part of it, but it wasn't the whole story," Chelsea says. "Jake owed Simon for keeping quiet about what happened to my father."

I've been avoiding Jake's eyes for a while, and now that I'm looking at him, he won't look back. I search his face anyway, desperate for answers. Is this true? Is it real? Did Jake go all-in with Simon not only because he was angry with me, but because Simon was holding on to an even bigger secret of Jake's?

His clenched jaw is all the answer I need. *Yes.*

Chelsea levels her gaze at Jake. "But God, Jake, you were seriously naïve for believing that Simon would *stay* quiet. You spent all that time with him, working on a plan that would ruin the lives of everyone he hated, and it never occurred to you that he hated you too?"

Jake glares at Chelsea as she continues, "After I read the letter, it felt like my father had died all over again. I couldn't stop watching his old ad campaigns, especially the one he'd been working on right before he died. Practice Makes Perfect. That was a better slogan than people realize, you know. It has so many connotations." Her voice hardens. "It went over big in Bayview, where they love to coddle boys like Jake. Always practicing, always perfecting. Weren't you, Jake?"

She nudges his foot with hers, and he jerks away like she scalded him. "But we all know what Bayview's real game is, right?" she continues. "Revenge. Except they keep doing it wrong. Nobody ever targets people who are *actually* guilty. Even though this town is full of them. So I decided it was time to change that. Once Juror X surfaced, I could tell Jake was going to be released—I would've bet every cent I inherited from my father's life insurance policy on it—so Gavin and I moved to Bayview in May. The day of Jake's hearing, I used my dad's old security credentials to hack the Clarendon billboard and let everyone know that this time, we're playing by *my* rule. *Practice makes perfect.* Something that would get justice for my dad, and honor him. Step by step."

"Step by step?" I echo.

She nods. "Step one was somebody who'd done something wrong, but not unforgivable. Someone who could learn. That was supposed to be Vanessa, because of the way she supported *him*." She jerks the gun toward Jake. "Enabled all his worst behavior. Guys like Jake are made bit by bit, you know? And Vanessa played her part better than anyone at Bayview High. But Phoebe stole the drink I'd drugged from Vanessa at Nate's party. After she nearly passed out in the backyard, she told me what really happened with Jared Jackson."

I blink, confused. "Huh? What do you mean?"

Chelsea cocks her head. "Phoebe didn't tell you? How her brother stepped in for Emma and kept the Truth or Dare game going until Brandon died? She's been covering for him all this time." My jaw drops at the revelation, and Chelsea snorts out a mirthless laugh. "I guess I shouldn't be surprised. She's a great liar until her defenses are down. Once the drugs kicked in, she couldn't shut up. I listened to all her pathetic justifications and made a spur-of-the-moment swap from Vanessa to Phoebe."

Phoebe. *Owen.* Oh my God, no wonder she's been a wreck all summer. I'm desperate to know more, but the last thing I want is to make Chelsea any angrier at Phoebe than she already is. I swallow my questions and ask, "What about Reggie?"

A spasm of something like angry regret crosses Chelsea's face. "Reggie had no problem telling the world that Jake was a good guy, even after everything he did to you and your friends. And to Simon. *He was always pretty cool to me,*" she says in a way that makes it clear that she, too, has memorized that *Bayview Blade* article. Jake, who's been uncharacteristically quiet all this time, gives a smirk that Chelsea fortunately doesn't catch.

"Plus, Reggie was a disgusting predator," she continues.

"I saw Katrina Lott's TikTok, just like everybody else who's ever lived in Bayview. The comments made it clear he hadn't changed, and I knew he never would unless he got the scare of his life." Her voice drops lower. "He wasn't supposed to die, though. That was an accident. Jake, on the other hand . . ."

Panic floods my veins, and I try to tamp it down. The most frightening thing about Chelsea is how *calm* she is. And how absolutely sure of herself. If I could put even the tiniest dent in that confidence, maybe there's a way to get everyone out of here alive. "Chelsea, this is horrible, and I understand why you're so angry, but Jake was just a kid when his father"—*Not his actual father,* I think, but she'll know what I mean—"killed yours. I'm sure Jake would have stopped it if he felt like he could. He must have been terrified."

"Really, Addy?" Chelsea asks, her voice dripping with scorn. "After everything he's done to you, that's your response?"

Time for a new tack, especially since she's making a fair point. If I think about that for too long, it'll be harder to do the right thing. "But you said that this is about getting revenge the proper way. Targeting people who are actually guilty," I say. "So why are you going after Jake instead of Scott Riordan?" Of course, it's a horrible punishment for Scott to lose the son he killed Alexander Alton to keep, but it doesn't seem *fitting*. Even though I haven't known this version of Chelsea for very long, that strikes me as the sort of distinction that she'd care about.

Chelsea's lips curve into that half smile I've come to dread. It's as though she's been waiting for me to ask the question, and she's pleased that I finally got there. "Because I haven't told you about the rest of the letter," she says. "That wasn't all that Simon said."

SIMON

Six Years Earlier

They listened for what seemed like hours.

Listened to Mr. Riordan give up on reviving Alexander Alton, pace the kitchen, and agitatedly stalk between rooms. It was a minor miracle, Simon thought, that he hadn't spotted them. Mr. Riordan had passed by the spot where he and Jake crouched behind the couch at least a half-dozen times. Simon was pretty sure he knew what Mr. Riordan was thinking: *Get rid of the body, get rid of Alexander Alton's car, and hope and pray that nobody ever noticed it was here.* It was dark enough, Simon thought, that Mr. Riordan might get lucky in that regard. The Riordans, after all, were the luckiest people he knew.

"You can't tell anyone," Jake said in a panicked whisper when Mr. Riordan's footsteps faded down the hallway. "He didn't mean it."

"You sure about that?" Simon whispered back.

"Simon, *please*. Promise me. Please."

"I promise," Simon whispered, just to shut him up.

Jake pressed his head into his hands, curled into a ball behind the couch. Mr. Riordan was still out of hearing distance, but he wouldn't be for long. Whatever he was planning next, one thing was for certain: he wouldn't want a witness. So when Jake started rocking back and forth, seemingly lost in his own world, Simon took advantage of the opportunity to get to his feet and slip outside, as quickly and noiselessly as he could.

All the way toward the patch of grass where he'd left his bike, Simon expected to feel a hand on his arm—Jake or Mr. Riordan pulling him back, begging him to stay quiet. Or maybe they'd insist on it. Get angry and threaten that he'd wind up like Alexander Alton. Simon was so caught up in the drama of what felt like an inevitable confrontation that when he reached his bicycle and glanced over his shoulder, he was disappointed to see nothing but the empty stretch of grass he'd just crossed.

He was a murder witness, and the Riordans were *still* treating him like he didn't exist.

Simon picked his bicycle up from the grass and slung one leg over the seat. Then he paused, unable to tear his eyes away from the Riordans' palatial home.

He didn't want to leave yet. He wanted to know what happened next.

Simon made his way to the Riordans' kitchen window and hoisted himself up onto the flower-covered trellis below it until he could see inside. Instantly he spotted Alexander Alton's body, all stiffness and unnatural angles. And beside it—there was Jake. Staring at the floor with wide, blank eyes.

Any minute, Simon thought. Any minute, Mr. Riordan would come back and see the boy he'd always believed was his son standing over the body of his real father. Simon couldn't even begin to guess what would happen then. This was the strangest, most surreal experience of his entire life, and he wasn't one hundred percent certain that he wasn't dreaming.

And then, the body twitched.

Simon nearly fell off the trellis, certain his imagination had gotten the better of him until he saw Jake recoil in shock. Neither of them was seeing things—Alexander's hand moved, and then his head. Faint, but definite.

He was still alive, which meant—what? Would Mr. Riordan call an ambulance? How was he going to explain what had happened? And what would Alexander Alton do once he got out of this house? *He could take Jake away,* Simon thought. *It's probably what he and Ms. Riordan were planning to do, anyway.*

Before Simon could wonder for too long, though, Jake grabbed a towel that was draped over the oven door and folded it in two. He knelt beside Alexander Alton and then, as Simon watched through the window, pressed the towel over Alexander's face. Even as Alexander struggled weakly, Jake held it there. After a few minutes that passed with agonizing slowness, there was no movement at all.

Simon dropped from the trellis, breathing hard. He could tell someone, he thought. He could rip the entire Riordan family apart and let Chelsea Alton and her brothers know exactly what had happened to their father. That was the right thing to do, probably, but it wouldn't bring Alexander Alton back.

He'd promised Jake that he would stay quiet. That was when they'd thought Alexander Alton's death was an accident, though. Simon didn't owe Jake anything now.

But Jake owed him.

Even before he'd watched Jake finish what Mr. Riordan had started, Jake owed Simon a staggering debt. The kind where Simon could tell Jake to do anything, and he'd have to do it.

He would wait, Simon decided, settling himself onto his bike. Wait and see whether Mr. Riordan got away with what he'd done. He and Jake might feel safe then, like they were still the picture-perfect family they'd always pretended to be, but they weren't. Not when Simon could reveal the truth at any time.

Secrets are power, Simon thought as he pedaled away.

CHAPTER THIRTY-EIGHT

Addy
Tuesday, July 21

A full-body tremor runs through me as I say, "Jake killed your father?"

"And his," Chelsea says.

"He wasn't my father!" Jake spits out. "Simon was lying."

"Simon never lied." This time, I don't look away when I say it.

I know what Jake is capable of; I barely lived through it. But all this time, I thought that I was the one who'd brought the monster out of him. I didn't realize it had been there before we even met.

"Oh, Simon's a paragon of virtue now, huh?" Jake sneers. "You'll believe whatever he said, even though he couldn't wait to ruin your life."

"Neither could you," I say quietly.

Chelsea was wrong about Jake; he didn't believe Simon

would take his secret to the grave because he was naïve. He believed it because he was arrogant and self-involved. If Jake had spent a single moment trying to truly understand Simon Kelleher, a boy he'd known since kindergarten, he would have realized Simon would never leave a secret like that untold.

What I can't figure out, though, is why Simon told Chelsea. Why not address the letter to her mother—who was still alive when Simon died—or one of her brothers? Was it because Simon had met Chelsea once? Because he knew, instinctively, that she'd do something like this? It seems impossible, considering how brief their interaction must have been. But somehow, more than a year after he died, Simon managed to hand a lit match to a powder keg.

Jake snorts. "You were lucky to have me."

"Bravo, Jake. Thank you for proving that you're entirely incapable of change," Chelsea says, taking a step forward. "You understand, don't you, Addy? I'm not just doing you and me and my brothers a favor. I'm doing the entire *world* a favor." There's a clicking noise as she releases the safety on the gun and lowers her arm, aiming directly at Jake's heart. "It's okay, you know. To admit that you want this."

"I . . ." I stare at the hunk of metal in her hands as Jake's breathing gets uneven. I want a lot of things right now: for Nate to be okay, for Phoebe to get out of here safely, for Bronwyn and Maeve to be working the kind of Rojas sister magic that means I'll get to see my friends and my family again. That I'll get to meet my niece or nephew this fall.

But I don't want this.

"You can put Jake back in jail," I say. "That's your revenge."

Chelsea snorts. "Are you serious? They wouldn't keep him

behind bars when he was caught with his literal hands around your neck. Think they'd care about a letter? Even if there's a way to prove it came from Simon, you heard him, right?" She lifts her chin toward Jake. "He'll never stop insisting that Simon was lying. And there's no evidence. What I *think* happened is that Scott Riordan drove Dad's car to the beach and tossed his body into the ocean—maybe with Jake's help, maybe not." Her voice hitches. "But that car was totaled in the accident that killed my mother, so I can't even try to prove it."

"You could prove paternity," I say. "That would show the letter is at least right about one thing. And it gives motive."

"It's not enough," Chelsea says. "You know it's not enough."

"This isn't the way," I say. My voice takes on a pleading tone, because I'm running out of arguments. "It won't make you feel any better."

"Maybe not," she says. "But I can't imagine it would make me feel any worse."

"Chels," Gavin says suddenly. He's been silent for so long, I almost forgot he was here. "Hold up. Do you hear that?"

I've been so focused on Chelsea that at first I have no idea what he's talking about. Then I hear it: the sound of tires crunching on the gravel driveway out front. My pulse takes a giant leap as Gavin crosses to the window and peers outside. "Who drives a black Subaru?" he asks.

"A what?" Chelsea asks just as I cry out, "Cooper!" Then I want to clap my hand over my mouth and swallow the name, but it's too late.

Jake starts laughing then, a mocking, bitter sound that puts a quick end to the hope that started fizzing through my veins.

"Cooper Clay to the rescue once again," he says, his lip curling. "But this time, you're the one getting punched in the head."

"He's with another guy," Gavin reports. "Big, dark hair. I don't know him." *Luis,* I think, but this time I manage to keep the name to myself. Gavin backs away from the window and adds, "Chels, I don't think I can take them. Even with the element of surprise." His gaze drops to the gun in Chelsea's hand. "Unless . . ."

"Jesus Christ, Gavin, we're not shooting Cooper!" Chelsea says, recoiling with what looks like genuine disgust. "That's not what this is about." Despite everything she's done, I feel a rush of gratitude at her words. I'm already sick with worry over Nate; I couldn't take it if another friend got hurt trying to help me.

"Then we gotta go." Gavin grabs hold of Chelsea's arm just as a loud, thudding noise comes from downstairs. It sounds as though Cooper and Luis are throwing all their weight against the front door. "Come on, Chels. You did the best you could," Gavin says.

"Just not quite good enough," Jake says, still smirking.

For the first time since I saw her in the kitchen, Chelsea looks unsure of herself. "I . . . I don't know what to do," she says.

"Out the back door, babe," Gavin says. "Come on. We'll disappear a little sooner than we planned."

Chelsea's eyes are like glass as she allows Gavin to pull her into the hall, the gun still in her hand, only now pointed at the floor. I'm frozen in place, my gaze ping-ponging between Jake's smug grin and Chelsea's slack face, and I almost miss the moment when her expression changes. The hard mask drops back into place, her mouth curves into that disconcerting half smile I've come to know too well, and she raises her arm.

"Just kidding. I know exactly what to do," she says, and then the thunderous crack of a gunshot fills my ears.

CHAPTER THIRTY-NINE

Phoebe
Tuesday, July 21

Chelsea exaggerated; this room isn't entirely soundproof. I hear things. A persistent thudding noise, a distant pop like the last bang in a fireworks finale, and a prolonged scream.

And then silence for what feels like a very long time, until footsteps finally approach. My heart stutters in my chest as I try to prepare myself for whatever's on the other side of the door. I'm praying for the police, but even Chelsea would be okay. *If she wanted you dead, you would be,* I remind myself.

But I'm almost positive that it was a girl who screamed. The worst possible scenario is that Jake did something to Chelsea, and now he's coming for me.

The doorknob turns but doesn't open. It shakes and rattles. *Not Chelsea,* I think, my stomach twisting with fear. Then there's the crashing sound of metal on metal, the door swings open, and Cooper steps through.

There's nobody in the world I'd rather see right now, and my entire body goes limp with relief. "Hey, Phoebe," Cooper says, looking equally relieved as he drops a wrench onto the ground. "You okay?"

All I can do is blink as he crosses the room and crouches beside me. "Let's get you untied," he says, his voice as gentle as the hands that circle my wrists, feeling for the knot that's binding them together. "Everything's gonna be all right."

"How . . . how did you find me?" I stammer. "Where's Chelsea?"

"Phoebe!" a familiar voice calls out before Cooper can respond, and my jaw drops even farther when I see Addy stumble into the room. "Are you okay?" she says.

I can't think of any answer to give except "What are you doing here?"

"I was with Gavin—that's Chelsea's boyfriend from high school; it's a whole thing," Addy says breathlessly. "When Nate realized who they were, Gavin attacked him and grabbed me and . . ." She turns her attention to Cooper, who's managed to loosen the ropes around my wrists. "Nate must be okay, right? He told you and Luis how to find us?"

"*Luis* is here?" I ask. Although I shouldn't be surprised, probably, that this has somehow turned into an impromptu Murder Club meeting.

"Upstairs," Cooper says briefly. The rope drops from my hands, and I massage my wrists as Cooper adds, "I don't know what's going on with Nate, Addy. I'm here because Marshall Whitfield came to my freaking house to tell me that he'd watched Phoebe go into an apartment building, and then he saw two people stuff her into a car and drive away."

334

Addy stares in disbelief. "Marshall Whitfield?" she echoes. "Juror X? You're telling me that guy actually used his creeper tendencies for good?"

"Guess so," Cooper says, turning his attention to my ankles. "He was afraid to go to the police, on account of us calling him a stalker and all, so he came to me instead. I texted the group chat, and Maeve gave me this address. She said it still belongs to the Alton family, so Luis and I came over to check it out." His mouth tightens as he adds, "She also said Nate was hurt, but . . . that's all she said."

"Oh God," Addy says, gazing wildly around us. "I need my phone. Gavin took it, he probably still has it—" She looks at Cooper with imploring eyes. "Can I use yours?"

"Of course," Cooper says, pausing briefly to pull it from his pocket and unlock it. "Luis might already be checking on that, or he might be . . . you know." He clears his throat as he bends over the knot at my ankles once again. "Telling the police what went on upstairs."

"Upstairs?" I don't feel relieved anymore; that short burst has already been replaced by fast-growing dread. "What are you talking about? And what happened to Nate?"

Addy swallows hard. "I'm . . . I'm sure he's fine. I just need to make a few calls. And I shouldn't have left Luis by himself with . . . that." She steps into the hallway, and I feel suddenly desperate at the thought of her leaving my sight.

"Addy, wait! By himself with *what*?" I call after her. "Does it have anything to do with Jake? Where is he?"

Addy freezes in place, stopping so abruptly that she has to place one hand on the wall to steady herself. Then, without turning to look at me, she says, "Jake's gone."

CHAPTER FORTY

Phoebe
Friday, July 24

Three days later the world is a very different place, although I haven't seen much of it. My family has been holed up in our apartment ever since the story broke. I've left only once, to visit Nate in the hospital after he finally regained consciousness. Bronwyn was by his side, like always, holding his hand while I perched at the edge of a chair beside his bed.

"Why are you always the one who gets hurt?" I asked.

"Because I'm an idiot who's easy to get rid of," Nate grumbled. "Doesn't matter what crime we're dealing with—when shit goes down, I'm out of commission."

"I was, too," I reminded him, which earned me a wry grin.

"Yeah, well, you've got some catching up to do. I'm three for three," Nate said. I held out a fist for him to bump, and he was nice enough not to leave me hanging.

Bronwyn brushed a lock of dark hair off his forehead.

"You're looking at this all wrong, Nate," she said. "We couldn't have figured anything out without you. If you weren't spending time with your dad, letting him know that he could count on you, we wouldn't have found Phoebe *or* Reggie. Plus, nobody but you could've brought Vanessa in, or put her and Ms. Riordan together, and you're the only one who knew Gavin—"

Nate grimaced. "Not sure I want to take credit for that."

"Still," Bronwyn said. "You're at the center of *everything*. Could you even have imagined that two years ago?"

"I couldn't have imagined this many scars," Nate muttered, brushing his fingertips against the new one at his temple. But he looked a little pleased too.

"I'm really glad you're okay," I told him. I feel like I know Nate the least of anyone in the Bayview Crew chat, because by the time we started hanging out, I was already keeping secrets. But I want to change that—especially because now, there's nowhere left to hide.

Everything about Owen is out in the open, and my family, once again, is being dissected by the media. I was braced for the worst, but *Mikhail Powers Investigates* set the tone early, descending on Bayview the night Chelsea killed Jake. "Chelsea Alton devised an elaborate and vengeful scheme aimed at punishing those she deemed responsible for Bayview's deadly, toxic past," Mikhail said in his first broadcast. "And now the town has a choice. Will they harass a grieving boy who made a terrible decision, or address the broader cultural problem of privilege and entitlement that has become this town's legacy?"

So far, at least, Bayview appears to be going for option B. People have gone out of their way to express sympathy for me and concern about Owen. It helped, I think, that Emma's lawyer, Martin McCoy, appeared on Mikhail Powers's second broadcast and shared the final transcripts between Jared and Owen. *That wasn't supposed to happen,* Owen wrote after Brandon died. In all the back-and-forth, Martin explained, Jared had never talked about actually killing Brandon until it was done. Owen hadn't realized he was helping to plot a murder. Emma, at age seventeen, understood that something about Jared was off and stopped communicating with him. Owen, five years younger, didn't have the same instinct.

A lot of the coverage is zeroing in on Mr. Riordan, although it's unclear what's going to happen to him. Bayview Police are trying to trace the letter Chelsea received back to Simon. But even if they do, Martin says, it could be considered hearsay. Still, there are enough details about what happened that most people believe it's a version of the truth. It's like Addy keeps saying—the main reason that Simon Kelleher had such a hold over so many people, for so many years, is because he never, ever lied.

Chelsea and Gavin managed to make it out of Bayview after she killed Jake, and no one knows where they are. She left behind detailed notes in her apartment—kind of like Simon's manifesto from two years ago—taking responsibility for everything that happened to Phoebe, Reggie, and Jake. *I'm sorry that Reggie died,* she wrote at the end. *I only meant to scare him. But I'm not sorry about what I'm going to do to Jake. He took my father away, he helped Simon Kelleher die, and he tried to kill Addy Prentiss. He was going to spend the rest of his life hurting people, and nobody would have stopped him. So I will.*

There's a massive hunt underway for Chelsea and Gavin, and the police keep asking for any details they might have let slip that could help track them down. I suppose I could share the fact that Chelsea once told me that if she could live anywhere, it would be Colorado, but . . . I haven't. I can't bring myself to hate her, and I'm not sure I want her caught. After all, half my family launched their own revenge plan after our father died, and Brandon jamming that forklift was an accident. I can't imagine the rage we'd feel if he'd done something like Jake did.

Plus, even though Chelsea was twisted, she was right about a lot of things. Especially when it comes to me, Emma, and Owen.

We've had *a lot* of family time over the past few days. A lot of time to try to explain to our mother why we kept quiet—that it wasn't a lack of trust, but a messed-up attempt to protect her when she'd already suffered so much. It was, as Mom has told us repeatedly, an absolutely horrible choice. One that we're going to relive in therapy indefinitely, starting with our first family session tomorrow, and individual sessions next week.

I'm kind of looking forward to it, to be honest. We all need it.

"Can we watch something else?" Owen murmurs from the couch when Mikhail Powers goes to commercial. He's sitting between me and Emma, our mother seated on a stool at the kitchen island, brow furrowed at her laptop. Lately, when we're home, we're never more than a few feet away from one another unless we're sleeping.

"I think Liz Rosen is doing a special report on Channel Seven," Emma says, reaching for the remote. "She's supposed to have Marshall Whitfield on."

"Ugh," I mutter. I'm glad Marshall isn't getting doxed

anymore, but I can't bring myself to view him as anything close to heroic. Even if he did help get me out of Chelsea's house.

"I mean, something that's . . . not this," Owen says, hunching his shoulders. "I can't stand hearing my name anymore."

Emma pauses the channel instead of turning it. "People are being pretty decent about you, though," she says.

"Yeah. That's the problem," Owen says. "I'm one of those guys everyone is talking about, you know? Who doesn't get any consequences for doing something bad."

I reach for his hand, a little surprised when he lets me take it. Even though he towers over me, he seems more like my little brother now than he has in months. "You *are* getting consequences. They're just age-appropriate."

Owen swallows hard, his Adam's apple bobbing up and down. "Even Brandon's parents were nice," he says.

I don't remind him that Brandon's parents are still living with the guilt of Brandon's carelessness being the cause of the accident that killed our father. I can empathize, now, with their reasons for protecting him; we did the same thing for Owen. "They know you didn't understand what Jared was planning," I say instead.

"I was so stupid. And don't say I was *twelve*," Owen adds before I can. "It's not like I didn't know better. I just . . . I missed Dad so much, I couldn't think straight."

"I know," Emma says, taking his other hand. "Me too."

"Me three," I say, thinking with a pang how happy Dad would be to see the three of us holding hands again. Even if it took all this to get there.

"Poor Phoebe," Emma says. "You're less guilty than anyone, but you always take the brunt of the fallout."

"At least I'm not Nate," I say.

"What are you three talking about?" Mom calls over her laptop.

"Our relative guilt," Emma says. Brutal honesty is one of our new family rules.

"Maybe it's time to watch something else," Mom says, looking at Mikhail Powers's frozen face on the television screen.

"That's what *I* said," Owen says.

"What about you, Mom?" I ask nervously. She's been at that laptop for a while. "Anything new?"

"Just going back and forth with Martin. He's been incredibly helpful," she says. "We're going to meet up for lunch tomorrow to discuss legal strategy. He doesn't think there will be any charges against Owen, given public sentiment and the fact that the messages show a clear lack of intent. But he says we need to be prepared for anything."

Emma clears her throat. "Mom, in the spirit of brutal honesty, I think that Martin might be *preparing* to ask you on a nonlegal date."

There's a moment of shocked silence before my mother sputters, "That's preposterous!" Owen sinks into the cushions, groaning, as I reach over to punch Emma on the shoulder.

"I was thinking the same thing!" I say, and we grin at one another.

"In sync once again," she says. "For good."

"Not for evil," I say.

"Well, yeah," Emma says. "But I also meant—from now on."

The intercom buzzes then, and Owen leaps to his feet like he's afraid of getting stuck in a group hug otherwise. "I'll get it," he says, heading for the door. I hear the crackle of an indistinguishable voice, and then Owen returns and flops back onto the couch. "It's Knox," he reports. "I buzzed him in."

"Oh." I blink at my phone, looking for some kind of notification that I missed, but there isn't one. "I wasn't expecting him, but . . . okay. Let me just, um . . ." I stand up and look around our cramped apartment, and at the three faces staring expectantly at me. Brutal honesty doesn't have to mean a total lack of privacy, right? "I'll meet him downstairs."

"He's coming up, though," Owen says as I head for the door.

"Then I'll meet him in the hall," I say, ducking out.

Knox must've gotten lucky with elevator timing, because as soon as I close the door behind me, he steps into the hallway. "Hey," he says, stopping in his tracks. "I was just coming to see you."

"I know," I say. "I thought we could go outside, maybe? It's kind of crowded in my apartment right now."

"Yeah, sure," Knox says. "Or we could go up on the roof deck, if you want."

I raise my eyebrows. "You? On a roof deck?"

"I'm getting used to them," he says with a rueful smile.

"If you're sure," I say, one hand on the stairwell door.

"I'm sure."

I push the door open then, with Knox at my heels. We've texted a lot since the police pulled me from Chelsea's house, but this is the first time I've seen him. I wanted to, but I don't know what to say. Given how quiet our climb up the stairs is, I'm guessing he doesn't either.

"I'm sorry for showing up out of the blue," he says when

we finally reach the roof. "But I was afraid that if I texted first, you'd tell me not to come."

There are tables here now, and I pick one closest to the center of the deck and sit. "Why would I do that?" I ask.

"Because of how I acted the night you told me about Owen." Knox runs a hand through sun-streaked hair as he takes a seat across from me. "I didn't handle it well. I said a lot of wrong things—"

"No, you were right," I interrupt. "About all of it." If I'd talked to my mom that night, Owen could've come clean before Chelsea had the chance to shove Reggie's necklace into his backpack. I wouldn't have gone to her apartment, and I wouldn't have gotten kidnapped *again*. Maybe everything else would've still happened exactly the same way, but my family might have started putting ourselves back together a lot sooner.

"Still," he says. "It didn't come across the way I wanted." He lets his gaze wander, then blanches at the open sky and quickly returns his eyes to me. "It meant a lot that you trusted me enough to tell me, and I feel like I let you down."

"You didn't," I say.

"Good. Because I hate not talking to you."

"Me too," I say, and we share a smile that makes me feel ten times lighter.

"You look great," Knox blurts out. Then his expression shifts, like he's not sure it's the right time for a compliment. "I mean, considering what you've been through."

My lips quirk. "So *great* on, like, a sliding scale?"

"No. Well, obviously, circumstances being what they are, it wouldn't be surprising if you were, um, affected by that, visually speaking, but . . ." I swallow a guilty laugh, enjoying his discomfort way too much, until he finishes, "But what I meant to say is, you look beautiful, Phoebe. Like always."

"Oh." The sudden intensity in Knox's gaze leaves me a little breathless. "Thank you."

"Do you want to, um . . ." He trails off as he looks around us. My heart starts beating a little faster, until he says, "Go back to your apartment?" I must look disappointed, because he quickly adds, "I know you have a lot of family stuff going on, so—"

"True," I say. "It's not a good time. But when it comes to you and me, it never is. And I'm tired of it. So . . ." I reach for his hand, threading my fingers through his. "I do want to go downstairs, but then I want to go to your house and watch movies. In your room." I smile as a blush spreads across his cheeks. He's ridiculously cute when he's embarrassed. "Unless you'd rather be in the living room, in which case, I'll make a giant bowl of popcorn to put between us and we'll never speak of this again."

"God, no," he says in a strangled voice. "No living room."

"Good. Let's tell my mom we're leaving," I say. Knox jumps up way too fast, still holding my hand, and I laugh when his knee bangs hard against the table. "Don't injure yourself," I tease. "And don't look over the edge. You'll get dizzy."

"Too late," Knox says with a grin, letting me pull him toward the stairwell. "For the record, though? It's not the heights."

CHAPTER FORTY-ONE

Nate
Tuesday, July 28

"Are you sure you should be going to a party?" my mother asks anxiously.

"It's going to be the most mellow party ever," I say, rising slowly and carefully from her living room sofa. My head doesn't hurt much anymore, unless I stand up too fast. "All I'm doing is going from your couch to a lounge chair in Bronwyn's backyard."

"I know, but you have to take it easy," Mom says, wrapping an arm around me like I need her help getting to the front door. I don't, but I let her hang on anyway. "I can't go through anything like last week ever again." A pleading note creeps into her voice as I wave to Addy, who's parked in Mom's driveway. "I love your friends, you know I do, but you can't keep putting yourself in these situations—"

"I won't, Mom," I interrupt. *I won't have to* is what I really mean, because I think Bayview has finally settled down for good. But it seems like bad luck to say that out loud.

"Okay. Give me a hug," she says.

I do, and she clings for so long that I clear my throat and say, "The party's going to be over by the time I get there."

"All right," Mom says, wiping her eyes as she releases me. "Tell Addy that I hope she has a wonderful time in Peru."

"I will."

When I get closer to Addy's car, I realize that she's not alone—somebody's in the back seat, leaning over the console and talking animatedly. "I'm in Murder Club now," Vanessa announces as I open the car door. Addy visibly winces, and Vanessa adds, "Sorry, are we not calling it that anymore? My bad. Hi, Nate. How's your head?"

"Still in one piece," I say, buckling my seat belt. "How was Cape Cod?"

"Amazing," Vanessa says brightly. "Keely says hi."

Addy's driving slowly and carefully down my mother's street, her eyes on the road. "And how was Cape Cod for you?" I ask.

"Good," she says quietly, pausing at a stop sign.

I lean forward and try to catch her eye, but she's still staring straight ahead. "You don't sound sure about that," I say.

"It really was," Addy says. "We had a lot of fun. It was kind of like old times, except we were all a lot nicer to one another—"

"Keely and Addy were *especially* nice to one another," Vanessa adds. "But it's fine. I'm a good third wheel; I know when to disappear."

346

"How about now?" I say, and she leans back against her seat with a loud sigh. "You okay?" I ask Addy in a lower voice.

"I'm fine. Honestly," Addy says. "It was a good trip. It's just . . ."

"I know," I say.

I got physically beat up the most in this round, but Addy . . . Addy, once again, took the hardest emotional hit. Jake died in front of her, and even though there's no way she could have stopped it, she's Adelaide fucking Prentiss, so of course she wanted to try. Despite everything Jake did to her— and would've done, given the chance.

"It'll get better," I tell her. Addy just nods, and I add, "You can't save everyone, Addy."

Her voice catches. "I know."

"But you did save me. Literally, this time."

She sends me a faintly puzzled look and asks, "When did I save you figuratively?"

"When you made me go to Bronwyn's piano recital and tell her how I felt. I would've been stubborn and stupid enough to let the best thing in my life pass me by if it weren't for you."

The ghost of a smile flits across Addy's face. "You would have told her eventually."

"Not without a push," I say. "I didn't think I deserved anything good, but you? You wouldn't shut up about it." Addy laughs a little, and I add, "You're a hell of a friend."

There's nothing but silence for a few beats, other than Vanessa's loud sniff from the back seat. Then Addy puts on her blinker for Bronwyn's street and says, "Cut it out. You're going to make me cry."

347

I wait until she pulls into Bronwyn's driveway to respond. "You know what? I always hated being an only child, and it's kind of like I've got a sister now."

"Oh my God," Addy says tearfully. "I'm wearing *mascara*, you jerk."

She shifts into Park and flings her arms around my neck, and I hold her while she sobs on my shoulder. I've spent a lot of time with Addy this week, and I can tell when she's about to break down. If she doesn't get it out of the way now, she's going to have a miserable time at the party. Vanessa, proving that she's a pretty good third wheel after all, stays quiet until Addy finally pulls away.

"You good?" Vanessa asks in such a kind voice that I turn around to make sure it's actually her.

"I'm good," Addy says, wiping her eyes. "Let's go."

We're the last ones to show up. Bronwyn's backyard is in full bloom, trees sparkling with lights that she and Maeve strung this afternoon. A picnic table is set up along a smooth stretch of grass, and the smell of grilled hamburgers wafts our way.

"I bet you anything that Kris is doing the cooking," Addy says. Other than her red eyes, she looks a lot happier than she did when I first got into her car.

"I'll take that bet, and you'll lose, because Javier just bought some kind of space-age grill that nobody's allowed to touch," I say as we turn the corner and the Rojases' deck comes into sight— along with Bronwyn's father, flipping burgers. "Told you."

"Hey, there they are!" Cooper calls, waving at us. He's the hero of Bayview once again; the guy who, along with Luis, swooped in at the last minute to save the day. Even though it's more complicated this time; for one thing, he couldn't stop

Chelsea from killing Jake and taking off, and for another, I don't think either Phoebe's or Addy's life was really in danger. As for me, I've made peace with the fact that Gavin bashed me over the head out of panic. I'm not worried about him ever trying to finish the job; wherever he is, I'm pretty sure his top priority is keeping his distance.

"Here we are," Addy says, waving back.

There's a lot of hugging after that. I mean, *a lot*. Anyone who didn't know that we'd all just been through some serious trauma bonding would have thought we hadn't seen each other in years. When everyone's finally done, we sit down at the table. Kris and Vanessa fall deep into conversation about his sneakers, which she seems to admire a lot. Stranger things have happened, I guess, than those two becoming friendly.

"You guys excited for Germany next month?" I ask Cooper.

He grins. "Man, I can't wait. I've only ever met Kris's family over FaceTime." He reaches across the table and taps Phoebe on her arm. "You're gonna check in on Nonny while I'm gone, right?"

"Oh yeah," Phoebe says. She's sitting next to Knox and looks happier than she has in a long time. "We have big plans. She's going to teach me bridge, and I'm going to introduce her to reality dating shows. You sure you want to go to Germany and miss all that?"

Cooper laughs. "Tough call, but . . . nonrefundable tickets," he says.

"Everyone's leaving," Luis sighs. "You guys, Addy and Maeve—"

"Only for a month," Maeve points out. "Then we come back and Bronwyn leaves." She wipes an imaginary tear.

"And I'll start applying to college, finally," Addy says. "That's just how it is now, I guess. Constant change."

"Not for those of us who still need to finish high school," Knox says.

Phoebe leans her head on his shoulder. "Just one more year," she says.

"Then I'm getting out of this hellhole and going straight to Europe," Maeve says. Luis blinks at her and she adds, "What? You can come. Wouldn't you like to earn your first Michelin star in Paris?"

At first, Luis looks like he's trying to calculate the distance between the Eiffel Tower and the nearest beach. Then he grins and says, "I wouldn't *not* like it."

"You know, I used to hate Bayview," Kris says, glancing at Cooper. "All I knew about it, at first, was that it was the place where Cooper couldn't be himself. Then it turned into something worse. I think we can all agree that nobody in their right mind would ever willingly move here. And yet . . ." He gazes around Bronwyn's backyard. "In a weird way, it's home now. And I might even miss it while I'm gone."

There's a long moment of silence, until Cooper says—in his calmest, most patient voice—"Kris, babe, you're out of your ever-loving mind."

Everyone cracks up as Javier Rojas calls, "Burgers are ready!" There's a mad scramble for the deck, but I put an arm around Bronwyn's waist to keep her beside me.

"Hold up," I say.

Her eyes go straight to the scar on my temple. "You feeling okay?" she asks anxiously. I've gotten woozy in front of her a few times this week.

"Yeah, I'm fine," I say. "But Addy got me thinking, with all that talk about change. You're leaving soon, and—"

"And we won't have any of the problems we had last year," Bronwyn says earnestly, grabbing both of my hands in hers. "We'll talk every day, and I'll come home every chance I get. And you'll visit me, right?"

"I will. I'm not worried about that. It's just—look, Bronwyn, I know you have a five-year plan, and a ten-year plan"—I can tell she's about to interrupt me, so I start talking faster—"and so do I. I have a fifty-year plan, and you're in it. It revolves around you, mostly. Because I've been in love with you since the fifth grade, and that's never going to change." She smiles then, and I turn her hands around in mine, running my thumb down the bare index finger of her left hand. "I don't have a ring or anything, because I know we still have a ways to go before that makes sense, and also, you don't like diamonds—"

"They're not sustainable," she says breathlessly.

"I know. So when the time comes, it'll be something different, but—that time's going to come, okay?" I gaze into her clear gray eyes, my chest aching with how much I love this girl. "I'm going to marry you, Bronwyn Rojas. Just so you know."

She puts her hands on either side of my face and pulls me close enough to kiss. But first, she says, "Oh, I know."

CHAPTER FORTY-TWO

Addy
Thursday, July 30

"I thought you were ready," Ashton says, gazing at the piles of clothes around my room.

"I am," I say. "I'm ready to put all of these into my suitcase. Soon."

"You're leaving tomorrow," she reminds me.

"I'm aware," I say, adding a pair of flip-flops to one pile.

Mom pokes her head in then, waving my passport in one hand. "Addy, you have got to stop leaving this lying around," she says.

"It's not *lying around*," I say. "It was exactly where I wanted it. I have a system, Mom. Can you put it back, please?"

She heaves a theatrical sigh before withdrawing. "Do not blame me if you miss your flight tomorrow because your system fails," she says on her way downstairs.

"Thank you, G-Ma!" I call after her.

Ashton perches at the edge of my bed, one hand on her ever-growing stomach. "You can't tell her it's not spelled G-E-E-M-A," she says. "She's started signing her emails like that. It's very cute."

"It'll be our little secret," I say, miming a zip of my lips.

"Is that the only one?" Ashton asks, arching her brows. I hesitate, not sure what she's talking about. "Eli admitted last night that he never actually threw away the note from the obstetrician. You're both so sneaky," she complains when I grin. "Did you take a look?"

"I didn't. Do you want it back?"

"No," she says. "I want you to destroy it, so I don't ask for it in a moment of weakness when I'm nine months pregnant."

"Done," I say. "I'll toss it into the ocean."

"You don't have to be so dramatic," Ashton says with a smile.

"Fine," I sigh, and flop onto my back beside her on the bed.

"Do you want to know another secret?" she asks.

"Obviously I do."

"We decided on names."

Instantly, I'm upright. "What are they?"

"If it's a boy, William Elijah. After Eli, of course. We'll call him Will."

"Love it. Perfect. And if it's a girl? Don't pick an *A* name," I say before realizing that's a terrible thing to say before Ashton reveals the name. "Unless it's an awesome *A* name, of course. Which I'm sure it would be. I'm just thinking about patterns, you know, and maybe . . ." *Maybe we need to start some new ones for the girls in this family.*

That's silly, though. We already did.

"It's not an *A* name," Ashton says. She pauses, enjoying the suspense, and I make a big show of gnawing on my knuckle. "If it's a girl, we're going to call her Iris Adelaide." I blink at her, tears springing into my eyes, as she adds, "After her kick-ass aunt."

"Oh my God," I whimper. Into Ashton's shoulder, since I'm half strangling her with a hug. "Really? That's . . . that's amazing. Thank you."

"What else would we call her?" Ashton says, hugging me back. "I couldn't use Adelaide for the first name, because there's only one Addy, but I hope she's just like you. I really, really do."

"Well." I gulp, thinking of all the mistakes I've made over the past few years. The past few weeks, even. I don't know if I could've done anything different to stop Chelsea, but I wish we'd been able to have a real conversation when I first got to know her as Evie. Before she did what she did and forever changed the course of her life. I think I would have understood, better than she might have imagined, how it felt to learn the truth about how her father died. "Maybe not *just* like me."

"Oh, hush," Ashton says. "I wouldn't change a thing."

I could use a good night's sleep before tomorrow's marathon flight, but there's one more thing I need to do, and I wanted the beach to be nice and deserted while I did it. It's chilly at midnight, though, and I'm glad for my extra-thick hoodie and sweatpants.

Back when I was in high school and we used to throw parties on this beach, I was never the one who started the bonfire. Jake always wanted to do it, and he liked to explain his methods in great detail. I'd made dozens of campfires with my father and Ashton when we were little, but I listened patiently instead of telling him that I already knew.

And he never asked.

The fire I make now is a small one, because this isn't a party. While I was packing, I dropped a pair of socks behind my bed, and as I fished around for them, I pulled out a scrap of paper. It was a photo booth picture of Jake and me, one from the sophomore-year school fair that I thought I'd thrown away long ago. We were fifteen years old, both of us making goofy faces—my eyes popping wide, his tongue practically touching his nose. A lot of my memories of Jake are bad in retrospect, but I remember this day as nothing but fun. Jake had a lot of charm, and when he directed it toward me, I felt like the most important person in the world.

I don't know when Jake's dark side took over. Maybe it was always there, given the kind of person the father he grew up with turned out to be. Maybe it was that sense of entitlement the media loves to talk about. I can't spend any more time wondering, though, because I've already tortured myself with enough what-ifs to last a lifetime. And I realized a while ago that I never really knew him.

I take one last look at our happy faces, then drop the photo into the fire. "Good-bye, Jake," I say as the edges blacken and curl. "I hope you're at peace."

Within seconds, the photo is nothing but ash. I watch the flames dance for a few more minutes, then take a crumpled envelope out of my pocket. I put a finger beneath the seal and tear, pulling out a sheet of paper. I unfold it, read the single line, and start smiling so wide that my cheeks hurt. Then I carefully refold the paper and put it back into my pocket. I'll get rid of it eventually, because I promised I would, but not yet. I'm going to bring this piece of news to Peru with me; it'll be our first adventure together. The first of many, I hope.

I toss the envelope onto the fire and say, "I can't wait to meet you, Iris Adelaide."

ACKNOWLEDGMENTS

With any book, there are many people to thank. For this one, I need to start with my readers, because without you it wouldn't exist. Thank you for loving these characters, and the world of Bayview, as much as I do. If it wasn't for your continued enthusiasm, *One of Us Is Lying* would have remained a stand-alone. Instead it's now a trilogy, and I'm so happy that I've been able to give my characters the ending that I've imagined in my head for years. I hope this book was worth the wait for all of you.

To my agents Rosemary Stimola and Allison Remcheck, thank you for being such fierce champions of this book and of my career. I don't know what I'd do without your wisdom and guidance (please don't ever make me find out). So much appreciation to the entire team at Stimola Literary Studio, especially Alli Hellegers for her work on the international side, and to Pete Ryan and Nick Croce for their help in operations.

I remember getting an email from my agent more than six years ago, saying that Krista Marino at Delacorte Press wanted to publish my debut, *One of Us Is Lying*. I was thrilled, but I didn't yet know how lucky I was. Now, after seven (seven?!

what is time?!) books together, I'm so thankful for all we've accomplished. I'm grateful to my publishers Beverly Horowitz, Judith Haut, and Barbara Marcus for all their support, and to the amazing team at Delacorte Press and Random House Children's Books, including Kathy Dunn, Lydia Gregovic, Dominique Cimina, John Adamo, Kate Keating, Elizabeth Ward, Jules Kelly, Kelly McGauley, Jenn Inzetta, Tricia Ryzner, Meredith Wagner, Stephania Villar, Elena Meuse, Madison Furr, Adrienne Waintraub, Keri Horan, Katie Halata, Felicia Frazier, Becky Green, Enid Chaban, Kimberly Langus, Kerry Milliron, Colleen Fellingham, Heather Hughes, Alison Impey, Ray Shappell, Kenneth Crossland, Martha Rago, Tracy Heydweiller, Linda Palladino, Tamar Schwartz, and Janet Foley.

Thank you to my wonderful international rights colleagues at Intercontinental Literary Agency, Thomas Schlueck Agency, and Rights People for finding homes around the world for *One of Us Is Back*. I'm grateful for the support of my international editors and publishers, and so glad that I've had the opportunity to meet some of them in person.

The young adult author community is something special; any time you have a question, these brilliant people have answers. Thanks to Krystal Sutherland, Adam Silvera, Becky Albertalli, Leigh Bardugo, Dhonielle Clayton, and Jennifer Mathieu for sharing your wisdom, and to Kathleen Glasgow, Samira Ahmed, Sabaa Tahir, Tiffany Jackson, Stephanie Garber, Courtney Summers, Kara Thomas, and Kit Frick for being tremendous colleagues and inspirations.

Many thanks to Beth Stevens for generously sharing your legal expertise, and thanks also to all the booksellers, librarians, teachers, and reviewers who have enthusiastically championed my books and helped to grow the YA thriller category.

And finally, thanks to my parents for always supporting me; to my son, Jack, for always inspiring me; and to the rest of my family for all the love and laughter.

ABOUT THE AUTHOR

Karen M. McManus is a #1 *New York Times* and internationally bestselling author of young adult thrillers. Her books include the One of Us Is Lying series, which has been turned into a television show on Peacock, as well as the standalone novels *Two Can Keep a Secret*, *The Cousins*, *You'll Be the Death of Me*, and *Nothing More to Tell*. Karen's critically acclaimed, award-winning work has been translated into more than forty-two languages.